From the reviews of *Mystical Circles:*

'intricate tapestry of human emotions and psyches with a romantic thread weaving through.'
Caroline Bailey, *creative arts specialist and ceramic artist*

'will captivate you from the first paragraph…like any good mystery the more I read the more questions I had.'
Marsha Randolph, *US reviewer*

'weaves romance…with spiritual searching and emotional needs, powerful universal themes.'
Marie Calvert, *arts psychotherapist and retreat leader*

'I fell in love with the beautiful house where the story is set and wanted to go there immediately…intense and compelling.'
Eleanor M. Watkins, *author*

'romantic…colourful…well observed cast of characters at the … esoteric Wheel of Love…the community's practices, and their effect on vulnerable individuals, ring true.'
Fay Sampson, *prizewinning author of 'A Malignant House'*

'a gripping read … I wanted to … find out who were the goodies and the baddies … and … what would happen to Juliet and her sister.'
Frances Smith, *Bookseller, Warwick and Kenilworth Books (voted one of the best 50 bookshops in the UK)*

Mystical Circles

SC SKILLMAN

First published in Great Britain in 2010 by Blue Lily Press
Second edition published in 2012 by Blue Lily Press
This paperback edition published in 2017 by Luminarie

Grateful acknowledgement is made to J.M. Dent, an imprint of The Orion Publishing Group, London for The Bright Field by R.S. Thomas; Hamish MacGibbon for Not Waving But Drowning by Stevie Smith; Faber & Faber for Valentine by Wendy Cope; Hodder & Stoughton for Celtic poem in The Celtic Way of Prayer by Esther de Waal; Denise Levertov for Writing in the Dark from Candles in Babylon, copyright ©1982 by Denise Levertov, reprinted by permission of New Directions Publishing Corp; University of Nebraska Press for For My Daughter by Weldon Kees, reprinted from The Collected Poems of Weldon Kees edited by Donald Justice copyright 1962,1975, by the University of Nebraska Press © renewed 2003 by the University of Nebraska Press; Penguin for The Great Gatsby by F. Scott Fitzgerald; Lenono Music for Beautiful Boy by John Lennon; Scholastic for The Subtle Knife by Philip Pullman; and Rev. Margaret & Rev. Richard Deimel for Liturgy for Midsummer Eve.

A CIP catalogue record for this book is available from the British Library.

ISBN 978-1-9997073-0-9

www.scskillman.com
www.luminarie.uk

Mystical Circles

To my father Ken,
who first gave me a stamped addressed envelope
to submit my stories to a London publisher
when I was twelve years old

and to David, Abigail and Jamie for their patience and support
throughout the creation of this book

Craig's farmhouse

N
W E
S

RIDGE

Narrow path
Tall stinging nettles
Hermitage
Woodland
Point from which Craig's group watch the sunrise on the summer solstice
Upward sweep of the valley
Path
Gate
Orchard
Pasture
Stile
apple & pear trees
Gate
Blue Cedars
Back gate
chairs
Scots Pines
Path
Gate
Gravel
Stile
Garden
Sunken garden
Car Park
House
Shrubbery
Gazebo
Barn
Woodland fence
Fir trees
Terracotta urns filled with marigolds & snapdragons
Wide Lawn
Hut with isolation tank
Goose House
Vegetable garden
Woodland
Road
Gates

1

Arrival

Juliet was trembling. It had all happened so fast. The explosion of anger between the two men. The rush for the car park. The engine roaring into life. As the rear lights picked her out, she dodged aside just in time. The next thing she heard was a loud bang. And the sickening crunch of metal giving way. And a fountain of fragmenting glass.

He'd slammed on the brakes too late.

And it was all her fault.

*****

Juliet's palms were slippery on the steering wheel; she wiped the sweat away from her upper lip. The air conditioning might offset the strong heat of this June day, but not the burning anxiety she felt. Even the spectacular beauty of the high limestone hills and deep valleys as she headed west from the A417 had failed to calm her. A sign half hidden by the trees proclaimed that she'd found '*The Wheel of Love*'. She turned in at the entrance.

Further down the valley, she could see the two steeply pitched gables of the farmhouse with its mellow honey-coloured stone. It looked idyllic. But that held no pleasure for her; her stomach twisted with apprehension for Zoe.

She drove round the house to the gravel parking area at the back. A Bentley and a Saab were parked up against the woodland fence. She was about to nose her Renault Mégane in between them then realised there wasn't quite enough room, and reversed into the space on the other side of the Saab. She drew to a halt and turned the engine off.

She pulled a copy of an email from the door pocket. A few phrases leapt out at her with the same force as when she'd first read them.

Hi, you in crowded, stressed old London from me in the peaceful, perfect Cotswolds…massive change of plan…I'm in love…Craig invited me out for supper…got to know him a whole lot better…gorgeous, sexy, intelligent…all I ever dreamed of…moved to his place…fantastic farmhouse a few miles from Cirencester…group called Wheel of Love…changes people's lives…won't be coming back…glad to leave London…paradise here…staying for ever…why not visit?… Material for a documentary here!..I'll tell Craig you're ringing…know what you're like with a story.

See what you think!

Love Zoe.

Juliet bit her lip, folding the sheet of paper. Zoe's tone still needled her as much as when she'd first read it. Zoe knew her sister wouldn't be able to resist coming to find out what was going on. And the suggestion about a documentary had worked out just as Zoe had proposed. Still, Juliet didn't like it, not one bit.

She was deeply suspicious of this Craig guy, for a start.

But friends and colleagues hadn't been at all sympathetic. One had said, *Hey, the love of her life and the truths of the universe all wrapped up in one package – great!* But Juliet knew she needed to come and see the situation for herself.

Another colleague had advised her to wait and see if this infatuation would blow over, despite the tone of the email. Not a hope. Not if Juliet knew Zoe. Too late now, anyway. She was here.

She had, in the limited time available, done a bit of research into whatever powers Craig might produce. Psychological powers, she thought most likely. Mind control. That sort of thing. But, as she'd discovered when she'd googled the subject, *Knowledge is power.*

Prepare yourself: that was the key. Know what you're up against.

So thinking, she stuffed the copy email into her shoulder-bag, pushed the door open and jumped out. Ahead of her she could see the north-facing wall of a fine tithe barn. The stonework all looked in perfect condition.

The atmosphere closed in around her. She drew a deep breath and felt strangely unsatisfied. Going to the back of the car, she opened the boot to lift her suitcase, laptop and portable recorder out. Setting them down on the ground, she locked the car.

As she turned, a champagne cork in the gravel drew her eye. She picked it up and twisted it in her hands, pondering. Then she glanced towards the back door, and saw the discarded bottle lying there. Going across, she took hold of that too.

She was suddenly aware of being watched.

A silver-haired man appraised her. "Found the champagne so soon?"

She straightened. "No. The bottle was empty when I saw it on the ground."

Might this be Craig? Did Zoe now prefer her men lined and wrinkled? But his Yorkshire accent soothed her. It hadn't seemed anything like so pronounced over the phone.

"Who are you?" he asked.

She put the champagne bottle and cork back down. "Juliet Blake. Zoe's sister."

He held out his hand to shake hers. His grip was firm, businesslike and brief. "McAllister's the name."

So it *was* Craig. She was about to ask where Zoe was, when he broke in.

"You caught me on a rare break. I've been slaving over a hot computer up there."

"Oh? How hot?"

"Scorching. Sweated over one cursed Excel spreadsheet all morning. Income and expenditure for the last year. Decided to take a break for the sake of my sanity."

"Auditing the accounts? Bit late, surely? We're more than halfway through June."

His glance sharpened. "Why? Not an accountant, are you?"

"No." *I introduced myself to him on the phone only yesterday. Surely he remembers.* "You know I'm a freelance radio journalist."

Silence cut between them.

"Journalist?" She could hear his breathing for a few moments. He moved a little closer. His eyes penetrated hers.

Why was he playing this game with her? She indicated her portable recorder. "It is still OK for the interviews?"

"Interviews?"

Is he testing my nerve, pretending he doesn't remember? Juliet gave a brittle laugh. But her BBC training five years back had taught her to get on with people of all types, and she was adept at disguising her true feelings.

"Want to start with me then?" he said.

"That would be a good idea," she replied. "After all, you've already enchanted my sister." *And you can begin by explaining how you managed to lure Zoe to your group.*

He stared at her and then burst out laughing. "Me? Enchanted her? Wish I had! No, you've got me wrong. That's my son Craig you're talking about."

"He's your son?"

"Expecting character instead of youth, were you?" he asked.

Her cheeks burned. She clenched her fists, rammed deep in the pockets of her combat jacket. How would she manage to keep up this restrained image? But she visualised Toby, her programme editor contact at Radio 4, who she hoped to sell her documentary to, and it helped.

"So he agreed to your coming to investigate?"

"He did."

"You fixed a fee?"

"Yes. Half payable on recording, the balance payable on broadcast."

"That's something." He nodded. "A step in the right direction, any road." He considered her. Then he deftly changed the subject. "Which matters most? Your keenness to quiz the group? Or your fears for your sister?"

She flushed. "Well, naturally, I'm worried about Zoe."

"No need. They're not axe murderers. Mad, I grant you; but harmless. Does that help?"

It didn't really. "Mad in what way?"

"Best you find that out for yourself. I won't tell you what to think. Last person to look to for that. Though you and I may have something in common."

"How so?"

"You're unhappy about your sister. And I… my problem's my son. He's created his own philosophy of life. Knows why we're here and what for. Always beat me. But when it comes to the practical stuff…" He shook his head. "No money sense at all."

Their eyes met and held. The atmosphere hung heavy between them. "You don't cast Craig in a very good light," Juliet said. "But he's mesmerised Zoe."

"True. Special ability he has with young women. He can be very charming."

She resisted an urge to follow him up on this subject. *So, Craig's charming is he? I'll be the judge of that, when I meet him.* "Good to have met you, Mr McAllister."

"Call me Don. Can I give you a hand?"

"Thanks, but no. I'll be all right." She walked back to her car, picked up her recorder case, and slung the strap over her shoulder. She was just about to grasp the handles of her laptop bag and suitcase when she saw Craig's father had followed her, and was standing close by. "Well, Don, I'd best be getting in."

"How long are you staying?" he asked.

"Few days at the most."

"You'll find the bookings diary in the front hall. Table near the stairs."

She nodded.

He studied her. "Good luck. You'll need it."

She stifled a smart reply.

"No sense in false pride," he said. "Let me carry your bags."

She moistened her lips. *You need to get on with him or you won't last long as an interviewer.* "All right."

As they reached the back door, her mobile phone buzzed. Digging it out of her pocket, she took the call, aware all the time of Don's searching gaze as she spoke to Toby's personal assistant.

"How are you getting on, Juliet?"

"Just arrived," Juliet answered in a low voice. "Can't say yet."

"Met Zoe yet? And Craig?"

"No to both. Tell Toby I'll call later."

"Fine. Bye – good luck."

"Thanks."

Don had the door open for her. Before she could step through, however, her way was blocked. Someone was coming out: a man. Early thirties. Tall. Dark haired. She swallowed. Was this him?

"Well timed," said Don.

"Oh, thanks, Father." Craig wore a deep-raspberry polo with white cotton twill trousers. He closely resembled a former English cricketer turned television personality. He looked athletic and relaxed, faultless in the role, completing the effect with gleaming Reeboks.

His eyes were fixed upon hers, dark and intense. He took her hand, and pressed it. "You must be Juliet. Delighted to see you here."

Her mind went blank. It was as if all thoughts cut out, for one second, two, three…

Craig broke the silence. "Did you have a good journey?"

"Yes thanks." She heard herself breathing. Almost as if she'd stopped, and restarted. Bizarre. What had happened just then?

He still had not released her hand. It seemed as if only she and Craig stood there, with no other person present.

Then, swiftly, she found words, as he dropped his hand back to his side. "Thank you for agreeing to the recordings."

"You're welcome."

"You impressed Zoe with your talk in Cirencester last week. She seems set on a long stay here."

Craig smiled. "She certainly is."

"May I see her? Is she around?"

"No, she's in the barn doing a group meditation."

"Not to stop before time's up. On pain of death," said Don shortly.

Craig switched subjects. "Like the house, Juliet?"

"I love what I've seen of it so far. To find a house so old in such beautiful condition…"

"Thank you," said Craig. "It was a bit run-down when we found it. But we've done some good work since then."

"Yes, haven't we?" said Don. She could have sworn he was trying to suppress mounting rage. "Very different state when we first saw it."

She looked from one to the other. It had taken only the very briefest exchange for her to register an odd blurring of the boundaries between father and son in the matter of who owned this place.

"See the date above the door there?" said Craig. "1532. As you might expect, a fascinating history. The first family who lived here were Catholics. This property was used as a safe house for displaced monks. Feel free to look around when you've settled in." He held her gaze for a few more moments.

"That's kind," she replied. "But I'm most anxious to see Zoe as soon as possible."

"Absolutely. I'll let her know you've arrived, once she's out of meditation." He still contemplated her. Then his manner became brisk. "As I said on the phone, take as much time as you like to explore the community. You're welcome to speak to anyone you wish."

"Good. We must have a briefing, Craig. When's the best time for us to talk? We need to discuss the contract, and get it signed. And then I'd like to learn something about your group members. And draw up a schedule of interviews."

"Of course, Juliet. Four o'clock suit you? Fine." He turned to Don. "You two clearly met a few moments before I turned up."

"We did."

Craig rubbed his hands together. "Would you please show Juliet round then, Father? I'm just off to deal with an urgent call. See you later." And without giving further details, he shot away, round the north side of the house.

Juliet turned back to Don.

"Come on," Don said, and they stepped into the house.

They stood in the passageway. The stone walls were whitewashed, and a variety of corn dollies hung along their length. To her left Juliet could see the utility area, and to the right a rack containing an assortment of boots and walking shoes.

"Aha," she said. "So the group are keen on walking then?"

"No doubt about that," said Don.

"Just as one might hope, among these rolling hills." She could hardly wait to get out there, crossing stiles and streams, following woodland trails that might lead her to the top of a high escarpment and open onto stunning views.

Don continued to look at her. *He's trying to read my thoughts. Such as – 'at least they do something normal like going for country walks'.*

Don led the way forward until he reached a right-hand turn. At this point, a door ahead banged open and someone charged out. She stopped just in time: a small, slight woman in a flimsy voile dress.

"Oh! Hello, Don," she said.

"Watch where you're going, Laura." He jerked his head towards Juliet.

Laura assessed Juliet with birdlike eyes, and Juliet returned the scrutiny. Laura could have been in her twenties, or her late forties, for all Juliet could tell. Her hair fanned around her head like a gorgon. *Looks like she hasn't brushed it in days. Wouldn't impress in a BBC production office. Not that she'd be likely to enter one.*

"You're Zoe's sister, aren't you?" Laura spoke in a breathless voice.

"Yes, I am."

"Thought as much. Recognised your hair. You look so like her."

"Yes. People often say that."

"You're a freelance journalist, aren't you? Zoe told us. And I was expecting a big power-dressing media type."

"Were you?" said Juliet, amused.

"Let me introduce myself. I'm Laura. Laura Greevey." She held out her hand, which Juliet took at once.

"Pleased to meet you, Laura." Laura's fingers felt light and insubstantial.

Disengaging her fingers from Juliet's, Laura turned to speak to Don. "You're taking Juliet through, are you?"

"Looks like it. Craig landed me the job."

"I'll do it if you like," Laura offered.

"Oh no," he said. "Suits me fine. Want to join us, Laura?"

"Be happy to." She looked at Juliet. "Zoe's booked you a room. We'll show you up there."

Juliet followed Laura and Don into the dining room. Shafts of light slanted across the flagstone floor, and the finely blended scent of ancient oak timbers and beeswax polish came to her nostrils. She gazed at the dark exposed beams and the deep window recesses. Her heart lifted, despite herself. This looked and felt like the sort of place you might dream of staying in for a country house weekend break.

Other elements combined in the fragrance. Looking about her, she recognised the source of these as the basket of apple logs in the fireplace, together with two shining bronze bowls of freshly cut roses.

"What an inviting room," Juliet said.

"Yes." Laura indicated a small black door to the left of the inglenook. "Beyond that's a secret spiral staircase. Not so secret any more of course. Winds up through the thickness of the wall, and takes you to the Monk's Room. I love it there."

"Good place to hide. If it all gets too much," said Don.

"Hope I'll have no need for that."

He chuckled. "Expect you will."

Juliet's spine tingled.

Without qualifying his last statement, Don nodded at the oak refectory table set beneath a low-hanging wrought-iron chandelier. "They eat here in the evenings."

Juliet turned to Laura. "I see you can seat sixteen."

"That's right. Enough to accommodate the permanent members, and any visitors like you. Come along." Laura led her past the table. Juliet stopped. On the wall before her hung a large tapestry panel. She gazed at it, her favourite medieval scene, from *The Lady and the Unicorn*, with its rich colours and exquisite details. There stood the lady at the entrance to her tent, beneath the words: *A mon seul désir, my heart's one desire*, jewels spilling from her hands as her maidservant held out an open casket. She was flanked by the seduced unicorn begging at her left, and the lion to her right. How appropriate for Craig to choose this, for the Wheel of Love.

They passed through the doorway and entered a sitting room. Late morning sun streamed through the leaded window panes, tinting the oak floor timbers gold, and enriching the colours of the silk long-fringed rugs.

"Another lovely room," murmured Juliet. But something wasn't quite right. Though she couldn't say what.

A gold-painted grandfather clock dominated the opposite corner. A number of flame-red velvet armchairs invited the three, from their position in front of the oak wainscoting.

Laura chattered on. "We won't sink into them now. We all gather in here for drinks before dinner."

"That's right. A whisky or two guarantees survival in this group," muttered Don.

On the surface, it all looked perfect to Juliet, with or without the addition of a cocktail hour. And it was clear why Zoe loved this place. And yet she still felt something was not as it should be. She managed a polite smile.

They passed through a further doorway into the entrance hall, again with low ceilings, polished oak floors and wainscoting.

Don fanned the pages of a bookings diary on the circular table. "Here's your room," he said. "It's up in the loft. I'll take your suitcase. Let's go."

"Oh," said Laura, "and have a brochure while you're at it." She lifted one from a pile beside the diary, and tucked it into Juliet's pocket.

They began to climb the oak staircase, which creaked with every step. Laura and Don led her past the first floor.

"Keep climbing," said Laura. They went up a steeper, narrower flight of stairs to the attic, which had been converted to provide extra accommodation.

"Here you are." Don opened the first door on the left. "Two more bedrooms along there. Can't think for the moment who's in them."

"I look forward to finding out."

"Now I come to think of it, might be Zoe's in one," he said. "There's a bathroom up here too. Settle in." He put the suitcase on the bed. For a moment he looked around thoughtfully. "Not bad up here. Me, I'm in the goose house."

"The goose house?" she asked.

He laughed. "Been converted into a bedroom and bathroom. Round the south side of the house, past the barn."

"And very nice too," said Laura, behind Don. "Almost wish I was in it myself. But I'm down on the first floor." She giggled. "Near Al's room."

Juliet looked at her. What did this signify? Who was Al? She'd make it her business to find out before long.

"Make yourself comfortable," went on Laura. "You'll find lunch in the kitchen. See you down there." And before Juliet could ask again when she might expect to see Zoe, Laura and Don disappeared.

Once in her room, Juliet sank onto the bed and took several deep breaths.

Well, she'd arrived. But she did wish she'd met Zoe. Her instinct was to set off and search for her sister at once. She had so many questions. What might Zoe's plans be for herself and Craig? Did the pair of them, in fact, have any plans? And the group: mad but harmless, Don had said. What did that mean? And did Zoe agree?

Unpacking could wait. She jumped to her feet again. Then she remembered the brochure. Quickly, she pulled the tri-fold format publication from her pocket, and opened it out.

If you've been searching all your life, but have so far not found what you've been looking for, you've come to the right place. Here at the Wheel of Love, you may sharpen your subtle knife and cut a window into heaven. There are no limits to what you can achieve here; only those you impose upon yourself. You've chosen to come so we promise to supply the necessary tools. If you accept these tools and use them well, you'll enter a freedom you've never dared dream of.

Craig will reach deep down into your spirit and touch a part of it you never knew was there.

She closed the brochure. *Creepy.* She didn't need him to reach down into her spirit, or provide her with tools to enter heaven. Nor did she trust the word *freedom*, until she knew how he defined it. How did Zoe get caught up in this?

But she had to admit the place didn't look like her idea of the headquarters of a weird sect. More like a luxurious English country retreat.

And there was Craig's father. A brusque Yorkshireman auditing the accounts. Sharp-tongued and clearly not a hundred percent in sympathy with his son.

She speculated about Craig's community. She'd only met one member so far, Laura. Quaint little lady. Elfin features. *Seems to have stepped out of a nineteenth-century children's novel. Probably meet her again later.*

Then she focused on her surroundings. A compact room, purple curtains, lilac carpet, fitted out in antique pine, perched beneath the black rafters. The dormer window had diamond leadlights and golden sandstone mullions. From where she was standing, she could see down to the front of the house, onto the gravel forecourt.

Then movement before the front door attracted her eye. Zoe. As Juliet watched, her sister made her way round to the back of the house. Juliet hurried from the room. If she was quick, she'd catch up with Zoe in the car park where she'd met Don earlier.

Retracing her steps back through the rooms Laura and Don had shown her, she went along the passageway to the back door. Opening it and stepping through, she just avoided tripping over the champagne bottle, and hastened forward.

"Zoe!" she called.

2

A Seductive Voice

Juliet grasped Zoe by both shoulders, and looked straight into her shining eyes.

"Juliet! When did you arrive?" Zoe flung her arms around her.

"An hour ago. And I've found my room." Juliet squeezed Zoe.

"Cool. Oh, Juliet, you're going to love it here."

"It all seems great so far. And you're looking pretty good yourself."

"That's probably because I've been doing yoga relaxation and creative visualisation this morning."

Juliet gave her sister a quick inspection. Somehow she'd imagined her looking different in this new life of hers. Though she wasn't quite sure what she'd anticipated: shaved head and druid's robes? She'd already seen the way Craig dressed, a clue to the fact that she'd have quite a few of her expectations defeated here. Zoe's brilliant red-gold hair – a colour both girls shared – was worn loose and wild as ever, and she wore a navy and white tie-dyed cotton skirt. Her cream cheesecloth shirt flapped open, revealing the black lycra leotard she wore beneath.

"Who knows what could happen?" said Zoe. "You may want to stay long term, Juliet."

"Hmm. Unlikely. It's a big enough deal to have interested Toby in this project. I can't afford to waste these next few days. I'm here to work, not to have a good time."

"Your plans may change. Be prepared for anything," said Zoe.

Juliet bit her lip.

"How are things going with Craig?" she asked.

"Fantastic. Couldn't be better." Zoe scuffed her trainers against the gravel, then pointed north. "Come on. Let's go round the house to the front garden. We can sit there and talk."

"Sure." Juliet hurried after her sister.

Unlatching the gate, Zoe went through, and Juliet followed. Before them appeared a flight of stone steps leading to a sunken lawn with a water-lily pond.

"This is stunning," she said.

"Isn't it?" Zoe indicated the Scots pines and the blue cedars over to the north of the sunken garden. The two girls went towards these. Scattered beneath were a number of white cane chairs.

As soon as they sat down, Zoe burst into excited speech. "So Juliet, what do you think?" Her eye fell on Juliet's pocket. "You already have the brochure."

"I've started reading it. Craig makes big promises, doesn't he? They certainly lead you to expect huge rewards."

"And you'll find them," declared Zoe. "Wait till you meet him."

"I have met him."

"That's wonderful. So you'll know. He's perfect."

"Well, I'm not quite sure about…"

"Whose side are you on?"

Juliet leaned forward, and took hold of Zoe by both shoulders. "Hey, I can see why you've fallen for him. He's the best-looking guy I've ever met."

Zoe visibly relaxed.

"If he feels the same about you as you do about him," continued Juliet, "then that can only be good news."

A smile of relief spread over her sister's face.

"You're here for the best of reasons, Zoe. And I'll give you the benefit of the doubt. Let's suppose Craig is everything you believe he is. But even so – what's with the Wheel of Love? Sounds a bit dubious to me."

"We're not like that Heaven's Gate sect, you know."

Certain key words hammered into Juliet's brain. *Sharpen your subtle knife...cut a window into heaven...freedom you've never dared dream of...* "This *heaven* stuff he goes in for... the bit about *freedom you've never dared dream of*, and him *reaching deep down into your spirit...* What's that all about?"

"You'd need to live as one of us to understand."

"Give me a break, Zoe. I won't do that."

"If you want answers to your questions, read the rest of it."

"OK." Juliet took the brochure from her pocket, and opened it out.

She skim-read: *express all your emotions, good and bad...interpretation of dreams...dynamic meditation...guided fantasies and group therapy...self-evident truths... destiny lies in our own hands...no such thing as chance or accident so far as human beings are concerned...any further questions, ask Craig...here to guide you. Use him. He wants to be used.*

"Doesn't that fill you with hope?" cried Zoe, "and inspire you with a vision of new life?"

"Can't be sure. Craig says we must *express all emotions, good and bad.* Bad? I don't want to express mine. He seems to think *our destiny lies in our own hands.* I don't accept that. I'm here because I'm worried about you. How can he say there's *no such thing as chance or accident*? Though, of course, I look forward to interviewing him about it, and finding out."

"Don't be so negative."

"I don't mean to be. Sorry it seems like that to you. Look, why not spend this week here, then return to London with me? If Craig cares for you, he'll stay in touch."

"No. I don't want to go back to London. I want to stay here."

"But you have so much ahead of you. And your job applications... don't give up on them, will you? You have a good degree."

"I know, I know. But..."

"You don't want to waste it."

"Whoever said I was going to?"

"Why are you so stubborn?"

"Because you don't understand how I feel about Craig. Your mind's closed."

"No it isn't. I'm here to learn the truth, just as you are."

"A different truth."

They glared at each other.

"Craig's hypnotised you, hasn't he?" said Juliet.

"How dare you suggest that?" Zoe sprang to her feet and flew across to the gate.

Juliet jumped up too. "Zoe! Stop! I didn't mean…"

Snatching the gate open, Zoe turned. "You've already made a judgement, haven't you? Call yourself a journalist."

Juliet opened her mouth to protest, but Zoe was racing across the gravel forecourt. Juliet tried to steady herself, shaking.

Looking about, the place still seemed deserted. Where was everyone? Then a figure appeared from round the north side of the house, crossing the forecourt to the garden gate: Don.

They might have had a sharp exchange that morning; but he was the only person she'd met so far here who had his feet on the ground.

"Your sister didn't look happy," he remarked, as he closed the gate behind him.

"No," said Juliet. "She thinks I'm unsympathetic."

"And are you?" he enquired.

"Of course not."

He rubbed his chin as he looked at her. "Been thinking over our little chat. Bit abrupt. Like to apologise."

"That's good of you." She stuffed her hands into the pockets of her combat jacket.

"Take a seat?"

"Why not?"

They went over to the white cane chairs, and settled into two placed opposite one another.

"You and me – we're both outsiders," he said.

"Yes. I'm here visiting Zoe. And you've come to look at the group's finances."

He gave a curt nod. "Cash-flow problem." He studied the ground, then looked up again. "This is by way of an annual holiday. Not how I planned it, of course. But that's by the by. Call it a family visit."

"So what line of business are you in?"

"Property management. For me, this place is a sizeable investment."

"Oh – I wouldn't have expected Craig to have such connections."

"That so?" His voice was barbed.

"Property business, you say. Is yours a demanding role?" she asked.

"Company director and chairman." This time his eyes remained fixed on hers. "My father ran it before me." Reaching into his inside pocket, he pulled out a business card. "Here."

"Thank you." She studied it. "Ah. Family firm. I'm surprised you decided to come here to your son's community, and take on the worry of troubleshooting his problems. Couldn't you have delegated that? Appointed an accountant perhaps? You must be a very busy man."

"Glad you appreciate it." A little of his tension evaporated. "Not sure Craig sees it that way." He probed the cane weaving on the arm of his chair with his fingers for a few moments. "But I had to come." He volunteered no further information on the subject. "And you, Juliet? Who'll broadcast your stuff?"

"BBC I hope. I'm offering this to an independent production company and they'll pitch it to Radio 4."

"And if they don't want it?"

"A local radio station might pick it up."

"You work for yourself?"

"I do." She slipped her hand into her own pocket, depositing Don's card, and finding one of her own business cards. "Here you are."

Taking it, he scanned it for a few seconds before looking up again. "So Craig's giving you your big chance here."

"You could put it like that." She hoped her newness to all this wasn't glaringly obvious. She'd never sold a documentary before. Just filler spots for features programmes and regional news items. And (until Zoe's email had knocked her off balance) her sole focus had been to win national acclaim with a documentary.

"So. Bit of a testing ground for you here," he said, adding Juliet's card to his own collection.

She nodded.

"Craig's scored one credit in his copy book, any road," said Don. "For having you to stay."

"Thanks."

"And he'll let you record what you like?"

"Certainly. He expressed no objection."

Don looked sardonic. "Might be coming. Once he's thought things through. You wait and see."

They both turned as they heard the garden gate being unlatched.

"Ah, Llewellyn," said Don. "Welcome."

"Our in-house poet," he explained to Juliet.

A young man approached. "Don," he declared, brushing a thick wing of hair back from his forehead in a theatrical gesture. "Just the man I wanted to see. I need marketing advice." He drew up sharply at the sight of Juliet. "I do apologise. Hadn't realised…" He regarded her with lively interest. "Hope I haven't interrupted anything." He stuffed an apple into the rucksack he carried over one shoulder.

"See you've fixed yourself a packed lunch," said Don.

"Yes. I'm off up to the ridge for a few hours." He extended his free hand to Juliet, and grasped hers firmly. "Don't think we've met."

"No." His accent put her in mind of the Welsh hills.

Don moved forward. "Juliet, meet Llewellyn. From Anglesey."

"Pleased to meet you," she said.

They shook hands.

"So, you're Zoe's sister. And you hope to make a documentary?"

She nodded.

"I'm surprised he's agreed to it." He glanced at Don.

"Me too," said Don.

"As I'm sure you both realise," she said, "I aim to be fair and accurate."

Don grunted. "I've spent thirty years doing that with Craig. And look where it's got me."

"You sound jaundiced, Don."

"Juliet's right there." Llewellyn laughed. "If only you had as much faith in people as I do, Don."

"Hmm," said the Yorkshireman. "Well, you must think something of them, else you'd write no poems at all."

"Ah yes." Juliet looked at Llewellyn. "Don did say you were a poet."

"That's right."

"Turn your back, and he runs up a verse," said Don.

"I've had a fair measure of success," the Welshman conceded modestly. "Won a couple of poetry slams. Performed at literary festivals – Cheltenham, Hay-on-Wye, Oxford… Brought out two slim volumes so far."

Juliet wondered why someone with such a record of achievement had turned up in a group like this, which promised tools she fully expected he, as a poet, already possessed.

But before she could ask, Don intervened. "Did you want marketing advice?"

"Yes," said Llewellyn.

"What's your product?"

The Welshman opened his rucksack again, and pulled out what looked like a rolled-up news sheet.

"Take a look. And you too, Juliet." He handed it to her. "Delighted to have the thoughts of a newcomer like yourself."

She spread it out on the table and glanced at the front page. The image of a saffron pathway winding up a viridian green mountainside to a sunlit peak, enclosed within an electric-blue sphere, made her think of something one might produce in a creative visualisation workshop. She could almost see the legend scrawled beneath it: *I am choosing to be successful.*

Pulling herself smartly back to the matter in hand, she read the masthead: *Wheel of Love Weekly News.*

Don came and glanced over it with her. "Might work," he said. "Planning to run off a few copies? Got a mailing list?"

"No," said Llewellyn, "Thought I'd sell it on the street."

"What's your cover price?" asked Don.

"One pound ninety-five pence." The Welshman moved close to Don, massaging his shoulder in a matey manner. "So, the two of you, just imagine you're window shopping in Cirencester, and I pounce on you with this. Would you buy it?"

Don and Juliet leafed through it together. The centre page spread was entirely taken up with *The poems of Llewellyn Hughes.*

"A money spinner, I do assure you," murmured the Welshman.

"It's a fundraising idea. I'll give it that," remarked Don.

"What do you think, Juliet?" asked Llewellyn. "Could it sell?"

"People might well be attracted to it."

"I thought so too," cried Llewellyn. "It's bright, it's positive, it's life-enhancing. The illustrations are all in full colour."

Don laughed. He handed the news sheet back. "Could give it a go."

"Glad to see you have faith, Don."

"Ah. Faith. Not so fast. You know me. I'm lacking in that department." Don dug his hand in his trouser pocket, brought out his handkerchief, and blew his nose. She suspected it was a device to cover his awkwardness, rather than because he was starting a cold.

"The only way to prove something true or false," Llewellyn said, "is to suspend disbelief, and agree to conduct an experiment, as if it were true."

Don shook his head. "Don't believe it. Recipe for a self-fulfilling prophecy."

Juliet gazed from one to the other. How would Llewellyn counter Don's argument?

Silence fell instead.

The Welshman's hair stirred in the breeze. "Perhaps you should take part a little more, Don," he suggested. "You haven't done that yet, have you? And you've been here nearly a week. We've all noticed. Why don't you join in?"

Don lifted his hands, as if raising a shield against an oncoming charger. "I'm here to sort the finances, not attend my own son's classes," he said. "Though he'd be keen enough to show off his skills, I'd be bound."

"Come to Dynamic Meditation in the barn tomorrow evening," said Llewellyn. "You don't want to miss out. I hope you'll forgive me for quoting one of my fellow countrymen. The poet R.S. Thomas speaks about seeing *the sun break through to illuminate a small field.* That might be the experience you're having now."

"Nonsense," said Don. "Expect me to swallow that?"

Juliet couldn't resist a smile.

"In the poem," continued Llewellyn, "he goes his way and forgets it. Years later he discovers it was *the one field that had the treasure in it.* Do the same, Don, and you might spend the rest of your life searching for it again."

His gaze swung round to include both of them. "*There are more things in heaven and earth, Horatio, than are dreamt of in your philosophy*," he remarked.

"Thought you'd quote that," grunted Don. Then he sighed. "Idealism of youth. Tell me. What do you know about gullibility, cheating and lies?"

"Plenty," Llewellyn said softly. "Put away your cynicism."

"You're persuasive, Llewellyn," said Juliet. "What's Dynamic Meditation?"

Don broke in. "They let all their emotions hang out. Be warned."

"You come too, Juliet," said Llewellyn. "It might open something up in you. Try it. It could help you understand what we're about."

Then he said his goodbyes and walked back through the gateway, leaving her alone with Don once more.

"So, Don?" she said. "What do you think?"

"Oh, I've heard a silver tongue or two in my time."

"But what about Dynamic Meditation?" she persisted. "Will you go? I certainly shall, to make recordings. Why not join me?"

"Perhaps. If I do, Craig may even…" He stopped short.

"Craig may even do what?"

"Nothing."

She felt rebuffed.

Then he said, "You'll want a bite of lunch. Come along." He set off towards the garden gate, and she followed. "Might meet a few more of them," he flung over his shoulder. "Won't join you though. Just show you the way."

Hmm. No more clues from him then, for a while. But never mind. She'd meet some others.

As they passed through the gateway, and emerged onto the forecourt again, a door on the north side of the house banged shut, and they heard voices raised in argument.

"What's that about?" she asked. "I thought this was a place of love and serenity."

"Did you?" Don crossed to the front door and held it open.

"Yes. Isn't that what Craig's brochure promises?" She walked through into the hallway.

"Look more closely," said Don, closing the door behind them. "Might find something very different."

"Oh?"

He nodded. "All that talk of heaven. And freedom." He went through into the sitting room, and as she joined him, he swung to face her.

"I'm well aware those two words are much misused," she said.

"Even more so here. *Express all emotions – good and bad.* That's what he tells them. And so they do. Especially the last."

"What do you mean?"

"Ha! Best not go into it." He held her gaze. "Wait till you've tasted it yourself."

Then she heard a sound like a nut being cracked behind her. She spun, and gasped. She was staring into the eyes of a parrot.

He balanced on his perch on one foot. His cage occupied the corner of the room next to the leadlight window.

"Meet Groucho," said Don. "He's Craig's."

"How did I manage to miss him before?"

"Ah. Keeps quiet when it suits him," said Don.

He waited while she went over to stroke the parrot's plumage of cobalt blue and deep yellowy orange. Then he moved alongside her. "Pricey he was too. Craig wouldn't have any other."

"Oh?"

"Yes. Set him back a thousand. And don't forget maintenance costs. He'll likely live to sixty," he added darkly.

They watched the parrot scattering bits of walnut shell over the floor, and using his blunt tongue to extract the nut-meat. She reached out, and scratched his wing. At this, he hopped off his perch and onto her hand. He walked up her arm, and began to rummage in her hair with his beak. She was so engrossed by him that several minutes had passed before she remembered Don again.

He touched her on the shoulder. She gave a start, causing the bird to rise to the ceiling in a flurry of sapphire and gold. He settled on the top of a bookcase, quizzing them with a glittering eye.

She turned to see Laura had rejoined them. How childlike she was. The dress was probably meant for a thirteen-year-old. Though Juliet reckoned Laura might be in her forties.

"Ah, Laura." Don took his opportunity. "I'll be off then, Juliet. Laura will show you where to find lunch."

"Thank you, Don."

He gave a curt nod and left the room.

"Come through into the kitchen." Laura led her to the farther door. "There are two others in there I can introduce you to."

"I'd like that."

As before, though slightly odd in her manner, Laura seemed friendly enough. Encouraged, Juliet followed her through the dining room, and out into the passage, where they turned left into an open doorway.

The kitchen she found generously supplied with copper implements, brightly polished, hanging from the beams overhead; and the whitewashed walls between the black timbers were decorated with large bunches of dried flowers. A pale youth in his late teens sat at one end of the oak table, stirring a spoon round and round in a soup bowl. At the other end stood a thickset man in a lime-green shirt, busy sawing at a granary loaf.

A list of rules pinned to a cork noticeboard above the fridge began with the statement: *On the following days, silence will be observed at breakfast and lunch.* She wondered if Craig liked to keep up a myth that the group had rules to be adhered to. But there again, she knew nothing to suppose it didn't. However, that day, Friday, was absent from the list.

Both men had stopped what they were doing to stare at her.

"Sam and Al," cried Laura, "meet Zoe's sister, Juliet."

Ah, thought Juliet, so one of these two is Al. The man whose bedroom was near Laura's, a fact which had caused giggles when she mentioned it. Which one was he?

"Juliet, the journalist?" The youth opened his eyes wide.

"Yes, Sam," said Laura.

Sam shrank back in terror.

"The media isn't that scary, is it?" laughed Juliet.

Then she realised what a big deal it was for this group of people to trust Zoe after only three days here to invite her journalist sister to visit. Though she supposed it was Craig they trusted, not Zoe, for he was the one who'd given permission. Odd though, when clearly he had issues with his father, and she'd have thought he'd prefer them not to be aired to a radio audience.

She remembered Llewellyn's words: *The only way to prove something true or false is to suspend disbelief, and agree to conduct an experiment, as if it were true.* She didn't think she wanted to live that out herself.

"Well, well, well," said the big man in a soothing bass. "Media hound or not, you don't look at all like we imagined you."

"Although we did guess you'd look a little like Zoe," said Laura.

Fixing Juliet with a luminous gaze, the man continued. "Same gorgeous red hair, same green eyes. You look more controlled than your sister. Neater. Zoe's a little wild."

Juliet laughed. "You are an American, aren't you?"

"Sure am. Born in New York. Raised in the Berkshire Hills around Pittsfield, Massachusetts. Alan Beckert. Call me Al." He thrust his hand out. It was large and well-muscled, and nearly cut her blood supply off. Fortunately he didn't maintain his grip too long.

"Pleased to meet you," she said, flexing her fingers. "What are you doing here in England, Al?"

"Touring. At least I was. Now I've wound up here. And I'm staying put." He cast a quick glance at Laura. "I'm hooked on you Brits. Love your hang-ups."

"Thank you. On behalf of British people, I'm flattered," she said.

Though, when it came to hang-ups, no doubt a rich treasure store of them lay waiting to be found here. But she had yet to meet the other members of the group to confirm that.

"Irony," said Al. "There's something else I love. You've all got it. But back to the hang-ups. Some of you people say I put my finger straight on your problems. That's great. I'll stay just as long as I'm needed." He gave a genial grin.

Wasn't it supposed to be Craig sorting out everyone's problems, not him? She noticed Al wore his shirt with most of the buttons undone. This exposed the silver medallion nestling among his chest hairs. He looked like something left over from Woodstock. She'd be none too happy to trust him with her problems.

"You haven't put your finger on mine yet, Al," observed Laura.

Al gave her a lingering look. "I'm pretty much ready to get going soon as you let me, honey." Then he turned to the youth. "You going to introduce yourself to our visitor?"

"Sam. Sam D-D-Dorling. I can't t-tell you about myself, Juliet. I can n-n-never do anything in f-f-front of anybody."

Al looked at Juliet again. "Sam has a bad time of it with his nerves."

"Enforced separation from his twin brother," said Laura.

"His GP green-lighted it," added Al. "Get the picture?"

Juliet didn't really, and took the nearest vacant seat at the table. She was beginning to glimpse what she'd let herself in for.

"So," said Laura, "how do you find us so far?"

Juliet played for time by fiddling with the silver bracelet on her left wrist. Though she was here to check up on her sister, and hopefully to rescue her, she could still feel the attraction of the place.

"I'm not here to judge," she said. "But one thing's for sure. The house is out of this world. It seems to have a personality of its own."

"I was sure you'd feel it before you'd been here long." Laura's face glowed. "Craig wants people to see what he calls *the true reality*, which isn't like the outside world at all."

"But don't you think living here for several months tends to make people not quite *real* themselves?" asked Juliet.

"No. Why should it? Look at me. I've been here since January," said Laura.

Juliet remained silent.

"Go on," urged Laura. "Say what you think. We can take it."

"Please don't misunderstand me, Laura," said Juliet. "But I already have a feeling that it might be a glass bubble, too good to be true."

"Stuff and nonsense," said Laura. "Trust me. It's real, all right."

The door opened, and another group member came in. "Ah, food. Just what I need."

Juliet turned. The newcomer had a circular bald patch on the crown of his head, rather like a monk, but offset this effect by sporting a luxuriant, almost Parisian, moustache. Rising to her feet again, and facing him, she found herself the subject of an unnerving scrutiny.

"Juliet, this is Edgar," said Al.

"Ah! Our media lady." Edgar thrust out his hand. "Very happy to make your acquaintance." His grip, too, was immensely strong, but swiftly released. "Edgar Swinton. In charge of Craig's forecasts, five-year plans, and statistics. I also interview the new recruits. I know what you're here for, Juliet. Craig prepared us well for your arrival last night at dinner. You'll want to mingle with the group and be as it were, one of us. I've a number of questions to put to you which I hope we can deal with quite quickly, perhaps after lunch."

She winced.

"Ah, you're a little uptight about this," smiled Al. "It's OK. Edgar's not from the FBI."

"Maybe not, but I hardly think it appropriate…" began Juliet. What would her fellow journalists make of this? How would they handle it?

Edgar drove remorselessly on. "You'll be thrilled by our little chat. I designed the questions myself. They cover every possible eventuality."

Well, if he planned to include her in his ritual, she'd need to set him straight – without causing offence. She could be treading on eggshells here.

"You've taken me aback, Edgar. What did you want to know?"

"I'm simply curious to learn about your spiritual position."

"I have no position. None that's relevant to you. I'm here as a journalist."

She'd stopped short at using the word *objective*. She knew it would be untrue.

"None of us believe you're objective for a moment," said Edgar, "but even if you want to dispute that, I still need you to provide me with some information about yourself."

"But…" She spoke courteously but firmly. "Afraid not. I'm here in a professional capacity."

Edgar ignored this. "To help you, I've put all the questions down in writing." He handed over a clipboard securing a wad of A4 paper.

A breathless hush followed. She sensed a power struggle. Perhaps she needed to try a different, lighter approach. "If I answer your questions, will you play your part, and give me an in-depth interview?"

The other three were all watching with a strange intensity.

"Very good, very good," said Edgar. "I can see you're trying to sidestep the issue."

"Don't be afraid to reveal yourself, dear," said Laura.

Juliet met Laura's gaze. "It's not that at all, Laura. I'm sure you understand perfectly."

Feeling it best to humour him for the time being, she scanned Edgar's top sheet.

"We've all come here in need of healing," said Edgar. "Don't be proud. Pride has no place here."

Juliet swallowed the words that had been about to fly to her lips.

She looked down at the form again. The first words that met her eye were: *What is your age and sex?* And then: *Are you receiving any form of treatment or therapy?*

"Don't delay lunch for it, there's plenty of time." Edgar reached for the Double Gloucester. "But I shall want it back for Craig by five."

Ah. A breathing space. Juliet helped herself to one of Al's thick slices of bread. "You haven't told me about yourself yet, Edgar. What's your background?"

He cleared his throat. "I used to systematically study man's religious experience."

"*Used to*? Why the past tense?"

"The unit I headed up closed down through lack of funding." He cast a severe glance at her, as if she was personally responsible for it herself. Then he went on. "So I'm here instead. I devised this questionnaire for Craig. The idea is to get proper scientific evidence about human spirituality. I know others have gone before me. But I have a passion to pin down the evidence, starting with you lot."

He wore a self-satisfied expression as he busied himself with the salad bowl.

"Sounds ambitious," said Juliet. "I hope you do get your evidence. Must admit I don't feel I have any to give yet."

He gave a dismissive snort. "Everybody here is raw material as far as I'm concerned. You're no exception even if you have come here to interview us."

Juliet looked down at her knuckles and saw they were white. That was the effect of Edgar's last sentence. She consciously relaxed her hands.

Edgar, meanwhile, speared a cherry tomato with his fork and began munching.

"We've all filled in one of his forms." Laura leaned toward Juliet, an intimate smile upon her face.

"Maybe," Juliet said. "But I'm here for a different reason."

"Oh, don't try that with us, Juliet." Edgar lifted his hands, palms uppermost. "We're all where we're meant to be, and you're here for a special purpose. I can see you feel you're somehow set apart from the rest of us. But you'll soon get over that. And we each have to learn it's no good holding back from the group. We are, after all, part of the Wheel of Love."

She countered him swiftly. "But does love demand the completion of a form?"

He raised his eyebrows.

"We're not railroading you into this, Juliet," said Al. "You just relax, huh? Perhaps you're one of these guys who like to make a big show of chewing it over." He placed a large dish of some unidentifiable-looking substance on the table. It steamed gently. "And I'll wait for this to cool down."

"What is it?" she asked.

"Tomorrow morning's breakfast for the parrot. Groucho. You weren't here earlier to see it prepared, were you? We run a rota to cook it up for him. Rice, millet, couscous, lentils and split peas garnished with chopped herbs, mixed veg and…" he unscrewed the top off a jar, "a generous helping of his vitamin and mineral supplement." He scattered a white powder in, and stirred with a wooden spoon. "Delicious."

"Groucho certainly gets excellent treatment," laughed Juliet. "He must love it."

"Sure does." The American seated himself opposite her, his plate piled high with a well-oiled salad. "Go on, answer the man's questions." He reached for the butter. "I haven't yet figured out this English obsession with privacy. I'm curious about you. We all are. How did you wind up here? How did you swing it by Craig?"

"Yes, Juliet," said Laura, "Craig said you wanted to make a documentary."

Al turned to Juliet again. "I'd kinda like to know a bit more about that. What's the thrust of your piece?"

Ah, she was back on home ground. She could easily explain her journalistic approach, without causing offence. She opened her mouth to speak, but Edgar broke in. "Naughty, naughty, Al," he said. "Don't put Juliet on the spot too soon." His eyes gleamed. He wagged his finger in front of the American. "Not, that is, until she's shared her experiences with me."

"Which ones?" she asked.

"Ecstatic ones," he said.

Who did he think he was? Why should she bare her soul to him?

"Take your time. But not too long. Evidence, that's what I like." Edgar rubbed his hands together. "Evidence of any type. There's no evidence so thin I cannot massage it."

"Take it from him. The man means what he says," observed Al.

Probably best to concentrate on her lunch. But she couldn't resist pushing Edgar further on the subject. "I'm not a member of the group, and have no plans to join. I'm here as an impartial observer. And there are various guidelines that I have to observe…"

"The broadcast media has the highest code of conduct…" murmured Edgar. A titter passed between the other three at this.

"What you suggest is impossible. If you're to achieve anything here, you'll have to take part, and live as one of us," said Laura.

Juliet swallowed two or three times. Deep down she knew Laura was probably right. But could she pretend to go along with their beliefs without compromising herself? Weren't they all nuts, in one way or another? And yet she knew she wasn't the only one here who felt like that. Surely Don did too.

They allowed her to spend the next five minutes eating, before Edgar took up the topic again. "Therapy or treatment? What about those, Juliet? Have you ever had any?"

"No. There's nothing wrong with me."

"There doesn't have to be anything *wrong* with you, dear." Laura turned an earnest face to her. "But you'll have needs. We all have those. And they are what have brought us here."

Juliet considered. Since her relationship with her last boyfriend had broken up, just two months before, she'd set her sights more firmly than ever upon her career, and upon trying to help Zoe. She needed recognition, acknowledgement, acceptance… and some truth from Craig about his plans for her sister, for a start.

"Well," she said, "I expect I do have a need to find some answers." She gave a half-smile.

Edgar quickly took his opportunity to get back to the all-important questionnaire. "So," he said. "You can't at this moment remember an ecstatic experience to share with me. Let's move on to another question instead. How have you been feeling in the past week?"

No, she wasn't going to be drawn. "As from Wednesday – which was when I received Zoe's email – I've been looking forward to the challenge of meeting you and your fellow group members." As Juliet levelled her eye upon Edgar, there came several loud knocks on the kitchen door. They all looked up, startled.

"Come in," called Edgar. The door banged back, and a dishevelled figure lurched through the doorway, dumping a well-stuffed plastic carrier bag down onto the quarry tiles.

"James!" cried Laura. "Why must you do this at meal-times? Every time you do, I swear you get filthier and filthier. It's a good thing Craig never saw you in this state up in Edinburgh. Otherwise, I'm sure none of us would be here now."

3

Being Drawn In

James wore a filthy, tattered gabardine coat, and his hair hung in oily dreadlocks. He seemed to have smeared his face with greasepaint. His teeth were a sickening mixture of black and yellow. The eyes he turned upon Juliet were filled with undisguised curiosity.

It was those eyes which gave him away. Despite being bloodshot, they fizzed at her, keen and intelligent – totally out of keeping with the rest of his image.

"So you're Juliet Blake, our radio interviewer?"

"Yes," she said, astonished.

"James Willoughby. We're all on first-name terms here, so call me James. I used to teach Craig at Edinburgh."

"How do you do, James?"

"Excellently, thank you."

She tried not to flinch as they shook hands – especially as his needed washing. "Would you mind telling me why you're dressed like that?"

"Ah," he said. "You haven't had the chance to meet me in my socially acceptable persona yet have you?"

She shook her head.

"Well, let me tell you," James said, "I dress very smartly when I'm in that guise." He slouched into the seat next to her.

"I "I first started dressing up like this," he continued, "shortly after I was appointed to my position at Edinburgh."

"Why?"

"I saw that everyone around me hunted honour and prestige. So it seemed a good idea to try shame and squalor instead. My plan was to do it every few days." He paused. "And then, I got hooked."

"That sounds fascinating, James, but I still don't see how…"

"*The Shadow*," interrupted Edgar. "That's what you call it, don't you, James?"

"Exactly." James seized upon the prompt Edgar offered. "*The Shadow* is Jung's term for the dark side of ourselves. And in my case, it's had one or two extra advantages. I've picked up a few cameo roles from film production companies – and not least when the BBC's been filming up my way."

"Isn't that cheating?" Juliet asked. "Earning money from it?"

"Not if you've got an Equity card it isn't." He leered at Juliet, displaying his ghastly dentures once more. She could only speculate that he must have a very well-stocked stage make-up kit.

He grabbed the cheeseboard, smearing it with grimy marks.

"No, James," cried Laura. "Wash your hands first."

"If you say so, lady." He scraped his chair back, lurched to his feet, and sloped across to the sink, where he began to run the hot water.

"So," Juliet said, when he returned with cleaner hands. "You were Craig's mentor, were you?" She struggled to suppress the laughter bubbling up in her.

"Oh yes," said James. "I met a need in him, one of the many unmet by his father, I might add."

Silence fell. She looked at Edgar, then at Laura and Al, thinking they might deny this picture of their leader as emotionally insecure. But they said nothing. She fought a brief temptation to spring to Don's defence.

"French dressing for your salad, honey?" said Al. "Help yourself."

"Thanks, I will." As she reached for the bottle, though, she kept half an eye on James. He was now plastering butter on his bread.

"What perfect manners," mused Laura. She turned back to Juliet. "Listen, my dear, you've yet to experience Dynamic Meditation. When you do, Craig will change you just as he's changed all of us."

"Not too much I hope, while I'm here," said Juliet, "for I'm really quite happy the way I am right now."

Edgar gave a bark of amusement. "Your goals will change if you become one of us."

"I think that's unlikely," said Juliet.

"When we give ourselves to him he changes our lives," Laura told her.

"And what does that mean?"

"Simply that we throw off our self-limiting beliefs," said Laura. "We wipe out negative messages from the past. And never speak of them again."

"In fact we forget them," said Edgar. "That's why my initial interview is so important. I can't possibly let people give themselves to Craig without offloading their past onto me first."

"That's an extraordinary statement," said Juliet. "So each person tells you their story and then forgets it?"

"Yes."

"But how can anyone forget their past? James clearly doesn't."

James chortled. "I'm the exception that proves the rule," he said.

Juliet wasn't quite clear how.

"For the rest of us," said Laura, "this process of forgetting starts when Craig begins his work on us. He's pulled me apart and reshaped me."

Juliet glanced at the faces of the others but they remained impassive. How could she take this seriously?

"You make Craig sound very physical," she said.

"I wish." Laura giggled for some while.

Suddenly Juliet's attention was drawn to Sam. His face had reddened. What was that about?

"Well, all right, not with me anyway," Laura admitted, "yet."

Nor Sam either, if his face was anything to go by. Juliet stored her observations away, together with the questions they raised. Plenty here for her to investigate later.

"Here you are, have some Branston pickle." Al cut into the conversation in a very deliberate way. A large jar with a fork in it landed in front of Juliet.

"Thank you, Al. So, Laura, what exactly is your relationship with Craig?"

Silence fell heavily. Laura stared at her. So did the others. Then Laura said, "Here in this group we all share love equally, and nobody is to have an exclusive relationship with anyone else."

"But *all men are equal and some are more equal than others*," Al added enigmatically.

At this, Sam's face burned even more.

Al's rather artificial laughter hung in the air until Laura caught it and slapped it down. She shot him a warning look.

He quickly said, "You've changed in every way possible, Laura, since I first met you. You're a different woman."

"Am I really?"

"Sure."

What must she have been like before?

Al and Laura held eye contact for several moments.

Juliet gazed at them. Clearly, passion was simmering not too far beneath the surface. If Craig wasn't available, then perhaps Al would supply the deficiency. On first acquaintance with Laura, she hadn't guessed she might be a candidate for such a relationship.

"I understand this is a wheel of love."

"Oh yes." Laura's voice was low.

"And what does that actually mean to you?" asked Juliet. "In a practical sense?"

"It m-m-means everything to m-m-me." Sam had spoken for the first time since James had entered the room. "All I care about is that Craig's in t-t-touch with the t-t-truth, and he's m-m-my m-m-master."

"In what way?" asked Juliet. Silence followed. Then Sam began to bristle, like a highly-strung poodle who'd misinterpreted a cautious pat. She waited. Did Sam bite?

At that moment, the door opened. Craig stood there. She rose and faced him. Her heart pounded.

"Don't ask too many questions too soon, Juliet," he smiled. "Have patience. It'll be worth it."

4

Wheel of Love

A near collision with Craig interrupted Juliet's progress along the first-floor passage later that afternoon, heading towards her four o'clock appointment with him. She'd been enjoying the sensation of walking on the smooth, almost slippery floorboards, worn by centuries of footsteps, when he emerged from a doorway.

"Sorry, Craig."

He lightly held her shoulders to steady her, then let go. But before he did, she had felt a current of electricity flick between them. What was going on? She stepped back quickly, disconcerted.

"Don't apologise." His eyes held hers for several moments; longer, perhaps, than she thought necessary. "How was lunch?"

She gave a wry laugh.

"Colourful bunch, aren't they?" he said. "Edgar's set on those statistics of his. Sam's scared of everyone. And James..." He hesitated. "Very talented man. Great loss to the acting profession."

"I understand he's your former mentor."

He regarded her steadily but said nothing.

"You must have looked up to him at Edinburgh," she said. "Did your father meet him then?"

His expression was unreadable. "I don't encourage talk about the past," he said. "Let's concentrate on the present, shall we. Come in. Make yourself comfortable."

And he held open the door for her. Holding her blue folder of paperwork under her arm, she walked into a well-furnished room which was evidently his study.

She took in two easy chairs upholstered in green velvet, which faced each other across a highly polished circular coffee table, on which sat a handcrafted terracotta incense burner. She recognised the oil he was burning at once: frankincense. Her favourite. Its seductive aroma permeated the atmosphere. How would she be able to hold a businesslike conversation with Craig, while that seduced her senses? She contemplated asking him to remove it from the room. But it was already too late.

"Take a seat, Juliet, please."

She obeyed, and began to relax.

He sat opposite, and looked at her. Again, his eyes held an intense quality she found almost irresistible. But she was determined to steel herself against that. She glanced away, beyond him. Her eye moved from the flat screen monitor and keyboard on the mahogany desk. Behind it was a wall of bookshelves. In the brief moment her eyes swept across it, she registered one or two titles about mental health and another about the Middle East. For some not quite identifiable reason, she hadn't expected such subjects on the shelves of a New Age guru.

The jade silk curtains exactly matched the colour of the carpet, and through the leadlights of the window she could see down to the front of the property, across the garden, and then up the thickly wooded slope to the ridge beyond.

The muted colours created a peaceful, dreamlike aura. She looked at Craig again. His presence, together with the angelic fragrance, continued to penetrate her mind and heart and soul. Quickly she laid the blue folder on the table. She was going to talk contracts and bank account details with him. Take a grip on yourself, she repeated inwardly.

Then she met his eyes once more. He was smiling. *God, this'll be difficult.* She began to forget her own reason for entering his study in the first place.

But he surprised her by getting straight to business. "So, Juliet. A briefing."

"Of course." She took out notebook and pen, ready to make notes.

"Edgar, Sam, and Al you've met. And James. You've learned a little about them. Now, we move on to Rory." He paused.

"Rory?"

"Rory Anstruther-Jones. Born in London. South Kensington."

"I know it well."

"Good. Go easy, though, on talking about his past. Initially, he'll impress with his gracious manner. But treat him with caution."

She looked up from her notebook. "Why?"

"Can't go into details. Confidentiality, you understand." His eyes danced. Was he playing a game with her?

"But I'll find out, if I ask the right questions," she said.

"Exactly." He leaned forward across the coffee table, put his hand out and gave hers a gentle squeeze.

Her reaction was disproportionate to the gesture. She felt as if he'd made some spiritual claim upon her. As if they had sealed some sort of pact. She started.

"Are you all right, Juliet?" He sat back, hands in lap again.

"Perfectly, thank you." This would never do. She was a confident, independent, professional woman. Not a naive, inexperienced young girl. She swallowed hard, and sat up straight. "Go on, Craig."

"Emotionally, he may test you. It will mean some extra sensitivity on your part. Which of course you have in abundance."

"Thank you, Craig."

"You're welcome. Next, Patrick O'Shaughnessy. From County Limerick. Coordinates all practical tasks. Very fond of Sam."

She looked at him. His face gave nothing away. He crisply continued. "Llewellyn, our Welsh poet."

"Ah yes, I've met him."

"Excellent. Then there's Oleg, our Russian friend. Once more, handle with care. Highly fragile. I'm working on that one. Next, Beth. Again, a troubled family background. Takes life too seriously. Oleg would help, but something holds her back."

"Which is..?"

"Attachment to the past," said Craig. "As is the case with most who come here. I offer healing for that."

"You do?"

"Yes. Laura you've met. And Zoe – well I hardly need introduce her."

"No." *Challenge him about Zoe.* But no words came. She made an extra effort. And said something different to what she'd intended. "You haven't mentioned your father."

"Of course. My father."

"You teach forgetfulness of the past, I understand. But I detected some ill-feeling between you."

He chuckled. "No, no, Juliet, you misunderstood. In any case I'm not open for discussion on that. Quiz my followers first. My time will come later." Then he swiftly changed the subject before Juliet could get another word in. "So you want to draw up a schedule of interviews. Fine. I'll make sure they all speak to you after dinner tonight, so you can get that sorted. Anything else?"

"Yes, your fee."

"I'm quite happy with the figure you mentioned," said Craig.

Again, she felt unsure whether he was taking this seriously. In fact she had feared he would want to raise the figure she had offered. Still, she felt she should accept this as a small act of grace. "And the contract," she said.

"Absolutely. You'll want a signature."

"Bank details?"

"In my drawer over there. You should have gone to my father first. He'll have them off by heart." He laughed lightly. Then he rose, and walked over to his desk.

From her position she could see into the drawer as he unlocked it. She noticed a piece of black-and-white checked material in his fingers as he lifted it out of the way, searching beneath. It caught her attention for a few moments.

"What's that, Craig?" she asked. "Looks like an Arabic headscarf." She had an instinct that it was a female headdress. Though she could have been wrong.

He pushed it back into the drawer. "James likes to dress up."

She raised her eyebrows. "As a woman too?" she was about to say, when her eyes fell on a piece of charred and broken timber lying at the side of the drawer. "A souvenir of the house? Was that the state it was in when you first saw it?"

"Something like that, Juliet."

"Had there been a fire?"

He smartly closed and locked the drawer, and pocketed the key. He said nothing, and didn't look at her.

Then he pushed the signed contract over to her. "Must rush now, Juliet. I'll see you at dinner."

He touched her shoulder. She rose, collected her papers and he ushered her to the door, closing it firmly behind them both. In the next moment he was gone.

What on earth was that all about?

She felt slightly bemused, unsure what to make of Craig and his behaviour towards her. She'd gained some bite-size pieces of information about his followers. But he'd left no time for any discussion about Zoe. And he himself had remained as mysterious and as unknown a quantity as before. And had already sown some doubts in her mind that would need resolving.

For several seconds, she stood silent and baffled. Her mobile buzzed. She answered.

It was Toby. "How are you getting on, Juliet?"

She summarised events so far, and he seemed pleased. That was encouraging; Toby believed her subject matter would make great radio. But it was the line he finished on that unsettled her. "Whatever you do, Juliet, hold a little bit of yourself back."

All very well for him to say that. But there again, Toby knew nothing of her anxiety for Zoe. And just as well too; she felt thankful for it.

"That's the observer part of you," Toby went on. "You don't want to end up getting too personally involved."

A few moments passed. How could she fully explain her ambivalence about it all? "No need to worry, Toby. I won't let them brainwash me."

But that, of course, wasn't what centrally concerned her. Rather, her instincts had been alerted by a number of scents on the trail: and they all clustered around Craig, and what had gone on between him and Zoe in the time since they'd met.

There were, firstly, Don's earliest words to her about Craig: *My problem…son…he's created his own philosophy of life…but no money sense…* and the words: *special ability…with young women…can be very charming.*

Then, there were James's words: *his mentor…met a need in him…one of many…unmet by his father.*

And finally, she recalled Craig's remark: *I don't encourage talk about the past. Let's concentrate on the present, shall we?*

What was all this telling her about Craig, the man her sister was besotted with? And then there was the curious way Sam had reacted when she asked about Craig being *physical.* She felt slightly disturbed. No way would she explain her personal fears to Toby. They weren't part of her brief at all.

"Must go, Juliet. You'll strike the right balance. Perfect position. About the right age for people attracted to this kind of community. And your sister … her being there gives you the ideal opportunity to live alongside the group members. So long as you don't take it too far, of course."

"No, Toby."

"This documentary should be good stuff. I've every confidence in you. Catch up with you again tomorrow." And he was gone.

With this conversation still preying on her mind, she headed towards the staircase. She was developing a different agenda to the one Toby had set. Was she up to it? And how would all this affect her sister? She needed to find Zoe, and try to put things right.

To her delight she got her chance almost immediately, down in the entrance hall, when her sister appeared before her.

"Zoe!" Juliet cried. "Sorry about this morning."

Zoe looked relieved. "That's all right. Been thinking about it too. Difficult for you to understand. But it's still great you're here. And hey, I know the others have been working on you. Laura told me all about what happened at lunch."

Juliet said nothing. What had Laura's slant been on that conversation? She dreaded to think.

"You won't believe what Craig can do for you," Zoe rushed on. "Just trust him, Juliet. Wait and see what he's like this evening."

Pointless to tell Zoe her forebodings about Craig. Yes, thought Juliet ruefully. See what the evening held. That was all she could do.

The buzz of conversation from the other side of the inner door increased. Juliet knew the group were already taking their seats at the dining table, ready to start the meal. She glanced through the doorway, entranced by the many candle flames. How sensuous the room looked in this light; the gleaming timbers held even greater depth and richness. And the fragrance of the roses and apple logs in the fireplace seemed more intense.

At that moment, Craig appeared before her, hand outstretched, a smile of greeting on his face. She stopped short, disconcerted by a tingling sensation in her stomach. If not for the evidence of her eyes, she could have sworn she'd just brushed against a lightly charged electric fence.

"Welcome to your first evening meal with us, Juliet."

"Thank you."

"Come in, come in," he said robustly. He took her arm. "Do sit here, close to me."

Juliet was still recovering from her initial reaction to his appearance. She wondered whether her being invited to sit near Craig would upset Zoe. But not at all. Instead, her sister touched her shoulder. "I'll slip in, opposite you."

"Sure," said Juliet. She looked for Don. Perhaps pinpointing his location would ease her mind and her nerves. Then she saw the Yorkshireman, near the top of the table. Zoe was already seating herself.

Juliet followed Craig past *The Lady and the Unicorn.* Craig moved with a fluid grace. For her part, she hoped her manner gave no clue to the insecurity she felt. This would be her first official introduction to the group. As she glanced around those sitting at the table, it suddenly occurred to her that the only non-speaker was the large, hand-carved wooden Buddha which sat in the chair opposite where she stood. How bizarre, she thought.

Now she sensed a change in the atmosphere. All eyes were upon her. Juliet almost expected everyone to push back their chairs and rise to their feet. Yet nobody did.

The table was laid with blue-and-white china and silver cutlery, together with ivory church candles set in wrought-iron candlesticks. At each place appeared a large wine goblet. Interspersed between three bowls of roses, she counted at least seven bottles of red and white wine.

Craig showed her to her chair, and waited until she was in her seat before taking his. Then he raised his voice. "May I officially introduce our new arrival to you all?"

Everyone fell silent.

"A few of you," Craig went on, "had the good fortune to meet our visitor earlier: Juliet, Zoe's sister. You'll remember from my explanation last night, Juliet's a freelance journalist, and has asked my permission to come and make recordings for a radio documentary. She hopes the BBC will take it up eventually. I speak for us all, Juliet, when I say we're happy to have you. We'll be only too pleased to answer any questions you may put to us."

Juliet squeezed her hands together under the table. From the lack of reaction to this preamble, she didn't feel at all confident that her presence met with one hundred percent approval. But all she could do was courteously accept his words.

"Thank you." She faced everyone. "I'm delighted I have your consent to make these recordings." She might as well play her professional role for all it was worth. "There'll be nothing underhand about it. You'll know what I'm doing, because you'll see this." She lifted her recorder and microphone, which she'd brought with her. "Also, may I set your minds at rest; I aim to be as fair and accurate as possible. And if any of you are worried in any way, I can show you my guidelines on consent."

She sat back in her chair. To her right, she glimpsed an ironic expression on Don's face. He was clearly amused at her performance.

After a mixed chorus of murmurs which couldn't be interpreted as agreement or otherwise, Craig said, "I've a suggestion so Juliet feels welcome. Why don't those of us she hasn't yet met, introduce ourselves in turn?"

A current of approval rippled up and down the table. Over the other side of the Beaujolais, next to Zoe, a smartly-turned-out man in his forties banged on the table with his spoon. "Well said, Craig."

"Thank you, James. Why don't you start the introductions?"

James! Juliet could barely believe it. He was so different from the vagrant in the kitchen.

From his neatly combed hair, distinguished features and elegant bearing, to the shiny brass buttons of his navy blazer, he looked like the sort of person who might command respect anywhere.

She quickly recovered from this slightly troubling reflection. "I met your alter ego at lunch, didn't I, James?"

"Indeed you did, Juliet."

She glanced at the dark smear from his collar up to his cheekbone. He evidently hadn't washed all traces of his disguise off.

She wondered when he got his Equity card. Presumably he'd fitted his drama training in prior to acting as Craig's PhD supervisor.

Craig began again in a smooth, urbane manner. "Zoe, of course, needs no introduction," he said, smiling. Then he inclined his head toward his left-hand neighbour. "Sam you'll remember from lunchtime."

Sam failed to make eye contact with her. She could see his lips were shaking. Poor boy, she thought.

The diner on Sam's other side hastened to his rescue. "Fear not, Sam," he said in a strong Irish accent. "You're not obliged to speak. I'll introduce myself, shall I? Patrick O'Shaughnessy. From Limerick. Delighted to meet you, Juliet, I'm sure."

Craig spoke. "Thanks, Patrick. Why not tell Juliet a little more about yourself?"

"Willingly. I'm the coordinator here. I order new supplies. In house or garden, if you have any practical problems, you come to me. I keep track of the toilet rolls, change blown light bulbs, you name it. The only thing I don't do is guarantee the destiny of your immortal soul."

Without giving Patrick the chance to qualify this, Craig went on, "And Al?"

"Had the pleasure of meeting the lady earlier," said Al heartily. He motioned to the seat at his left-hand side. "Sorry, this happy-smiley Buddha here gives me the creeps. And I've been here… how long?" he appealed to Laura.

Craig turned to Juliet and spoke before Laura could supply the information. "I thought it would be an amusing touch for the Buddha to join us tonight and over this weekend. At the beginning of next week he'll be superseded. I'll explain later."

He lifted his gaze above the candles and wine bottles to the two seats at the opposite end of the table. "Oleg and Llewellyn will be sitting there, when they've served our meal. And Edgar?"

Juliet leaned forward to greet that keen researcher of religious experience. He still looked as if he should be wearing a habit, and leading a Gregorian chant. The candlelight heightened the effect. Edgar's lips curled. His glance was edged with steel. "Juliet and I chatted this afternoon, too. I have her questionnaire ready to fill in, just as soon as she has a few moments to spare."

"But…" began Juliet.

Craig interrupted her in a low tone. "Probably best to humour him."

She gazed at him, astonished. He made no further explanation.

Then Craig lifted his voice again. "Juliet wants to draw up a schedule of interviews. See her afterwards in the library to make an appointment. I'll shift any other commitments you have to make way for this."

"I'll be first," said Edgar. "And you can start by filling in my questionnaire." A light wave of chuckles ran up and down the table.

There was a small pause. Oh dear. Juliet was about to speak, then thought better of it. Turning back to face down the table, she met

Don's eye. It held a strangely knowing expression. But he resisted any urge to comment. For the moment, so did Edgar.

Juliet exchanged a wave of acknowledgement with Laura, seated opposite the American, before turning her attention to the next diner, beside Laura.

This was a sharp-faced young woman with dark hair pulled tightly back in a French plait, which emphasised the severity of her expression. She gave Juliet a frosty stare. "I'm Beth. Beth Owen," she snapped. "I prefer not to say anything else about myself."

Well, thought Juliet, Beth wasn't very friendly. How had Juliet managed to earn her hostility so soon? Beth continued to look tense and suspicious. Perhaps she misunderstood what Juliet was trying to do. But if she didn't say anything, Juliet couldn't put her mind at rest.

Then Juliet's glance was drawn on to the next diner. He for his part gave her a watery smile. His pink shirt was teamed with a blue-and-white polka-dot bow tie. Even though seated, he was head and shoulders above his neighbours. How, she wondered, did he manage with all the low ceilings in this farmhouse? She tried to recall the date she'd seen engraved above the front door. Ah yes – 1532. Certainly they must have been shorter in those days.

"Rory. Anstruther-Jones," he said.

Ah-ha. The one she had to handle with caution. "Good to meet you, Rory," she replied.

Tall as he was, Rory presumably managed somehow. She observed too that he'd blow-dried his blond hair. He leaned forward, across Don, extending long, slender fingers to clasp her hand. She registered the slippery quality of his touch. She was also struck by the curious unreality of his porcelain complexion.

He drew back into his seat. "I suffer from a *thorn in the flesh.* Won't tell you what it is right now. You can guess as you get to know me a bit better. Do I suffer from migraines? Am I epileptic? Or gay, perhaps? I don't have one leg shorter than the other. You can see I'm not a dwarf. So, each time we meet, you might get a little closer to guessing my problem."

"Well, Rory, what can I say to that?" murmured Juliet. She was unsure how she felt about his remarks; certainly, she didn't trust him. But there again, neither did she trust anyone else. With the sole exception, she realised, of Don, the terse Yorkshireman. Meanwhile it was important to listen carefully and miss nothing. There was much to learn, not least everyone's names and personal quirks.

Before Juliet could speculate further, Craig broke in. "Read much of the brochure yet, Juliet?"

"Yes, I have. A lot to take on board. I shall go through it again very carefully a few times, I expect."

"And your feelings so far?"

"Mixed. You make big promises."

Before he could respond, the door swung open behind Patrick and two figures emerged, each bearing a covered silver dish. Juliet was reminded of a Greek myth in which a character served the head of his enemy's son to him at dinner in revenge for some wrong done to him. Pushing this image aside, she studied the two chefs. Llewellyn she recognised immediately; he looked cheerful, but his shorter, fair-haired companion seemed jittery. Her curiosity was aroused. She wondered what lay behind his mood. As the dishes were placed on the table, everyone applauded.

"Ah, Llewellyn and Oleg," said Craig. "Well done, friends. Soon the feast will begin."

Oleg evidently didn't share his positive frame of mind. He wore a taut expression. "Burned the rice."

Llewellyn squeezed his arm. "No need to tell them, Oleg. The next lot we cooked was fine."

The Slav looked unconvinced. "This always happens to me."

"Nobody minds," insisted the Welshman.

Craig intervened. "We'll happily accept whatever you give us, Oleg. You've cooked it, and that's all that matters. Dish it out."

"Do community members take it in turn to prepare meals?" Juliet enquired.

"Yes," said Craig. "They also serve on a rota of other practical tasks around the house and garden. Each day everyone does two hours' work."

"So you aim to make the community as self-sufficient as possible?"

"Indeed."

Juliet had a hunch that whatever Craig asked, his followers carried out without question.

While the food was being served, James raised a bottle in the air. "Red, Juliet?"

"Yes, thank you."

As he poured, Craig said, "Surprised we have such a high standard of living?"

"Surprised but very pleased," she replied.

"I see it as all part of my group therapy," he went on. "Remember, any questions, ask me. I'm here to help and guide you. Use me. I want to be used."

She gazed at him. Use him in what way?

"That word makes you feel anxious, doesn't it?" he said.

He picked up on her emotional state with an almost feminine intuition. This in itself gave her pause for thought.

She still didn't trust him. And what worried her was the fact that Zoe clearly did. Her attention had barely swerved from Craig during the past ten minutes.

Craig clapped his hands. Silence fell once more, and all eyes turned to him. In those faces she noted a quality of warm engagement. This was true of the men as well as the women.

"Before we begin, I'd like to make an announcement: one I feel sure will delight you all. On Monday evening, we'll have Theo Lucas with us again. He's agreed to come and be our guest speaker for the week."

A buzz ran round the table.

James snapped his fingers. "Excellent. The Reverend Theo Lucas," he said. "Splendid man. Though I still can't believe how he managed to get himself ordained."

There was a good deal of table-thumping and laughter at this, until Craig's voice dropped into the swell of sound. At once, hush descended. Juliet allowed her eye to skim the diners. Craig's presence and personal style exerted a powerful effect upon them.

"The Wheel of Love is a tribute to the dynamic power of change," observed Craig. "And Theo fits in with that perfectly. We all bear witness to it ourselves. Which one of you can say you're now exactly where you were on your life's journey when you first arrived?"

No one spoke. Again Juliet glanced around at the faces; some dreamy – as was Zoe's – some wistful, others intense. Beth's and Oleg's even looked distressed. This puzzled her. As she studied Oleg, she saw his eyes dart to Beth's face, with a yearning expression. Ah. He liked her, it seemed. But were his feelings returned? It appeared not. Beth herself spent more time looking at Craig than at anybody else.

Emotions were simmering, and evidently not everyone was happy. And how, Juliet wondered, *did* people change once Craig *got to work on them and reshaped them*? And did that include her too? She hoped not.

Once again she looked at Don. At the sight of him, edgy laughter welled up inside her. He took hold of the nearest bottle, and refilled her glass.

As he did so, Craig continued. "As we all know, only the present moment matters. Not the past."

"Yes, yes."

"True."

"Absolutely."

These words skittered up and down the table.

Then Craig's expression sharpened. "We create our own reality," he said. "That's what I've taught you. And what I stand by."

"Tough for some," remarked Don.

A shaft of enmity passed between father and son. Juliet was on full alert. Then swiftly Craig changed the mood. "Don't let me keep any of you from your food! Eat and enjoy."

The group burst once more into animated chatter, alongside much clattering of cutlery and glasses. But Juliet felt faintly oppressed by her vulnerability. She had no idea what to expect over the coming days. How would she balance her commitment to do interviews with the need to keep track of Zoe?

One thing was for sure. She certainly wouldn't be seduced by Craig's brand of healing and wholeness, if that was what it was.

She turned to Don. "Have you met Theo?" she asked in a low voice.

"No. But this lot seem to give him high marks. Doesn't inspire much confidence, does it?"

Leaning forward, Rory supplied some new information. "I met Theo at a talk Craig gave in Tetbury last November. Chatted to him for twenty minutes. Wondered what he was doing there. Then I discovered he'd had a wilderness experience. Lasted eighteen months. Crisis of faith. And I understood."

"You did?"

"Yes. Felt I'd met a soul mate."

This startled Juliet. "He doesn't sound like a *regular* sort of clergyman."

"He isn't," said Rory. "Though of course my knowledge is limited." His lip curled. "Haven't darkened a church door for years."

"Theo sounds more than a little unorthodox," she remarked, "if he's willing to come here." She heard Don chuckle.

"Oh?" Rory queried.

"Well, for instance," she said, "it's clear from the brochure that Craig believes we're in charge of our own destiny."

"Quite right, he does," agreed Rory. "But Craig welcomes anyone who's in retreat from the outside world."

This intrigued her. "What of you, then, Rory? Are you here to renounce the world?"

"Sort of."

"You do it in style."

Before he could reply, Don distracted her, holding out the dish of risotto Beth had passed him.

"Like some, Juliet?" he asked.

"Oh, yes please. That smells and looks very good," she said.

Rory, she noticed, had handed the serving dish on without helping himself, and his plate remained empty. She wondered whether he knew something about it the rest of them didn't. He put his water glass down, and continued. "After Theo was ordained he served for a couple of years, then vanished from the face of the earth for several months. When I met him, I understood he'd not long returned."

James interjected. "He visited us here in February. Rory missed him that time. You remember that was the week you fell ill, Rory?"

"Oh yes. Dreadful week."

Laura spoke. "We'll all be delighted to see him again. Such a dear man. Not a spark of hellfire in him. He knows all about me. He's very forgiving."

Rory fiddled with his linen napkin. "I expect you'll find him interesting, Juliet," he said. "And you too, Don."

"Last person to judge." Don shrugged. "Count me out."

Before Juliet could say more, Don added, "Put it this way. When Theo shows up, he may need protecting. From my influence."

She started at this. Rory took upon himself the task of satisfying her curiosity. "Why?" he said. "You're not tattooed with the number 666, are you?"

Don nearly choked on something he'd eaten. Juliet found Rory's remark highly amusing. She struggled to stop herself bursting out into hysterical laughter.

Rory banged Don on the back.

"Stop that," Don said testily, with an abrupt change of mood.

"As you wish. Only trying to help."

At this point, Craig entered the conversation. "Come, Father," he said. "You don't really believe Theo will need protecting, do you? From you? Because you're an agnostic?"

Rory looked ominous, and sipped again from his glass of water. She noticed he still hadn't taken any food. "Theo will need protecting from Satan most likely," he said.

"Indeed?" said Juliet. "You truly think so? Does such a belief fit in with your teachings, Craig?"

"No," said Craig.

Rory lowered his voice to a confidential whisper and again leaned across Don. "You'd be surprised what fits in with Craig's teachings."

She raised her eyebrows, careful not to commit herself.

"Since I arrived here," Rory went on, ignoring her caution, "many strange things have happened to me. Now, I think that has to do with the effect of being in Gloucestershire, which is renowned for occult activity."

"Planning to bite her, are you?" said James from across the table.

Craig silenced him with a look. "What kind of occult activity, Rory?" he prompted.

"Such as," persisted Rory, "the fact that things started going wrong for me as soon as I arrived. You remember?"

"I do. Very well," said Craig cryptically.

"Last June it was. You told me you had no room."

"Not true. I simply asked you to commit to a short fixed-term stay."

Juliet looked from one to the other, alerted. Why had Craig not been keen for him to stay longer? Clearly Rory had ignored this and stayed on anyway. If Craig wasn't happy about it, why hadn't he chucked Rory out? She didn't doubt the strength of his personality. She found it difficult to believe he wouldn't deal firmly with wastrels and hangers-on, if such Rory was. But for now, the matter must remain a mystery.

She turned back to Rory, who continued unperturbed. "I remember opening my mouth to give Craig a piece of my mind, and my words came out all wrong. I was jabbering incoherently."

"Yes," said Craig.

A sharp silence fell. James applied butter to his bread roll in short, terse strokes of the knife.

"Can you account for that experience of Rory's, Craig?" asked Juliet.

Then she dropped her fork. Craig's features had changed. She wasn't at all sure how, but his face was unrecognisable. She stared. Her fingers had turned cold. All the charm of his handsome features had melted away, and now she saw something that looked to her like an ancient face, like a stone carving on a rock in the rose-red city of Petra in Jordan.

Most creepy of all, Zoe appeared totally unaware of it. So did Rory and Don.

Juliet continued to stare at Craig, dumbstruck. As she did so, his former identity returned, shifting back into place like the next frame on a movie reel.

"Thank you, Rory, that's enough." Craig now evidently considered it time to insist upon a change of subject.

But Juliet could barely continue eating. Her fingers were trembling too. What had she just witnessed? Or had she imagined it? Had somebody spiked her wine? Certainly, nobody else seemed to have noticed Craig doing anything untoward.

At this moment, Craig caught her eye. She read in his glance, *Don't worry. You'll understand, later.*

Zoe had now clearly noticed something. She looked suspicious.

Taking a grip on herself, Juliet lifted another forkful of food, trying to push down her disbelief at what she'd seen. She determined to find out later what had happened. But most definitely she couldn't think of Craig in the same way again.

She turned to Rory, once more grasping for some kind of distraction. No food had touched his plate. Neither had he permitted any wine in his goblet. Instead he sipped intermittently at his glass of water.

"Not eating, Rory?" she enquired.

"Oh no." He shuddered. "Never in public."

"Why's that?"

He reached across Don again, and placed slender fingers upon Juliet's wrist. "Don't ask," he begged. "It can wait till another day."

She gazed at him, mystified. Why did he so dislike eating in front of other people? It didn't add up. But worrying about it seemed futile.

Craig meanwhile looked as if he was starting to draw himself inward. James had raised his eyebrows. Juliet glanced from one to the other, her spirit of enquiry on full alert.

It was left to Oleg to break the impasse. "If I can get into this place, anyone can."

"Why?" said James. "I considered you highly suitable, with your existential angst. Of course, your family's escape across the Russian border years ago impressed me."

These words should have mellowed Oleg. Instead it was as if a knife with a serrated edge had slipped between him and the academic. Juliet looked at Oleg's face. For one microsecond she could have sworn he hated James. Then the impression passed.

She shifted position so she could also observe Beth, who'd so far remained silent. She wanted to see if Beth was reacting to Oleg in any way. But no, her eyes were on Craig. She was in love with him, Juliet had no doubt about that. Poor girl. What prospects did she have, with Zoe so ahead of the game? Her sister was chatting animatedly to Craig. Sparkling and pretty, Zoe had everything going for her to win first place in Craig's affections.

Suddenly Beth leaned back as Don became caught up in a conversation with Rory. She faced Juliet in a conspiratorial manner. Her eyes hardened, and she spoke in a low, tight voice. "When you interview us, Juliet, do hold off from asking us about our past won't you?"

"Why?" asked Juliet.

"Because none of us here are supposed to remember it. Craig teaches us to cut ourselves off from that."

"But your background's one of the first things my listeners will want to know about."

The colour of Beth's face deepened. Juliet guessed that to be the effect of the wine. She decided to try the direct approach. "How do you feel about Craig, Beth?"

Cold hostility glimmered in the girl's eye. "What's that to you?"

"I've been invited here to ask questions," said Juliet gently.

Beth drained her glass of wine and refused to look at her again. Instead she switched her glance to Oleg, who'd left his seat at the end of the table, and come up to speak to her. She gave him full attention for the first time during the meal. He leaned down towards her, and laid his hand on hers. She jumped as if someone had laid hot metal on her bare flesh.

He spoke in a low, urgent voice. "Why so nervous when I touch you, Beth? Relax."

Instead of having the desired effect, this seemed to destabilise her further. She pushed her chair back and sprang to her feet. "Goodbye, everyone." With that, she headed round behind Juliet's chair, whirled past *The Lady and the Unicorn*, and vanished through the doorway into the sitting room.

Everyone turned to stare.

"What did she mean by that?" asked Juliet. "She's not leaving for good is she?"

"Of course not." Craig jumped up. "I'll go and talk to her." But before he followed, he met Juliet's gaze. His expression was perfectly calm. "Remember," he said. "We're not responsible for how others choose to react to us."

His words hung in the silence. He walked out of the room. Everyone left at the table exchanged uncertain glances.

5

Jealous Designs

"Does James like dressing up as a woman? What an extraordinary question," said Edgar, shooting a piercing glance at Juliet.

"I don't think so at all," she rejoined, "from what I've learned of him so far."

They both sat in the oak-panelled library early the next morning. Rays of sunlight slanted through the diamond-paned windows. Juliet's recording machine was between her and Edgar, and the microphone close to his mouth.

"What about people of other nationalities?" she asked.

"Not since I've been here," said Edgar, still staring at her.

"Does Craig support him in his cross-dressing?" she asked. "Or even join him in it?"

"Why d'you want to know this?" he demanded.

"Just thought you might know something of Craig's background, that's all," said Juliet.

A conspiratorial gleam entered his eye. "Digging, aren't you? For stuff he won't give you himself?"

"Could be," she said. "It's worth a try."

"I can certainly tell you a thing or two," he hinted. "But only if you complete my questionnaire." At this, he jumped up, knocking the microphone out of her hand, and lunged at a well-stuffed concertina folder that had until now stood unnoticed by the occasional table.

"Go easy, Edgar," she said, getting up too, and bending down to pick up her mike.

Suddenly she found the researcher looming over her, and coming uncomfortably close.

"Edgar, I really don't think…" she began, trying to veer away from him. She could feel his breath on her cheek.

"Let's do a deal, you and me," he said, close to her ear. "I'll dish the dirt on Craig if you tell me all sorts of personal information about yourself."

"Certainly not," she said, rising abruptly to her feet, causing Edgar to lurch across the rug on top of his concertina file. Oh dear, this wasn't a very good start to her schedule of interviews. "Sorry Edgar, I do apologise," she said, helping him to his feet. "But if that's the price, it's not on."

"Why so secretive?" he asked, springing to his feet once more, with handfuls of crumpled papers, and turning on her. "Why so fearful?"

"I'm neither of those things. You've completely misunderstood me, Edgar," she said, smoothing her hair down and trying to regain her professional poise. "I'm not afraid of anything. Simply concerned to remain objective."

"Ha!" he cried. "Objective. And yet you've already tried to turn up titbits on Craig."

"Titbits?" she said coolly. "Your word, Edgar. Not mine."

They both stood, looking at each other, each breathing faster than usual. She didn't like this at all.

"This is almost like Dynamic Meditation," he remarked.

She frowned. "What do you mean by that?"

"Find out tonight." He tapped the side of his nose, and gave her a knowing look.

"Very well, Edgar," she said. "I'll do just that."

Dynamic Meditation took place that evening in the barn. Surely, thought Juliet, as she stood at the rear of the spacious meeting room, with her portable recorder and mike, the original builders of this glorious sixteenth-century tithe barn would never have imagined that such use would ever be made of it. She gazed at the roof, a dazzling criss-cross of beams and wooden vaulting. Yes, the tenant farmer may well have held barn dances; but surely nothing of the nature of what Craig was leading his followers into right now.

By nine o'clock the lights had been dimmed, and the sound of heavy metal music echoed up to the roof trusses, ricocheted off the hayloft and rebounded all around the stone walls. The hayloft, or upper room, could be accessed by two spiral staircases, one at the west side, and one at the east. Juliet had positioned herself beside the foot of the west one. She was trying to make herself heard as she explained her digital recording equipment to Don. Following Llewellyn's words, he'd clearly felt sufficiently emboldened to try this session, but meant to stay at the back watching and listening.

He moved closer to Juliet in order to hear her words.

"This machine is a Nagra Ares BB Plus," she said. "I record on flashcards. Each has only about one gig of memory, not that much, so I've brought several for all my interviews."

"And your mike? Will it cope with the noise levels?"

She laughed. "It's omnidirectional. I'll hold it as close as possible to Craig when he's speaking, if I get the chance. Must admit I'm a bit doubtful whether I'll pick up any speech."

"Me too," he said cryptically.

She smiled.

"However," he continued, "Craig dropped me a few hints. So I steeled myself."

"Certainly looks and sounds chaotic." She gazed at the scene in front of her. She suspected that tonight would yield nothing her listeners could make sense of. But her concern for Zoe was far greater. What would her sister get up to with Craig in an atmosphere like this? And as for Craig himself, she'd be watching him very closely; for she found it impossible to believe he wouldn't take advantage of his position, especially with the women, in such circumstances.

And as if to confirm Juliet's worst suspicions, Laura, her hair wilder than ever, was already tearing off her cotton print dress. Juliet feared Zoe would soon follow her example. She and Beth, however, had so far both kept their lycra leotards on. But, to Juliet's confusion, Zoe was curled up in a foetal position in the corner, sobbing as if her heart would break. Should Juliet go over and comfort her? Or was this all part of the Dynamic Meditation and meant to serve a cathartic purpose?

Her instincts told her it was the latter. The other members of the group were scattered across the available floor space, in a variety of postures and states of undress. Several danced; some had curled themselves into tight balls, and others writhed across the flagstone floor like snakes. Juliet followed Craig with her mike, as he strode around amongst them, looking authoritative and crackling with sexual energy, in a bottle-green leather jacket and Levi's, shouting at each in turn.

She recorded him as best she could, whilst trying to keep an eye on Zoe. But her sister, it seemed, won no more from him than anybody else; and neither did Laura or Beth. To Craig's credit, and Juliet's mystification, he seemed to share his attention equally.

His attention consisted largely of a verbal lashing. With each person he varied his remarks, depending, as he explained to Juliet a little later, upon their emotional situation. At Beth, who clearly had a problem with self-esteem, he hurled personal abuse; when Sam confessed fear and timidity, he compelled him to imagine the kind of exposure he most dreaded; finding Oleg full of anger, he provoked him to an even higher level of rage. The Slav then strode over to Beth and accosted her. Juliet watched closely. She'd already picked up emotions simmering between these two. What would happen now, in this overwrought situation?

But before she could satisfy her curiosity, her attention was distracted. Laura, in a desperate attention-seeking measure, had finally peeled off her lacy knickers. But even this failed to win a special response from the group leader. However, the same could not be said of Al. Laura then gave herself over to what looked like a Dionysian frenzy. Edgar rolled around the floor giggling hysterically, creating a surreal effect with his monastic appearance. James, too, added to the madness of the scene by kicking his legs in the air and screaming like a child having a tantrum in a high-street store, without any regard to the state of his tailored trousers or natty cravat.

The only question in Juliet's mind was at which point one of the men would snap, leap onto Laura, and sexually assault her. Or settle for Craig instead, as some, in her view, might well do. She'd already begun forming opinions about their sexuality. It was when she began to focus on Craig's, that she felt ambivalent. He was supposed to love her sister. But… Her mind went foggy beyond this. All she knew was it was a big *but.*

Meanwhile, miraculously, here in the feverish atmosphere of the barn, no assault, sexual or otherwise, ever happened.

Oleg now seemed to be performing t'ai chi; James was grinning inanely and blowing bubbles, and Al, who'd begun the evening in a benign frame of mind, was beating his head against the wall.

At this point Craig turned the music off, and Juliet hurried across to him with the mike. Before she could speak he plunged himself into a lotus posture, and apparently into a state of deep meditation. Meanwhile, the participants lay around weeping or working out their distress in whichever way seemed best, or emerging slowly from hysteria. So Juliet moved among the group members instead with her mike, though there seemed no need to ask any of them to describe their feelings to her. Eventually all sounds faded into silence. Juliet set her Nagra on automatic voice-activated recording. Craig allowed stillness to reign for several minutes. Then he opened his eyes, stood up, and, looking around among his followers, began to speak.

"This Centre has been going for exactly fourteen months tonight. Fourteen months from the day James and I moved in. In the time that's elapsed since then, the Wheel of Love has become a tribute to the dynamic power of change."

"Who has changed?" asked Juliet. "And in what way?"

"Guilt has gone," announced Craig. "Feeling bad about yourself because of the negative messages you once received, is in the past. Your former life can no longer hold you. All that matters is now."

His glance swept once more around the meeting space. "By

coming here and joining us, you've shown you correctly identify your longing. You recognise your birthright. And you want to regain your inheritance. You seek spiritual experience in your own bodies. We all do. I'll guide you to a place where you can say, not *I believe* but *I know*."

Absolute concentration gripped the members of the group.

Then he said, "Remember, we create our own reality. That's what I taught you. And what I stand by."

The expression in his eyes intensified, as for a moment they settled on Juliet. Then they moved to the middle distance again. "What you give out, you receive back. Simple as that, once you've learned to understand and harness the universal system. Your new life starts here."

With that he dismissed them all.

Juliet breathed a sigh of relief as Laura started putting her clothes on again.

She found herself intensely curious about Craig's failure to react to Laura's exhibitionism. The first obvious explanation that sprang into her mind – that he was gay – just didn't ring true. Other facts went against it. The group members, of course, were distracted by their own emotional states. But not so Craig. He'd been perfectly poised and centred throughout. She found herself gazing at him wonderingly.

"What a relief," said Don. "One thing's for sure. I feel drained. And all I've done is watch."

Juliet moved across to Al with her mike. "How d'you feel, Al?" she asked.

The American looked relaxed and in good humour, and walked with a spring in his step. "Great, Juliet," he said. "You should have given it a go."

Juliet then looked for Beth and Oleg. Had they resolved anything between them? She wouldn't find out tonight. Both seemed to have made a quick exit.

"And you, Laura?" she queried.

"Totally purged," said Laura. "You must join in next time, darling. It would have done you the world of good."

Zoe joined them. "Fantastic," she cried. "I was afraid I might curl up in humiliation and die. But not at all. I feel a hundred miles high."

Juliet held her mike in front of Llewellyn. "Amazing," he declared, and pranced along the path like a mountain goat. "I must rush back to my room. I have a brilliant idea for a new poem."

"Good for you," grumbled Don as they reached the path leading to the goose house.

"Will you have a go next time, Don?" asked Juliet.

"You joking?" he said. "I'm off to bed." And with that, he turned right.

"Good night, Don," cried Laura.

"Join in next time," called Al. "It'll blow you away."

Once back in her room, Juliet collapsed onto her bed, and spent several minutes trying to understand what she'd witnessed. She had mixed feelings about the behaviour of the group members. On the one hand, she thought they were all totally out of their minds. On the other, she recognised that some who'd taken part claimed they'd benefited.

But, how could it be right for Laura to dance naked among all those men? Juliet had seen the way Al reacted, but Craig had completely disregarded her. How did he respond on other occasions? She imagined Laura's performance wasn't a one-off. She wondered, too, about Beth and Zoe, and whether they'd simply chosen not to follow suit tonight.

And did Craig love Zoe, as she'd implied, or was all the love on her side only? He'd given her no special attention. Juliet felt confused. At that moment her mobile buzzed.

"Juliet? It's Don."

"Hi, Don." What did he have to say that couldn't wait until morning? But she was grateful he'd rung. She needed somebody to talk to.

"What d'you make of tonight?" he asked.

"Crazy," she said.

"I agree."

Thank God. The only other sane person here. But… "Some of Craig's claims make sense," she said.

"Which ones?" asked Don.

She thought about this. "Before he left the dining room earlier, he said something about bad emotions, which we need to express in order to be rid of them."

"Do you believe that?" he snorted.

"I'm not sure whether I do, but I feel mixed up."

"Which means," Don said, "that part of you thinks it could be true?"

"They believe it works…"

"Course they do. They'll believe anything."

"Placebo effect?"

"Yes. That's what I put it down to."

Both fell silent for a few moments.

"Well, Don," she said, "what shall I try tomorrow morning?"

"The Dream Yoga walk."

"Dream Yoga? What's that?"

He chuckled. "Go on it and find out. Then tell me."

When the group gathered around Craig at the back door at six a.m., Juliet was encouraged by the brightness and freshness of the sky. A steady heat, enlivened by a crisp breeze, ensured that most walkers had chosen T-shirts and shorts this morning.

Craig, in bushwalking khakis, swept his arm out over to the north west, where a fence separated the car park from a thick stand of horse chestnuts and field maples. "That's where we're going today."

Juliet spotted a footpath accessed by a stile. Beyond the trees, the side of the valley rose steeply through pasture to a wooded ridge. Her concentration returned to Craig, who was now telling the group that the first part of the walk was to be conducted in silence.

So that meant she wouldn't get the chance to quiz Zoe further on what she really felt about last night.

Craig led his followers along a track that disappeared among the trees. Zoe walked way ahead of Juliet, who couldn't see whether or not her sister was sticking close to Craig. Beth, she noticed, seemed to be missing, though Oleg was present. Everything about him suggested depression, even his tired-looking floppy beige hat. So much for the effect of last night's Dynamic Meditation.

They tramped for several minutes, sometimes through dense undergrowth that contained a lot of bramble, and eventually emerged on the top of the ridge. A glorious panorama of hills and fields spread out before them. But Craig didn't allow them long to admire it. He instructed them to gather round.

"This is where it gets interesting," murmured Zoe to Juliet, before Juliet moved forward to put her mike in front of Craig's mouth.

"Now, in a moment I'll ask you to start walking again," said Craig. "But this time I want you to walk backwards. Don't turn round. Just trust me. I'll tell you when to stop."

Juliet shot him a look. He seemed serious. And they were all obeying. She had no option other than to join them, sticking close to Craig so she could be ready with the mike for his next utterance.

After about ten minutes of this, Craig's voice rang out again. "That's it, everyone. Stop. Who found it difficult to trust me? Who struggled with an urge to look behind, to check they weren't going to crash into anything, or fall over a sheer drop? Laura? Sam? Zoe? As I expected. And who thought it was extremely silly? Juliet? Good. You're here to unlearn everything you've been taught to believe about the world and how to behave in it, from the moment you were born."

Juliet caught sight of Oleg. He was in deep gloom.

She stepped aside with her mike. "You don't look enthralled, Oleg," she said. But before he could reply, Craig's voice cut in again and she swung round once more.

"See that beech tree? Look at the very topmost branch. Concentrate on those leaves. Next, imagine a spot in the centre of your forehead. Visualise a silver cord extending from it, reaching out, further and further, and finally connecting you to the leaves at the top of the tree. Keep your eyes on them. Now walk very slowly toward it, never letting your eyes drop."

Juliet joined them, unable to notice the reactions of the people around her until they'd completed the exercise. Then Craig seated himself on a fallen trunk, and asked how they'd felt when asked to do it, and during the walk; and whether those feelings had changed now they'd stopped. Juliet could detect no sign of dissent among them, apart from Oleg, who continued to look miserable. He seemed to be weighed down by some heavy problem; she resolved to get him to open up about it as soon as she had the chance.

Craig sprang from the fallen log. "I want you to do this every day. As you walk around, think: *This is a dream.* Whatever you're doing, say to yourself: *I'm dreaming this.* Any questions?"

Juliet looked around, mike at the ready. Silence. Surely, someone other than herself must have doubts? But nobody expressed any. Were she and Don the only people in this community who still saw things from the perspective of the outside world?

"This," said Craig, "is part of my strategy to teach you all the art of lucid dreaming. Remember, if you master this art – the art of knowing you're in the middle of a dream, and then taking command of the dream at that point – I tell you, if you master this art, death will be a breeze."

Not one of his followers spoke, or moved. A dreamlike quality had settled upon them all.

Craig spoke again. "If you follow what I've taught you this morning, lucid dreaming will become second nature. And, I might add, one of our number has already had a lucid dream."

A murmur spread among them.

Craig turned to Oleg, blushing deeply beneath his floppy hat. "Yes, Oleg; don't be so self-effacing. Our friend here had a lucid dream last night, which he told me about before this walk. He's well in tune with his higher self. Congratulations, Oleg."

Juliet looked at the Slav. The flush had diminished to a dull purplish hue. She couldn't work out whether Craig's praise pleased him or not.

She then caught sight of Rory's face. His eyes held a cold glitter. Was he jealous? But before she could consider this further, Craig's voice interrupted her thoughts.

"Right, let's all turn round and go back."

They all set off, following the path down to the farmhouse. Zoe followed immediately behind Craig, and Juliet couldn't catch up with her. Instead, she fell in step with Rory. "So how do you feel, Rory?" she asked.

"Life is but a dream," Rory said.

"You really believe that?"

"Of course. Who'd have harsh reality when they can live here?" he replied.

Oleg moved within range. "Life's no different from what it was outside. Still goes badly for me most of the time."

She glanced at him, bemused. "I noticed you last night in the barn with Beth, Oleg. Didn't you two sort things out at all?"

He glared at her. "What d'you mean by that? Sort things out? How? And why were you watching us?"

She took a deep breath. "I can't help noticing how much you care for her."

"She doesn't care for me," he snapped.

Silence fell. She sought words. "Perhaps you've misunderstood her true feelings, Oleg. Perhaps you think too little of yourself. Be encouraged by Craig. He says you're in tune with your higher self."

"That depends upon what he actually chose to tell Craig." Rory spoke in a snide tone of voice.

"Rory's jealous," said Oleg.

Rory moved as if he was about to strike him.

Juliet, alarmed, quickly stepped between them. "What's up between you two?" she asked.

Rory looked surprised. "Nothing," he replied, and sauntered on.

Then she turned back to Oleg. "What have you done to upset Rory?"

"Other way round." His voice filled with self-pity. "It's him who upset me."

"Oh?" She ducked under a low branch. "What did he do?"

He looked dejected. "He asked me if I could possibly love him."

Juliet took the risk of flippancy. "Didn't you say 'yes, as a friend? But I love Beth more'? This is, after all, a wheel of love."

"No, I'd never tell him that," he retorted, in a fierce undertone. "It doesn't work that way. Not with Rory. He gets violent."

"Oh?" She started. Her heart missed a beat. "Violent? D'you mean he beats you up?"

But Oleg was clearly unwilling to say more.

Juliet now felt a frisson of fear when she looked at Rory. She knew she shouldn't judge anyone here simply on the basis of what someone else said about them. Even so… She would treat Rory with just a little extra caution until she knew him better.

But what she really wanted to know right now was: how did Craig mean to deal with all these conflicting desires? Was he really equipped to handle them? Or was this, for him, a dream he never intended to wake up from?

They'd reached the back door of the house, and the rest of the group were busy taking their boots off and throwing them on the rack in the utility area. She found herself drawn aside by Craig, several metres away from the others, closer to where the cars were parked.

"Meet me after lunch, Juliet. I'm busy this morning. But I'll have an hour to give you then. I may be able to explain a little for you."

"Thank you Craig. I hope you will."

"Have faith, Juliet. Perhaps I can do even more than you hope for."

And with that he strode in through the back doorway.

6

Uncertain Hopes

An interview with Craig: that was Juliet's first priority.

The scene in his office had aroused her curiosity. And every meeting she'd had with him since then had sharpened it. The Dream Yoga walk that morning had served to whet her appetite even further. She was keen to challenge him on several of his statements, and equally determined to resist his magnetic appeal. She needed to understand the reason for her own strong mistrust. She had further questions not only about the group, but also about his relationships in it, with both men and women; and that, most importantly, would throw light on his relationship with Zoe.

The fact was, he fascinated her.

True to his word, he appeared in the kitchen just as lunch finished. Everyone else had left. She and Craig were on their own together with the Nagra and mike. They sat at the top corner of the oak table; she'd placed her audio equipment on the table beside her. He regarded her with his dark eyes. She struggled to control her reaction to him. She'd resolved to keep a firm eye on any psychological tricks of his, like seeming to change his appearance without warning.

She plugged her cable in and switched on. "I'm grateful to you, Craig, for allowing me to make these recordings." Good idea to disarm him with the courtesies first, she thought.

"Nothing gives me greater pleasure, Juliet."

Looking at him, she felt encouraged by the openness of his

expression. Right ankle resting on his left knee, he sat at an angle to the chair, one arm casually slung along the back. He appeared relaxed, and had changed into a navy tracksuit. Everything he wore, no matter how casual, he wore with perfect style and ease. This was the third time she'd seen him in sports gear. She wasn't aware the property boasted a squash or a tennis court, or anything like that. She could only conclude he wore the gear because it conveyed just the impression he wanted. And she for one could not deny he looked gorgeous.

She sat up straight. No unprofessional thoughts. What she wanted here was iron-hard control. She studied the level reading on the display. All was in order. She met his eyes again. They were touched by a faint smile. Plugging the mike in, she held it in front of Craig's mouth and pressed record.

As she did so he spoke. "Enjoy last night, Juliet?"

"Yes thanks. I found that, and this morning's walk, very entertaining."

He looked amused. "Ah. I detect scepticism."

"Yes. I find it difficult to believe we can be one hundred percent positive all of the time."

"Oh?" he said lightly. "Do leave room, though, for the possibility that I may yet convince you."

She had no intention of being thrown off course by any smooth talking on his part, even though she already felt that now-familiar instability in the pit of her stomach. She maintained an even tone. "Would you give me an image that you think represents this community?"

He seemed to like this question. "It could be represented by an eagle: an eagle on its eyrie."

Her eyes widened. "But we're not high up, here. We're in a valley."

"Physically, maybe. But spiritually, it's a completely different story."

She considered this. It was difficult to find a simple, single meaning in his words. Rory? Oleg? Sam? Beth? They all had their problems. "Wouldn't you prefer the symbol of a dove?" she asked.

"No."

"Yet you teach love and peace. Am I missing something?"

"Yes," he said.

Juliet knew plenty of the things that happened in this house stood way outside the bounds of peace and love.

At that moment his face seemed about to change. She held her breath. Was he going to do it again? That strange and frightening thing which disorientated yet engrossed her?

He apparently thought better of it and gave her a calm, steady look. "You've missed something all right," he said. "I teach freedom first. Peace of mind flows from that. And the eagle, as you know, symbolises freedom."

"But being set free isn't all good news," she remarked, "especially if you're unprepared for it."

He smiled. "What sort of freedom do you think I give, Juliet?"

"No idea," she said.

"Freedom from one of the most enslaving of all false notions, that other people are somehow responsible for our happiness."

"I don't think I believe that," she replied, disconcerted.

"Don't you? You've never felt your wellbeing depended upon what your friends or your lover or your family members were doing?"

She blushed, furious with herself for falling into the trap. And as she did so, Zoe's face floated to the forefront of her consciousness. She was afraid she'd break the cardinal rule of her guidelines as a radio journalist, and betray her personal feelings.

"What about you then, Craig?" she asked. "And the members of your group? It seems some of them feel you hold the key to the rest of their lives."

"They've still a long journey ahead," he said. "I don't hold the key. They do."

"Have you told them that?"

He looked faintly patronising. "No need. It's something they must learn themselves."

She tried another angle. "You mention past negative messages and the power they have over our lives. You help break that link, do you?"

"Yes."

"It's a big claim," she said. "Don't you suppose *you* have a responsibility to your followers? You've given their lives purpose and meaning. You can't expect not to arouse strong, even sexual emotions. As you did in the dynamic meditation session last night."

He looked quizzical.

"When Laura stripped off, for instance, in a desperate bid for your attention." She was beginning to struggle. Why did he now look so lofty and detached? Though, of course, it did occur to her as she said this, that she may have misunderstood Laura's intentions, *and* the reasons for Craig's self-control.

She held Craig's gaze. Had she expected him to appear uncomfortable? Fool, she told herself. Rather, he just looked faintly tolerant.

"I think you've misinterpreted her message," he said. "Sexual emotions, you say? I can handle them."

What else might she have imagined him to say? She felt hot and trapped. Her glance shifted to the rows of highly polished copper kettles and jugs hanging from the overhead beam, and the corn dollies on the wall opposite.

She fought the feeling that, so far, the score stood at *Craig: one*, and *Juliet: nil.* "But do you care about them, Craig?" she asked. "Do you believe what you're doing is right?" Those questions burst from her without warning. Her hand tightened round the microphone.

"I don't think you need be concerned about that." He chuckled.

What was that supposed to mean? "How do you see yourself, Craig? What's your ultimate objective here?"

His voice took on a hard edge. "You want to know what my end product is?"

"Yes."

He set both feet on the floor, leaning forward so his elbows were supported by the table. Interlocking his fingers, he rested his chin on them as he looked at her. "Let me answer that by asking *you* a question, Juliet. What are you searching for?"

She battled the temptation to break eye contact. "Nothing at the moment, Craig, apart from a good interview with you."

Would he fall for it? She felt small and weak, hiding behind a smart-tongued façade. After all, it had been a good question. And one she found difficult to answer honestly. Her focus had, until now, been solely on discovering what Zoe was up to, and getting her home again. Why should she feel bad about that?

Aloud, she said, "All right. Let's suppose I want to be a very serene, loving being, in tune with the universe."

Craig's eyes regained their warmth. "I'd say you've come to the right place." He sat back again, in a relaxed pose.

"Ah-ha," she said. "So that's your end product." Had she got the better of him, in this exchange? She hardly believed so.

"Maybe," he replied. "But it's by no means easily achieved. After all, we have ourselves and each other to contend with. One of the things I make clear to my new recruits is there'll be a lot of hard work."

"Hard work?"

"Oh yes." He laughed. "My students work. And that doesn't just mean window-cleaning, polishing and vacuuming – though they do all that. No, I mean psychological work, and spiritual work. I mean work to release negative emotions, rubbish that's accumulated over the years."

Juliet viewed him narrowly. This kind of talk made her glad *she* wasn't a member of his group. To her it all sounded very risky. Where might such self-analysis and soul-searching lead? For some it would bring release. For others it might cause breakdown. Who could tell? Of one thing she was absolutely sure. No way would she allow Craig to reach into her, and try to change *her* mental state.

"What about the past?" she said. "I've heard a number of confusing things about your attitude to that. Some say your aim is to blot it out."

He shifted position in his chair once more. "A misunderstanding. Though I do encourage my students to *erase their personal history*."

A small silence fell.

"Yet you keep souvenirs of your past in your desk drawer," she remarked.

His face darkened.

"If that is indeed what they are," she said.

He jumped up, startling her. "What…?"

She twisted round to look at him in alarm, as he paced across the kitchen away from her.

"Just take care, Juliet." He spun to face her. He looked livid.

She too got up, confused and fearful. She still clutched the microphone. "What's the matter, Craig?"

"I hear you've been asking Edgar if I help, or indeed join, James in his cross-dressing."

"That's right. Well, it looked like a woman's headdress to me. In your drawer."

The colour of his face swiftly changed, now deathly pale. "That's none of your business, Juliet."

"But I –" she began, then just as abruptly stopped. A few moments passed. Then she said, "And the burned timber. You never did say whether there'd been a fire."

He lifted the kettle, and slammed it down with unexpected violence. She gasped. Her heart was racing.

He strode back over to her, and took her by both arms. His touch wasn't gentle. "Just listen, Juliet. No, I don't help James with cross-dressing. Or join him. Primitive. I don't need it. I can change my appearance at will."

She felt a jolt in her abdomen. "You mean suddenly look like a different person?"

He nodded, keeping her within his gaze. "Completely different. It's all about having a fluid and flexible ego. The shamans have mastered it. Once you've learned the skill, it's like a classic sorcery tale. Shapeshifting. Close friends will fail to recognise you."

A creepy sensation travelled up her spine. He released her. She flexed her shoulders and arms for a few moments, trying to calm her breathing. She didn't trust herself to pursue the subject further. "Shall we sit down again?" she suggested.

He did so. She settled into her chair once more then held the mike out close to his mouth. "We've mentioned the past. Your father Don is here with us right now. Let's talk about him."

Craig reacted with a gesture of light dismissal. But she could see through that. "I understand," she said, "that he runs a property management company in Yorkshire. He's a man of the world, rooted in practicalities."

"True."

"He must struggle to come to terms with what you're doing here." Did Craig find this line of questioning offensive? She couldn't tell.

"Perhaps so," he said coolly. "If by *practicalities* you mean *the worship of profit*, then naturally his values fly in the face of all that the community stands for."

"But he was involved in the purchase of this property, wasn't he? And he freely chose to join you here."

His lips tightened. He said nothing. She'd hoped he might open up on the subject. But it didn't look like he planned to provide her with any clues. They both remained silent for a few moments.

She rested her elbow on the table. "Let's talk again about some of your teachings, Craig."

"Go ahead."

"Do you believe in reincarnation?" she asked.

"Yes."

"You believe we're perfecting ourselves through many lives? What evidence do you have? How do you account for the existence of evil?"

"I don't waste too much time agonising about it, Juliet." A cryptic gleam entered his eye. "Shall we say the destiny of an evil man is to come back as a slug?"

She could detect no sign that he was joking. She felt like slapping him. "Really? That seems a bit hard on the slugs. Are we to understand that they are what they are as a punishment for wrongs done in previous lives?"

"Yes. Tough, isn't it?"

How she'd have loved to shake him! But that was out of the question. She sensed his hostility increase. Perhaps it was better to move on to the next subject: the fears for her sister that had brought her here in the first place. "I'm worried about Zoe."

He nodded. "I know."

"I still can't see what effect your ideas might have on her. She's looking for something to focus her life; but what sort of focus is this that you offer?"

He laughed. "Your worry is totally misplaced."

"You think so?"

He gave her a long, steady look. "Would you turn your machine off?"

She obeyed, then regarded him again challengingly. "Zoe's going through a very changeable stage. No wonder she was attracted to this Centre. She hasn't stuck at anything at all since leaving university. Not, I admit, that that's too big a deal. Many go through it. But the point is how can this be the right place for her to end up?"

"Who says she is to *end up* here?" He wore a frank, even innocent expression.

"Zoe herself says so." Juliet made every effort to withstand his look. How dare he not take this seriously? "She got the idea from you, Craig."

There was a small silence. "Coffee?" he said.

"Oh. Yes. Thanks."

He got up, and took two pottery mugs down from shiny brass hooks. Then he moved across the kitchen to the kettle. As he did so, he said, "You underestimate Zoe's intelligence, Juliet. She knows what she's looking for. She's far more likely to find it here than anywhere else outside."

This remark incensed her. "No, Craig, I don't see that at all. I don't think she does know what she's looking for." Before he could reply, she went on. "And there's someone else I want to ask you about. Laura."

"Laura? What of her?"

"You say I misinterpreted her message. So why did she feel the need to strip off and dance naked in Dynamic Meditation?"

"Why?" He smiled. "She likes it."

"Well, leaving aside the mystery of your failure to react, what about all the other men here?"

Craig threw his head back in mirth. "What kind of question's that? Does Laura's nudity worry you? It doesn't worry me."

"Craig, you make me angry."

"So I see." He eyed her in a tolerant manner. "Juliet, I know what's going on for all these people. You're here to observe and listen, not worry yourself about it."

"I'm not," she said in a tight voice. Yes, she was. And really, she'd have liked to throw one of the copper kettles at him.

"Good," he said. "And remember, you're here on my terms."

His words silenced her for a moment. Although they infuriated her, something warned her not to challenge him. "Very well, Craig," she said instead. "If I agree to abide by your terms, then I expect you, at the very least, to answer my questions fairly."

"I'm doing my best, Juliet, depending on the nature of the questions being asked."

"They're not that difficult," she said coolly.

He raised his eyebrows. "I make up the rules," he said.

"But you call this group a wheel of love!" she cried.

"And so it is," he replied.

"That's not love. That's dictatorship."

"Dictatorship?" His next words were delivered with an air of knife-edge finality. "Let's call it quits for the time being, Juliet. We've both said enough."

But his eyes flashed as he put a mug of coffee in front of her. And she felt once again a shock as if she'd brushed against an electric fence.

Laura, wearing pink gardening gloves and a canvas apron over her flimsy cotton voile dress, was kneeling on a cushion beside the flower bed, weeding. Juliet watched her for a while, as she tossed weeds into a trug beside her. She still couldn't relate the prim little figure to the whirling dervish in the barn last night.

Still, it was rather nice right now to think that she didn't have to do two hours of household or gardening duties. She preferred her own work.

She'd already replayed her interview with Craig, using her headset. Her laptop open before her on the cane table, she studied the sound waves on screen. It would have been even more pleasant sitting out here beneath the blue cedars, near the perimeter of the sunken garden enjoying a warm light breeze, if only she wasn't still feeling furious with Craig for his slippery answers to her questions.

She'd now escaped the highly charged aura surrounding him, but she felt like gritting her teeth at the memory of his arrogant manner.

After a few moments she removed the headset, lifted her cup, and took a long refreshing sip. She cast her mind back over the events of the last few hours.

Some of Craig's sharp rejoinders had at least refocused her on her own primary motivation in coming to the community. For what was that other than to check up on Zoe, and try to reorganise her sister's life? OK, certainly it was also a perfect opportunity to do interviews. Especially as Toby had sounded really keen. But in every conversation she had so far had with Toby, she had underplayed her feelings about Zoe. Otherwise he wouldn't believe in her ability to remain objective.

But looked at from another angle, it did seem to her ironic that she'd now reached a turning point in her career entirely through the rash, impulsive actions of Zoe. This was something she could never have anticipated.

Back to the problem of Craig himself again. She'd need to quiz every one of the group about their views of him as their leader. But she felt certain that if he guessed she was inviting criticism of him, he'd turn her out at once. Then there'd be nil chance of rescuing Zoe from this place.

And yet the farmhouse and its surroundings were enchanting. Here she was, out in the garden enjoying a mild, balmy atmosphere and a radiant blue sky, taking afternoon tea at a white cane table. And just beyond the hedge was the soft weathered honey-and-cream stone of the house. She lifted her eyes to the slate tiles on the roof and then allowed her glance to dip just below to the dormer window with its diamond leadlights and golden sandstone mullions, behind which lay her bedroom in the eaves.

Who could wish for anything better, in the heart of the Cotswolds? The comfort of the house, the perfection of its setting, and the generous supply of good food and wine were like a foretaste of heaven. It was just Craig who worried her.

She sighed. As she did so Laura got to her feet, collected her trug, and moved further along the border, away from her and out of sight behind the trees.

"Mind if I join you?"

She looked up. Don stood there, silver hair gleaming in the sunlight. His eyes rested on her.

"Feel free," she said. The way her thoughts were tending, she felt glad of his company.

He pulled another cane chair closer to hers, and sat in it. Then the mood unexpectedly changed. "I hear you've been stirring things up," he shot at her, eyes fixed on her face. He indicated the audio recorder and laptop.

She felt stung. "Yes. That's what I'm here for."

"I've never seen Craig so edgy," Don said.

"Oh?" She pretended to be cool, but was sure her heartbeat had increased. "That's his choice."

"No it's not. It's yours. What are you up to, Juliet?"

She felt goaded to self-defence. "Investigating, that's all."

He laughed. Then quickly the warmth left his eyes. "Don't probe him on family matters, Juliet. Just don't. It's fatal."

"Why?" she protested. "I'm interested. I want to know."

"I forbid it," he snapped.

She came back strongly. "Surely not you too, Don? Come on. I'm onto a story here. I want to light up dark corners. What else d'you expect of me?"

"Not this dark corner. No chance." Suddenly he caught hold of both her hands. "Promise, Juliet. You'll stay out of family stuff."

"No," she cried.

His jaw tightened.

"Relax, Don," she said. "Hey –" She tried to lighten things up. "I'll bet you pester them with enough questions – about the finances."

She succeeded. He released her with a chuckle. "I try. But they're all on guard against me. Scared stiff I'll come round with a collecting box. Ask them to cough up for a support fund. Something Craig ought to have organised at the start."

"A support fund?"

"Yes. Donations – for those who can't really afford to be here."

She shot him a curious glance.

"In other words," he said crisply, "hangers-on with empty pockets."

She thought this rather an unkind way to describe them. Though she knew what he meant. "Are there many of those?" she asked.

"More than a few. Booked up, paid, then stayed on. My generous son. Generosity at my expense, might I add."

"But Craig's well able to deal with malingerers, I'd say."

"Ha. You'd have thought so, yes."

They sat for a while without speaking.

"Why wasn't it set up properly?" she asked.

He snorted. "Long story. If he'd listened to my advice in the first place… But no, went his own way."

She waited. Had he forgotten his ban on family stuff? But he offered no more information.

OK. Play it low-key. She'd try and gain his confidence later. Meanwhile, better move on to another subject. "You should have been on the Dream Yoga walk, Don. You'd have loved walking backwards."

He gave a guffaw. "Sure I would," he said.

She rubbed her finger across the smooth surface of her laptop. "Well, I'm trying hard to see the benefit in being forced to experience the world upside down, and even inside out for a bit."

He nodded, and would have spoken again but for the musical

Welsh lilt of a third voice to be heard behind him.

"When the world's turned right way up again, it'll make sense."

"Llewellyn," said Don, twisting to face him. "Here. Take a seat."

"Thanks." The Welshman bounced into the chair Don offered, his thick hair rising before flopping down once more across his forehead. "What do you make of lucid dreams, Juliet?" he asked.

"Never had one," she confessed. "What of you? Do you think death could be a breeze?"

"I'm a poet," he declared. "It's my business to consider every option." Moments passed, during which he held Juliet in his gaze.

He was attractive. She had to give him that. Warm brown eyes – why couldn't Zoe go for him instead? No, she shouldn't think in this way. But at least it was testimony to the positive light in which she saw this Welshman. "You know, Llewellyn," she said, "I'm surprised you're content to join a group like this, and follow in the footsteps of Craig."

He held his hands wide. "Why not? Time for everything, isn't there?"

"I suppose so, if you see it like that." But she still felt curious.

He considered her. "Tell you what, Juliet. Come to my room later, nine o'clock, say, and I'll explain further. If you're willing, I'll show you some poems."

She gave him a sharp look. "No etchings?"

"Absolutely none."

They both burst out laughing; in glancing sideways, she noticed a rather jaundiced expression on Don's face.

"Then I might just join you as you suggest," she said.

Don cleared his throat.

Juliet leaned forward and touched him on the arm. "I hope you don't mind us making these arrangements in front of you, Don."

"Not at all. You go right ahead."

"If it's any comfort to you, Don," said Llewellyn, "I'm in no doubt at all that she'll bring her recording equipment with her."

"That remark leaves me with a perfect excuse to make no comment," said Don.

But Juliet remained mystified by the look he wore. Was he labouring under the burden of some strong emotion?

"This is a safe environment," said Llewellyn. "Craig keeps telling us that. A safe environment in which to do whatever you want and not to be misunderstood."

Don was quick to come back at him on that one. "Safe for whom?"

"For each one of us, to be true to ourselves without fear of judgement."

Don chewed his lip for a few moments. "True to yourself? If I was that, I'd tell you to keep your hands off this girl. And double your payment to Craig."

The Welshman was about to reply, but Juliet broke in. "Really, Don, I'm sure Llewellyn has no intention of getting his hands on me," she said. "Of course, I can't comment on your second remark." This stopped conversation for a few moments.

Llewellyn's expression remained neutral. He said nothing.

Very wise, thought Juliet. Then she said, "I know this isn't really my business. But even so, Don, whatever it was that went wrong between you and Craig when you set this place up, I do hope you two can put it right soon."

"Remember what I said." Don looked warningly at her. Then he seemed to relent. His gaze softened, became more reflective. "You can hope, any road," he said. "We can all hope. No harm in that."

"What do you mean?" she asked.

Llewellyn, too, was scrutinising the Yorkshireman with an ironical eye.

Juliet turned. A fourth person had joined them. "Zoe!" Juliet said.

Zoe's hair appeared tangled and unbrushed, not to her disadvantage, for she always looked pretty. She wore jeans and a T-shirt with a big blue heart on it. Her face was much paler than normal. What was up? Had she and Craig had a disagreement?

"Come and sit here, Zoe," said Juliet.

"Oh, no, I won't, thanks." An awkward pause followed. Zoe stared at Don, then at Llewellyn, then at Juliet, in a searching way.

Juliet realised she'd left her laptop on, and closed it down.

Don got to his feet. "Want me to go?"

"Thanks," said Zoe, startling Juliet.

Don jerked his head at Llewellyn. "Come on."

The poet seemed hesitant. Don put his hand on his arm. The two men stood up, and headed off back through the garden toward the house.

"What is it?" asked Juliet.

Zoe still refused to sit, but stood in front of Juliet, hands on hips. Her eyes were bright with accusation. "I've just been with Craig."

"Good for you."

"Don't give me that, Juliet," Zoe flashed. She ran her fingers through her hair, and went on. "You've been stirring Craig up. What d'you mean by it?"

"Me? Stir him up? I didn't mean to." Juliet took Zoe's hand, and her sister snatched it away.

The breeze tugged at Zoe's hair as she grasped the lowest cedar branch, and bent it back. Then she spun. Juliet looked at her in alarm. "Craig's sold on you," Zoe stated.

"Get real, Zoe." Silence fell. Juliet felt herself trembling – her arms, her fingers. This was the last thing she wanted, the very last. She hastily spoke again. "You're way off course." She took a grip on herself, and switched to a cooler tone of voice. "He was very high-handed with me, actually," she said.

"That doesn't mean a thing."

Juliet stared incredulously as her sister snapped a stick off the branch, and began stabbing it repeatedly into the grass underfoot. "I've just been talking to him about you," said Zoe fiercely. "And trust me, you've already got under his skin."

"Shut up, Zoe!"

Zoe studied her with growing distrust, then looked away again. Both fell quiet for several moments. Then Juliet tried again, in a softer voice. "Listen, Zoe. I'm here because I care about you."

"You're here because Craig liked the sound of you on the phone. When he saw you, he was even keener. And now…"

"Cut it out, Zoe. His manner towards me at best has been one of cool courtesy. At worst he's been either detached or slightly patronising."

Juliet hoisted the strap of the carrying case over her shoulder. She bit her lip. She felt hot all over and was not going to play into Zoe's hands by betraying it to her.

Zoe slapped the palm of her hand against the side of her head in exasperation. "Cool and detached?" she scoffed. "Just an act."

"You're fantasising."

"All right. Refuse to see the obvious. At least I can recognise it when it's staring me in the face."

"Zoe, stop this." Juliet spoke angrily, almost afraid of her own reaction.

"No. You wise up. If you do fall for him and let him have his way with you, you'll find yourself in big trouble."

Juliet's mouth fell open at this. Had Zoe gone crazy? "What do you mean?" she cried.

But it was too late. Her sister had turned and hurried away, leaving Juliet mystified and worried.

7

Signs of Mutiny

Dust motes floated in the beam of morning sunlight from the east-facing window. A Gothic clock on a wall bracket near Juliet, which she noticed had the phases of the moon on its dial, struck the hour of ten. Again she felt the dreamy, serene atmosphere in the house, at odds with the inner lives of the residents. And yet no house of this age would have long escaped political intrigue, fear and betrayal in the past. The same emotional turbulence within these walls prevailed right now – only the immediate causes were different.

She paused as she arrived at the bottom of the narrow staircase leading down from the attic. The many feet that had passed over them had worn the timber treads smooth and slippery. As she placed hers on the silken surface of the oak she needed to balance carefully. She placed her hand on the structural post to her right, which was helping to support the floor above. She wondered what the fissures in the timber were. Maybe a few Roundheads had tested the point of their swords as they searched the house for hidden priests or monks?

Some of the current residents would probably like to be armed with those same swords, despite this being a wheel of love. After Zoe's explosion yesterday afternoon, there'd been a tense atmosphere between the two sisters at dinner. But Craig had said nothing to Juliet about any subsequent conversation with Zoe. So Juliet could only speculate that Zoe had kept any further thoughts to herself. Or had she completely misread the situation?

And then there'd been last night's meeting with Llewellyn in his room. She'd been pleasantly surprised by the Welshman's restrained behaviour. They'd spent an enjoyable time discussing and looking at poetry, both his and those of his favourite writers; she could find no fault in his manner towards her at all.

Now she stood on the first-floor landing, the Nagra slung over her shoulder in its carrying case. This was, she knew, a free morning for the group, but all seemed especially quiet today.

Floorboards creaked at the far end of the passageway. She slipped back behind the timber post, which served well as a hiding place. James was making his way towards her, looking faintly displeased. His pastel- pink shirt, however, perfectly complemented the mauve cravat. Both in turn harmonised with his smartly pressed cream trousers. She was in no doubt most of his wardrobe originated from a bespoke tailor. Despite her interest in his dual personality, some instinct told her not to accost him. His manner was restless. She remained hidden from view.

She watched as he knocked on the study door opposite. A low voice came from within the room.

"Yes?"

"It's me. James."

"Come in."

He pressed down the black wrought-iron latch, and opened the door. Juliet saw Craig, seated alone before the computer screen. He turned his face in James's direction as his mentor entered. Juliet registered Craig's dejected expression.

James hadn't closed the door behind him, and Juliet could see and hear the two.

Craig spoke first. "I need a break from the notes on the accounts."

"Page-turning stuff?" James moved out of Juliet's line of vision, and she heard him taking another chair.

Craig sucked his breath in between his teeth. "We're in a mess."

"So I guessed."

Craig nodded. "Expenditure's way above forecast, and income's static. My father reckons he's thrown money at this place, and we've nothing to show for it."

James gave an impatient exclamation. "Nothing that he values. But everything you and I value is here in plenty."

"True. But I've been wondering. Am I too extravagant?"

James scoffed. "Of course not."

"Hmm. The antiques, the first editions, the wines… Talking of the wines, we seem to be getting through those at a rate of knots."

"Can't cut back. Ruin the spirit of the place," said James.

"Perhaps. But I'm a bit stumped by the champagne."

"The champagne? Why?"

"There's hardly any left."

"What do you mean?"

"Just that," said Craig. "Had a word with Patrick after breakfast. He says a case of *Dom Perignon* is missing. A dozen bottles."

James tutted several times. "You think we have a secret indulger?"

"Looks like it," said Craig. "Particularly worrying, now my father's checking us over and finding fault where he can."

"Don't worry. I'll get to the bottom of it. Tomorrow we'll be up on the eastern ridge at daybreak for the summer solstice. We've enough champagne for that, haven't we?"

"I hope so."

"Good. I'll find out what's happened. Sure there'll be a simple explanation."

"Thanks, that would be a great help. But, another thing, James…" Craig indicated the computer screen. "Take a look."

Silence fell for several moments. Juliet waited. Then James spoke once more. "Perhaps I'm biased, because I came up with the idea for this project in the first place."

Craig nodded.

"It's vital we make this thing succeed," continued James. "Defeat isn't an option. Don't give in to him. We'll sort it."

"How?"

"Through increasing our income, of course." James swept out his arms in a vigorous, authoritative manner within Juliet's line of vision. "New recruits. That's what we need. And I know where to get them."

"Where?"

"I have contacts." And with this, James jumped up and strode from the room. The door swung closed behind him. Juliet flattened herself against the panelling as he swept past, a new energy in his step, and hurried importantly down the main staircase.

So James was going to fix it, was he? She acknowledged to herself it was no bad thing to discover hidden depths in people. But she wouldn't have thought James had it in him. After all, this rather pretentious academic with the curious taste for brief appearances as a tramp, would on first acquaintance not have struck her as the mover and shaker behind this operation.

Her thoughts turned to Craig. At that moment the study door opened again without warning and Craig came out. She held her breath. But he failed to notice her, and instead rushed past, in the same direction James had taken.

For one moment she paused. Craig had disappeared. She moved forward to the open doorway. Looking in, she saw a buff folder with a mess of papers on the desk, and a tracksuit top thrown carelessly over the chair.

She went quickly in, and quietly looked through the papers. Accounts sheets, printouts of online bank statements, receipts, credit card statements, final demands. Pages of handwritten sums and angry crossings-out and curt notes.

Her eyes fell upon the tracksuit top. It was Craig's jade-green one. She could just see a silver panther key-ring hanging out of the pocket. She moved quickly, grabbed the bunch of keys, and went back round to the front of the desk. The first key she tried fitted the top drawer. She opened it.

A jumble of items met her eye. Biscuit wrappers, sellotape, loose rubber bands, open tube of glue. It seemed out of character for him to be so disorganised. The headscarf was still there, under the other things: and the piece of charred timber. She lifted it out and turned it in her hand to inspect it. She didn't know what to make of it. Fire-blackened. Was it from this house? Or from somewhere else? What did it mean? And why did he keep it in his desk drawer?

Then her fingers made contact with a folded wad of notepaper.

She took it out, opened it up, and realised it was a handwritten letter. Not very legible. Blobs of inks on several lines indicated a cheap ballpoint pen had been used. No address at the top. But there was a date, quite a recent one, only a couple of weeks ago. And below that, simply a salutation.

My darling Craig…

She shouldn't be reading this. But she wasn't going to stop now.

I think of you so much. There followed several sentences she could not decipher, only a word or phrase here and there: *when you first came… guilt… now… you've forgiven me…*

Her interest quickening, she turned the sheet over and scanned the next page: *pain…mess…remain here…don't run away…desperate to see you again…come as soon as you can.*

She heard the floorboards creaking outside in the corridor. Quickly she folded the letter and put it with the other notepaper back where she'd found it. She locked the drawer and snatched out the key. Then she slipped round and stuffed the bunch on the key-ring into the tracksuit pocket. The footsteps were nearly at the door now.

Diving round in front of the desk again she squatted down low, out of view. Someone came into the room and stopped. They appeared to be waiting for something.

Her heart was pounding, but she remained silent. Whoever it was walked across to the chair, and then back to the door again and out of the room.

When all was quiet again she stealthily rose. The tracksuit top, together with the contents of its pocket, had gone. Her thoughts and her feelings were a chaotic mix.

Who was that letter from? Whoever it was loved Craig. And he looked at the letter often she guessed, certainly whenever he was in his study. It was highly emotionally charged. Certainly enough for him to keep it safely locked away from prying eyes. The writer seemed to be pleading with him to come. But come where? And the writer also mentioned guilt. Though Craig had apparently forgiven this person, whoever they might be.

She burned with curiosity. Was this a girl he loved? And if so, where did that leave Zoe? Without a doubt, Juliet could not tell anyone about it, not Don, not Zoe, no one. And if Craig knew she'd sneaked in and read it, he'd throw her out at once.

But she must find out who it was. How, she had no idea. What could she do now to try and reassemble some rational thoughts? Brisk exercise. That would do it. She slipped back up to her room, changed into jogging trousers, sweatshirt and trainers, then set off again.

She knew the route well now: across the car park, over the stile and through the woodland, where she hoped to find a cooler temperature. But steady heat and a still atmosphere meant that she soon felt rather overdressed. She'd have been better off in shorts and strappy top. Zoe would have chosen to dress like that without thinking twice. She headed up to the ridge via the pasture.

"I see you've had the same idea as me," said a voice behind her.

"Ah! Llewellyn!"

He looked jaunty as ever, fresh and eager, with his thick wing of hair flopping over his forehead. She could never imagine him sharing Oleg's depressed states. She wondered if he had any mysterious ongoing relationships outside the community. Or any highly charged letters hidden in his room. Still, she undoubtedly had more to learn yet about this Welshman.

They walked side by side, exchanging occasional remarks, until they reached the top of the ridge. All the time, by an effort of will, she forced herself not to think about Craig, and his letter. Not for more than a few seconds at a time, anyway.

For several moments then, they stood in silence, gazing at the Severn Vale spread out before them.

"Almost as good as the view from Beaumaris," he observed wistfully.

"Looking across the Menai Strait to Snowdonia, you mean?" she said. "Beautiful."

He regarded her warmly, clearly touched by her empathy.

"I might be a Londoner," she said, "but I do appreciate the countryside. And I love North Wales."

"I'm so happy to hear that," said Llewellyn.

A companionable silence fell between them, as they turned their attention back to the landscape. It was broken by the Welshman. "I wish there was more contentment among the others down there in the valley."

"Yes, peace seems in short supply, doesn't it?"

"It's inevitable you've noticed, Juliet. I dread to think what you'll have uncovered by the time you leave."

She chuckled but made no reply. Her stomach still felt twisted. Craig… Craig… she thought.

"You probably wonder why I defended the group when we first met," he said, "and I persuaded Don and you to come to Dynamic Meditation. It's because I believe in the principles behind it all."

"Maybe. But do those principles work out in practice? I certainly didn't expect to find this level of frustration, anxiety and anger. I've found it in Oleg, Zoe, Sam…" She would certainly not mention Craig's name.

"I don't deny that," Llewellyn said. "But, for my part, I'm convinced I'm in the right place. OK, we've all brought our hang-ups with us. And that prevents it from being paradise. But would paradise inspire me as much?"

"Surely it would." She liked his grin. "It was good enough for Wordsworth, Keats and Tennyson, wasn't it?"

"No. Poets need this imperfect world. What sort of effect d'you think *La Belle Dame Sans Merci* had on Keats? Hardly the ideal relationship, was it?"

"No," she admitted. "I'll take your word for it, Llewellyn."

But what she really wanted to know was who wrote that letter to Craig.

Llewellyn didn't say anything for a few minutes. Then he said, "Let's talk instead about your part in this, Juliet."

"Mine?" She was immediately on guard.

"Yes, you, of course, Juliet," he said impatiently. "You've changed everything."

She threw a glance at him, and stumbled over a tree root, which nearly winded her. "How so?" she said, regaining her balance. "I'm only here as a journalist, Llewellyn."

"No, you're not," he said unexpectedly.

"Oh?"

"Last night," he added, "was a step in the right direction."

"A step in what direction?" she asked.

"In the direction of getting to know you better."

"I hope you haven't misunderstood me," she said. "I enjoyed reading and talking about your poems, but…"

"Come on, I want to know what you really feel; not just about the poetry but about many things."

She shook her head. "That's not in my plan, Llewellyn."

"*Life is what happens to you while you're busy making other plans*," he quoted in a flippant manner. Then he laughed. "Let's see how long you can keep me going before I run you to ground."

Whether his flushed appearance resulted from the emotions stirred up by his last remark, it was difficult to tell. She chose not to pursue the subject any further; it seemed wisest that way. She felt she needed to tread warily with the Welshman. He smiled again, and they walked back to the farmhouse.

Their chat remained casual during that time. All the while, though, her emotions were agitated. It was bad enough Zoe making pointed remarks about Craig's supposed feelings for her… and then finding that highly personal letter from somebody else he was clearly very close to. So many deep feelings were involved. *Love… guilt… forgiveness.* What was going on?

She chided herself. Stop thinking about it. Llewellyn will start to suspect something.

As they approached the house, he turned and said, "Juliet?"

"Yes?"

"Do you trust Craig?"

She felt herself flush. He looked at her with a slight frown.

"I'm interested in what led him to set this place up," she said quickly. "Wonder where he got his inspiration from. James has quite an influence, doesn't he?"

"Sort of, I suppose," he said. "But you don't want to worry too much about that."

"Worth taking note of, though, isn't it?"

He shrugged. A few moments passed. Then he said, "Will you share all your concerns with Don?"

She was puzzled by his tone. "Why do you ask?"

His face seemed to have shut down. "Excuse me." He stepped past her and disappeared.

What was that all about?

That night at dinner, Juliet noticed Don's mood had definitely plummeted since they'd last met. She suspected he'd been looking at his notes on the accounts again, and found them even more depressing than he'd previously supposed. Certainly she'd been on the receiving end of a few sharp words. His demeanour was echoed by that of Beth, who'd been persuaded to swap places with Llewellyn.

This arrangement clearly met with Oleg's approval. He looked bright for the first time Juliet could remember, because Beth was next to him. But Juliet wished Beth would reciprocate, and loosen up and show some warmth to Oleg. His hopes at this moment were touchingly transparent.

Meanwhile, Juliet knew the poet had manoeuvred the situation to suit not so much Oleg but himself, so he might be close to Juliet. This evening, having first taken Beth's place, he'd then moved up two and claimed Don's seat before he got there, to win the role of Juliet's neighbour. Well, that was all right, if he merely wanted to be her next interviewee. Though she suspected that wasn't his prime motive.

Don looked none too pleased at the situation when he arrived. Meanwhile, the well satisfied poet absorbed Juliet's attention with his chatter. Beth for her part kept darting yearning looks down the table at Craig. Soon Oleg's euphoria vanished, owing no doubt to Beth's coldness. Juliet felt sorry for Oleg. All Beth needed to do was back off from Craig a bit and give the poor guy a bit of encouragement.

Juliet studied the candles. Tonight they were all black. This surprised her; it even gave a rather macabre impression. Perhaps it had something to do with Craig's ritual for midsummer. Then she realised the Buddha was missing from the seat next to Al, and remembered that tonight they were expecting a new guest: Theo, the unorthodox clergyman. She wondered what difference he might make to the group, and whether he'd be willing to join them at dawn to greet the summer solstice.

Meanwhile Craig was moving up the table behind the chairs with a long taper, lighting the candles. He looked very much in command – of the occasion, of himself, of his role here. Who would have thought that raw, vulnerable letter lay in his desk drawer?

"Tonight is the eve of the summer solstice. With these candles we welcome the dark," he declaimed.

Llewellyn and Rory were both leaning forward talking to each other; and behind their backs Don and Juliet exchanged a questioning look. They appeared to be the only ones slightly puzzled by the ritual. Was this emphasis on the dark appropriate or wise, for the uneasy emotional state the group was in?

Craig returned to seat himself once more at the head of the table. "All concentrate on the candles for thirty seconds, then come together."

James, impeccably attired in a burgundy velvet jacket with a white carnation in the buttonhole, appeared calm and composed. But the glitter Juliet noticed in his eye seemed to belie this. He gave Don a brief nod, not quite friendly, but civil. Juliet checked her Nagra, which sat on a small chair just behind hers. She had permission to make recordings during dinner so long as she was reasonably unobtrusive about it, and she meant to use her opportunity to the full. The levels seemed OK and she could just see her mike behind the nearest bowl of roses in the middle of the table, positioned so as to pick up the voices of those opposite. She wore a clip-mike on her jacket to record the words of her neighbours.

"Let me know if I'm monopolising you," said Llewellyn, close to her ear.

"I will," she replied evenly. "Right now I'm glad to see you so eager to be interviewed."

At the other end of their side of the table, next to Laura, Edgar shuffled notes on his clipboard. It appeared that he insisted on bringing these to the dinner table with him. Was he afraid someone would steal them if he left them unattended for a moment? Al came in from the kitchen wearing a large canvas apron over a flamboyant checked shirt, and placed the dish of the day on the table.

"Which transatlantic recipe's on the menu tonight?" asked Patrick.

"Steak and fries?" enquired James. He looked like a senior member of the Washington Administration who'd just received news that the CIA had caught America's Public Enemy Number One. Juliet wondered what he'd been up to since she last saw him. She studied the faces of the diners opposite. Zoe's glance was rarely anywhere but upon Craig's face, unless James engaged her in conversation. On James's other side Sam resembled as ever a moody sheep. He always made her feel uncomfortable.

"Th-th-thank you f-f-for helping me th-th-this afternoon, Don," he blurted out unexpectedly.

"It was nothing."

"Don't know what I'd have done without you."

James looked suspicious. "Why? What did you do, Don?"

"Nothing to stir you up, James," replied Don. "Kept watch at the door. That's all. While Sam was in the tank."

"The tank? What's that? And what happens in it?" asked Juliet.

Conversation halted. James, Craig and Sam all swivelled their eyes to her face.

"Let me explain, Juliet," said Craig. "I teach my students to seek their answers in the unconscious mind. A tried and tested way of doing this is in the isolation tank."

"How?" she enquired.

Craig wore an enigmatic expression. Opposite, Zoe threw her a sharp glance. "The answers will come," said Craig, "as you float. The tank's filled with a thick, warm saline solution. You climb in, close the lid, and you're in total blackness."

Juliet shuddered. "I should hate that."

Craig gave a tolerant smile. "Many love it. They find bliss there. It all depends on your viewpoint."

"Where is the tank?" she asked.

"In a cabin of its own. The former cart hovel. Halfway between the barn and the goose house."

"Ah yes, I've seen it."

Craig waited a few moments. "Some of my methods may appeal to you more than others."

They regarded each other slowly. "I doubt it," she said.

"Try them anyway, Juliet," he responded, "otherwise you won't be in a position to form an opinion, will you?" He lifted his voice. "Everyone agree with that?"

Not one voice of dissent could be heard.

"And that provides a perfect introduction to our guest speaker, Theo," said Craig. The atmosphere lifted at once. "Theo Lucas in fact needs no introduction, except perhaps to you, Zoe, and you too of course, Juliet. His last visit was in February. He's always welcome among us."

"That's because his boundaries are fluid and flexible," whispered Llewellyn in Juliet's ear.

"What does that mean?" she asked.

But before he could reply, a figure had appeared in the open doorway from the sitting room, to the left of *The Lady and the Unicorn*. Blond and neatly-bearded, in his early thirties, Theo looked smart in a black shirt and crisp dog collar. His grey, discerning eyes took them all in.

"Greetings, everyone." His tone was pleasant and well-modulated. At his appearance, the group broke spontaneously into a round of applause.

"Welcome, Theo." Craig gestured for him to come and join them, and occupy the space recently vacated by the Buddha at the end of the table. "I hope you've fully recovered from your journey?"

"I have, thank you, Craig. Thank you indeed." As Theo seated himself, he let his glance travel around the table, encompassing everyone in its warmth. "How delightful to be here with you all, once again! I can hardly believe four months have passed since my last visit."

"We've looked forward immensely to your return, Theo," said Craig.

The young clergyman smiled at him. "Thank you. I was flattered to be invited a second time."

Well, thought Juliet, Theo certainly seemed to have the gift of making himself agreeable.

"But there are some here I haven't met before," Theo went on.

"Of course." Craig swept his arm out. "Seated beside Llewellyn, may I introduce Juliet?" He gave a brief account of who she was and why she was there.

"Fascinating," said Theo. "I look forward to the opportunity to chat to you about that, Juliet. Used to be a freelance broadcaster myself."

This information came as a surprise to her. "Is that so, Theo? What kind of work did you do?"

"Recorded a few video diaries for the BBC. Must be five or so years ago now. Sadly lost touch with the programme editor since then."

She opened her mouth to question him further, but James broke in. "I'm sure you'll catch up with Theo later, Juliet. But for now shall we let Craig get on with the introductions?"

She stared at him. Why had he interrupted like that? Did he know something about Theo he didn't want aired publicly at the table?

"And sitting here, to my left, Theo," said Craig hastily, "is Juliet's sister Zoe, who's come to try us out, and may possibly join us if she likes us enough."

Juliet looked at Zoe, struck by the way Craig had introduced her. It certainly didn't sound as if he regarded her as the love of his life.

Zoe turned from Craig to Theo, a slightly hurt expression still on her face.

Theo's eyes met hers. "Pleased to meet you, Zoe," he said.

The look they shared lasted longer than Juliet would have

considered appropriate. His manner was modesty and gentleness itself, but she sensed something lay beneath the surface, telling a very different story.

James started clumsily refilling his neighbours' glasses, spilling wine on the table. What was going on?

Al raised his voice. "Say, Craig. How about some fizz to celebrate Theo's arrival?"

For a moment, he became the centre of attention. James held the bottle aloft, frozen in mid-pour, his eyes holding a curious expression. "Champagne, you mean?"

"Sure."

"Is that necessary?" James asked. "After all, we'll be taking it up to the eastern ridge for sunrise tomorrow."

"No reason why we shouldn't have some now though," said Craig. "Both to celebrate Theo's arrival, and to begin the midsummer festival. An excellent idea, Al. Go and get a couple of bottles."

The American instantly obliged. Laura leapt up to help.

Juliet continued to view James, speculating. He had stopped her enquiring about the break in Theo's freelance broadcasting career, which she was intrigued by, especially in view of Rory's words to her on her first evening about Theo *vanishing from the face of the earth.* She was engaged by Theo's amiable smile and his gracious manner, and curious to know why he'd cut off that career, and what he did afterwards.

After a few moments, Al came back in with two bottles of *Dom Perignon.* Laura, behind him, carried a tray full of champagne flutes. She set this on the table. As Al began the process of opening the first bottle, Juliet noticed James concentrating all his attention on the removal of some minor mark from the sleeve of his velvet jacket, in a manner which was both fastidious and edgy. The cork popped, and everyone else cheered.

Al was now pouring champagne and handing the flutes down the table, which were accepted by everyone but Rory, who as always confined himself to water.

Juliet felt apprehensive as she looked at Rory. Violent, Oleg had said. When? How? Why? It couldn't be the effect of drink. He never touched it, so far as she could see. Only water.

Craig stood up. "To Theo," he said. "To Theo. Welcome," chorused the group. All who had champagne took their first sip. Then Craig continued. "Let's celebrate this midsummer festival."

All eyes were upon him, and Craig began: "*These are the long days when the sun rides high above us; at this time of shortest night and longest day let us touch that vein of eternity in us all as we open our arms wide and say: Sister Death, we know you are coming and yet we greet you.*"

Suddenly she looked at Oleg. She saw new distress upon his face. Oh dear. What could possibly be the matter? Surely nothing in Craig's words had struck the wrong note for Oleg?

Craig continued his recital. "*We are held in a life that beats for ever and a light that cannot end. Let us celebrate; let us touch eternity at this midsummer feast.*"

"Let us celebrate," the group repeated in unison, and drank more champagne. The lids were removed from the dishes.

"Pass your plates," said Al. "I'll be mother."

Theo reopened the conversation. "So how have you all been since I last saw you?"

"Continuing our journey of growth," said Rory in an unctuous tone of voice, flicking his blond bouffant hairstyle back.

"But not healed yet, by a long way," added Oleg darkly.

"Of course not," murmured Theo. "These things can take a lifetime. I still struggle in every area possible."

Craig moved swiftly on from this. "Are you still with the Golden Chalice Foundation, Theo?" he queried.

"Yes. They keep me busy travelling up and down the country. Guest spots at residential retreats, and so on. But no community gives me greater pleasure than this one. And that's not simply due to its location, here in this lovely Cotswolds valley. Though I must admit I do have an affinity for priest holes and monks' rooms."

Laughter rippled around the table.

"But most of all, it's because of you, every one of you here. Certainly there's nowhere I feel more at home than in the Wheel of Love."

Chuckles of appreciation travelled up and down the table. Laura gazed at him over her champagne flute with shining eyes.

Juliet watched James for his reaction to these words. His eyes were hooded. Was he jealous of Theo at all? She didn't know enough, yet, to imagine a cause for this.

"Therefore, I'd like you to be first to hear my news. Not good, I'm afraid. I'm in trouble with my bishop. Or so I hear from stories that reached my ears early this morning." Gasps of alarm escaped from the group: which members of it, Juliet couldn't tell; but certainly not from James.

"How terrible." Laura clutched the table for support.

"What have you done, Theo?" enquired James. "Professional misconduct?"

Patrick crossed himself. Rory gave James a chilly stare. But Theo went on, unruffled.

"I wrote and published a short book on Synchronicity; a subject which, as some of you may know, I'm very interested in. It is, of course, a term coined by Carl Jung. But I'm beginning to regret having published it now. It appears some of my colleagues think it's heretical." He stopped. The room had fallen silent.

"What does your bishop think?" said Zoe.

"I don't know yet," he admitted.

Don wore a wry expression. "When will you?"

"I expect a call later," said Theo.

Craig spoke in a gracious tone of voice. "Theo, we accept you as you are. You need make no defence of yourself here." He lifted his glass as he said this.

"Hear, hear," said James; Juliet noticed a slight shiftiness in his manner.

"Thank you, Craig." Theo put his champagne flute down, and was about to help himself to more potatoes when Rory burst out, across the table: "Theo, you remember Craig's words about Sister Death?"

Theo nodded, and looked at him in faint surprise. "Why do you ask?"

"Because you may be able to help me. You see, I had a near-death experience last night," said Rory.

"Intriguing. You must tell me all about it after dinner."

Patrick sucked his breath in between his teeth. "Yes. Thank you for sparing us from it right now, Rory."

"Oh, no. I don't want to do that. I want to share it with you all," said Rory in a determined manner.

"No," said Craig. Rory looked at him. Their eyes held for a few moments, then Rory subsided.

Juliet liked Craig's handling of this. She thought the reference to *Sister Death* a beautiful and strangely consoling phrase reminiscent of St Francis of Assisi, but even so she recognised that some of the more vulnerable people in the group might see it differently. And evidently Craig had reason to believe Rory's experience was best kept to himself for the time being.

Clearly Craig did hold some kind of power over his community members. She'd seen that in Zoe, in Laura, in Beth, and now Rory. She'd make sure, though, that he never tried to claim the same kind of power over her. She was becoming quietly confident that if he had any such plan it would fail.

"Honey-braised carrots, Theo?" enquired Patrick.

"Oh. Yes please."

As Patrick shovelled them onto his plate, though, Theo addressed Rory again. "Nevertheless, I should be happy to chat to you about this experience of yours later, Rory. I've had several such experiences myself in the past."

While he said this, Juliet's attention had been caught by Oleg again. He seemed to have gone rigid, gripped by some powerful emotion, held severely in check. What was the matter with him?

Patrick, meanwhile, was apparently choking, having swallowed too much champagne. Sam anxiously patted him on the back.

A loud clatter of cutlery at Oleg's place commanded everyone's attention. The Slav had abandoned his meal, pushed his chair back, and leapt to his feet. Even Beth looked slightly startled. At last! An emotional reaction from her, thought Juliet.

"What is it, Oleg?" said Craig.

"I want you to release me," cried Oleg. "I've seen the darkness. I need to leave this place at once."

Juliet stared at him. What had brought this on? Was it Rory and his near-death experience? Oleg seemed oblivious even to Beth's hand, which had crept out to stroke his arm, offering some comfort. At last! Some compassion for Oleg. But was it too late?

Meanwhile, perplexity reigned among the group. Oleg was now bending forward, almost double, his forehead upon the table. Edgar, on his left side, had placed a restraining hand upon his shoulder.

"Food poisoning?" asked Rory sympathetically.

Edgar glared at him.

"I feel so inadequate," moaned Oleg, lifting his head.

"What makes you feel that, Oleg?" asked Theo.

Oleg shot upright again, shocking Juliet with the ferocity of his body language. Beth sprang back from him as if bitten by a spider. "I'm on the edge. Can't cope with life any more. Sometimes I wake feeling as if my bed is suspended in space out from a sheer cliff face, and the nearest ground is a thousand metres below."

"Interesting," murmured Edgar, scratching something with his pen on one of his sheets of A4 paper.

Oleg ran for the door. James rose too, but with more dignity, hastening round the back of the diners on his side of the table to intercept him. Beth had begun to cry silently.

"Come and sit down again, Oleg." James took his arm. "Finish your meal. We can talk about this. We usually do."

"Talking never solves anything," snarled Oleg. He shook James's hand off, but remained in the room.

"Who started this?" asked Edgar.

Beth smothered her face in her napkin. Theo reached out to her gently, and squeezed her shoulder. She didn't react.

Rory broke in. "Me. I'll take the blame. Why not? I usually do."

Patrick swiftly rose to the bait. "Yes! It was you and your near-death experience, Rory, that set him off."

Before Rory could react, Craig interjected. "That's enough,

Patrick. Rory, calm down. You remember the exercises I gave you."

What were they? Juliet wondered. As far as she could see, Rory was now hyperventilating, which she would have thought made matters worse. Beth sniffed loudly, and bowed her head almost to the table, her face still buried in the napkin. No one else said a thing. Instead they stared first at Rory, then at Oleg and James, who remained by the door, and then at Beth, and finally at each other with baffled expressions.

At this point, Theo got up and walked round the table to where Oleg stood poised close to the open door, ready to flee. He laid his hand gently on Oleg's shoulder. Then he turned to address everyone else. "Perhaps," he suggested, "Oleg is opening your eyes to something you need to acknowledge. Something you all need to *come out* about."

A few moments passed, during which Oleg visibly relaxed. A kind of peace had seemed to settle on him at Theo's touch. Then Oleg slowly returned to his seat. So did James, looking stunned.

A miracle! thought Juliet.

Next Theo went over to Rory, who was shuddering, and touched him as he had just touched Oleg. "Peace," he said. A few seconds passed, and Rory's breathing steadied.

Is Theo a spiritual healer? Juliet asked herself. For the first time since all this had begun she glanced across to Zoe to see how her sister was reacting. Zoe's eyes were on Theo and she looked captivated.

"Thank you, Theo," said Craig carefully.

"You're welcome," said the clergyman. "But I'd like to ask you all a question." He held his hands out. "What do you all think love really means?" A pause followed. "And with that, I'll leave you for the evening. Sorry, everyone. Would you excuse me? I've had a long journey. I think I'll go straight to my room."

"Oh please do. Feel free." Craig sounded taken aback. Juliet looked at Theo in surprise. This was completely unexpected.

"We understand perfectly how you feel, Theo," went on Craig. "Do go to your room. You must be tired. Let me know if there's anything you need."

"Yes, yes," said Theo.

"I'll help." Al rose to his feet.

Juliet thought Theo might be about to faint. She gazed at him in concern.

Seeing her face, Theo said, "Nothing to worry about, Juliet. This is nothing to do with what has just happened in this room. No, it's just I suffer from migraines. Fortunately I recognise the early warning signs, so I'm able to take action before it's too late." At this, he left, with Al at his side.

A subdued atmosphere settled upon the group.

"I quite understand how Th-Th-Theo feels," said Sam. "I th-th-think I'll adjourn as well."

"I'll collect you for the sunrise ceremony," said Patrick.

Sam nodded shakily. And he too left the room.

Craig wore a detached expression. It was left to James to take charge of the rapidly disintegrating group. "Eat up, everyone."

"More champagne?" enquired Edgar.

"Not for me, thank you," said Rory.

"You weren't having any, anyway, were you?" said Laura.

Edgar touched her elbow. "Leave it, Laura. We all want to believe we've just witnessed a miracle."

Craig stood up. Juliet looked at him. For a moment he held her gaze. She saw nothing but calmness there. He inclined his head, and left the room. There was no indication that Zoe held a special place in his affections. His departure acted as a signal for everyone else to disperse. Beth, she noticed, had slipped out at the first opportunity, without a word to anyone, least of all poor Oleg. She wondered how Zoe was feeling. She tried to catch her eye but failed.

She noticed, though, that Oleg hung behind. Here was her chance. She went to join him. "So, Oleg, will you stay, or go?"

"Go," said Oleg.

She waited. "May I ask you something? What did you mean when you said you'd *seen the darkness*?"

He hesitated.

"It was just after Rory had started talking about his near-death experience last night, wasn't it?" said Juliet.

Oleg lost colour. "Yes. Rory has *the darkness* in him. When Theo touched him, I saw it start to roll back."

She was silent. She couldn't trust herself to comment on what Oleg thought he'd seen.

"But I'm afraid," said Oleg, "that it will soon return. And I don't want to be around when it does. Last night I was unlucky."

"Last night? Something happened between you and Rory, didn't it?" She touched his shoulder. "Would you like to talk?"

"Yes," he whispered.

"Come with me then," she said.

8

Outside Fielder

The following morning a steadily climbing temperature, blue skies and a defiant breeze announced midsummer's day. Juliet had only slept about four hours, having been up on the eastern ridge earlier to watch the sunrise. A magical occasion – aside from the fact that it was partially spoiled by the guarded atmosphere following the disruptions of last night's feast.

And she'd been oppressed by a greater weight beyond that. For Oleg's revelations about Rory's behaviour towards him had once more thrown the spotlight onto Craig. The group leader had evidently tried to put Rory off coming here in the first place. The fact that Craig had ended up, instead, letting him overstay his original booking increased the mystery. Why hadn't Craig chucked him out? Was he weak? Or, worse, was he in Rory's debt in some way?

This, combined with her ongoing worry about Craig's other secrets, intensified her desire to know the truth about him, whatever that was. She had come to see what Zoe was up to and rescue her from him. She hadn't expected to find so many treacherous undercurrents. If the waters around Craig were so disturbed, how much less suitable a partner for her sister did that make him?

As these speculations filled her mind she strolled across the forecourt and unlatched the gate. Beyond the sunken garden she followed a cobbled path which wound through dense shrubbery. Past the lavender bushes, azaleas and rhododendrons she found a delightful African thatched gazebo with enclosed wooden sides. She went in at once and admired it for several moments: a perfect place to sit and enjoy a quiet uninterrupted hour or so.

Or so she imagined as she made herself comfortable on a redwood timber seat set against one wall of the octagonal structure, with her laptop and Nagra. But before she could settle down to her work, Edgar materialised in the doorway.

He looked, as ever, as if he'd just been gliding along the cloisters with a copy of the Daily Office under his arm. Except it was his clipboard of notes instead. His solemn expression contributed to the effect. "Ah, Juliet. Not having a lie-in either?"

She shook her head. "Couldn't sleep."

"Enjoy sunrise?"

"Of course," she replied. "Who wouldn't?"

"Theo, for one," he replied. "Our faith-healing cleric. What a shame he's laid up with a migraine."

"Yes," she replied, "but I think it's early days yet to credit him with healing gifts. After all, we don't know yet whether Rory or Oleg are going to show any long-term improvement, do we?

"That's true." He contemplated her. "You still look tired."

"Yes. I lay awake thinking, until there was nothing for it but to get up again."

She pushed her hair back from her forehead. She certainly didn't intend to share with Edgar the details of what had passed between her and Oleg after dinner last night. Fortunately he didn't ask. The only person she'd entrust with that information was Don, whom she hadn't seen yet that morning.

"Mind if I join you?" He indicated the seat opposite her.

"Please, feel free," she murmured, resigned to losing her blissful solitude. She closed down her laptop.

Seating himself, he placed his clipboard and papers beside him in a businesslike manner. Her heart sank. He began to cast keen glances at her. "You're just starting your fourth day here, Juliet," he observed.

"I am indeed."

"And I'm sure you already have many interviews."

"Yes. Few more to do yet, though."

His expression turned even more purposeful. "What do you make of our esteemed leader?"

She was taken unawares by the directness of this question. "Fascinating," she said, before she realised what deductions he might draw from this.

"Good," he replied. "Juliet, as I said, you've been here for a full three days now, and this far into anyone's experience of the Wheel of Love we like to get their impressions."

"And quite right too," she said. "But I'll need several more chats with Craig before I can understand what he's about. And Sam: he's terrified of me. He only seems to feel safe with Patrick, and perhaps Don. As for James, he's hiding something. And not just the fact that he occasionally dresses up as a tramp."

Searching for signs of humour in Edgar, she found none. But there again, she expected perhaps she too sometimes came over as a bit of a killjoy. "And Rory's a problem," she added. "Later this afternoon I may tackle him about it."

"No. Don't. That's Craig's job," said Edgar abruptly.

Her spirits lowered. Her time here was strictly limited. So was her ability to pay for an extended stay. She'd have to seriously look at the other commitments in her diary if she wanted to stay on. Next Monday she'd planned to be back in London. But she couldn't possibly leave Zoe behind with Craig.

Edgar said, "You don't like things getting out of control, do you, Juliet?"

She felt stung. How dare he? But relaxing her professional mask, she laughed. "I admit it's not a nice feeling, Edgar."

He regarded her with a sardonic eye. "You won't continue here for much longer and remain in control."

"But that's exactly what I propose to do." She had no desire for a battle of wills. But if he wanted one, so be it.

However, when he next spoke he used a softer, more conciliatory tone. "I understand how you must feel, Juliet. Desire for self-determination; that's true of each person here. When we first come we all intend to stay in charge of our lives. Look at Llewellyn, for example."

"Llewellyn? What of him?" Juliet felt her jaw tighten.

Edgar now slipped into a more bantering style of speech. "Well, I understand he's thought of little else but you, Juliet, since you both chatted together in his room on the night before last."

She gripped both sides of her laptop. So he was leaping to conclusions about her and Llewellyn. She stayed quiet, but her face burned.

His eyes remained on her. He went smoothly on. "Don't think I haven't noticed. Since you first came, he's quizzed me about you several times. It's plain he's got his eye on you. Go for it. You can't stand back for ever."

How presumptuous he was! She refused to dignify his speech with a reply.

A few moments passed. Edgar evidently considered it politic to switch back to his original agenda. He picked up his clipboard, and rearranged several sheets of paper on it. "Now, Juliet, let's look at your questionnaire."

"I'd prefer not to."

"Oh I insist," he said.

She resisted the urge to react. Instead, she watched a magpie flapping over the rhododendrons and coming in to land on the path near the window where she sat. Then he started a series of sharp jabs into the soil beneath the shrubs, as if he'd found a particularly fat worm just beneath the surface.

She willed herself to breathe more slowly. It wouldn't serve her purpose to get angry with Edgar.

"I tell you what, Juliet," said Edgar. "Why not try one of Craig's meditations first?"

At this point footsteps approached, and Don came into view bearing a tray, vacuum flask, mugs and a plate of cookies.

Juliet felt an enormous sense of gratitude and relief. What a well-timed entry on the scene. "This is civilised of you, Don." She put her laptop down on the seat beside her.

"Not at all." He walked through the doorway and set the tray down next to Edgar. The researcher, she noticed, looked sour at the interruption. But it struck her as pure serendipity.

"I'll pour," said Don. He indicated the cookies. "Patrick's work."

"How lovely. On baking duty today is he?" she asked.

He nodded. "And a dab hand too." He began to unscrew the top off the flask. "Just took breakfast to Theo. Our below-par cleric."

"How is he?"

"Too early to say. Poor chap."

She smiled. Trust Don to be economical with sharing personal information. He began pouring coffee into the mugs.

"Shame he missed the sunrise ceremony," she said.

"True. Nowt to be done about it though. If you're sick, you're sick. Asked for croissants, by the way." He tutted. "And an omelette. Cooked soufflé-style."

Juliet laughed. "Migraines do that to some people," she observed, as he handed her a steaming mug of coffee.

"Yes."

"How long is he staying here? Do you know?" Juliet asked.

Edgar supplied the answer. "Another six days, I understand. Craig's keen not to lose him again on Sunday. Wants him to stay much longer."

Juliet's investigative instincts were alerted by this. "I'd still like to know why he's here at all. He mentioned, didn't he, that he works for the Golden Chalice Foundation. What do they do?"

"Run a healing ministry," said Edgar, taking a mug from Don.

"There you are. That explains it then doesn't it?" said Don.

"Why?" she asked.

"Well, plenty of people here need healing," replied the Yorkshireman. "And Craig could certainly do with back-up."

She looked at him curiously. "But not from a Christian cleric, I would have thought," she said.

He shrugged. No joy from him. Well, she'd ask Theo as soon as he was better. "I'm surprised though that he finds it *most easy to be himself* here," she said. "He must disagree with several of Craig's teachings."

Edgar waved his free hand in a gesture of light dismissal. "The significant thing is the amount of soul-searching Theo's done. Craig's convinced that with his gifts, he'll be an asset to the Wheel of Love."

"And what sort of gifts are you referring to?" asked Juliet.

"Discernment of spirits. Very important here," said Edgar cryptically.

Juliet wondered at this. How could a soul-searching clergyman in danger of being defrocked be relied upon to decide which spirits were charlatans and which genuine? Rather she suspected Theo might even come under the influence of the Wheel of Love himself. And that brought her thoughts back to Craig again.

Don handed round the cookies. He and Juliet exchanged a glance. Neither said anything. A few moments passed as they all concentrated on munching.

"I'm just about to take Juliet through Section 3," said Edgar, wiping crumbs from his lips.

"No you're not," said Juliet.

"Ah. The famous questionnaire." Don picked up the plate again. "Dig in, Edgar. Tell you what. I'll take over." He sat forward on the edge of his seat.

As Juliet sipped her coffee, she felt like laughing. Don was doing his best to distract Edgar, and she deeply appreciated it. In fact he'd rescued her for the second time. She wondered what lay behind this unexpected act of grace.

"I don't know…" began Edgar. He looked from one to the other, suspicious, his second cookie poised in his fingers.

Don drank his coffee. Edgar relented. "Very well, if you can persuade Juliet to answer these questions, Don. Very good of you…"

"It's nothing. You eat up. I'll give Juliet the third degree," said Don. He and Juliet conferred together, as he went through the form, circling numbers on her behalf.

Then he stabbed the questionnaire with his forefinger. "What's this? *How certain are you that you understand your leader's teachings… agree with your leader's teachings… secretly think your leader is a waste of space…* Call this scientific?"

Edgar looked secretive. "The wording of the questions is very carefully designed. Rest assured. It's scientific."

Don gave a bark of laughter. "No comment. That's my motto."

"Not one I've noticed you live by," said Edgar in a spiteful tone of voice.

Their eyes locked. Juliet watched intently, whilst drinking her coffee. The tension mounted, then inexplicably slid away. Edgar moistened his lips. "You'll be giving our visitor here a bad view of us, Don."

"Too late for that." Don bit into another cookie. "She's three steps ahead. She already knows that nothing adds up."

"Including the balance sheets, you mean?" said Edgar. "That's no concern of mine."

"Ought to be," Don retorted.

Juliet viewed the researcher. He seemed unfazed. "James is working on recruitment," he said airily. "Entry has never been dependent on means."

"Don't I know it. What's James's news? Anything to show?"

"Nothing he's told me about. Give him a chance. These things take time."

Don grunted. "Look at me. Businessman. See what's in front of me, and act on it. Like to be the same? Straightforward; honest; unsentimental."

Juliet listened to this with rising amusement.

"I regard the prospect of being like you with total revulsion," said Edgar. He passed his hand across his brow. "I fear I'm getting Theo's problem too."

Don made a grimace. "Another one taken poorly?"

"Yes. I shall follow his example, and go and lie down."

"Up well before the crack of dawn, weren't you?" Don spread his hands. "Don't hang around. Off you go."

Unusually obedient, Edgar gathered his clipboard and papers, put his mug back on the tray, and departed.

For a few moments Don and Juliet both gazed at the blossoms outside the windows. Juliet suspected the charms of living here had lured people to drop all their commitments in the outside world. And Craig's talents lay in popular psychology, inspirational speaking and charismatic leadership. By now, she'd had enough conversations with Don on the subject to know that financial wisdom had been left out somewhere along the line.

"Before Craig got into all this, was there any other career you had in mind for him?" she asked.

"Yes." He didn't hesitate. "Business management."

She suppressed an urge to laugh.

"A fine career," went on Don. "Instead he's here. With this lot. Let's look at a case or two. Start with Beth."

"Beth?"

"Yes. Financial drain. Pays the least."

"An emotional drain too I should imagine," she remarked. "On Oleg as well as Craig."

He gave a chuckle of assent. "Too soft on the wrong people. *Healing* is what he calls it. What good's that? Needs efficiency. He'll go bankrupt if he carries on like this."

"Does anyone pay their way?"

"Yes. Oleg. Unbelievably. Beats me how."

"The very one who's threatening to leave."

He shuffled his feet and looked at her searchingly. "Had a word with him last night, didn't you?"

She'd been waiting for him to ask that. "Yes," she said. "He made several worrying claims about Rory."

"Oh?" Don listened, eyes keen as a bird of prey.

"Reckoned he attacked him on Sunday night," went on Juliet.

"Assault?" asked Don.

She nodded.

"What kind?"

Their eyes met and held.

Don groaned, holding his head in his hands. Then he looked up. "Suspected something of the sort."

"I still only have Oleg's word for it," she added hastily. She knew she couldn't necessarily believe everything she heard. Even so, she felt sick to the stomach at the thought of what Rory had allegedly done, and what he might yet be capable of doing, here in this community.

And if Oleg was telling the truth, how could Craig let this pass? Why did Rory behave in this way? What reason could there be for his aggression? She for one felt very unwilling ever to go into a room alone with him. "So how's Craig going to deal with this?" she asked.

"You tell me." Don's eyes narrowed. "What was that about *a near-death experience*?"

She drew a deep breath. She'd wondered whether that might have been self-delusion. "I think it was poor Oleg who had the near-death experience, not him."

"Perhaps I can explain." A third voice had spoken. They both started. Craig stepped in.

Juliet tried to steady her breathing. Why did Craig have this effect upon her? The breeze had stirred his dark hair. She was conscious of the warm colour in his face and the brightness in his eyes, as if he'd just been running. He wore a scarlet polo with pale-blue jeans. He looked very sexy. She couldn't avoid acknowledging this to herself.

"Push people far enough," he said, his glance passing from Juliet to Don, "and there's no limit to what they might do."

"Which means…?" asked Don.

"Which means Rory wants watching," said Craig. "You can trust me for that. No need to fear."

Juliet didn't know what to say. Was this good enough?

"Who started it?" asked Don. "Rory or Oleg?"

"Oleg claims it was Rory," said Juliet.

"Of course he does," said Craig, moving across to the seat on Juliet's right. "But we cannot say. None of us was there at the time."

"Has Rory ever done anything like this before?" asked Juliet.

Craig didn't reply immediately. Instead, he seated himself and settled back comfortably, right ankle crossed over his left knee. Juliet felt intensely aware of his presence. She was also conscious of the distrust between father and son. Maybe she could help. But did she have a right to intervene? And – worse – did it mean she was in danger of falling under Craig's spell?

She checked herself. The Wheel of Love would not draw her in. She was sure of that. Or believed so anyway…

As she wrestled with self-doubt, Craig spoke again. "Rory does have special difficulties. Naturally, you feel a little fearful, Juliet. But I do intend to take action."

"Let's see it then," muttered Don.

Craig held up a hand. "My strategy with my followers is to break down their defences. I still have work to do on Rory."

"But what's going on with him?" asked Juliet. "I understand he's been here several months. One of the group made the comment that he's overstayed his welcome. Now he's assaulting people."

"Well said," Don remarked.

She waited for Craig to justify himself. Instead, he gave her a winning smile. "We still don't know the true cause of the incident, Juliet. But I want to calm your fears. As I said, I have the matter in hand. This is a safe environment. A few respond at once, one or two take longer."

"And put others at risk while they're at it." Again she felt something swirl through her, threatening to break her self-command.

"Not at all," said Craig. "Just trust me, Juliet."

"Why should she?" retorted Don, evidently keen to cut in to this.

"Every reason," said Craig smoothly. "And remember too, both of you, there are those who like to cast themselves in the role of victim."

Don was not impressed. "Psychobabble. That's all it is."

"No, Father. The victim role is one we can choose or not, according to our will."

Don refused to take this idea on board. "Heaven help anyone who meets Rory down a dark alley," he said.

"Don't overreact, Father. I'll speak to him in a few minutes. Then I'll have a word with Oleg."

Juliet was struck by how masterful Craig had seemed during the last few exchanges. She found herself beginning to believe in him. She'd seen him change appearance. He practised what he talked about. Perhaps he did have real insight into these people and would indeed succeed in resolving their problems.

Don, however, clearly did not share these feelings. "You need to bring Rory to heel. If you lose Oleg, you lose our best payer. Where does he get his money from, by the way?"

"Haven't asked," said Craig.

"Organised crime in one of those breakaway Soviet republics probably."

"Watch your tongue, Father." Craig's voice was steady but his eyes flashed.

The distrust Juliet had seen smouldering between them a few moments ago now burned fiercely. What might Don be hiding behind these threat displays? Was it possible that Craig put up his theories as a shield to protect himself?

Meanwhile, a curious emotional shift stirred Don's features, resolving itself into a blend of triumph and regret. "I funded this place. My patience soon runs out."

Now Craig's eyes spat fire. But he said nothing. The atmosphere seemed charged with static electricity.

Despite her fear that she might worsen matters, Juliet risked intervening. "Why not ask Theo's advice? He seems a caring, thoughtful sort of character. When he's better he may be able to mediate between the two of you." Immediately, she wished she hadn't said it.

Craig released Don from eye contact, and swung to face her instead. His expression wasn't friendly. "I didn't invite you, or Theo, here for personal counselling services, Juliet."

"Of course not. I only meant…"

"Theo has his own issues to contend with," said Craig.

Juliet shot a querying glance at him.

"What's that mean?" asked Don. "We know he's in trouble over that book of his. But…"

Juliet continued to study Craig's face. She felt perplexed. Then she remembered the conversation she'd had with Rory about Theo at the dinner table, on the evening of her arrival. Rory had referred to a *wilderness experience.* Juliet had since then learned enough about Rory to know that not every one of his words could be trusted. Even so, she would like to confirm at some stage the truth of this claim about Theo.

Craig's voice broke into her speculations. "The fact remains, Juliet, you'll be well advised to keep out of this."

None of them stirred.

"Why?" she asked. Several moments passed.

"Because…" and now a new, but much less hostile, expression came into Craig's gaze, "if you probe too far you may discover things you'll wish you hadn't."

"Oh, I doubt it," she said. "In fact, Craig, I'm prepared to investigate just as far as I need to in order to discover the truth."

"Is that so? Good luck then. You'll find out during the next few days that nothing here is what it seems nor is it intended to be. You agree, Father?"

9

Shifts of Allegiance

None of her efforts to discover what Craig had intended by that remark yielded any fruit to Juliet. Did he suspect she'd rifled through his personal papers? Did he already guess she'd read that letter? And knew she believed it to be from a lover? There were no more opportunities to borrow his bunch of keys, or to slip into his study undisturbed. However she was vigilant and alert for any new openings. And one arose very unexpectedly.

An hour or so after lunch, she stepped out of the front doorway and nearly trod on a rake that had been left lying in the gravel. Avoiding it just in time she stumbled aside, steadied herself, and looked round. Somebody was crouching down not far away, wearing black jeans and T-shirt, his back to her.

"Oleg!" she said.

He twisted, jumped up and backed away from her in one amazingly swift motion. The look he darted at her made her think of a former Soviet defector being suddenly introduced to an ex-member of the KGB at a London drinks reception. *The Cold War's over, Oleg,* she felt tempted to say, but kept quiet.

"Didn't mean to leave the rake lying there," he said abruptly.

She shrugged. "OK, I forgive you."

He didn't smile. A brief moment passed. She decided she had more important things to discuss with him than his dangerous behaviour with garden tools. "So you decided to give Craig another chance," she remarked.

"No. He bribed me," Oleg said.

Her mouth fell open at this. "Bribed you?"

"Yes. To keep quiet about Rory."

"Why? What might you reveal?"

"Ha! You suppose I'd tell you? I'm not that much of a fool." And he snatched up the rake handle.

"Well," she said casually, "I can only speculate that it must be something the police might be interested in."

He gave a bleak, almost mocking laugh. "And the rest of the emergency services too. And not a few shrinks."

"Shrinks? You mean…?"

"Nothing. I said nothing." And he threw himself back into the task of raking the gravel, with the fierce energy of someone working out an inner demon.

"Oleg…" she began.

But he made a threatening gesture towards her with the rake.

Better disappear, she thought. He's dangerous; almost as bad as Rory. And she slipped quickly away.

She won no more confidences from Craig either, during dinner, and it seemed he saved his more interesting conversation for Zoe rather than Juliet. She had no wish to interrupt, so she ignored them. She found this uncomfortable and frustrating, but struggled hard to mask her feelings, especially every time she looked in Rory's direction. He scared her. She couldn't deny it.

As she left the table, Al strode up to her. "Hey, Juliet, Laura and I are heading to the top of the valley later on. Do a bit of star-gazing. Like to join us?"

"Are you sure?" she asked. "Perhaps you two…"

"No, no, no," he rejoined. "You come too. We'd love it."

So she relented. After coffee and brandy in the sitting room, the three of them walked up through the pastureland to the ridge. There at the top, way above the farmhouse, they stopped and fixed their gaze on the sky.

And how much sky there was here. Juliet realised this was the first time she'd fully noticed. The midsummer night, its profound silence, surrounded them.

Unexpectedly Al put his arms around both Laura and Juliet and drew them close. "Don't let Craig work his way under your skin," he murmured to Juliet.

She looked at him, startled. "How do you..?" she began.

"Watched you at dinner," he said. "I get the picture. Can see what's up with you guys."

"But…" she said, then stopped. It was pointless objecting to his interpretation of this; far better to let it pass, and enjoy the moment.

Laura too was regarding her with an expression of warm understanding. "That's right, Juliet," she said.

What ideas was she harbouring now? Despite their good intentions, Juliet felt discomposed. And yet the perfect contentment that flowed between Laura and Al couldn't but affect her too. She relaxed. Her feelings towards these two began to change. Both were people she'd previously had reservations about. Perhaps it was the influence of the landscape. And that, she now believed, was probably a strong element in what kept all Craig's followers here, too.

But the next morning told a different story. She awoke feeling disoriented. Had it all been a dream, a matter of fickle emotions? Initially, she couldn't marshal her thoughts at all. What day was it? She didn't even remember!

Sitting up abruptly with a rising sense of panic, she swung her legs down by the side of her bed and grabbed the diary that lay on her bedside table. Leafing through, she confirmed it was Wednesday. Putting the diary back she sat and reflected. All she'd achieved so far was a few unresolved conversations with Craig, warnings to keep her nose out of the deadlock between him and his father, and no guarantee that Zoe had any plans other than to stay for ever. And a few hints from Oleg that there might be things going on relating to Rory that were illegal, a serious health risk and of interest to the psychiatric services.

She looked at her watch and groaned. She must go and get some breakfast. It was always a good idea to be up early, otherwise she could never tell what she might miss. But as she hurriedly washed and dressed, she continued to fret. Friday was two days away now, and she'd only allocated a week at most for this project.

She must decide what to do. She felt sidetracked by Craig, though she couldn't be sure why. He had no power over her whatsoever, she was certain of that. And it was still vitally important she stick to her goal and get Zoe out of the Wheel of Love.

So thinking, she went out of her room and down the stairs. In the deserted kitchen she made herself a cup of tea, wondering whether the rest had set off on another Dream Yoga walk.

But on her way out of the room she passed James going in. A wave of Armani cologne assailed her nostrils. Her eye was immediately drawn to his gleaming collar studs. Whatever he did, he did to extremes. Either perfectly turned out or totally disgusting. It made her feel insecure, not knowing when the expensive aftershave might be swapped for the reek of the gutter.

"Morning, Juliet." James used a hearty tone of voice. "Pleased with your interviews?"

"Certainly, James, thank you." She sensed the artificiality of his manner. Was he, even now, in the process of transforming himself into the mindset of a vagrant? Perhaps he was wrestling his mental focus away from the world of elegance and good manners, towards that greasy wig hanging in his wardrobe.

"Excellent, excellent," he said. "So we're giving you value for money so far?" He chuckled and squeezed her shoulder, a gesture she greatly disliked. She was just about to make off along the passageway in the direction of the utility area, when she heard someone unlatch the dining room door behind her and come through. Turning, she saw Craig enter the kitchen. He left the door ajar, allowing her to overhear a short exchange between the two men.

"Any news yet, James?"

There followed the clink of coins being sifted in a pocket. Then came James's voice. "None from the email I sent all my Edinburgh contacts. Perhaps I need to be more discriminating. Reword it more directly. Target only those I believe to be on an income higher than the figure you mentioned."

Ah, so James had been in action. What would the group members think, if they knew the sole criteria for entry now was a healthy bank balance?

"Let's hope some of them bite," said Craig.

James's mood continued buoyant. "We'll soon have someone new. The moment I hear of it, I'll let you know."

At that the door closed behind them.

Hmm, thought Juliet as she strolled along. It sounded like they were making a genuine attempt to lift the community out of financial crisis. But would it be enough? Then she saw Don ahead of her. He'd just picked up a pair of walking boots from the rack in the utility area. He was examining them as if deciding whether or not they were fit for purpose.

"Off to the hills, Don?" she said.

He looked at her with a crooked smile. "Perhaps. You in search of interviews?"

"Yes."

"Could try Theo," Don said. "He's out and about."

Her heart lifted at this news. "Is he?"

"Saw him an hour ago."

"I'll try and catch him," she said. "Yesterday I mentioned he might be able to help break the deadlock between you and Craig. Didn't go down very well with Craig though, did it?"

"Nor me." He looked at her defensively for a few moments, then flung his arms out in a display of frustration. "Neither of us wants anyone else poking their nose in. I admit it." He dropped his hands to his sides once more.

"But…" she ventured, "it might help."

"Hmm." He hesitated, a slight frown on his face. "But would he listen? Pride. That's his trouble."

"Craig's? And not yours?" Juliet studied him for a few moments. She believed she saw some of his defensiveness begin to crumble.

The signs were very subtle, but she still detected a change, a loosening up.

"All right," he grumbled. "You've got a point, Juliet."

"What did Craig mean about Theo having *his own issues*?" she asked.

"No idea. Apart from that book of his." Don shrugged. "But Craig's a fine one to talk. Look at the hole he got himself into. Took disastrous financial advice, from an unqualified would-be accountant."

"Who was that?"

"Pal of his from Edinburgh."

Not another of James's students, thought Juliet. She was getting closer and closer to understanding how Craig had gone wrong. At the very worst, it still seemed to her to be through misplaced generosity rather than any serious misdemeanour.

"What happened to his accountant?" she asked.

"Sacked him."

"Oh dear," she said. "And you came down here yourself. That's sad. It gets worse and worse."

"Shame you see it like that."

"You know what I mean, Don."

He nodded. It seemed he was in the mood for rumination. "As for Craig… can't get any further with him. Me and him – we hardly ever talk. When I try, where do we end up? Down the same blind alley. Saw that yesterday."

"I did. Difficult, isn't it?" She remained determined not to offer advice. But she did feel the two of them needed to communicate better.

He set his boots down on the floor, straightened, and swung to face her. Evidently a decision had just fallen into place. "We need help. Never admitted it before. But now's the time."

"Good for you, Don."

This certainly sounded like a breakthrough: even the acknowledgement that both of them would benefit from support, not just Craig. But she needed to take care. His tone of voice and the way he was looking at her made her slightly apprehensive about who exactly he had in mind, and whether he was still thinking of Theo. "Sounds great, Don, but what do you want out of this?"

He reached beneath a shelf, and pulled a three-legged stool forward for her, then sat opposite on an upturned wine-crate. "Number one, he agrees to close the Centre down. In an orderly fashion."

"That's unrealistic," she said in dismay. "Craig wouldn't do that."

"If he doesn't, he goes bankrupt."

"What if he gets new recruits in who can pay their way?" Juliet asked.

"Probably too late."

"But does he realise?" She spread her hands. "Don, I don't know the true facts and figures. But from what I've seen so far, that solution is hardly likely to mean reconciliation for you and Craig, is it?" She scrutinised his face for signs that he might relent. "Wouldn't it make the bitterness between you far worse?"

"Probably," he said. "But what's the alternative?"

"Not for me to say. What's number two?"

"He comes back to Barnsley with me. And rethinks his life."

Silence fell. "I've a suggestion," she said.

"What's that?"

"First, put aside your plans, and carefully consider his dream."

"Craig's dream?" Don looked outraged. "What about mine?"

Juliet sighed in exasperation.

Don shuffled his feet as he sat on his upturned crate. "My business. I hoped he'd take over. When I'm gone."

"But does he want to?"

"Listen." He raised his voice. "I've come here, sacrificed my holiday. What for? To help him. But…"

"But what?"

"He doesn't respect me." Don looked despondent. He stopped, seemingly robbed of further words.

Juliet wanted to supply them: *…or behave as if he loves me.* But she felt unable to. She had no assurance he could take such a swift exposure of the wound. Don studied her. She waited.

The frustration in his eyes was miraculously replaced by the light of new hope. He wore an earnest expression. "Juliet, listen. Suppose I save Craig from bankruptcy."

"OK. How?"

"Give him the cash injection he needs," said Don.

"And then what?" she asked. "I thought you wanted him to abandon the Centre to please you. And come on line with your agenda."

He gazed at her, speechless.

"Look," she said, "if you do bail him out, who stands to gain long-term? You or him?"

He chewed his lip.

"Come on, Don," she said. "Would it not be better first to accept that Craig's now established in a career of his own choosing?"

He looked so weighed down by this challenge, she pitied him and indeed felt tempted to put her arms around him; but resisted. Instead, she continued to speak. "Running this group is what Craig wants to do. And I believe he cares about everyone here."

"But, Juliet… my side of the story. D'you see that?"

This provoked her. "Don't sink into self-pity," she said sharply. "That won't help."

He started, evidently impressed by her stance. "So where does it leave us?"

"With the fact that you're here," she said, "and that you won't leave until you and Craig have sorted this out between you."

"Right," he said. Then he leaned forward, and took hold of her hand. "Juliet. You might play a part."

"How?"

"You can help. You're just the…"

"Yes?"

"The sort of girl I once hoped Craig would marry."

She caught her breath, shocked. Craig? Her? Incredible, out of the question… For a moment her mind blanked. Craig? Marry? She wasn't even a hundred percent sure the guy was straight. Certainly, it was Zoe's infatuation with him that had drawn her here. And because of this she'd expected, at the very least, to find him a red-blooded male, possibly returning Zoe's feelings, and taking advantage of them anyway. And yet, as she'd begun to observe him and his relationships with others… She hadn't reached any clear conclusion yet. But there'd been a number of subtle signals, the lithe way he moved, the flamboyant colours of his polo shirts, his almost feminine bursts of intuition, the intense way some of the other men looked at him…

She shook herself. Her emotions were in turmoil. Snatching her hand from Don's, she jumped to her feet. "Now, stop right there."

"Why?" he asked.

"I won't listen to talk like that," she said.

The back door opened. "Mind if I join you?" said a third voice.

They both looked around sharply. Craig stood there.

He had such a talent for these sudden appearances. Again she felt a shifting sensation in the pit of her stomach. She was furious with herself. On no account must Craig ever learn of his power to do this to her whenever he showed up on the scene. As he passed he brushed lightly against her. She felt the electric-fence effect once more. She fervently hoped he hadn't noticed.

He nodded to his father, then wheeled to face them both. "We meet again – Father, Juliet."

Today, he'd teamed his pale-blue jeans with a casual open-necked shirt, this time in jade green. Again, the colours he wore suited him perfectly, as she couldn't help observing; and lingering on. Damn. She nearly cursed beneath her breath.

"Going for a walk?" he asked Don.

"Not yet."

"Do. It's a wonderful day. I highly recommend it." Hooking his thumbs in his pockets, he leaned against the whitewashed wall opposite Juliet, in easy style.

Despite his manner she believed Don was glad of the interruption.

"So, Craig," Don began. "Punished Rory yet?"

"Of course not. The concept of punishment has no place here," said Craig.

"Why not call the police?" demanded Don.

"I never do that," said Craig.

Juliet gazed at him. What an extraordinary statement. Strangely disturbing. Especially the word *never*, implying that this kind of thing had happened on more than one occasion.

"Beats me why Oleg didn't call them himself," muttered Don.

"He knew that wouldn't be wise," replied Craig.

"Why?"

"Because," said Craig, "I've told my students that if ever any of them gets into a fight with anyone else, they're to put the problem in my hands. And trust me. If they do that, then everything will be all right."

"How do you know?" demanded Don. Craig's last words had clearly incensed him. He was so heated he failed to notice another figure in the open doorway as he threw out his next challenge to his son. "Call yourself a prophet? You forget where you're from. A humble terrace in Barnsley."

At this the new arrival spoke. "And why shouldn't a prophet come from a humble terrace in Barnsley?"

Juliet turned. Theo stood there, dressed all in white – short-sleeved shirt, cargo pants and trainers. For a moment Juliet almost expected a halo to complete the effect. His sudden appearance, together with his remark, made her feel utterly disoriented.

It seemingly had the same effect upon the others too, judging by their failure to respond.

"A simple question, that's all," said Theo. He put his hand on Don's arm in a friendly manner. "Perhaps I shouldn't have broken in there."

"Glad to see you up again, Theo," said Juliet quickly.

"Thanks," he said. "I look forward to a chat with you later. But I've agreed to meet your sister in the hermitage first."

"Have you?" she asked, startled.

"Yes." He swiftly changed the subject. "A heavenly place, this, Craig."

"Thanks."

"Ever considered a sculpture courtyard here?" asked Theo.

Craig looked taken aback by this question. But he soon recovered. "A nice idea, but no. To be honest with you, Theo, the money ran out."

"And other things took priority," murmured Theo.

Juliet glanced at Don as Theo said this. His face was impassive, but the colour had noticeably begun to drain away. Odd. Why had Theo said that?

"Just a thought," said Theo. With that, he stepped back out through the doorway again and was gone.

Juliet looked at Don, who was struggling to regain his former mood, and then at Craig. "What's the hermitage?"

"A cabin I built in the woods," he replied. He touched her hand. With a firm resolve, she managed to disguise her reaction.

Craig allowed several moments to pass. "What about a walk, Juliet?" he offered. "Just you and me?"

Earlier, before Don had made his remark about her and Craig, she might have taken him up on it. But now the situation had changed. "No, Craig. Later, perhaps."

"I can see I've offended you, Juliet. You doubt me, don't you. Why?"

"Not now, Craig. This isn't the time."

"I believe it is the time. Come with me, Juliet."

"See you later, Craig." She walked briskly away.

Small wonder that she'd turned down Craig's invitation, Juliet thought to herself as she hurried across the car park away from the back door. What an outrageous comment Don had made, just before Craig's entry on the scene (which she feared Craig may have overheard). With an effort of will, she forced the issue to the back of her mind. What she needed to know right now was why Zoe had been so quick to book a one-to-one chat with Theo in this hermitage place. Was Zoe hoping for advice about her relationship with Craig?

She climbed over the stile and set off up the woodland track which led to the top of the ridge. Halfway to the ridge, another track branched off to the right, and she took this. After a short walk she reached a small clearing. And there, indeed, was the simple tongue-and-groove pine cabin which she took to be the hermitage. It was evidently another place for silent retreat and solitary contemplation. And this morning, as Juliet approached, she saw her sister inside with the young clergyman.

She ventured closer. She felt she couldn't pass up any opportunity to find out what was going on.

With the warmth of the weather, the windows of the hermitage were wide open. A glance through the nearest one told her that Theo was perched on the small wooden table. Opposite him, Zoe's posture as she sat on the single chair was one of rapt concentration. She leaned well forward towards him. And her focus was solely upon him, and his words. This puzzled Juliet.

"Don't be afraid to commit yourself, Zoe," Theo said. "You've nothing to lose."

Hearing this, Juliet bristled. What on earth was he suggesting to her?

"Juliet thinks…." Zoe began.

"That doesn't matter. All that matters is what you think, Zoe. Even what I've said to you is purely a matter of instinct. In simple terms, it's this. Take part in everything; and don't worry what your sister thinks about it."

Again, Juliet started.

"She thinks I'm crazy," said Zoe, "I know she does."

Theo smiled. "Accept all that Craig offers, and everything your fellow community members offer. And leave Juliet to take care of her own problems."

Juliet could barely contain her fury at hearing these words. What right did this interfering cleric have to say such things? Then her sister's words cut across her thoughts.

"And you, Theo?" Zoe asked. "What opportunities will you offer?"

He laughed softly. Then he reached forward, briefly took her hand, and squeezed it. "That's for you to find out, Zoe. Come on. Let's go."

Troubled by unsettling thoughts, Juliet sped back through the woods.

10

Not the Marrying Kind

Lunch had long finished; alone in the kitchen, Juliet stood by the window looking out onto the car park at the back of the house, fiddling restlessly with the bread knife. She felt agitated as she tried to decide on her next move. She hadn't managed a single word with Zoe since she saw her in the hermitage with Theo. That was because her sister had claimed his sole attention all through lunch, too. Nor had Juliet managed to pick up any details of their discussion, as they'd remained at the opposite end of the table conferring together in low voices. She could only imagine Zoe had been seeking further suggestions on her relationship with Craig.

Juliet felt a little sore that Zoe had chosen to confide in Theo, rather than her. And the emotions aroused by that earlier overheard conversation remained strongly with her. He'd told Zoe that what her sister thought didn't matter, and that Juliet should *take care of her own problems*. Who gave him the right to say that?

An afternoon of interviews lay ahead. But none of them were with Theo. That was no good. She must speak to him first. She could rearrange the others. She now suspected it may be Theo, not Craig, who held the key to unlock Zoe's mind. This disturbed her. She continued to stroke the serrated blade of the knife, not quite sure why.

The door opened suddenly. She looked up to see Theo walk in, and her finger slipped. She dropped the knife on the floor as blood welled up.

Theo started forward, a look of concern on his face. "What are you doing, Juliet?" he asked.

"Don't worry, Theo," she said lightly. "I wasn't self-harming."

"I should hope not," he said. "Here, let me staunch the flow of blood before the next group member in wonders what's been going on in here."

"No need, I can do it."

He ignored her, and quickly brought the necessary items to deal with the cut. As he played the role of first-aider, she observed him closely. There was no dog collar to be seen. She supposed he only wore it when on duty. But what did being *on* or *off* duty constitute for him in this Centre? Perhaps he was *on duty* when he was being a *guest speaker*. Or so she imagined. If not, what was his role here? Did anyone know?

It was clear he noted her look of sharp appraisal. "Come on, Juliet. Have I upset you already?"

"Not at all," she said.

"So you're all right?"

"Couldn't be better, Theo," she said breezily.

"Let's talk," he said. "I'm about to head for the woods. Join me there?"

"Fine by me. I've got my Nagra. I can record anywhere."

"Of course," he replied smoothly. "I decided to leave Craig to take care of the group therapy. All he wants from me today is a talk after dinner. No need to prepare for that. So it's a perfect opportunity to speak to you."

"Glad about that, Theo." She must remain courteous, regardless of how she felt about his comments to Zoe in the hermitage. "Are you fully recovered from your migraine?" she asked as they walked through to the utility room.

"Yes. Feeling much better now, thanks. It had me in its grip for a full twenty-four hours this time. I've been subject to these attacks since I caught malaria in the Middle East four years ago."

"Sorry to hear that." Juliet felt unsure of her ground. But she couldn't help warming to him, despite everything.

"I'm determined to make the most of these few days in the Cotswolds," said Theo, choosing some walking boots.

"Good idea." It had seemed an innocuous remark, but she sensed something else lay beneath Theo's words which he wasn't revealing. "You and Zoe had plenty to say to each other at lunch. I couldn't get a word in edgeways."

"I do apologise." A warm look, signifying either amusement or some other emotion Juliet couldn't read, flitted across Theo's face at mention of this.

For a while they were both occupied pulling their footwear on. But Juliet turned this observation over in her mind, all the while. When they were ready to set off, she looked straight at him.

He wore an open expression on his face. "What your sister wants," he said, "is to experience the spiritual reality here on this earth, in her own body." He opened the door and stepped out.

She followed. "And has Craig delivered on it yet?" she asked.

There was a pause, as she wondered how Theo would take this question, together with all its implications.

Theo smiled. "I don't think so. If he had, I imagine she would have told you, Juliet."

He began to stride across the car park. Juliet had no time to consider her riposte to this evasive answer. She hurried to keep up with him, holding the omnidirectional mike. She checked the sound levels as he walked briskly past the north side of the house, and across into the orchard. It looked as if he'd settled on the same route that she, Al and Laura had taken last night on their trip to the top of the valley to look at the stars.

"Zoe's told me nothing, Theo. So I'm relying on you. How do your beliefs and certainties stand up against Craig's?"

"Certainties?" Theo's tone continued amicable. "I'm human. And God's God. He doesn't need me. He chooses me. So sometimes I say: *What's going on?* and *Why am I doing this?* or *Why is it so hard?*"

"And yet," she said, surprised, "you seem to have it all together. Mostly."

He smiled, and headed on through the orchard, toward the gate at the other side. "I'm glad it looks like that to you," he said.

"If this isn't the whole picture," she said, matching his pace, "how come you're in the position you are?"

"A long story," he said, "and one my bishop's probably running through right at this moment."

"I don't imagine your bishop's very pleased that you're here at the Wheel of Love."

Theo gave a chuckle in response to this. "I'm a renegade," he said. "I'm all about working with people on spiritual journeys. I'll go anywhere, come in on anything."

"How do you find Craig's teachings?" she asked.

"Some have wisdom in them," he replied crisply. "And you?"

"I admire Craig's idealism. I don't accept all his theories. Nor do I believe in God." They reached the gate.

"What sort of God don't you believe in?" asked Theo.

"The Judaeo-Christian one, of course," she replied, feeling slightly ruffled by this question. "The fire and brimstone one. The one who punishes the children for the sin of the fathers, even to the third and fourth generation. The one who is supposed to be so loving, not even a sparrow can fall without Him knowing about it, but He still lets the good suffer and the evil go unpunished." She stopped. "You know the one I mean."

"I certainly do," he said. "And I've known what it's like to feel very angry with Him." Theo unlatched and opened the gate. "Are you angry too, Juliet?" He swung round to face her as he stood in the gateway.

She was nearly thrown off course by the directness of this question. But she quickly recovered and was ready with her reply. "I probably was angry when I was younger, and turned my back on it all. But nowadays – most of the time I don't give it any thought. What really matters to me at this moment is showing Zoe that there's someone who cares about her, and has her best interests at heart – and that someone is me." Juliet walked quickly through to the pasture beyond, and Theo closed the gate behind her.

They set off up the track. "Is there no one else?" Theo asked.

"Our mother died years ago," she said, feeling compelled to defend herself. "We were both quite young. I was thirteen and Zoe five. My father's health wasn't good. He couldn't cope."

He nodded.

"So I suppose I've taken on that role for her," she added.

"Very caring of you, Juliet." He swept his arm out to indicate the farmhouse now falling behind them. "Remember, Juliet: to everything there is a season. Especially in that community down there."

"Which means…?"

Perhaps her question got lost, for he didn't answer, but continued to the far side of the pasture. They made good progress as the narrow path they joined at the field boundary began to climb the side of the valley. Talk ceased for a while, as they tramped upwards, dodging the tall stinging nettles. Eventually they both came out at the top of the ridge, and stopped to survey the panoramic views.

"We're looking west here," observed Theo, "across the Severn Vale to Wales." A cluster of rays emanated from behind white clouds, intersecting the landscape, creating wedges of golden green and blades of light, increasing in transparency to the most distant hills. "Why do we love patterns so much?" Theo asked.

"Because we like to make sense of things," she said.

He nodded. "True. It's all so geometric. Wherever you look, you can see scalene triangles, obtuse angles and intersecting line segments. Did you know the Ancient Greek astronomers found God in geometry?"

Juliet gave a wry smile. "Did they?" she said. "You mean it helped them believe in a Great Designer?"

Theo nodded. And with that he set off again. Instead of going straight along the ridge, he followed a trail that curved round and down the other side.

"You seem very sure of your way," she commented.

"Remember it from my last visit," he threw over his shoulder.

After a descent that took several minutes, they could hear water bubbling beneath the woodland shrubs a short way below them.

"The voice of God is like the friendly chatter of a stream," said Theo.

Juliet walked down to the brook. "Why have I never heard that voice?"

"Maybe because you don't listen."

"But I think of myself as a good listener. But what of you, Theo? You do a lot of listening. How long have you known Craig?"

"Eight months now. We first met last November."

"And he invited you here in February?" she queried.

"That's right." He smiled at her. "I liked his idealism, and his desire to help people. I felt I had something to offer, with my experience in healing. And he agreed. So I came. And now I'm back again." He stooped to pick up a pebble and throw it in the stream. "What do you want to know, Juliet?"

"Do you know anything of Craig's background? His past relationships?"

Theo gave her a long, penetrating look.

"Or even Craig's present relationships?" she added.

"He has confided a few things to me. But I'm certainly not going to pass them on to you, Juliet."

"I suppose I asked for that," she said. But she still felt stung and frustrated, and resolved to somehow – either during this conversation, or later – bypass Theo's discretion. Catch him in an unguarded moment. She believed now he knew interesting things about Craig. Perhaps, even, the secret of who wrote that letter.

Meanwhile, she crouched down to trail her hand in the running water. As she did so, a green dragonfly wheeled before her eyes. She reached out as if to brush it away, but it had already gone. How could she persuade Theo to open up to her?

"I came here," she said, standing again, "because Zoe said she was in love with Craig. Of course, I didn't know how he felt."

Theo nodded, but remained quiet.

Determined not to be put off by her companion's silence, Juliet forged on. "But now, I don't know what to believe, except for one thing. She must come home with me, to London."

"And she thinks differently," Theo said.

She cast him an annoyed glance. Then they set off again, walking beside the stream.

"Craig's goal for his pupils," Theo said, "is to loosen the hold the past has on them, to help them let go of the roles their parents cast them in. And in Zoe's case, that probably means the role you've cast her in. Yes, Craig has mentioned it to me. But, Juliet – and I hate to be the one to tell you this –"

"No, feel free," said Juliet, although she felt like hitting him.

"– I think Craig may already have achieved that goal with Zoe. In a very short amount of time."

"What?" she cried. She was about to protest in no uncertain terms. But then she was silenced by a strained, questioning quality in Theo's eyes.

He led the way forward once more.

Pushing her feelings down and regaining control, she quickened her step until she was alongside him. "That was an interesting comment you made on Monday evening at dinner," she said.

"Which one?"

"The one about feeling more at home here than anywhere else."

Theo's smile briefly touched his eyes. "I have wanderlust in me. And also perhaps I have a fellow feeling for people who are avoiding pain."

She gazed at him, full of curiosity and wonder. "And so, you've come here to…"

"…do a bit of soul-searching along with the rest of you. People always surprise me. Everyone's unique. First impressions are often completely wrong."

"Especially here, perhaps."

"Yes. At the moment I feel most who come here are hoping to find a safe retreat from the world. And, of course, they're attracted by Craig's personal magnetism."

"That makes sense," she said.

"And it applies to you, too, Juliet."

"Me?" At this she lost track of where she was going, and found herself in a clump of tall stinging nettles. Theo quickly came to the rescue and helped her out again. He looked at her in concern, but she refused his sympathy. She walked smartly on to conceal her agitation. What was Theo suggesting? No way would she fall into Craig's power.

Theo persisted. "Naturally, having only been here since Monday, there's much I don't know. I have little to go on yet, of you and your feelings."

"You're right there," said Juliet coolly as they began moving along the track again.

"Let's take Craig's followers, the ones who have fallen under his spell," went on Theo. "Beth, for instance. She has her sights set on Craig. But it's Oleg who loves her. Jealousy has nearly driven the poor boy out of his mind. Add another couple, Al and Laura…"

"So you know about that pair too?" interrupted Juliet.

"Yes. Al mentioned the situation to me as he showed me to my room on my first evening. Laura, like Beth, can't make up her mind whether her heart belongs to Craig or not."

"Oh? I'm surprised. I thought Laura and Al…"

"Oh no. Al would like it to be so, of course, but…"

Perhaps she'd misread the situation, then, when she'd gone up to the ridge with them yesterday evening.

"So you see," went on Theo, "it really is like a night in Shakespeare's wood outside Athens."

Juliet laughed, pleased with the image. "So which part has Craig cast himself in?" she asked. "Oberon?"

"Not really," said Theo. "For Oberon has his Titania. Whereas Craig… oh, it's just a passing idea I've had… but sometimes I think he's unlikely ever to commit himself. To any woman, that is."

Juliet's heart lurched. Was this the indiscretion she'd been hoping for? But it didn't make sense. It didn't fit in with her embryonic theory about Craig. If that was what you could call it. Not commit to any woman? But she'd thought…

She tried to pull her mind back on track. And failed. Of course, there'd been no indication whether the writer of that letter had been male or female. She stamped down on that line of thought. And quickly tried to cover up her reaction, fearful Theo had noticed. But she felt oppressed for some time afterwards. She'd have loved to probe further, but didn't dare. Her objectivity had vanished.

"And is there a role for me to play in all this?" she asked lightly instead. "Puck, perhaps?"

"Are you skilled with enchanted sleeping draughts?" enquired Theo.

"Probably not."

"Whereas I might do for the role. I've abused a few illegal substances in my time," remarked Theo.

Juliet pulled up at hearing this. "What was that? Ecstasy? Crack? Or worse?"

"Never mind the details of what it was."

"So when did you do drugs?" she asked.

"Back in my university days," said Theo. "Managed to kick the habit eventually."

"You went cold turkey?"

Theo nodded, but would say no more on the subject. "So what I'd do, if I was Puck, then," he went on, "is pour a potion into the eyes of Beth, and declare, *When you wake, you shall fall in love with the first thing you see.*"

"And then put Oleg in her way?" suggested Juliet.

"Exactly. A pair of star-crossed lovers." Theo took the lead as they climbed up to the ridge again. The sky was still bright, but a cool breeze had blown up and was tugging at their hair and clothes.

When they reached the highest point, Theo paused. Juliet did too, watching him expectantly, and drawing her combat jacket closer around her.

"My words down there about my role as Puck were pure fantasy, of course." He shrugged. "I will, naturally, mind my own business, and leave matters to take their course. If anyone wants to talk to me about it I'll listen. But that's all." An unreadable expression on his face, he gazed down the valley to the orchard.

"But I imagine you must be highly practised at troubleshooting people's problems," Juliet said.

Theo stooped to pick up a stick, and used it to scribble in the dirt. "Answers don't come to me as easily as that." He finished writing on the ground. "Perhaps I've found a few solutions. But often not until long after the problem first arose. And by then it's far too late."

"Hmm." Juliet considered him doubtfully. They set off back along the path leading down to the orchard again. "So, Theo, I hear Craig's given you an open invitation to stay as long as you like."

"He has, much to my amazement," said Theo. "But I'm still waiting to hear from the bishop. I've no idea what the future holds. I need to know what he plans to do about my book, and whether I'm to be excommunicated – though it is, admittedly, an extreme measure rarely used – and then probably only in cases where a vicar has murdered his parishioners." He entered the orchard.

"Oh, so then it won't be relevant in your case," said Juliet as she joined him.

Theo cast a glance at her. "Have to be prepared for any outcome."

Was he being flippant or not? It was difficult for Juliet to tell from the expression on his face. They crossed the orchard and reached the gate that led out onto the gravel forecourt. Juliet turned to Theo again. "Why not stay here and write your next?" she suggested.

"Oh no, I wouldn't do that. This is Craig's territory."

She sensed he had something further to tell her.

He jerked his head toward the farmhouse. "Do you know how I first heard of this place? A colleague of mine came to dinner here a few years ago with the previous owners, a shepherd and his wife."

"Really?" This was unexpected. "What sort of state was it in then? Did he say?"

Theo looked rueful. "Sadly run-down. The owners couldn't afford the upkeep."

"And that's why they sold it to Craig?"

"Yes." He was about to add something, when his mobile buzzed. "Excuse me." He took the call. "Good afternoon, Bishop." He listened for a while, then began, "But, Bishop…" He fell silent. Then he said, "Oh, I think you've misunderstood the point I was making…" His words were evidently cut off. Another few seconds passed as the voice at the other end continued. Then he said, "Very well," and ended the call. Juliet studied his face. It was pale and distraught.

"Bad news?" she said.

Theo nodded.

"So he doesn't like the book?"

"No."

"What was it about again?" she asked.

"Synchronicity."

"What's that?"

"A term coined by Carl Jung to describe the apparently meaningful patterning of events that are not causally connected."

She opened her eyes wide. "Like you coming here?" she said.

"That's right," he replied with a wry expression.

"I'd love to read it."

"I'll let you have a copy." Theo's mouth twisted. "My book explored whether such events might be random, coincidence, or God's intervention. I never imagined there'd be a problem writing it. But it seems I thought wrong. Some of the bishop's colleagues feel it's heretical."

She remembered him using this word before, on the evening of his arrival, at dinner. However, she hadn't taken it seriously at the time. But perhaps it meant more to her, now she'd had a chance to set it in the context of their present discussion. "Heretical?" she said. "That's a bit strong, isn't it? Mary Tudor used to burn heretics at the stake, didn't she?"

"Yes," said Theo. "But no need to worry, Juliet, the last person to be burned at the stake for heresy in England was executed in 1612. So I don't think they'll use that punishment in my case. But nevertheless, my bishop is a conservative evangelical and he's surrounded by advisers who think along the same lines, some of whom aren't too happy with my angle on things."

He stood, arms at his sides, both hands fidgety. "Perhaps I'm to be cast into the outer darkness, where there is wailing and gnashing of teeth," he said. "The bishop has summoned me to a disciplinary review first thing tomorrow morning."

11

Something Not Quite Right

Sprawling on the sofa in an Edwardian tea jacket he must have picked up from a theatrical costumier's, James listened to the tea-time conversation but did not participate. Every so often, Juliet noticed, he moodily sipped from the bone-china cup placed beside him on the occasional table. Theo, despite his modest manner, was the centre of attention for the others in the oak-panelled library. Seated between the slight figure of Laura and the nervously twittering Sam on one of the sofas, he answered all questions shot at him.

Juliet too had stayed quiet for the past twenty minutes. As ever, her Nagra hung from her shoulder in its carrying case, and she was equipped with her microphone. But just at this moment, she didn't feel like making any recordings. She was still struggling to come to terms with the mixed feelings that had arisen from Theo's observation about Craig up on the ridge earlier that day. So Craig was unlikely ever to commit himself to any woman, was he? Well then, in principle she should be feeling pleased. She imagined Theo would have told Zoe that too, and Zoe would quickly realise she was better off leaving this place and coming back to London with Juliet.

But in fact Juliet didn't feel pleased at all. Rather she felt a tumult of conflicting emotions. Why? Craig meant nothing to her personally. Though if he had a problem with commitment it was, of course, interesting, and she should probably investigate it in a further interview at some stage.

The powerful feeling of hurt that had overtaken her when Theo had first mentioned it had now diminished somewhat. But even so she resented feeling like that.

Pushing this observation away into a dark corner, she refocused on the curiously anachronistic figure of James. He looked as if he should be lolling back against the brass fender of a gentleman's study, pipe in hand, at an Edwardian house party. From time to time, she noticed, he'd been on the receiving end of a quizzical glance from the clergyman. It was clear James wasn't happy about this. However, for the moment, he seemed prepared to remain silent and attentive.

"Even if you are in trouble, Theo…" Laura laid her hand on his, "you know you can always stay here with us."

"Don't go," said Sam. "Who cares about the bloody bishop?"

Theo smiled. "Thanks, Sam, but I must go. There's no getting out of it. My boss at the Golden Chalice is concerned too. I have to face the music. But I'll be back, I hope. I've looked up train times, and there's one I can catch from Cirencester in two hours."

"I'll give you a lift," said Don.

"Thanks, Don; most appreciated."

The Yorkshireman sat back, arms folded.

Zoe, eyes large and appealing in her oval face, gazed at Theo from the seat opposite. Juliet could hardly fail to notice. This level of concentration on him from her sister was beginning to give her serious qualms. It was Craig she loved, after all. Or so she supposed. And if not, what was going on?

Although she liked Theo, his penetrating questions, discernment and insight made her uneasy. And Zoe was a headstrong drifter. That was still how Juliet saw her, despite all Theo's words during their walk. Certainly it felt like no time at all since she'd claimed to be in love with Craig. Indeed it was only just a week, she reflected. Surely she wasn't cooling off from him? Was she starting to prefer Theo? Impossible. And yet… if she was, to do this so soon seemed feckless at the very least, not that Craig would have been any better a choice, of course.

She resolved to speak about it privately to her sister at the next opportunity.

However, as tea finished and the group gradually dispersed, Zoe slipped away before Juliet could intercept her. Suddenly Juliet's path to the door was cut off by Don.

He stood four-square in front of her. "Glad I've got you alone."

"Why's that, Don?"

"Your sister. This new liking of hers. For our friend Theo. Can't help but notice."

"Neither can I," she said in a tight voice.

"We'll be off at six. He may be back tomorrow, of course. There again, may not. But meanwhile…" He stopped.

"Yes?"

"While he's gone… Might be a case of *out of sight, out of mind.* Zoe could set her sights back on Craig again."

Juliet frowned. "What are you trying to tell me, Don?"

"When she first came…" he said, then stopped. He quickly continued. "Hung on his every word, she did."

Juliet listened with quickening interest. It seemed undeniable that a new attraction to Theo might be drawing Zoe away from Craig.

"Does this worry you, Don?"

The colour of his face intensified. "It ought to worry both of us."

"Why?" she asked, prickling with suspicion.

"Do you like him?"

She stiffened. Somewhere in the background she heard the library door open, but her focus was upon Don.

"Who?" she said. "Theo?"

"No. Craig."

"What are you getting at, Don?"

"I'm sure you like him. And the feeling's returned." He broke off.

She sat upright in her chair. She'd need to stamp on this, fast. "Look, Don. Even if I weren't here to do interviews… He's charismatic. No one denies that. But if you're suggesting…" She looked up. Craig stood there. Her eyes met his. She could have kicked herself.

Craig moved to the armchair opposite, and occupied it.

She sat up straight. The honest approach was best. "You'll have overheard our last few remarks, Craig. So perhaps you can put your father right on this?"

"No, Juliet, I'm afraid I can't."

"Why not?"

She struggled to settle her inner turmoil. But, instead, whilst groping towards some kind of exit from the fog gathering around her, she slipped further in. Now she felt a curious instability, as if she was on a jetliner that had flown into an air pocket. In the next moment she received the impression that Craig's features had melted and realigned themselves.

Instead of looking at him, she believed she faced someone infinitely old and wizened, and Peruvian in appearance. The image of an ancient carved face on a rock in an Inca city, presented itself to her. It shifted again, and a new face emerged, that of a shabby, travel-stained New Age traveller.

With a desperate effort of the will, she regained her awareness of Don beside her. But he was set into a freeze-frame. His hand had risen, perhaps to admonish Craig, but had then been arrested in mid-air. He wore a glazed expression.

Craig smiled, and as he did so the spell, or whatever it was, lifted. All returned to normal. Don's hand dropped to his side.

Juliet realised she'd held her breath for several moments. She gasped the air back into her lungs. Her heart was pounding. Craig had done it again. Changed appearance. What was it with him? How did he do it? It frightened her. Her eyes were fixed upon his face. She hardly cared if he thought her rude to stare at him.

Then Don spoke. "Well, Craig? What's your answer?" It was as if nothing had happened. Hadn't Don noticed? She was astounded.

Craig interlocked his fingers, and laid them lightly upon his knee. "I believe we must learn to live at a high level of uncertainty," he said.

Juliet continued to search his face, but he offered no further explanation. Turning back again, she caught a glimpse of Don's expression, a fine blend of expectancy and frustration.

Struggling to regain her composure, she took a slow deep breath.

But her heart was still beating wildly. As she exhaled, her mind went into overdrive again. What lay behind Don's words as Craig entered the room? Surely he didn't want to throw her and Craig together. That was ridiculous! The very last thing she could ever possibly want to happen.

So thinking, she jumped up and headed for the door. Pausing in the open doorway, she caught the looks on both their faces: Don edgy, Craig calm and unruffled, yet still somehow mentally reaching out to her. Both men now were on their feet, moving forward, perhaps in an attempt to stop her.

"No, Don. And you, too, Craig. Get one thing clear. I will not be used by either of you."

With these words, she fled the room.

Juliet hurried across the hallway, and unlatched and opened the sitting room door. As she entered the room and shut the door behind her, the thrilling sounds of a rich bass voice assailed her ears. She stopped short. She recognised this music. It was the final scene from Mozart's opera *Don Giovanni.*

She knew this to be Rory's taste in music. Was he in here? Yes. Those shiny shoes appeared over the end of the nearest sofa.

Her mouth went dry. Rory had assaulted Oleg. He was unpredictable. There was some kind of psychological problem with him, which Craig wouldn't be open about. Capricious mood swings turned him to violence. He could be dangerous. Had she escaped the scene with Don and Craig, only to find herself at far greater risk, alone with Rory?

Not quite alone, she saw. Groucho, the parrot, sat on his perch, head on one side, listening intently. Rory had draped himself over the sofa, a crystal goblet of water on the occasional table beside him. His face wore a devout expression. She knew enough about him not to trust this. And somehow, from this angle, his legs looked longer than she'd ever seen them before. He was dressed in black from head to toe. He reminded her of a giant spider.

As she stood poised, wondering whether to flee the room, he saw her. Swinging his feet neatly down onto the carpet again, he sat up and patted the newly created space beside him. "Juliet, do join me."

No way. But if he did try something, maybe Groucho would come to her aid? His sharp beak, surely, would provide some kind of defence. But all things considered, the possibility seemed thin.

Right now, it would hardly look good to run back out. She chose the armchair opposite, setting her carrying case containing her audio equipment down on the floor. "I'd sooner sit here. Thanks all the same."

Since she'd arrived in the community, she'd found Rory nothing but courteous towards her. And yet Oleg's tale rang warning bells in her mind. Not to mention his odd words out there in the forecourt, when he'd been raking the gravel. About knowing too much. And Craig being afraid he'd talk. Already her fingers had chilled, and were beginning to tremble.

He acknowledged her decision with a gracious wave. "The opera, as you're no doubt aware, is rising to its magnificent climax. Don Giovanni is about to be dragged down into the fires and everlasting torment of hell, as a punishment for his sexual excesses."

She didn't like the way he said this. Anxiety stirred in her stomach. His eye lingered upon her in a curious manner. She fought to disguise her ill-ease. "When the music's finished, may I ask you a few questions?"

"But of course." He picked up the remote control from the arm of his chair, and immediately silence cut in.

"There was no need for that. You were perfectly free to listen till the end."

"Not at all, not at all. I'll save it for later, when I'm alone again." He licked his lips, as his eyes slid across her.

All her senses were razor-sharp. She was ready for anything. But she'd got herself into this situation. She must calmly prepare to interview him. She set up her Nagra, plugged in the mike, and switched on. Then she held the mike close to his mouth.

"Rory, what did you hope for when you first came here?" she asked.

A secretive flicker passed across his face. "As you might expect, to try Craig out and see if I like what he offers," he replied.

"And you've been here a year, so you must know more fully than anyone else what that entails."

His eyes hardened. She mentally pulled up. Take care. Don't provoke him. Ask any innocuous question. As long as it doesn't offend him.

"You're sure you're not here to sit in judgement upon us?" said Rory.

Yes. Here it was. An abrupt switch to a hostile tone. Groucho rummaged in the nut bowl beside him, withdrew a pistachio, and began to crack it. "Of course," said Juliet. "I told you before, Rory. I mean to be fair and accurate."

"Very well." He fell to studying her once more. His pointed, elongated features accentuated his insect-like quality. He held his hands, palms uppermost, in a gesture of transparency.

"So, then, Juliet. What he offers, first of all, is work on breaking down our defences."

"Your defence of yourself, against other people?"

"Yes."

"That must be challenging for you. How does this affect the way you all get on together? Do Craig's promises apply to your relationships with each other… you and Oleg for instance?"

She held her breath. Why did she say that? Fool. If she angered him, she was lost. And yet, what a perfect opportunity to perhaps win a few admissions from Craig's most unstable follower.

He bristled, like a hunting dog about to spring. She watched him warily. He leaned forward and placed his hand over hers, with a light but menacing touch. "You're treading on dangerous ground there, Juliet."

She was well aware of that. She withdrew her hand quickly. "I'm sorry. I was hoping you might be willing to tell me what happened from your own viewpoint."

He scuttled his long fingers over the arm of the sofa, in a cockroach-like motion that made her shudder.

"Don't do that, Rory," she said.

"Don't you like it?" he asked.

"No." She saw and felt how tense he was. Perhaps she could defuse him. "I'm giving you the chance to justify your actions, if that's what you'd like to do."

Groucho flew off his perch, and back into his cage for a drink of water. Rory stared at her, his expression increasingly unfriendly.

She felt perspiration prickle her forehead. She'd miscalculated. Pull back. Now. Before it's too late. "If you'd prefer not to, I quite understand," she said. "Perhaps later instead. What about your plans for the future? You do seem to be looking to Craig for freedom and peace. Do you believe you'll find it? Will he succeed in pulling out that thorn from your flesh?"

Oh God, no. She'd done it now. Even as the words left her lips, she knew it. She'd pushed her luck too far. But she still didn't expect what followed.

After a fractional hesitation, he sprang from the sofa, knocking the mike from her hand. Groucho erupted into the air with a screech. In one bound, Rory was onto her, his hands around her throat.

She gagged. Tried to scream. Fell from the sofa. Rory on top of her. As he increased the pressure on her neck, she kicked out. He recoiled in pain. The Nagra fell to the floor and the microphone rolled across to the fireplace. But Rory held on.

Groucho circled the room, letting out a series of squawks. Rory increased his grip. Squeezing. Squeezing the life out of her. He was choking her. Panic clawed its way up from her stomach. He'd kill her. He was mad. She was going to die. Here in this beautiful room. Her hands flailed. Her legs were pinned to the floor by his weight.

Chaotic images followed. Body on the floor. Bulging eyes. Purple tongue.

Who'd find Juliet? Zoe. How would she react? What would she feel? And Craig… Juliet couldn't bear to think of him. Too late now. Was her life flashing past her? When did she last say the Lord's Prayer? No. No. No…

Suddenly Rory let go. He jerked back. She coughed violently, fighting to swallow. Then she scrambled to her feet.

Now he crouched in the far corner of the room, eyes glittering, his chest heaving. Something had broken into his mind. He'd decided to stop. If he hadn't, she'd be dead. He'd tried to strangle her.

She flew to the door. Chest heaving. Exploring her burning throat with her fingers. Desperate for life and sanity. She pulled the door open and sprang through the doorway, into the arms of Craig.

"Juliet! What's happening?" He held her for several moments, steadying her, then released her, his eyes on her throat. "Have you upset Rory?"

"Craig!" she burst out before she had time to process this extraordinary remark. She could barely speak, but mustered what was left of her energy. "Thank God," she croaked. "Call the police. Rory tried to kill me."

"Oh, I don't think so." His eyes had widened. He spoke the words as if he thought her reaction over-the-top.

Patrick appeared from the library, Edgar close behind him. Both men stopped short, and gaped at her.

"Holy Mary and Jesus! Have you been provoking Rory?" asked Patrick, delicately touching her neck. She flinched. Her heart was pounding.

His words appalled her. She turned to indicate the sitting room. "Rory's still in there," she gasped. "He's lethal."

Craig moved closer again, and gently inspected the raised weals on her throat. Meanwhile, the Irishman scuttled back into the library – to collect, she was to learn in a few moments, the first-aid box. Edgar, left behind, became absorbed in scribbling something on a sheet of paper on his clipboard.

"I'm very sorry, Juliet," said Craig. "This is quite inexcusable. I shall have words with Rory about it."

Juliet's mouth had fallen open. Was that all he meant to do? "Words, Craig? Nothing else?"

Patrick emerged from the library with the first-aid box. Setting it upon the hall table, he opened it up and produced a tube of Savlon. Seeing this, Juliet's sense of unreality increased. They had a homicidal maniac in the sitting room, and all they could do was produce antiseptic cream and pathetic remarks.

"Now, calm down, Juliet. Let's think clearly about what's happened." Craig laid his hand on her arm as he said this.

"But, Craig," she whispered. "He needs to be locked up."

"Juliet, please be patient. I do care about what's happened to you. But I've learned that when Rory's done something like this, it's best to leave him alone for a while to calm down."

"You're protecting him. Why?"

Patrick dabbed Savlon on her injured throat. "There. That'll help."

"I can't explain right now," continued Craig. "Just believe me. In most cases he's perfectly harmless."

"*Most cases*? What does that mean?"

Patrick interjected before Craig could answer. "Juliet, we all have to protect Rory. I agree, he can be too physical; but that makes him no more guilty than you or I, for, as the Good Book says, *what a man thinks in his heart…*"

Craig silenced him with a severe look.

"Have I heard you right, Craig?" asked Juliet. "You mean – all he'll get from you is a tongue-lashing? Shall I call the police myself?"

Craig regarded her sympathetically. "Do you really think that would be a good idea?"

As she held his gaze, she felt a change. Her breathing calmed. Her mind cleared. She started to relax again.

"You don't want to jeopardise your documentary," he said softly. He took her hand.

"No," she agreed hesitantly.

"That's right," Craig said. "Now listen. I told you a few days ago, didn't I, that nothing here is what it seems? Well, that's probably truer of Rory than of anybody else. I'm very sorry this happened. I'll go straight in there to speak to him." He squeezed Juliet's hand lightly, and released it.

She looked at him. He turned, and went towards the sitting room door. She couldn't bear to wait and watch or listen. Instead she went up the staircase, intending to retreat to her bedroom.

For a few moments she studied herself in the mirror, fighting back tears at the sight of her neck. It looked terrible. Fiery. Red. Soon to be swollen and bruised. How dare Rory? How dare Craig? She felt like screaming.

But no sooner had she sunk onto her bed than there came a knock on her door. Not Craig again so soon, surely. "Who's that?"

"Don." She felt enormously relieved. "What timing." She opened the door.

He entered. "Just a quick word before I drive Theo to the station…" He stopped, and studied her throat in horror.

"Your neck. What happened to it?"

"Rory tried to throttle me."

"What?" he exclaimed, his face flooding with colour.

"He did it in the sitting room a few minutes ago. I got away from him, and met Craig just outside in the hall. But I couldn't believe his reaction. He said he'd *speak to* Rory about it. That was all he planned to do."

Don was dumbfounded.

"How many times has he done this before?" she asked. "Craig mentioned something about *in most cases* – what did that mean?"

Raising his hand to stop her questions, Don moved forward, and examined her throat. "Looks nasty. Patrick has the first-aid box."

"I know that," she said. "I've already had the benefit of it."

Don nodded. "He's well-trained. Small comfort to you, of course. What happened?"

"I was interviewing Rory. Asked him about his thorn in the flesh."

Don tutted. "No good. No good at all," he said. "Did you record the attack?"

"God, I had no time to think about that. Possibly."

"Good. Evidence," he said.

"Well, yes, but what use would I make of it? Craig advised me against calling the police. And, I hate to say, I came round to his way of thinking. I realised it could backfire on me. Wreck my documentary for a start."

Don sank heavily into the chair by the window. "A mess, isn't it," he said.

She didn't reply.

"You even keener now to rescue your sister?" he asked.

For the first time since the attack, she laughed, though her neck still burned ferociously. "Yes."

A few moments passed. "How do you feel about Craig now?" asked Don.

"Angry. I know I should really leave at once. Grab Zoe and go."

"No point. Forget about sorting Zoe out. That's my advice," he said.

"Why?" She felt a flame of fury at his interference. She couldn't believe he'd spoken those last words. How hypocritical of him. Was he criticising her now for her attitude to Zoe? Wasn't he at least equally guilty himself of trying to organise someone else's life for them: Craig's?

"Goodbye, Don." She couldn't trust herself to continue with the subject.

He got up, touched her shoulder, and walked out of the room.

She sat for a few moments, breathing deeply, unsure what to do next. Then, on inspiration, she jumped to her feet. Go and find Zoe. That was it. She'd be shocked at what had happened to Juliet. She might want to leave straight away. But first, Juliet pulled a blue Liberty scarf out of her drawer, and loosely knotted it around her sore neck. Somehow the gentle warmth it created was comforting. It would also cover the redness and the bruises she expected to appear soon. Hurrying out of her room, she nearly collided with Theo heading down the passageway, travelbag slung over his shoulder.

Instinctively she put her hand to her throat, but the silk covered the evidence of Rory's aggression. She felt she'd had quite enough conversations about that subject for the time being. She surveyed Theo. She could understand the initial attraction between him and Zoe. Her sister was pretty and charming; and Theo gentle, considerate, caring – and not at all bad-looking himself, in a neat, blond kind of way.

But, clearly, from what she had heard so far about him, Theo had suffered in the past. It seemed to her, too, that he might be in the wrong job. Surely he was no better a choice for Zoe than Craig had been.

And yet, studying the young clergyman, she did feel sorry for him. Nearly as sorry as she felt for her injured self.

"You look out of spirits, Theo. This must be so difficult for you. This disciplinary review tomorrow morning won't be much fun, will it?"

A warm, appreciative light came into his eyes. "Thanks. But it's no more than what I've been asking for, ever since I was ordained. I'm sure I shall just be ordinary Mr Lucas again, after the bishop has chewed me up and spat me out tomorrow."

She reached up to finger the folds of soft material round her neck. "You know, Theo, I've an odd feeling that isn't going to happen." She didn't know why she'd said this; she certainly hadn't planned to.

Their gaze held. He sighed. "I hope you're right. But it's only a faint hope."

"Why?"

"With a past like mine… well, perhaps I'm in the right place after all, here in Craig's group."

"What an odd thing to say."

He smiled faintly. "I've just spoken to Rory, by the way."

She started. Then she swallowed. Her hands dropped to her sides. Theo's expression told her he knew all about the attack. "Is Rory behaving like a human being again?" she asked.

"I had a short but rational conversation with him," said Theo. "Yes, I know what he did to you. I'm so sorry, Juliet. Craig assured me that he'll deal with it in his own way. Rory even plans to apologise to you. I did lend him a book I thought might make a small difference."

Her jaw dropped. A book? Did Theo reckon that Rory's difficulties might be resolved by reading a book? He must be deluded. She decided not to pursue the issue. Not right now, just as he was about to leave. And yet, something else he'd said nagged at her. "What happened to you in the past, Theo," she asked, "that makes this community the right place to be? You don't have anything in common with someone like Rory, surely?"

He gave a small chuckle. "I'd like to share the truth with you, Juliet, but not right now."

"Is it a long story?"

"Yes, you could say so. Instead, let me share another tale, from the last time I was in the Middle East, four years ago. I climbed the fence of the Garden of Gethsemane – against the rules, I might add, as it's now closed to visitors to stop them stealing bits of the trees as holy relics. I did it because I wanted to record an audio diary about how it felt being in the very place where Jesus thought about packing it all in."

She considered this. "And did you finish your recording?"

"Yes. I was all alone in there. Been recording for about ten minutes, when suddenly I realised several machine guns were trained on me. Clearly the soldiers thought I was up to no good, and were taking no chances."

"Scary. How did you get out?"

"I convinced them I thought I was the Son of God, and they let me go free. There are plenty of people around with Jerusalem Syndrome."

"That must have been a relief," said Juliet.

"It was. But still a very close thing." His eyes rested upon her.

"So why did you tell me that?" she asked.

"Only because of the fact that sometimes being mad can get you out of a tight spot."

"But you're not mad, Theo," she said.

"No?" He shook his head. "You can't be sure of anything here, Juliet. Remember what you've heard. Nothing is meant to be taken at face value."

She frowned, looking at him. Mild-mannered Theo? Mad? Impossible. He was teasing her.

"Including," he added unexpectedly, "any ideas you may have about what truly *is* in your sister's heart."

She started. What an unexpected thing to say. Had he read her thoughts earlier? About him and Zoe? The two of them had certainly been close enough in recent hours for her favourite perfume, one Juliet recognised at once, to linger on him.

At that moment, they both heard the sound of a car horn, out on the forecourt.

"That's Don," said Theo. "I must be off. He's going to drive me to the station."

He held out his hand, and she took it. "Goodbye, Theo. Good luck."

"Thanks. And you look after yourself, Juliet. Go and get some first-aid from Patrick." He smiled, squeezed her hand, and then let go.

She stood watching him go down the stairs. Now he'd told her that little story she felt different about him. She drew a deep breath. It seemed some kind of traumatic experience did lie in his background, from what he implied, just as it very probably did in Rory's. Although of course, the results, in terms of their personalities and actions, were very, very different.

And, from his remark about Zoe, she had her suspicions her sister might be about to fall for him. Maybe in a big way.

And that, in her book, was unwelcome news.

12

No Halfway Meeting

Echoes of her recent conversation with Theo chased each other round Juliet's mind. And so did fragments of emotional fall-out from her encounter with Rory. She felt very sore – in more ways than one – and a dark shadow of insecurity lay in the pit of her stomach. Rory was still around and she might find herself alone with him at any time.

As she hesitated, Beth pushed past, carrying a huge armful of sheets and pillowcases.

"Can I help?" Juliet asked.

"No," said Beth grumpily. "Work duty."

She stomped down the stairs, trailing sheets behind her. Juliet winced as her neck throbbed. Beth vanished.

Juliet decided to return to her room. Arriving at the door again, she saw Beth had left a pile of clean bed linen on the floor. She bent to pick it up and took it back inside her room. She'd rest for a while, to prepare herself for whatever the evening might hold. If she could, she'd have liked to lock the door. Just in case Rory came up here to get her. No, that was silly. She must pull herself together.

And in any case, there was no door key.

Refreshed, Juliet reached the bottom of the staircase an hour later, and entered the hall, just as Don closed the front door behind him and Craig stepped out through the library doorway.

"Theo caught the train OK?" Craig asked his father.

Don gave a curt nod.

Craig then turned to Juliet. "Feeling better, Juliet?" he asked in a low voice.

"A little," she said guardedly. "Have you spoken to Rory yet?"

"I have," Craig said.

At this, Don broke in. "Like a word with you, Craig," he said. "Before supper."

"Fine by me," said Craig.

Juliet immediately went on full alert. Craig for his part looked unperturbed. Was Don planning to take him to task about Rory? She half hoped not, for she herself felt that matter was best left for discussion between her and Craig.

Craig strolled back across to the library door and opened it. "Happy for Juliet to join us, Father?"

"Quite happy. Concerns her as much as you." Craig gestured for them both to join him. They followed him into the library, where they took easy chairs facing each other. Not for the first time in this house, Juliet wondered at the contrast between the tranquility of the surroundings – the mellow oak panelling, the dreamy atmosphere, the softly glowing lamps – and the turbulence of the people who inhabited them.

Her neck still hurt strongly. And her heart fluttered from time to time. Would she have nightmares tonight? Would Rory's face haunt her dreams? And images of his long, spider-like fingers? She shuddered.

Craig noticed this at once, and looked at her, concerned. Leaning forward, he reached out and lightly laid his hand on her arm. She remained perfectly still. For one moment, she felt a sense of peace. Then he removed his hand. Her anxiety returned.

Craig sat in a relaxed position, crossed his legs in a slow, deliberate manner, and slung his arm along the back of his chair. Ah, the studied casual effect. This was in sharp contrast to Don's prickly manner.

"First, Rory," said Don.

"Oh, come on, Don," protested Juliet, "I think Craig only has me to answer to for that. I was the one who suffered."

"Then ask me anything you like," Craig said to her.

"Why is Rory so aggressive?"

"Yes, Craig. Tell her," Don burst in. "And not only that. Why didn't you warn Juliet about him?"

"First of all, because I like to believe the best of people."

Don was almost apoplectic. "Never heard such … this your idea of an experiment?"

Craig looked mildly irritated by Don's words. "I am already dealing with Rory in the way I choose."

Don bristled but remained silent. Juliet drew a deep breath. Was he preparing for another onslaught?

Craig turned to her as she breathed out again. "As we're on the subject of Rory… I've been thinking since our last conversation, Juliet. The last thing I want is for you to feel badly treated. And I intend to make it up to you."

She was greatly surprised. How did he mean to do that?

"I cannot be at peace if I know you're unhappy here, or anxious about anything."

She wanted to reply, but found no words. She was only aware of his face, and his dark eyes. And of the passion with which his own words had been spoken. He did seem to genuinely care about her. And that meant a lot.

But before she could respond, Don sprang to his feet. "Not enough. Rory's violent episodes are on the increase. And nobody else seems any the more content for your teachings."

"I never promised contentment."

"Freedom then," Don insisted. "Where's the evidence?"

"I don't need to supply any, Father," said Craig. "Not to you. As you've evidently been round gathering information on their mental state, you're probably best placed to pronounce upon it yourself."

Don snorted at this.

Juliet interrupted. "What I'd like first of all, Craig, is for you and Don to start talking to each other properly. And stop behaving like two sides in a Cold War."

Craig's face clouded. She had an instinct that this came as both an unexpected request and an unwelcome one. And she found herself regretting that she hadn't claimed some other far more radical and personal compensation from Craig for the part he played in her mistreatment at the hands of Rory.

"She's right," said Don. "Craig, you and I… We can't carry on like this. Been thinking. Got a suggestion to make."

"Oh?" Craig threw a sceptical glance at his father. "And you're happy for Juliet to hear it?"

"Perhaps I'd better leave the room," said Juliet, and waited. She didn't really want to go, although she was finding it a strain to be so stoical about her injuries; the pain had still not subsided. Perhaps she would ask Patrick for some more first-aid after all. She got up from her chair.

Don was so focused on what he planned to say, he failed to answer Craig's question. "Came to me last night," Don continued. "This ship of yours here. Heading for an iceberg. We need to change course."

Craig listened. Juliet reached the door and lifted the door latch, ready to go.

"But where to? We haven't discussed that. Reckon you and me…" Don hesitated. "Let's agree on a plan. One that looks good to both of us."

Craig shifted his position in the chair. "If you've got one to lay on the table, then I'm willing to consider it."

Don immediately took the opportunity this afforded him. "Craig, everything I have is yours. Or will be one day. And you know it. But you want to be here running this outfit. Why not sell up? Come back to Barnsley. You can start over. In premises owned and managed by the company."

The library fell quiet, and unnaturally still. Neither man seemed aware of Juliet's continued presence. She barely breathed as she waited for Craig's response. Don wore a look of intense expectancy. But a minute passed, and Craig said nothing.

"Speak, Craig," said Don. "Are you still alive?"

The expression on Craig's face wasn't easy to fathom. But Juliet felt absolutely sure he'd reject this proposal out of hand.

"Well?" asked Don.

"No, Father."

Clapping both hands to his head, Don groaned. "Will we ever call a truce?"

"Yes. When you stop trying to map out my life for me."

Don subsided back into his easy chair again. "That all you can say?"

"For God's sake, Father, you don't seriously expect me to sign up to such a plan." Craig rose to his feet in an abrupt movement. "There'll be any number of get-out clauses in it."

"Like what?" Don buried his head in his hands. Then he looked up abruptly. "Why don't you trust me?"

"Hell's teeth! What a question. You know full well why. You only need to cast your mind back to the conversation we had in here, earlier, after tea." Craig began to pace up and down the silk-fringed rug, past the well-stocked bookshelves, arms tightly folded. Juliet watched, nervous and concerned.

Craig wheeled to face Don again. "Why not simply invest more in this place?"

Don was, she saw, trying to smother rising rage. "Explained that before. The way you're running it isn't cost-effective."

Craig's expression was impassive.

Newly emboldened, Don forged on. "If you relocate to Yorkshire, I won't judge. Nor veto anything. All I ask is this. You use property owned and managed by the company."

Juliet was seriously alarmed. Would Craig fall for this?

"I need time to think." Craig continued pacing.

"Fine, fine. Only remember. What's in it for me is what's in it for you, Craig."

"What sort of penance would you exact from me?" demanded Craig.

"Penance?" Don's voice had acquired an almost falsetto pitch. "No such word in my vocabulary. And you know it." He cleared his throat, and began again in a more even tone. "The company would buy whatever you like. A redundant church. Georgian mansion being sold off to pay death duties. Converted abbey. Best on the market. Think of that, Craig. What do you say?"

Juliet could not believe Don had resorted to bribery. But there it was, undeniable. Bribery to fulfil Don's dream of an ideal future, with his son where he wanted him. Juliet knew Craig would reject the proposal.

"I say this." Craig held his finger up close to Don's face, as if to accentuate his words. "In the story of the prodigal son, the son first freely returned; and then the father killed the fatted calf. But I haven't returned yet; and here you are offering me that fatted calf. That's bribery."

Juliet felt her heart beating faster.

"What more do you want? Blood? The only reward I ask is peace." Don let his hands drop once more to the arms of his chair. "Nothing else."

Peace? thought Juliet. What sort of *peace* did Don think he meant? Juliet saw none between these two, until they came clean with each other. She almost shrank from his disingenuousness with his son. And it was clear to her that Craig saw through it, as she'd fully expected he would.

"Nothing else?" he asked. "Not even for me to let go of my beliefs?"

Don straightened, and stared at him again. Juliet looked from father to son. She saw Craig's body language was hostile, hands on hips. She couldn't predict Don's reply.

"I never asked your mother to change her beliefs, did I?" said Don in an icy voice.

Juliet tensed. What was this all about?

Craig had frozen. His face was white. "No, you just drove her away instead."

Don turned from him. Juliet couldn't see his expression. But he took several moments to regain emotional control.

Then he swung round, and tried a new angle. "This philosophy of yours. It's no hurdle." He looked brighter. Juliet sensed he was about to say something disastrous. But she of course was powerless to stop him. She shouldn't even still be in the room, listening to this.

"Why not offer *Devil's Advocate* sessions?" suggested Don. "I'll run them. Want to take me up on it?"

Craig scoffed contemptuously.

The fact that Don could make such a misjudged remark, proved to Juliet that Don didn't understand Craig at all. And Don still seemed to imagine the ideal solution lay within easy reach. If he won Craig's agreement, he'd call in an estate agent to sell this place, exchange contracts, complete the sale, and be off back to Barnsley in a flash. Except…

What about Craig's followers? They loved the Centre. Craig couldn't betray them. She felt sure they'd all believe Craig was selling his soul to… not the devil exactly, but to something very close.

"I have a proviso," said Craig.

"A proviso?" repeated Don. "What's that?"

"That you agree to change the name of the company."

Don's jaw dropped. So did Juliet's. This was completely unexpected.

"Change the company name?" said Don. "What's wrong with *McAllister Developments Ltd*? Perfect."

"No it isn't," said Craig. "I challenge you to swap it for *McAllister & Son Life Transformation*."

Now Juliet felt she could barely withhold the laughter that would give her away and reveal that she'd overheard the entire conversation. But Don didn't share her amusement.

"*And Son*?" He nearly fell off his chair. "*Life Transformation*? Got to be joking."

"Ah," said Craig. "There I have you, don't I?"

"I'm … I'm…" Don stumbled over his words. "Before you've proved your worth? You expect the fruits first?"

They faced off like birds of prey, each chained to a tree stump to prevent them flying at each other and attacking.

For Juliet, despondency re-emerged. They were at it again. She knew Don had difficulty articulating his feelings. But even so, she wished he was much less controlling. As her mood dropped, so her aching throat became worse.

She resisted the urge to draw a deep sigh. Instead, she redirected her attention just as Don renewed his appeal to Craig. "Give it another day or so. Then we'll look at it again. I realise I dragged you up after your mother left."

"That's what you call it," murmured Craig.

"Can't you forgive me?" Don fired up again. "It's not all bad news. I put you through Edinburgh. You loved it there. Wouldn't be where you are now, if not for me."

Craig said nothing. Juliet now began to wish he'd make some kind of concession to his father, some move towards him. The words *thank you* or *sorry* would open things up for them; she felt convinced of that.

Craig turned. She quickly stepped aside. He passed her without a glance and left the room.

Don crumpled back onto his seat. "So you heard all that, Juliet," he said.

"Yes. Sorry."

"Don't be," said Don. "Just as well you heard. I need your help."

"Perhaps you do," remarked Juliet.

"Could kick myself. Where do I go wrong with him?"

They both listened as Craig's footsteps crossed the hallway, and as the sitting room door opened and closed. She watched Don quietly for a few moments. Then she came and sat down on the chair Craig had just left. "Don, what matters to you more than anything?"

He looked up. Outside, a crow flew past the leadlights. They were both distracted by the flash of movement for a moment. She wondered whether Don considered a short life as a vagabond bird infinitely preferable to the journey he'd taken, one of several decades, leading into clouds of puzzlement.

Then Don spoke. "All I want is to settle this business with Craig. To change things."

"In what way?"

"So that every time we talk to each other we don't end up in a fight. So I don't..." He paused. "... make the same mistake my own father made with me."

She leaned forward and put her hand on his. She couldn't think of anything to say.

"When I see Craig's attitude to me, I..." Don hesitated. He looked nonplussed. "It just seems the hardest thing in the world."

"How would it be if..." she began.

"Yes?"

"...if I were to talk to him for you?"

"You think that would work?" He searched her face. "After all, *you* are the one..." He stopped.

She looked straight at him. "What were you about to say?"

He seemed embarrassed. "Never mind, Juliet. Forget I said it."

Supper was nearly ready, and Juliet felt hungry, as she sipped her sparkling mineral water. Tantalising smells emanated from the kitchen. She knew a good hot meal by candlelight, together with a glass or two of a fine red wine, would help to deaden her discomfort and calm her nerves. She'd received so much sympathy from the group members by now that she heartily wished never to be reminded of the attack again, even by kind words. News of it had spread round the community at once. Zoe had been shocked, and very concerned. Even now, she was standing one side of the inglenook with a dry Martini in her hand, watching Juliet carefully, as if searching for any tell-tale signs of post-traumatic stress syndrome.

This show of sympathy was of small comfort to Juliet. She dreaded seeing Rory again. And she knew she would, at the meal table. She wondered how the other group members would behave towards him, or whether Craig had already briefed them on this.

Meanwhile, she watched Llewellyn steadying himself against the other side of the inglenook, his third gin and tonic in his hand, and unruly hair tumbling over his eyes. Beth and Edgar had been at work for some considerable time, preparing the evening meal. Beth must have dumped the bed linen in the laundry room, and gone straight off to the kitchen. She was certainly working hard today.

"Edgar was told very clearly he was not allowed to experiment with any new recipes when cooking for us all," said Llewellyn. "So why is it taking the two of them so long? I'll have polished off the entire contents of Craig's cocktail cabinet by the time they serve up."

"Yes, I think it's probably about time I hid that gin bottle, Llewellyn," said Juliet. "And Zoe – go easy on the wine won't you? There'll be heaps more at dinner."

Instead of taking offence at her sister's bossy instructions, Zoe gave her a tolerant smile. "I'm in no hurry," she said.

"Come on." Juliet rose from her seat. "After all, they might have had an accident with the Aga. Let's go in, and see what they're up to."

Zoe followed Juliet as she marched towards the kitchen door and pulled it open. A scene of disorder met their eyes.

The kitchen table was barely visible beneath the mess of dishes and store cupboard ingredients. A fine white film of flour covered most objects. Other spilt items included chopped onions and breadcrumbs. An aroma of mixed herbs permeated the air.

What was going on in here? Well, Juliet could see the original intentions, but the reality seemed to have veered way off course. They were only supposed to be doing a tried and tested recipe.

Beth was by the sink, attempting to wash various implements and bowls that Juliet supposed wouldn't fit in the dishwasher, her face flushed. Edgar was busy keeping a check on the progress of four saucepans at once.

"Go away," Beth cried. "We're not ready yet." She sniffed, and wiped her nose on her sleeve.

Juliet considered her. Then she glanced at Edgar. It seemed as if they'd both overstretched themselves this evening.

"Smells delicious," she said encouragingly.

"Thanks," said Edgar, "though we may have been a little ambitious with the pudding."

She looked from one to the other suspiciously. Had they been arguing? Beth's eyes were red, and Edgar's face unnaturally flushed.

Had he been going on at her about his questionnaire? Was he demanding she provide him with extra information about her psychological history?

"Can we help?" asked Juliet.

"No, no. You go and relax. None of us have a train to catch."

"Are you sure? Beth?" murmured Juliet.

"No, go away!" she cried.

"OK, fine."

Zoe and Juliet swiftly backed out, and closed the door behind them. They stood in the passageway, looking at each other.

"What is it about this place?" asked Juliet.

"Nothing. It's the people who're the problem," said Zoe.

Juliet stared at her. "You admit it?"

"Well, of course I do. And you of all people must agree, especially with what you've just copped from Rory. But I'm beginning to see the answer to that." She wore a beatific smile.

"Is this Theo's influence?" asked Juliet suspiciously.

"Could be," she murmured as she drifted away. "Edgar and Beth can take all the time they want. I'm happy."

Juliet was about to ask, "What's up with you?" But she didn't need to. Her heart sank.

She slipped through to the library. She still felt uncomfortable about the idea of spending time in the sitting room, the scene of Rory's recent violence. She didn't know how she'd feel about being on the very sofa from which she'd fallen, or gazing at the very rug where she'd struggled beneath Rory's weight as he attempted to throttle her.

Refusing to give power to any flashbacks, she threw herself into an easy chair in the library, and set to thinking. She wasn't happy about this new behaviour of her sister's. And neither was she happy about Don's words in this room earlier, just after she'd offered to talk to Craig for him. In fact, she'd regretted the offer soon afterwards, and had been worrying about the implication of his words ever since.

"*You are the one…*"

He'd broken off mid-sentence, but she had an uncanny intuition of what he might have been about to say next.

How was she to make it clear to him that, even if Zoe had been sidetracked, and therefore no longer stood between her and Craig, that didn't mean she was after him herself? And neither was there any possibility whatsoever of her changing her mind. That was quite out of the question.

She called to mind some of Craig's teachings. She'd already spotted the flaws in them. *Erase your personal history… create a fog around yourself… learn to stop the world.*

Where had she heard that before? From a young anthropology student who set off from the University of California, Los Angeles, and headed into the mountains of Mexico, to meet up with the Yaqui Indian sorcerers, men of awesome psychological powers. Now where could she check that she'd remembered it correctly? Might Craig have the books on the shelves in here? She'd read a few of them in the past.

Getting up, she went over to the nearest bookshelf and began to scan the titles. As she did so the door opened, and Craig came in.

Her body tingled. Her fingers tightened around the volume she'd partially withdrawn. As he looked at her, every part of her felt poised, alert, ready for… what? She couldn't be sure.

"Juliet," he said. "How are you feeling? Does your throat still hurt?"

"Yes," she said.

He moved swiftly to her side. "I'm so sorry about what happened. Certainly you won't trust Rory again. I quite understand that. And I expect you feel afraid to be alone with him. But don't worry. I'll keep an eye on him, and make sure that never happens."

"Thank you," she said, not sure if she could rely on this or not.

"Believe me," he said softly, his eyes on her face. Silence fell. He broke it to add, "Our third meeting in here today, Juliet."

"So it is." She waited a few moments. Then – "Craig, about Don."

"Yes?"

"I asked him what matters to him more than anything."

"You did?" He studied her intently. "And what was his reply?"

"He hopes to change things between you and him. He doesn't want to repeat what happened between himself and his own father."

Craig's face registered no emotion. "Did he share the details of that with you?"

"No," she said.

"Good." Craig still wore an inscrutable mask. Then he softened slightly. "My grandfather was an old tyrant. No doubt about it."

She was taken aback by this remark. "That's a little harsh, surely, Craig."

He didn't reply.

"Your father wants a truce," she persisted. "I know I'm putting myself on the line here, but…"

"Go on," he said coolly. He looked at her, and she recognised the expression in his eyes. It was one that she knew had the power to destabilise her.

Immediately she began to feel unsafe, as if she was toiling up a scree-covered slope. With all her strength, she resisted this feeling. She had now had more than a few opportunities to witness the effect of his gaze upon those around him. And she resolved that he would not succeed in claiming *her* poise and self-assurance.

She renewed her effort. "I only want to say this, Craig: what stops you going halfway towards meeting him?"

Craig's manner took on a steely character. "Not an option, Juliet," he said sharply. Then he changed the subject. "I see you're looking through the shelves here. You're welcome to borrow any book you like. Take this one." He stood up and removed a volume from the shelf behind him.

"*Conversations with Don Juan*," she said, "by Carlos Castaneda. Just what I was searching for, Craig. Thank you."

He looked at her reflectively but said nothing.

"Do you really think you'll succeed in erasing your personal history?" she asked.

His voice when he spoke was low and soft, but also held a warning note. "Yes, I believe so. Don't take what my father says too seriously, will you?"

She felt stung by his words.

He continued to regard her. "You heard everything we said earlier, didn't you? Admit it, Juliet. His offer was outrageous, wasn't it?"

"I agree it was bribery," she said. "But, Craig, he's desperate."

He came close to her. "So am I," he said.

She was aware of nothing but him.

At this, the door opened, and James looked in. She broke away from Craig. "I'll certainly bear that in mind, Craig," she remarked for James's benefit. "And in turn, I hope you'll remember what I've said."

"Supper's ready," said James.

Juliet barely tasted the meal. She could concentrate neither on food nor conversation. Two people separated her from Rory: Llewellyn and Don. But she was still painfully aware of his presence not far away. And on top of that, every time she looked at Craig she saw a different face. Who was he? She no longer had any confidence that she was even close to guessing the answer to that question.

Juliet's disquiet about her sister also continued. Zoe's afterglow had now lost its high sheen, and she appeared to be in a daze. Clearly she was missing Theo. Later, after coffee had been served in the sitting room, Juliet caught up with her in the hall.

But before Juliet could open the subject of Theo, Zoe deflected her. "What were you and Craig doing in the library before dinner?"

"Why do you want to know?" retorted Juliet.

"Because of the mood he was in all through the meal, of course," said Zoe.

Juliet sidestepped the issue of her power to affect Craig's mood, and quickly went on. "Never mind that. What about you, Zoe? How do you feel?"

Zoe's manner threatened to turn brittle. Then a flash of understanding passed between them. "Juliet," she said, "I know Theo only came on Monday. It seems incredible, all that's happened since then. But I've never met anyone like him before."

Juliet felt torn. It seemed hardly any time at all since Zoe had been saying the same thing about Craig. And yet, in the hothouse atmosphere of this community, she understood how quickly new emotions could flourish. Erotic love grew fast here – but with a weak root system.

Which was even more reason to be anxious for her sister. "Yes, Zoe, he's different. But go easy, won't you? This isn't the real world."

"No need to lecture me on the subject." Zoe was about to react further, then pulled herself in. She glanced quickly at Juliet. Still thinking about the attack, no doubt, and feeling she ought to perhaps be a little gentler with her sister and make allowances for her.

This irritated Juliet. And she still felt the sharp prick of Zoe's distrust just below the surface. She reached out to touch the cloisonné enamel vase which stood on the occasional table, and lightly traced the design on the surface with her fingers, trying to disguise her unhappiness at Zoe's attitude. "It's just… I can't help worrying about you."

Zoe quickly forgot her desire to walk on eggshells around Juliet. For a moment, it seemed to Juliet that her sister would complete Rory's work, snatch the vase, and hurl it at her.

"Juliet, I know you've played mother to me ever since mum died. We were both very young then. I was only five. But things have changed. We're grown up now. My life's my own."

Juliet considered this. It was true she'd first begun to behave protectively towards Zoe when her younger sister was very little, and she in her early teens. And somehow it had stuck. But she still felt she must continue to fill the role of the mother they'd lost to cancer nineteen years before. And also, if Zoe was to fall for someone Juliet feared unsuitable, then she couldn't possibly remain silent.

Zoe broke into Juliet's reflections. "Theo is special. Leave us alone."

"Zoe, lighten up," Juliet flashed. "I like the guy. He's caring, intelligent… I respect him. But, remember, there was a period of time when he just disappeared…"

"What are you talking about?"

"Rory told me on the day I arrived – at dinner," persisted Juliet. "He said Theo served as a curate for a couple of years after being ordained, then *vanished from the face of the earth* – whatever that means. Oh, I know Rory himself doesn't have the full story, and he could have misunderstood. Even so, it makes me wonder. Did Theo lose his memory? Did he take on a false identity? He might even have roamed round Florence as a Hannibal Lecter type..."

"Oh shut up, Juliet," retorted Zoe, her face flushed. "This stuff is way over-the-top. You're getting paranoid."

"I'm perfectly sane, thank you. And you'd be amazed at what people can do."

"But not Theo. I won't listen to this any more. I can have any man I choose. And if it's Theo – that's for me to decide!"

With this, she turned, and ran up the stairs.

13

Between Two Worlds

Time seemed to crawl the next day. By four o'clock Juliet felt she'd been waiting for ever. But for what? She'd seen no sign of Craig since dinner yesterday evening. And even more disturbing – at least to her, in her present insecure state of mind – nothing had been heard from Theo either. He was supposed to have had his disciplinary review with his bishop in London that morning. Juliet had expected that he might at least have called Zoe on her mobile, to let her know what happened. Had he gone off on another of his *disappearances*? She shook herself. She must rein in her fevered imagination.

Then she turned her mind to that row with Zoe last night. Juliet had tried to smooth things over a little this morning at breakfast. And she'd asked Zoe to let her know if she heard from Theo, and Zoe had said yes. So her sister would have no reason to hide any news from her…

Unhappy, and vaguely fearful, Juliet stood near the fence that divided the car park from the woodland, looking towards the house.

As she did so, the back door opened, and Edgar appeared with a watering can. He wore a solemn expression. Then he began to water the hanging baskets, suspended on black chains from the wrought-iron brackets. How refreshing! For once he was without clipboard and notes.

Walking in measured steps from one basket to the next, he looked like a monk gliding through the cloisters of the monastery of the Grande Chartreuse in Grenoble. When he was like this, he occupied a totally different world from the one in which he went round pestering people with his research questionnaires. It was amazing. Quite rapt, he concentrated on his task. The balmy weather and still atmosphere contributed to the trance-like feeling. His bald patch gleamed in the afternoon sun.

She experienced a pang of wistfulness. The farmhouse looked very peaceful: a visual representation of everything Juliet felt a community like this ought to be. Loving, tranquil, harmonious…

And yet, here she was, being eaten up by all sorts of worries. Zoe, and her infatuation with Theo. The doubts over Theo's background. Then the fact that she still hardly knew who Craig was, and what he was about.

Was he hiding something? What really lay behind his dysfunctional relationship with his father? And was it any business of hers anyway? But the answer to that, she knew, was *yes*. Because she cared about it – despite all her best intentions, she cared deeply. And she still hadn't resolved the mystery of who wrote that letter to Craig. The writer clearly loved Craig, longed for him to come quickly, had felt guilty about him in the past, but had now been forgiven by Craig. Juliet wanted to know who that person was. She felt she had a right to know. And she wanted to be rid of this terrible feeling in her stomach whenever she saw Craig. Was it yearning? No, impossible! All she knew was that it was tearing her apart.

And then there was the question of Rory and his unpredictable outbursts of aggression. Juliet knew Rory needed to be locked up. But that wasn't going to happen. Not while Craig, for some twisted reason of his own, allowed him to run loose in this community. Rory had said sorry to her, in Craig's presence, but it rang hollow. And she still felt sick when she found herself revisiting the sensation of his hands around her neck.

And yesterday she'd listened in on a very private exchange between a bitter and rigidly opposed father and son. Later she'd offered to help. And she'd foolishly used the word *desperate* to describe Don's state of mind. Then Craig had stunned her by using the same word of himself. Craig desperate too? Desperate for what?

And before he could show her, James had come in and Craig had slammed down the barriers again.

She looked almost tearfully at the house. Though she was in less physical pain now, an undercurrent of anxiety was never far away.

The back door opened and Don walked out. At once she brightened. She couldn't help but see the Yorkshireman as rather like a lifeboat, cresting the waves of anger and desire and secrecy she found herself struggling in… Crazy, she knew, especially as he was probably part of the problem, but she needed something to hang onto.

As she watched, he headed in a northwesterly direction across to the woodland path. The afternoon sun slanted through the copper beeches, marbling the gravel and fence with an intricate pattern of light and shade, reminding Juliet that it had been her earlier intention to take a brisk walk. She ran after him, catching up with him on the other side of the stile. "May I join you, Don?"

"Of course, Juliet," he said.

They began walking up the track together. "Any news of Theo?" she enquired.

"None at all," said Don. "Worried about him, are you? A fair few others here are getting twitchy about it too."

"Which is odd really, when you come to think of it," she said. "I mean, why should it upset them if he's defrocked?"

"No idea," said Don. "After all, lot of pagans, aren't they?"

She chuckled. "Apart, that is, from Patrick."

"A lot of that stuff's mumbo jumbo too," grumbled Don.

Juliet decided to let the subject go. She was in no position to argue any theological points with Don. And now she heard footsteps approach, scrunching the leaf litter on the track. Rory came into view, with an open book in his hand.

"Take it easy, Juliet," murmured Don. "I'm with you. It'll be all right."

She felt a surge of warmth and gratitude to him for these words – and for guessing her feelings. Not something she'd have thought Don excelled in. Her response to this took her by surprise. Don seemed so dependable, so solid, so real. And then she reminded herself that she'd listened in to a conversation where Don had bribed his son, and backtracked from dealing honestly with him. So she had her reservations about the Yorkshireman too. Even so, for a moment she almost felt like hugging him, but reined herself in just in time. She wasn't at all sure how Don would have taken it.

And then she realised Rory was very close to her. She stepped back quickly. He wore a black string singlet, drawing Juliet's attention to his white bony shoulders and arms. He'd teamed this with a pair of black wet-look trousers. This outfit distracted her for longer than she realised. All the time her heart was pounding. Would he attack her again? No, of course not! Don was with them. Don would protect her. She knew she'd be safe.

"Good book, Rory?" asked Don. "Or something depressing of Oleg's?"

"No, no. *The Celtic Way of Prayer.* Theo lent it to me yesterday." Rory said this in a strained tone of voice.

Ah! said Juliet to herself – so this was the book Theo told her he thought would help Rory. She still strongly doubted whether it would. Then a fanciful idea struck her. Perhaps Theo was praying for Rory right now. If so, she hoped Theo was praying for safety for her as well.

She examined Rory's face, which was pale and gaunt, but she didn't achieve eye contact. Nor did she want to, particularly. "Is the book helpful?" she forced herself to ask, thrusting her hands into her pockets, and ensuring that she kept at least one metre of clear space between herself and Rory.

"A little," said Rory. "Though I must admit, I wasn't actually reading it just now. I was looking at this." He held up a sheet of notepaper, closely covered with handwriting, then slipped it back inside the front cover.

"Oh. A letter," said Juliet. "Someone from the outside world?"

Rory nodded, looking slightly sheepish.

"My sister. We keep in touch from time to time. She's in a Buddhist retreat centre up in the Highlands."

Juliet felt a stab of surprise to learn that Rory had a relative at all, especially one whom he took the trouble to exchange chatty letters with, in between his violent episodes. She wondered if his sister knew how far Rory was from the Buddhist ideal of non-violence and compassion. "So you and your sister are both in spiritual communities?" she said. "But what a coincidence."

Rory shot her a suspicious flicker of a glance. It was just like the one he had given her before she asked about his *thorn in the flesh.* She withdrew another step. Don put a reassuring hand on her arm, then dropped it back to his side.

"So why doesn't your sister email you?" asked Juliet.

"Never!" said Rory with alarming force. "Her retreat centre forbids the use of computers."

"Does it?"

"Yes. So we always write letters to each other instead."

"I can understand that. It makes sense. People take more care with letters." Juliet was conscious of her own efforts to keep the conversation amiable, now she knew how easily an incautious remark could light his tinder-box.

Rory unexpectedly turned, and looked down the slope, at the honey-coloured stone of the farmhouse, just discernable through the trees. She and Don followed the direction of his gaze.

"It looks so peaceful," Juliet ventured. A harmless remark, she believed. But once again she was thrown off course by Rory's response.

"Craig's too soft on who he lets in," he said sharply.

"Who do you mean?" she asked.

"Theo, for a start," said Rory. "Means well, but… why did Craig invite him? A Christian cleric? What does he have to do with us?"

This astonished Juliet. Why target Theo? Especially as Rory had once described him as a *soul mate.* And then it occurred to her that Rory might be flailing out at Theo as a first target, before closing in on his main quarry again: her. She felt Don move closer to her as if he too sensed a warning in the air.

Rory picked up a stick and started stabbing it into the nearest tree trunk with vicious thrusts. They reminded Juliet of a Viking putting eyes out. She tried to see the funny side of it, and couldn't. And then her suspicion was confirmed. Rory's finger shot out accusingly. And it was pointing at her. "You too, Juliet," he rapped out. "Why did you come? Since you turned up, Craig's changed."

"Changed? In what way?" she protested.

"Craig adores you," Rory brought out through gritted teeth. Juliet fell back, shocked. "He wants you," stated Rory, "for himself."

She couldn't bear to listen to any more of this. "No, Rory," she cried. "You've got this all wrong."

Rory ignored her. "I say Craig should keep his hands off." Juliet's face was on fire. She didn't dare look at Don. Then Rory blurted, "He wants the best, doesn't he? Both worlds. The heaven and freedom stuff. *And* sex. All in the same package."

"I think this is all in your imagination, Rory," pleaded Juliet. She held her breath. If she put up any further defence, or tried to argue, Rory might turn ugly again. Though she did now feel that Rory's words had begun to explain the kind of twisted thinking that might have led him to attack Oleg last Sunday night, and then describe it at dinner on Monday evening as *a near-death experience.* In that case too, he had probably imagined that Oleg was much better off than him. And his feelings of jealousy had overpowered him.

But of one thing she was sure in this case – Rory's speculations about her and Craig were deluded.

Rory continued his rant. "Craig's got it all. But look at me. What have I got? Nothing." His voice took on a tone of self-pity. "My sister. What would she think?" he lamented. "She's so happy where she is. But I…" He began to sob.

Don and Juliet looked at each other helplessly. Neither of them could help Rory: he made it so difficult for himself. And Juliet was afraid to let her guard slip; nor could she forget what those hands of his had done.

But in the next second Rory's tears had vanished, and he clenched his fists with frustration and anger. Juliet's heart was hammering against her ribs. Rory's unpredictability frightened her. "But Craig,"

Rory went on bitterly, "gets the best of both worlds." A few beats of time passed. Then he clapped his hands to his face, in another sharp mood swing. "I've even offered Craig more money, and he's refused."

"What?" Don gasped.

"Didn't you know?" Rory asked in a disconcertingly low-key tone of voice.

Don's mouth hung open. He broke a twig from an overhanging branch, and then split it in two. He looked to Juliet as if he was about to explode himself. What she would do then, she didn't know – other than run for it.

"Perhaps it's best if you take this up with Craig later, Don," Juliet suggested gently, hoping to defuse the situation.

Neither man spoke. She turned back to Rory, and quickly switched the subject to something she hoped would be less sensitive.

"Tell me about your sister, Rory. She sounds very kind and thoughtful, if she writes so many letters."

Rory nodded. Juliet noticed this subject seemed to calm him down. He visibly relaxed.

"You say she's in a Buddhist retreat," Juliet prompted him.

"Yes," Rory said.

Juliet looked at him, intrigued. "How does your sister find their teachings?" she asked.

"She finds they make sense."

Don shook his head. This clearly meant nothing to him.

"The Buddha teaches that we should tread the *Middle Way* of compassion," said Rory, as if reciting a passage from a handbook of Buddhist doctrine. Certainly Juliet thought the words sounded strange on Rory's lips, when compared with his own past record of behaviour towards others. However she simply nodded courteously, determined to tread carefully with Rory.

Don on the other hand seemed to have lost some of his caution, and now opened up another line of conversation which threatened to become contentious. "So the Buddha taught that, did he? Well, I must admit I've always found it very difficult, especially with Craig.

Not that I'm saying *I* have always been in the right, of course."

Ah, thought Juliet. So Don was in confession mode now, was he? Did he believe this might defuse Rory?

"Craig's mother liked me well enough," continued Don. "At first. But walked out one day. Craig was six months old."

"Six months?" A sense of pity held Juliet.

"After that, bit of coming and going. Then she disappeared for good. Age seven, he was." Don shrugged. "There you have it. All in the past. Nothing to be done about it."

Rory looked dubious.

"Did Craig ever try to find her?" asked Juliet.

"Yes. But nothing came of it." Don drew two or three deep breaths. "Craig still blames me." He took several moments to recover from this admission. Neither Rory nor Juliet said anything. Meanwhile, two wood pigeons rushed at each other in the uppermost branches of the closest beech tree.

"So," said Rory, "What do we do now?"

"Beats me," muttered Don. "So hard to satisfy, Craig. Truth. That's what this place is supposed to be about. He can't face it himself."

Rory's face darkened. "Truth?" he said.

Something in the way he said that word warned Juliet to retire a few steps back, further behind Don's left shoulder.

"Yes." Don regarded him with a puzzled expression.

"You, Don, are the last person here qualified to use that word," said Rory. He slapped his hand hard against the nearest tree trunk. "Especially as a blunt instrument to hit Craig over the head with."

"I never meant it in…" began Don. Then he stopped. Perhaps he was reconsidering his words. "Do you think I'm a hypocrite?" he asked.

"No," said Rory. "Blind."

"Blind to what?" asked Don.

"The truth about Craig."

Don subsided. His next words were uttered in a much lower tone. "As it happens, I have my suspicions. But I won't name them."

"D'you want me to name them for you?" enquired Rory.

Juliet looked from one to the other expectantly.

"No," said Don.

"I've known the truth about Craig for months now," said Rory.

Don lost his sense of caution. "How dare you suggest you know my son better than I do?"

"Because it's a fact." Rory grabbed the older man by both shoulders. Juliet cried out. This was it. Don had done it now. If Rory started beating him, how could she help? If she ran off to fetch help, what state would Don be in by the time the rescue party arrived?

Reckless, desperate, she leapt forward. "No, Rory. Let Don go at once."

For a moment she succeeded in distracting Rory. He loosened his grip on Don. The older man fell back. But Rory grasped hold of him again. "Not until you admit the truth about Craig. How can you be such a fool?"

14

A Fear Not Yet Overcome

The next morning, Friday, opened with muted skies; and even when the sun cut through, a sullen humidity worked relentlessly to lower Juliet's spirits yet further.

What *the truth* was about Craig, she still did not know. Rory's battle-hungry approach had worked against him. Both Don and Juliet had been so intent on loosening his grip, and then putting plenty of distance between themselves and Rory, that the question remained unanswered – although she herself had her ideas. A gnawing sensation in the pit of her stomach reminded her of this. Rory's revelation was going to be about Craig's sexuality. She felt sure of that.

But what she couldn't be sure about was whether Rory's opinions on the subject would bear any relation to the truth at all. Although Rory himself might have intense feelings towards Craig, that in itself proved nothing about Craig's own sexual preferences – unless, of course, Craig had responded to him in some way, and given him cause for hope.

But nothing had been resolved up on the woodland track. Rory's behaviour had put paid to that. Always the same, thought Juliet. Violence never solved anything. And yet Rory still seemed to believe it was worth a go. Why, she didn't understand. What was it all about? She had her theories, and yet did they really fit? There was no time for theories anyway. She had to keep on the alert. Watch out for Rory. *Don't ever let him get you alone. Not if you value your life.* She touched her throat as she thought this, and shuddered.

And another serious question remained unanswered too. There was still no news from Theo. Zoe had heard nothing, and had been in tears the last time Juliet spoke to her about it. Juliet felt even more fearful that Theo was indeed planning to stage a second *disappearance.*

And meanwhile, Craig, too, was being elusive; and with Zoe now maintaining a chilly distance, Juliet felt restless and on edge.

But an hour after lunch, the skies held a much brighter aspect, and with the atmosphere fresher, she strolled across the forecourt, portable recorder slung over her shoulder, all set up to record, and microphone in hand. She stopped to watch Patrick painting the garden gate. His eye-catching overalls nearly matched the colour he'd chosen for the gate: peacock blue.

He seemed totally absorbed in his work, and it wasn't a task that provided good sound effects. She didn't consider it worth breaking into his concentration with a request for an interview, and began to walk away. At this he unexpectedly spun round.

"Hello, Patrick." She was at the ready with a friendly smile, and held the microphone out. "Would you like to tell the listeners what you're doing right now?"

He supplied a brief description, in a surly voice. Oh dear. What was the matter with Patrick?

He laid his brush in the tray. His expression was guarded. He muttered something about Theo. The name seemed to occur in the same breath as *committed a mortal sin*, and *outside the grace of God.* Then he added a remark in which she caught the words *languish* and *years in purgatory.*

"Purgatory? For Theo? What makes you think that?" she asked.

Patrick wore a secretive mask.

"Has Theo shared his past with you?" Juliet persisted.

"As it happens, yes, I do know a thing or two about what he's been up to. It'll be purgatory for him, all right," maintained the Irishman.

"How many years do you think he'll get?" she queried, hoping Patrick would lighten up. But her flippancy belied her true feelings.

She hardly knew Theo, after all. And neither did Zoe. And Patrick's words had increased her doubts about the clergyman even more.

The Irishman's face darkened. "It's not for us to know the exact timings. But he's been too lax. An earlier word from his bishop might have pulled him into line. But by the time he arrived here the rot had already set in."

"In what sense?"

"That book of his. I've read it. It has the devil in it."

"Does it? How fascinating!" She resolved to read it as soon as possible. Meanwhile, she reckoned Patrick needed careful handling. "I haven't read the book yet so I can't comment. And Theo may not be back again. He's already been away two nights."

"Oh no, he'll be back." The Irishman set about reloading his paintbrush. "He phoned Craig half an hour ago."

She pulled up at this news. "Did he? What happened at his disciplinary review?"

"No idea. But I reckons they're far too liberal, the Anglicans. They probably gave him a second chance." Patrick's expression hardened. And he fell silent. Clearly he felt they'd both said enough. Juliet thought it unwise to push him. He resumed his painting, and she walked on until, reaching the fir trees at the western perimeter of the vegetable garden, she found a bench to sit on.

Then she noticed three figures crossing the forecourt from the house towards the garden gate. Shading her eyes from the now-dazzling sun, she focused on them.

Laura and Edgar were easily identifiable but not their companion, a wild-looking character with matted hair, in unsavoury rags. For a moment she wondered whether he'd wandered in from the lane at the top of the drive, and they were just escorting him off the premises. He clutched a well-stuffed plastic supermarket bag, and every so often he poked his fingers in it and spent some time exploring the contents.

Then she snapped her fingers: of course. James. He'd once more slipped into his alter ego. He was at it again. What a spectacle he made. When she compared it with the elegant man who usually graced the community with his exclusive tailoring and Noel Coward-like manner, she found it hard to believe.

She got up again and walked towards them, Nagra once more set to record, holding the microphone to her mouth and setting the scene with a few well-chosen words. She held the microphone out close to the group. The trio approached Patrick, who turned, paintbrush in hand, seemingly unconcerned by the sight of James in full costume and stage make-up. Juliet moved closer with her mike; if they objected to her activities, no one mentioned it. In fact, they ignored Juliet throughout. It was a perfect fly-on-the-wall piece of recording.

Laura, Edgar and Patrick embarked upon an animated discussion. She adjusted the levels, and made sure it was all coming over clearly.

Laura gesticulated in the direction of the main entrance gate at the top of the drive. "Theo will be back soon. But I agree, Patrick. When he returns, he'll need to make his stance clear. Either he's a straight down the line *one of them*, or he's *one of us*."

"He's *one of us*." Edgar looked exasperated.

"How can you be sure?" asked Laura.

"Theo listened when we wanted to talk, didn't he?" said Edgar. "He enjoyed being here. He accepts us. Which one of us has seen him get up on a soapbox? He didn't when he came in February, and nor did he this time, either. I can't understand you, Laura. You had a crush on him back then."

This silenced her for a few moments. Her face burned.

Yes, Juliet had guessed this much.

"All right. But when he returns, he can't carry on like he did on Wednesday," Laura insisted.

"Why not?" said Edgar, provocatively.

"You know full well. We can all see the way things stand with Zoe."

Juliet stiffened.

"They make a lovely pair," dribbled James, producing a beer bottle from his bag.

"No they don't," Laura flared. "Theo was so sweet to me back in

February. But this time, he's ignored me. He's been all over Zoe instead. And I even swatted up *1 Corinthians 13* for him."

"Perhaps you'd have done better learning a piece from the *Song of Solomon*," said Patrick. "He'd have preferred that. Plenty there about erotic love." He looked disapproving.

"I don't think that would have worked either," said Edgar, looking like a jolly monk who's just blended a new liqueur. "You would have gone to all that trouble to please him, and all to no avail. Why? Because he only has eyes for our pretty little Zoe. And so, Laura," he added, "my advice is: stick to Al. There's no point in keeping your options open."

Laura tossed her head.

James's rags flapped in the breeze. He lifted the beer bottle to his lips, allowing most of the contents to spill down his chin. Laura drew back in disgust.

"So we are agreed," said Edgar. "Theo and Zoe should be allowed to have their fun."

"I don't think we've agreed that at all," said Laura in a snide manner.

"Well, James and I have," said Edgar. "You and Patrick can beg to differ if you like."

This produced a range of reactions from Laura and Patrick. Juliet felt she detected annoyance, moral outrage and even a hint of envy.

Then Edgar said casually, "And that book of his… Hot stuff. What do you think, Patrick? You read it after me."

This guaranteed the renewed attention of Laura.

Patrick snorted. "Burn it! That's what I think."

James lurched closer to the hedge and leaned back against the leaves.

"You're biased, Patrick," continued Edgar, clearly satisfied that he now had the upper hand over them, "I think it's stunning. My God, I wish I'd had something like that to show those bastards who axed my research grant."

"Well, all well and good, but small comfort to me," began Laura again. "When Theo returns, we must call a halt to his play-acting."

"In what role?" enquired Edgar with a sly smile.

"You know full well," she said. "*Lustful priest.*"

"*Licentious cleric,*" growled Patrick.

"Very popular literary and dramatic role, goes back to medieval times," said Edgar. "And may I add to your list the *flirtatious friar*? We meet one of those in Chaucer's *Canterbury Tales*. Chaucer's friar loves associating with the fairer sex, and is kind enough to perform marriages which he has made necessary."

"That's enough on the subject, Edgar," shouted Laura. For one dangerous moment, Juliet thought Laura was going to slap Edgar's face. But Laura restrained herself.

Edgar, however, still didn't seem to think the subject had been pushed far enough. "You and Al can bend the rules," he said to Laura, "then you call the censors in when Theo falls for Zoe."

"Well…" Laura spluttered for a few moments. "That's outrageous, Edgar. Al and I have no reputation to maintain, if that's what you mean. Whereas Theo…"

"…has standards to live up to," maintained Patrick. "Constantly changing ones, too. But that's the Church of England for you. Always shifting their goalposts."

This remark was met by stony silence from Laura and Edgar. Humming tunelessly to himself, James sank back into the hedge, perilously close to the wet paint. The Irishman snatched up his brush, and plunged it into the paint pot, as if planning to give James a new colour scheme along with the gate.

Whilst pleased with the recording, Juliet felt dismayed by what she'd learned. All this stuff about Theo. She couldn't trust him. What *were* his intentions towards Zoe? And when she'd questioned him on the subject of his past, he'd steered her away from the mystery of his disappearance, and had instead told her a tale about the Garden of Gethsemane. That had been interesting, of course, but he'd still not thrown any light on the other dark areas of his life that really concerned her. James, Edgar, Patrick and Laura had evidently seen enough of Theo, though, to begin forming strong opinions about him.

"Personally," said Edgar, placing a warning hand on the Irishman's arm, as Juliet closed in with the mike again, "I'm at a loss to understand all this fuss. I've no problem with Theo. I like him."

"Maybe you do," Laura sniffed. "I appreciate you and Patrick have read his book, whilst none of the rest of us have yet had that advantage."

"Borrow my copy," advised Edgar. "Patrick has it at the moment. He'll give it to you."

"I'll throw it on the flames first," growled Patrick.

Laura stared at him. "You said that before, Patrick. And I most definitely do want to read it. I'll get it off you as soon as possible."

Then James created a diversion. He shambled over to Laura, and put his hand on hers. "Gotta few pence to spare, lady?"

Juliet couldn't help laughing. He was a good actor. No wonder the casting directors liked him. Ideal for those cameo roles he'd mentioned.

Laura found voice again. "I'll slap your face, James, if you come near me again with that disgusting stench. Where do you get it from? And keep your bottle away from me, too."

James backed off slightly, drooling. Laura foraged in the sleeve of her cardigan, brought out a lacy handkerchief and scrubbed at her hand. But she couldn't resist returning to the subject of Theo. "I thought he was going to be our saving grace."

"Did you?" Edgar's bald head glimmered in the sunlight that had just broken through the clouds again. "Why?"

"Never," declared Patrick, "not with his background."

James sloped over to the Irishman again, and plucked at his sleeve. It struck Juliet as rather appealing that the tramp among them should be playing peacemaker. "Aw, go on," drooled James. "Give Theo a break. He only did it for a year or two…"

Did what? Juliet wondered.

Patrick retreated from James.

Edgar now seemed more determined to take the lead. "But there's one more thing I wish to say."

"And what's that?" Laura asked.

"Simply this," continued Edgar. "A few years ago, as we well know, through no fault of his own, Theo was tested, and cracked under the strain. So? Are we to condemn him for that? It could happen to any of us. That's why we're here – and because of Craig, too, of course."

Juliet fought her urge to dash forward and ask him to explain. They were in full flow, the Nagra was capturing everything, and she didn't want to interrupt.

"Although," Edgar went on, "I happen to know Craig still has one big fear he's never overcome – and this despite all his workshops on the subject."

Silence cut in. "Not exactly a *fear*, surely?" said Laura. At that point her mobile buzzed. She answered it. Then she began to simper.

Edgar started to walk away. "It's lover boy. I'm off. Finish painting, Patrick. We'll discuss this again later."

And they all separated, leaving only James, who slowly sank to the gravel, where he remained in a heap of rags, looking like something that had been tipped off the back of a recycling lorry.

Juliet debated inwardly whether to go over and interview James. She decided not to. Instead, she finished recording, and walked away. She was more interested in asking Patrick to give her Theo's book before the Irishman burned it. She might at least find clues there about Theo's background. And Theo himself would be back soon. She was more than ever determined to ask him directly, and hear it from his own lips, rather than from the gossip of Craig's group members.

After all, she didn't want her sister ending up with someone even more dubious than Craig himself. And as for Craig, she still had too many questions about him, including whether he was straight or not.

Later that afternoon, at five o'clock, she was just about to leave her room with her recording equipment when she saw James making his way stealthily along the passageway away from her. She stopped short. His face shone with cleanliness, his hair had been shampooed and brushed. He wore a silk shirt with a pair of cream linen trousers. Her heart beat fast. She still couldn't get used to these changes of appearance. They were almost as spooky as Craig's.

What was he up to? There were four rooms in the roof: hers, Zoe's, the bathroom, and the room set aside for Theo. She waited just inside her ajar door, her eyes upon his back.

He reached Theo's door, and stopped. Then he turned suddenly, and looked back in her direction. She froze. But, fortunately, he didn't spot her.

She continued to watch as he put his ear to Theo's door and quietly knocked. Was he back then? They both waited. No response. He then slowly turned the handle, opened the door, and entered.

She trod carefully along the floorboards, flattened herself against the wall near Theo's room, and listened. She could hear drawers being opened and closed. What was he hoping to find? If she stayed any longer, he'd see her when he came out. So she turned and stole back towards the staircase.

Once down on the first floor, she glanced at the alcove opposite Llewellyn's door. On a chair lay an open book. She picked it up and looked at it. Poetry, of course. The title of the poem was *Writing in the Dark.*

She saw he'd underlined certain phrases in black ink:

Wait till morning, and you'll forget.

And who knows if morning will come.

Was this how Llewellyn felt about being here? What did *morning* mean to him? Waking up and finding himself in the outside world? She read on. Again, she found words underlined:

Fumble for the light, and you'll be
Stark awake, but the vision
Will be fading, slipping
Out of reach.

As she finished reading, Llewellyn's door opened. She swung round to see the Welshman standing there looking, as ever, wide-eyed and eager. "Sorry, Llewellyn," she said. "I was glancing at your book."

"You're welcome. Would you like to know why that particular poem has special meaning for me?"

"Well, yes."

He gestured to the book. "Just imagine fumbling for the light and throwing yourself into a glaring wakefulness."

"Uh-huh," she said cautiously.

And now his puppyish manner was evaporating, taking on a darker quality. "That's how I see myself, as I would be if I returned to the outside world."

"That would be good, wouldn't it?" she said, surprised, but intrigued.

"No, it wouldn't. But let me explain. OK, I realise we're all sleepers here." He let his glance rest thoughtfully upon her. "And I prefer the dream world to the real one."

"You could never expect it to last, though," she said.

"But I do," he declared, "because here, I need explain nothing."

She considered this, following through the steps of his logic. "That's not true, Llewellyn. Because I, for one, have plenty of questions."

He made a sudden movement. His wing of hair lifted from his forehead, and settled back again. "But not questions seeking facts which define you. I wear a mask most of the time. *What do you do?* is the question I hate most of all."

"Why?" she queried. "You're one of the lucky ones, Llewellyn. You can say *I'm a poet.*"

"That's no advantage," he retorted. "The world doesn't respect poets."

"Yes it does," she protested. "We love our poets. We flock to literary festivals to hear them perform. We read the latest offering by the Poet Laureate; and we enjoy poems on the underground."

He looked glum. "That's all true," he admitted, "and progress is being made, but still…"

"I respect poets," she said firmly, "Laureate status or not."

He reached out, closed his fingers over hers, and slid the book and the microphone from her hands.

"What…?" she began, disconcerted.

"Come into my room, Juliet. We can talk better there."

"And may I record what you say?"

"No."

She took a quick breath. What was she in for now? Not a poetry recital, surely, for he'd certainly want that to go out over the air. Something more intimate, then, perhaps? A warning sounded somewhere in her head. Nevertheless, she followed him through the doorway.

He indicated a sheet of A4 paper stuck to the wall. Two lines had been written on it. "This is how I feel about being here," he said. "*Words may have the power to make the sun rise again*. I've remained faithful to the poet's calling," he went on. "And that's why it's important to me to *keep a record of the night*."

"But you feel you're among friends here," she said. "And you clearly don't want to leave. When you speak in these terms, you make it sound like you're unhappy."

He didn't directly answer, but instead paced the room for a while, then swivelled to face her. "Juliet, you know why I asked you in here, don't you?"

She had her suspicions, but she didn't like to voice them. Better cover up her doubts with a firm reply. "Yes," she said, "because I've shown some sympathy for the life of a poet."

At this, he pulled up a chair. "I'll take this. Come and sit on the bed."

Was this a good idea, in the circumstances? Probably not. But she obeyed him. He sat opposite. "So, Juliet, you've told me your thoughts about this community. You don't expect it to last."

She shook her head. "I was referring to the dream world you're living in," she said carefully, "not Craig's Centre."

Llewellyn's eyes narrowed. "How will it end?" he asked.

"Your dream world?" Juliet said. "You want me to predict that? Impossible. And I won't be around to see it. I've spent a week with you all. Yes, unbelievably, I first came here last Friday. So this is my last working day here. I have a full diary next week. I must be back in London on Monday."

"Ring up and cancel those appointments," he suggested. "Then stay on. Give yourself a holiday. Just stepping out of your official role might change your view of us – and me."

"I don't think so," she said.

"Oh I do," he responded brightly. "I'd love to see you break out."

"Break out from what?"

"From this stance of yours." He paused. "If you're here to please yourself, not whoever you hope to sell your documentary to, you'll be free. You won't need to hold back any more. You can join in fully."

She bit her lip. That was the last thing she wanted. It was not that she feared falling into Llewellyn's arms. No. It was because Craig hadn't opened up to her yet. And she hadn't yet asked him her most important questions. And many of those she had asked still remained unanswered. And she also needed to convince herself Zoe and Rory had both been deluded in their ideas about Craig's feelings for her.

Llewellyn held her in an intense scrutiny. "You do want to stay, don't you?" he said. "But you won't share your true reason with me." He rose to his feet. A knock came at the door. For a few seconds he refused to release her from his gaze. Would he ignore the interruption? But the knock was repeated.

"Juliet, Llewellyn. Are you in there?"

Don, Juliet thought.

"I want a word with you, Llewellyn," called the Yorkshireman. "And so does Craig."

The poet's eyes were still on her face. "I thought so, Juliet," he said quietly. And before going to open the door, he gripped both her wrists tightly. "Don't do it. It's all wrong. It won't work."

"Don't do what? What do you mean?" she asked, nervous and unsettled, shaking herself free of his hold on her.

At this, the door opened. Don's glance travelled from Llewellyn to Juliet and back again. Beside him stood Craig.

"I mean, it, Juliet. It would be disastrous," said the Welshman softly.

"Llewellyn," Juliet began, "you've got entirely the wrong…"

Craig took Juliet's arm and pulled her out of the room. Don gave Llewellyn a scorching look, and slammed the door in his face.

15

Pushing Back the Tide

From his position in front of the sitting room window, Llewellyn studiously ignored Don. Juliet could hardly fail to notice this as she entered the room. The Yorkshireman, for his part, having claimed an armchair in the corner by the gold grandfather clock, accepted a cup of coffee from Patrick with a grim look. She longed to step between them and break the impasse, but that wasn't possible as Theo had now rejoined the group and was on one of the flame-red sofas, commanding the attention of the whole room.

Seated beside Theo, Zoe clearly had no need of words to let everyone know of her joy at his return. Everyone could see that all she wanted was to be close to him again. Juliet disguised her sense of unease by drinking her coffee too fast and nearly scalding her lips.

"Sorry to arrive this late," said Theo. "So glad you saved me some dinner. I'd have hated to miss out on Rory's peach melba."

Rory, who'd been hovering near the door into the hallway, with an ambivalent expression on his face, and his fair hair recently blow-dried, turned pink, and gave a flurry of pleasure. What a change from yesterday. Juliet could hardly make it out. Then, he'd been seething with resentment against the young clergyman.

James, meanwhile, was stylishly arranged in an armchair opposite Theo. He adjusted one of his cufflinks and spoke. "We've been longing to know what happened at your meeting with the bishop, Theo," he said.

"Yes, what's the deal, Theo?" asked Al, who'd squeezed into the smaller sofa with Laura, his robust form straining against a cowboy checked shirt, again with most of its buttons undone.

Despite what Juliet imagined to have been an ordeal, on the outcome of which hung his future career, Theo's manner was easy-going. Smiling, he stirred sugar into his coffee. "When I arrived," he said, "the bishop had a car waiting. He told me we were expected at Lambeth Palace in twenty minutes."

Juliet surveyed Laura, knowing her mercurial views on Theo. But Laura's face, at this point, gave nothing away, ensuring her feelings remained a mystery to Juliet.

"What did the Archbishop say when you got there, Theo?" Laura asked.

Theo continued in a soft tone of voice. "He told me he liked my book. Kind enough to mention he enjoyed the way I *weave unorthodox strands* into my thinking."

The group of listeners visibly relaxed. Smiles of relief broke out on most faces, and laughter rippled through the room.

"And that means…?" prompted Rory.

"That I'm subversive. *Open-ended in style.* That was how he put it."

"How exciting! What happened next?" asked Laura.

"He asked me to sign his copy."

A cheer arose. Theo quietened them all with a raised hand. "Nevertheless, my bishop still thinks I want watching."

"But why, Theo?" asked Zoe. "What was it in your book that so upset him?"

Theo gave a wry smile. "He misunderstood me. And still does. Claims I deny God. Thinks I challenge His sovereignty. But I don't. I probe behind laws of nature, and ask why things should be. I believe God's big enough to cope with my questions. The bishop doesn't."

Zoe fell silent, apparently awestruck.

"Was that why you were away two days?" asked Juliet. "You and the bishop must have had a long discussion."

"You could put it like that, Juliet," said Theo. "The bishop suggested I attend a theological refresher course. He recommended one in Nottingham, which starts in three months' time."

"Will you go on it?" Zoe turned anxious eyes upon him.

"Not sure yet," said Theo. "For the present, therefore, I'm in No Man's Land."

"Good description of this set-up," muttered Don, though everyone but Juliet ignored him.

Zoe, meanwhile, laid her hand on Theo's, winning a warm glance from him. "I'm so glad you're back, Theo."

Craig, who until now had been standing on the silk rug, watching and listening, stepped forward. "So you'll stay for the rest of the summer?"

"Possibly not," said Theo. "The Golden Chalice – who don't share the bishop's view of this either – rang a short while ago and invited me to lead a healing retreat in two weeks' time. An invitation I may accept."

Craig looked disappointed. "Unless we can tempt you to stay with us instead."

"Let's chat about it later," said Theo.

Juliet noticed that Patrick in particular withheld his congratulations. Knowing, as she did, his views on the contents of Theo's book, she was hardly surprised. Meanwhile, her eye kept being drawn back to Zoe and Theo. It was clear Theo returned Zoe's feelings totally. Every touch, every glance was reciprocated. Juliet's own emotions were a capricious mix she couldn't keep up with, flitting between wistfulness, panic and fear. How could she feel all this in the space of a few moments? she asked herself. And what exactly was she afraid of, anyway? She was unable to say.

She was almost grateful to be distracted by Craig, who had crossed the room to join her in the corner by the empty birdcage.

"This is good news for Theo," he remarked quietly.

"Of course." She struggled to regain her self-composure. It was important that she did – for she had other things on her mind beside Zoe, and questions for Craig to answer.

"And what of you, Juliet?" Craig asked. "May I persuade you to stay too?"

But she was determined not to be sidetracked. "Before we speak of that, Craig, can you clear up my confusion? Yesterday afternoon, I met Rory on a walk. He mentioned knowing *the truth* about you."

Craig laughed softly. "And did he then go on to reveal what that was?"

"No," Juliet admitted. "He threatened to beat Don up, so we got away from him quickly."

Craig shook his head. "I'll need another chat with Rory."

"What's the matter with him, Craig?" asked Juliet. "Why does he behave like this?"

Craig wore a strained expression she'd not seen on his face before. His disquiet seemed genuine. "Juliet, I know you're mystified. Let's say he has difficulties: serious ones. I am trying to help him. But he's not always responsible for his actions."

She swallowed, several times. "But, Craig…"

"Soon, I'll explain. But not now. Just remember. You don't want to take anything Rory says too seriously."

"Including claims to know the truth about you? Don said he had suspicions, but wouldn't name them. Rory said he'd name them, but Don forbade him."

Craig looked at her appraisingly. "Rory *knows* nothing. But certainly I can tell you, if you're interested, that he has a crush on me."

She nodded. "I thought that was part of it."

"And did you suspect anything else, Juliet?"

As Craig said this, she noticed Llewellyn, keeping them both in his line of vision. She wished the Welshman would stop playing this game, especially as she felt powerless to take action.

She turned back to Craig. "Do you encourage Rory at all?" she asked.

"Of course not," he replied in a sleek tone of voice.

She didn't know whether to believe him or not. Llewellyn still watched them. So did Don, from the other side of the room.

"When I came across to speak to you, Juliet, I didn't plan to discuss Rory," said Craig.

"No I don't suppose you did."

"I was concerned," he said, "about our last little chat together just before dinner on Wednesday, in the library."

She called that conversation to mind. "Yes. You said you were *desperate.* Did you mean, desperate to make the Wheel of Love work?"

There was a pause. "Let me explain something to you, Juliet," began Craig. "After we parted I was afraid I may have left you with a misleading impression."

"Which was…?" she prompted him.

"That I don't fully realise the material advantages to me of yielding to my father's pressure."

"Don's bribe, you mean? To set you up in another property, fully owned and managed by his company?"

"Yes," he replied, watching her closely.

"I do believe that you fully understand the value of what you're turning down," she replied. "And I must say that my sympathies swing from you to your father and back again in a most unnerving way. But the fact is, I am trying to see the deadlock between you from both sides."

"You have to support one or other of us," Craig said.

"Oh?" She felt seriously alarmed by this.

"It's very important," Craig went on. "Something lies beyond all this. Something much more important – to me anyway," he added in a low voice.

She looked at him intently. Was this her opportunity? She took it. "Craig," she ventured, "do you have any strong regrets about the past? Is there anybody in your life who once desperately needed your forgiveness?" Their eyes held for what seemed like several moments. She thought he was going to open up, confide in her, tell her everything…

And then it was as if he slammed that door in her face. "I'm not interested in discussing the past," he said. Immediately he went on. "Now, Juliet, I want an answer from you. What do you say to my earlier question, about whether I may persuade you to stay? What are your plans for the future?"

"The f-future?" she stammered. Strangely, this last question disorientated her. She began again. "My plans? You already know those, Craig. And they haven't changed. I intend to return to London on Sunday, plus enough interviews for a documentary. And I very much hope to take Zoe with me."

Craig's face darkened. "No chance of..." he began. At that moment, Patrick approached them with the cafetiere. "More coffee, Juliet? Craig?"

Juliet was glad of the interruption. She suspected she knew well what Craig had been about to say. He wanted to keep Zoe here, and draw her into the Wheel of Love at the same time, didn't he? And she was having none of it.

Stepping out of the front door the next morning in her waterproof, Juliet confirmed that midsummer had apparently retreated. A dreary pall covered the sky, and now a drizzling rain had added itself to the close atmosphere she'd noted last night, especially when Craig had tried to get her to commit to joining his group. She was really worried about him – and about herself.

And it was now Saturday. She must make a decision in the next couple of hours. A number of people expected her back in London next week.

Pulling her hood up, she crossed the forecourt, heading in a northerly direction. A damp organic odour hung in the air, of rotting woodchip or decomposing leaf litter. It seemed to harmonise with how she felt: despondent. What should she do about Zoe? And Craig? She unlatched the gate and saw Theo approaching from the opposite end of the orchard. She greeted him, but his sole reply was a warning glance, not directly at her but a little to her right, over her shoulder.

"What's up?" She was keen to make the most of this meeting; she wanted a word with him in private, out of Zoe's earshot.

Looking behind her, she realised Craig, in a waxed jacket which looked suitable for a deer shoot on a country house party weekend, was gaining on them.

"Ah! Glad to see you two," Craig said. "And Theo – I very much hope you'll stay with us until September." There was an urgency in his tone that hadn't been there when he'd broached this subject before, and Theo picked it up.

"Any special reason, Craig?" he asked.

"Yes," said Craig, "I need your moral backing. Some here no longer give me the support I've had in the past, and expected."

"And the suspects?" enquired Theo lightly. He pulled a wet apple from the well-laden branch of the nearest tree, showering himself in the process. Weighing it carefully in his hand, he came and stood before Craig. "OK, Craig, how can I be sure I'm thinking the same as you?"

"Try me," said Craig.

"Rory? Don?" queried Theo.

"They're two," returned Craig. He looked at Juliet. "Basically," he continued, "what my father longs to do is seize me, bind me hand and foot, and transport me back to Barnsley in his Black Mariah."

Theo broke into laughter. Juliet couldn't resist joining him; she found the image so comical.

Then Theo became serious again. He passed the apple to and fro, rolling it from one hand to the other, before another unexpected change of subject. "About four and a half years ago, alongside my work as a freelance broadcaster, I led a small charismatic group. Doesn't exist any more, unfortunately. But, during its short lifespan, several members developed the gift of prophecy. Words of knowledge, that sort of thing. And some would get a picture."

"An image that appears before the mind's eye?" asked Juliet.

"Exactly. And one has just appeared before mine."

"… which you're about to describe to us," remarked Craig.

"Yes." Theo polished the apple. "I have a picture of you, Craig, trying to push back the tide."

Craig's brow became shadowed. "You're likening me to the boy who put his finger in the hole of the dam, to stop the Netherlands from being flooded."

"Absolutely," Theo said. "But, remember, it's temporary. You'll need reinforcements and a long-term solution, or the water will overwhelm you."

Craig's expression became unreadable. But, to Juliet, Theo's picture made sense. Certainly, she'd noticed a slackening off among Craig's disciples in terms of behaviour, self-discipline, loyalty… If this was allowed to gather pace, Craig's influence could weaken and give way just as Theo had envisaged.

Theo was speaking again. "How long do you think you can hold out for?"

Juliet waited anxiously for Craig's response. It startled her.

"As long as you did, Theo, during your wilderness experience."

Theo became very still, hand out, palm upward, apple balanced there. The rain had stopped, and the breeze died down, as he looked searchingly at Craig. "Well, let's hope it doesn't take *you* that long, Craig, to come through, and out the other side. And meanwhile, let's concentrate on you rather than me. Remember, you cannot hope to address the problems of your followers until you find the courage to come clean with your father."

And with that, he was gone.

Juliet met up with Theo again later that evening in the dining room, in front of *The Lady and the Unicorn.* They were the first two to enter before dinner.

"Well done," she remarked, "for what you said to Craig earlier."

"Thanks," Theo responded. "My words may be totally ignored, of course."

She raised her eyebrows. "Surely not! He respects you."

Theo didn't reply.

"We're both very early tonight, aren't we?" she said, to break the silence.

"We are," he replied. "Let's take one day at a time, shall we? And gaze at this bewitched unicorn."

"You feel sorry for him?" she said, intrigued.

"Perhaps. For now he cannot resist the lady." He smiled.

She immediately related this remark to him and Zoe. She didn't feel like discussing his romance with her sister. Instead, she hastily cast about for a different subject. "I don't suppose it was this room where your colleague had dinner with the shepherd and his wife?" she asked suddenly.

"It was," Theo said.

"I imagine it was different then."

He nodded. "Very rough and ready, none of these rich furnishings."

"I expect they were sad to have to sell up," she observed.

"So I understand."

"Why did you ask Craig about a sculpture courtyard?"

"Oh, I remembered one of the ideas my colleague came up with, after his visit."

Before Juliet could question him further, the door opened and her sister came in. Theo turned at once, stepping forward to take Zoe's hand.

At dinner Juliet sensed a tightly coiled atmosphere, and not only that between Theo and Craig.

The Mediterranean pasta dish was delicious. Sam, who prepared it, turned out to have done an international cookery course with his brother a year ago. The wine flowed more freely than ever, as did the numerous dishes up and down the table, yet she couldn't escape a sensation that something rapacious was prowling among them, ready to spring. And she had a nasty feeling this came from Rory. Not that she could see him, on the other side of Beth, and that was the way she liked it. Even so, she sensed hostile intent emanating from that direction. Her fingers tingled too, and her stomach felt uneasy. There was going to be a crisis tonight, she felt sure of it: here in the dining room.

She'd positioned her microphone in the centre of the table, discreetly hidden by a vase of roses. If the wolf amongst them pounced, she'd record the event. Just so long as nobody got seriously hurt. And she couldn't be sure of that at all. Edgar, too, despite his Benedictine-like appearance, seemed to be stoking up for something: and that impression gained strength with every look she intercepted between him and Craig. Meanwhile, Beth, hair plaited tightly around her head, maintained an icy silence beside her; and immediately opposite, Oleg, gaunt and colourless, looked as if he'd developed a nervous tic to match Sam's. And for some reason this evening he'd chosen to wear a hooded track jacket and navy baseball cap to the dinner table.

Things were only partially right at the other end of the table, where Zoe sat between Theo and Llewellyn. Juliet watched her sister with the clergyman. Their tender glances and warm chatter recalled his comment to Juliet earlier about the unicorn. And as for Llewellyn, he kept up a straight-faced conversation with Patrick. Since the meal began, he'd totally ignored Juliet.

She could feel a current of unexpressed desires beneath the surface froth of the conversation. Every so often, looking across the table, she met Don's eyes, bemused and questioning. She was sure he too expected something to happen. She'd told him of the exchanges between Theo and Craig in the orchard that morning. Don's only question was: "When will the dam burst? Will it be tonight?"

Craig, nevertheless, had begun in gracious mood, appearing undaunted by the less than perfect ambiance among the diners. "So glad you all came promptly this evening."

As they filled their plates, James, in a midnight-blue brocade jacket, looking every inch a dapper thespian at a post-show reception, leaned across and poured her a glass of wine. The atmosphere lifted slightly. Suddenly, Edgar's voice rose above the general chatter. "We marked Theo's arrival with champagne, Craig. Why don't we celebrate his return?"

Craig smiled and said, "What a good idea."

James interjected before Craig could add anything else. "We've enough wine on the table to be going on with, don't you think?"

Craig looked at him in surprise. "Yes, I suppose so, James."

Juliet became alert. What was going on here? She glanced at Don. She noted the ironical gleam in his eye.

He looked at Juliet's glass, saw it was still nearly full, and held out his own for James to recharge. "Thanks, James. Generous of you. Pity about the champagne. But we must make economies."

"Naturally," said James with barely moving lips.

Over to you, Don, thought Juliet.

But Don forbore to reply. Instead, Al broke in with what appeared to be a complete change of subject. "What say you cancel Dynamic Meditation tonight, Craig?"

Juliet leaned forward to look at him, further down her side of the table.

"Why?" Craig lifted his voice. "I expect everyone there tonight at nine: without exception."

This won disconcerted stares from every diner whose face Juliet could see. They appeared stung by the uncharacteristic belligerence of his tone. Al shrugged. Then he returned his attention to Laura.

Everything about Laura tonight said waif, elfin, gamine – perhaps because she appeared even more petite in proportion to the amount of space her hair took up. This evening her hairstyle was full-bodied with lots of volume. Clearly the new look won Al's admiration. He gazed at her ardently.

Craig pushed his chair back and stood up. Did he plan to make a speech? Maybe he'd found an excuse to bring out the champagne. "I'll leave you now," he said instead. "I have something important to attend to. I expect you all in the barn promptly at nine o'clock for Dynamic Meditation." And, with that, he disappeared. His departure was followed by a rising murmur of bafflement.

What was that all about? Juliet wondered.

"It's a disgrace," muttered Patrick.

"What is?" asked Juliet.

"This group," said the Irishman. "The Wheel of Blighted Love. Where's the love? Distinctly lacking. Instead our spokes are getting choked up with satanic dross." Patrick crossed himself. "I've long suspected his teachings had the devil in them."

A chorus of objections arose from the others. Juliet watched Patrick. Was this what Craig had been referring to when he spoke to her and Theo earlier about needing Theo's moral backing?

Laura raised her voice. "I disagree, Patrick. There's nothing wrong with Craig. He's turned my life around."

"Good for you," said Oleg. "I'm still stuck in a ditch somewhere along the slip road." He banged his wine glass down. "I should be chucked onto a dung heap. Can anyone here give me a reason why not?"

"Yes," thundered James unexpectedly. "What Craig teaches, works. That's why not. Pull yourself together, man." His face was highly flushed. Juliet wondered how much he'd drunk. Perhaps that was why he didn't want the champagne brought out: he didn't have confidence in his ability to do it justice. "Let's put it to the vote," James continued. "Who'll be first to say openly, what they have, if anything, against Craig?"

Up and down the table, the group formed a freeze-frame, heads turned to James.

Juliet's gaze swept around. She felt a strong sense of foreboding. Who'd be first to respond? James had inspired Craig to set this place up, after all.

James clicked his tongue against his teeth. "Come on. Your true thoughts. We can be honest here. Who'll kick off? Edgar?"

Edgar sprang into life, moustache trembling. "Makes no odds to me what he teaches, so long as it's completely far-fetched. All the better for my research project."

A low, grumbling sound followed this comment.

"But," went on Edgar, "I must say I don't accept that *if we're in tune with ourselves we'll always be in the right place at the right time.* What about innocent victims?" He wiped his mouth with his napkin, and lifted his wine glass to his lips with an air of self-satisfaction.

"Good man." Don popped the last piece of bread in his mouth. "Bugs me, too."

Then Rory blurted, "But who's innocent?"

A sharp silence cut in. Juliet felt her spine prickling.

Llewellyn spread his hands. "Fair point, Rory. Who *is* innocent?"

"Hear, hear," cried Patrick. "Nobody. That's the answer. I put it all down to original sin."

Incredibly, Rory remained silent. Was he refusing to rise to Patrick's bait? Or was he just biding his time?

Al laid his cutlery neatly on his plate. "Don't you think you guys are being a little uptight about this? When I first came here, I thought this country was a peach. Gentleness, mild air, muted light. Back in the States, I visualised peaceful lakes, rolling hills and dreaming spires." He now wore an expression of injured longing.

"You make it sound like heaven," said Juliet. "But surely everywhere we live, it's only the quality of our relationships that matters."

"Well said, Juliet." Theo had spoken from the opposite corner of the table. Zoe's concentration remained solely on him.

"I'd already figured that," responded Al. "I signed on for the whole thing. The place, the people. You Brits… subtlety and irony. I'd heard about that. But right now, it doesn't seem to be working."

"So we're not allowed to say what we think?" Rory slammed his hand down on the table. Everyone jumped, and looked at him nervously. "I've been restraining myself ever since I arrived." Rory's voice quivered with barely-controlled loathing.

"News to me," murmured James.

There was a barely audible intake of breath round the table at this. Very dodgy, thought Juliet. James was goading the wolf with a stick. Beth had slumped back in her chair, and Juliet could see Rory shaking. She felt a sense of dread.

Rory shot a toxic glance at James. "Not one of you here stands innocent of callous, cynical self-regard."

There was a chorus of dismay and protest.

"How can you say that?"

"That's not true."

"I don't recognise myself from that description. Although," added James smugly, "I'd be the first to admit I'm no angel."

Rory's mocking laugh unnerved Juliet.

"I'm sure no one else would claim to be angelic, either," smiled James.

"Demonic, more like." Rory's eyes glittered, and he rose unexpectedly from his chair. "Satan would love the way he's managed to slither into the hearts of the members of this community."

"I take exception to that," shouted Patrick, also leaping to his feet, oblivious to the danger he was in. "I'm the only one here with the right spiritual safeguards to handle using that name at this table."

Amidst the ensuing uproar, Juliet looked for someone to restore calm. In Craig's absence, she held James responsible. He was second-in-command, wasn't he? Or had she got that wrong? Theo, then? But she failed to make eye contact. Don, perhaps? If not him, then perhaps she should say something. "Come on, Rory," she urged. "Sit down again. Please."

Astonishingly, he did so.

"I don't think anyone here is callous or cynical," Juliet said gently. "I wouldn't use such words for anyone I've spoken to."

"What words would you use, then?" Rory demanded.

Juliet hesitated. Was it wise to express her true opinion, or not? Rory would probably see through her if she lied. "The words I'd prefer, Rory, are *insecure*, perhaps. Or *vulnerable*." The group fell silent, but a menacing undercurrent prevailed. "I think you've all come here for protection," Juliet continued. "Protection from the world. In this community, you exist in a glass bubble. It's very structured, on the fringes of life, but it's not reality."

Rory leaned forward, and grasped the water jug. Her heart missed a beat. He was going to throw it at her. But he didn't. Instead he refilled his glass, and put the jug back on the table.

"Not that I think there's anything wrong with that," she went on desperately, playing for time. "It's just that at some stage you'll all need to return to the outside world, to put what you've learned to the test."

"The outside w-w-world?" repeated Sam blankly.

"Juliet's point," Zoe suggested, "is that this is a game we're all playing."

Juliet's eyes widened. Had Zoe herself at last come to recognise the Wheel of Love for what it was – a make-believe world? But, with the use of the word *game*, she sensed an immediate rise in tension again.

"A game?" repeated Rory.

"I only meant to say…" Zoe raised her palms in a dismissive gesture.

"What about me?" Rory snapped. "Do you see me as a player on that board? Moving at the throw of a dice?"

"No, Rory…" Zoe didn't get the chance to finish.

Rory shot up from his chair once more, and this time began to prowl past the terrified diners, heading first to Zoe and Theo's end of the table. "You all know my background," he said. "The past Craig teaches us to forget. I came this close…" he held up thumb and forefinger two centimetres apart, "to never being here at all. Upon first learning of my existence, my mother tried to abort me. As you can all see, she failed. Shortly after my birth, she abandoned me and my sister. Her parents took us on. They brought us up. If you can call it that."

The other diners formed a silent tableau, listening fearfully to his potted life history.

Theo was first to respond. "Bitterness won't help, Rory. Can't you forgive your mother?"

"No. She's dead."

"You can still forgive her," said Theo. "How about your sister? How does she feel?"

Rory spun back to face the clergyman. "My sister is in a Buddhist retreat house and has detached herself from suffering."

"All right then, Rory," persisted Theo, "so why do *you* feel like this?"

"Because my mother rejected me," cried Rory.

"Perhaps not. Perhaps, rather, she was rejecting something in herself," said Theo. "Forgive her now, my friend."

"Then you'll reach closure," muttered Al, "and the rest of us will get some peace."

"No!" Rory's shout nearly flattened the startled American against the back of his chair. Juliet held her breath.

Al had twisted round, to keep the volatile Rory well in sight. As he did so, Rory stepped back, and cracked his head against a wrought-iron lantern hanging from the ceiling. Juliet flinched. That would do it. Now Rory's rage would boil over.

Al spoke in sympathetic tones. "Gee, you all right?"

Rory rubbed his head, and his next words emerged in a wail. "I came here to set myself straight. Yet my life's a cesspit."

Juliet bit her lip. Rory was being a bit melodramatic, and more than a little self-indulgent. She also knew no one trusted him. She certainly didn't. She still vividly remembered the feel of his hands around her neck, and his body pressing her into the floor… She watched closely. When and who would Rory attack?

Rory addressed everyone. "I came here," he said, "because I believed it would be life-enhancing. Instead, I'm frustrated, powerless and stuck."

"How can that be?" asked Laura. "I don't see it in that way at all. I feel perfectly restored, as if I've looked down the years and seen myself."

"We're very happy for you, Laura," Edgar said. Al put an arm around her shoulders. "For you, all is as it should be. But Rory, it seems, is about to give up on us."

"A consummation devoutly to be wished," muttered James.

Juliet watched Rory, still stationed behind Al, focusing on Laura's face.

Theo hastily put in a suggestion. "We're all unique. Each one of us reacts differently to the same situation."

"But we're not all in the same situation," said Laura. "That depends upon our state of mind when we first come here, of course."

"And what state of mind do you believe I was in when I arrived?" Rory shouted.

"I don't know," she twittered, seeming to perceive at last how perilous her situation was. She edged closer to Al on her right, as if he might afford her some protection. Then she persisted with the point she was making. "Speaking for myself, I've become a new woman since I joined this group."

Before anybody could comment, Theo stood up, and moved round behind Edgar, to join Rory. "Listen, Rory; despite what anybody else may say, you can still come through this."

"On whose terms?" asked Rory sharply.

"Nobody's but your own," said Theo.

Rory considered this. Theo held his gaze. No one else dared speak. But Juliet sensed the fight going out of Rory. Theo placed his hand on Rory's arm. As he did so, Rory's ferocity evaporated, and he visibly relaxed. Then Theo swept his free hand out, in a gesture that encompassed the whole group. "We cannot depend upon others for our happiness. That comes from self-worth, and it's a journey we can only take alone."

He moved away from Rory, and both men took their seats again in absolute silence. Juliet felt relief, but a sense of restlessness still hung in the air. And a question persisted in her mind: could Rory really come through this *on his own terms?* She strongly suspected what those terms were, in regard to Craig; and she didn't believe they'd ever be met. Was this the reason why Rory claimed he'd achieved so little peace in the time he'd been here? Craig, who perhaps held the key to the mystery, had conveniently slipped away.

Nobody disputed Theo's summing up. Juliet wondered if Don would comment, but it appeared that even he had nothing to add. A few seconds passed, and then Oleg rose from his seat and slunk round behind Don's back and Craig's empty place. He headed past *The Lady and the Unicorn*, navy cap pulled down over his eyes, hands thrust into the pockets of his combat pants. Clearly, he was aiming for the door, and had no intention of waiting for Sam's dessert. Juliet doubted whether anybody else would have an appetite for it either, after tonight's events. She looked around, baffled, for Theo; he, too, had disappeared from the scene. Zoe was gazing distractedly at the open door.

Then Llewellyn spoke in ringing tones, making them all jump. "Don't forget Dynamic Meditation this evening, whatever you do.

It's vitally important that every one of you attends."

"Why are you telling us this?" demanded James.

"Because, in view of what Rory has said at this table, I have a very important announcement to make."

"Does Craig know about it?" James asked.

"No," said Llewellyn. "And I forbid any of you to mention it, either. It must come as a complete shock to him."

16

A Bear in the House

The hayloft with its timbered gallery had seemed at first to be a good vantage point for Juliet to stand and record the group members in Dynamic Meditation. She'd been even more pleased when Llewellyn positioned himself right next to her, full on mike, in order to make his pronouncement.

Down below, Craig strode across the width of the barn, from east staircase to west and back again, goading the group members into pushing themselves even harder. Some interpreted this as a signal to race across the meeting space, up the west staircase, along the gallery, and down the east, as if in training for a marathon.

Perhaps this would succeed in burning away all the negative emotions of the last few days, she reasoned to herself: self-doubt, jealousy, distrust, mutterings of mutiny, frustrated sexual longings…

But something important was lacking; the wholehearted dedication and fervour she'd sensed the first time she'd attended Dynamic Meditation. Some, she suspected, were merely going through the motions of obeying Craig. Theo did not participate. He stood beside the long oak table set against the west wall of the barn, watching thoughtfully. She wondered what was in his mind. Don, she noted, was also sitting this one out. She glimpsed him in the shadows at the far end of the barn.

Meanwhile, she speculated about how much longer the beautifully crafted staircases would withstand the pounding of the group members' feet, as they thundered up one spiral, streamed across the gallery, and down the other at the far end.

Then Llewellyn spoke out. "I'm here to announce the end of this madness," he declared, raising his hands in the air like a priest bestowing a blessing. "The Wheel of Love needs to change direction. With me in the driving seat, we'll take a different route. Tomorrow night, you'll see the old order destroyed."

At this, the frantic activity of the group came to a halt. Everyone seemed set in a freeze-frame, staring at Llewellyn. Then they all seemed to break out into speech simultaneously. "What did he say?" "What does he mean?" "What's he on about?"

Juliet looked at Craig for his reaction. So, too, did the group members, each arrested in a different pose.

"Llewellyn," said Craig in an authoritative tone of voice. "Come down here."

The poet remained where he was. Shocked whisperings broke out at this defiance. Beth bit her nails; Al stood hands on hips, sweat dripping down his face, his jaw hanging low. Sam started to shake. Theo's face was in shadows, and Juliet couldn't gauge his response. She felt a rising sense of panic. How was Craig going to deal with this? Surely he could not possibly lose a battle of wills? This behaviour seemed so uncharacteristic of Llewellyn, too. She could barely believe this was happening.

"Enough, Llewellyn," said Craig again, in a level tone of voice, but with icy control. "Come down here. Do as I say. You have some explaining to do."

All waited. Not a sound could be heard in the lofty space of the barn. After what seemed like several agonising seconds, Llewellyn moved, and went slowly down the eastern spiral to join Craig. The two men walked out of the main doorway together. What happened between them after that, Juliet had no idea. Everyone else stood around, robbed of energy, conversing in low, scared tones, until after about ten minutes, with no reappearance by Craig or Llewellyn, they began to drift away in twos and threes.

Juliet didn't even have the chance to speak to Zoe or Theo, as they left together before she could ask for their reactions. She too walked out of the doorway with her recording equipment. Everyone seemed to have disappeared. There was nothing for it but to go back to her room.

And so the evening ended.

Early the next morning, she leaned her elbows on the balustrade and looked down into the tranquil meeting room, marvelling at the beauty of her surroundings. The artistry of the timber construction and the graceful proportions of the space delighted her, as did the house and outbuildings, not to mention the gardens, orchard and valley in which these were all set. And yet this perfection and charm was marred by the growing anarchy within its boundaries.

She sank her chin in her hands. Today was Sunday, and it was to be her last day at the community; she was due to pack her bags and leave after lunch. But how could she go? Llewellyn had promised something disruptive this evening. Last night he'd declared that they'd all see *the old order destroyed.* He'd challenged Craig's authority. The Wheel of Love was in a dire state. Surely she needed to see what happened tonight, and record it. And yet…

Heavy-hearted, she moved along the gallery, down the eastern spiral, and out through the great central doorway of the tithe barn. She found the atmosphere even milder and warmer, if possible, than when she'd entered the building forty minutes ago. She glanced up to a fair, bright sky. Then she looked across the car park. Was that where Theo's colleague had envisaged a sculpture courtyard? It would be quite good….

As ever, she carried her recording equipment, slung over her shoulder in a carrying case. Just then she heard sounds of movement behind her. Turning, she saw Edgar approaching from the south east corner of the barn. Immediately she switched on her microphone and went to meet him.

His face was flushed and his eyes strangely bright.

"Hi, Edgar," she said. "What's up?"

He stopped short at sight of her. She held the mike out.

"Have you voted, Juliet?" he asked.

"Voted? What for?"

For a second, he remained still. Then he raised his hand, tapped his finger against his head, and hurried past her in the direction of the farmhouse, soon disappearing from view.

She frowned. What was that all about? She turned and saw a flash of movement ahead. She felt the familiar thump of her heart. Craig was jogging along the path towards her. She must get his news. Had he managed to reassert authority over Llewellyn, or not?

He slowed down, waving in acknowledgement. This morning he wore an indigo tracksuit with another pair of designer trainers. She gazed at him. His breathing was not yet fully under control, and his hair ruffled with the exercise he'd had so far that morning. She felt furious with herself for failing to master her physical reaction each time she saw him; the racing pulse, the stirring in her stomach…

He must have had women falling into his arms for years. But did he prefer men? Or was the truth even more complex than that? She still had much to quiz him about. Now was her chance. The mike was still on, and she held it up. "Good morning, Craig."

"Good morning, Juliet," he said. "Lovely day."

"Certainly is," she replied. "Did you find out what Llewellyn meant last night?"

He searched her face, then replied with another question. "Have they pulled you in on this vote?"

She felt bewildered. "Edgar mentioned something about a vote but it's a mystery to me."

He looked at her strangely, then completely changed the subject. "Pleased with the interviews you've collected, Juliet?"

"Come on Craig, why are you being so distant with me?" she burst out. "You know there are things I want to know about you, questions you haven't answered."

He gazed at her. Moments passed. Was he going to change appearance, to evade the need to supply an answer?

"Ask, Juliet," he said. "Feel free."

"I asked you about your experience of guilt. About whether

you've ever struggled to forgive. And you refused to respond."

"Yes. That is an area I do refuse to talk about. Sorry Juliet."

"And I'm sorry, too."

"Planning to leave us later on, aren't you?" he said.

She felt a rising sense of despair. How could he be so cold?

"Yes," she said quietly."I hope…" Craig began, then stopped. She decided to come back for a second attempt. "Craig, I must ask you something else."

His expression was guarded. "Of course," he said in a cool tone of voice.

But the question she asked wasn't the one she'd intended to pose. "Do you love your father?" she asked.

Several moments passed. He focused on her all this while, his eyes darkening. "I won't answer that question," he said. Then he reached out and switched the mike off.

She nearly cursed under her breath. "Craig, you still feel bad about the past, don't you? And let it affect your relationships, despite what you tell your followers."

"Tell me something, Juliet," he said. "Do you believe I'm qualified to be a spiritual teacher?"

This question disconcerted her. She felt like saying, "No." But instead… "Qualified? How can I judge? And surely it doesn't matter what I think."

"You're quite wrong there. It does," he said, "very much."

She looked at him, anxious excitement prickling beneath her skin.

"But," Craig continued, "I fear you've shared more of that with my father than you have with me."

"And you're surprised?" she cried. "When every time I try to move beyond a certain level with you, you shut down the barriers?"

"And why do you think I do that?" he shot back.

She was taken aback by the edge of bitterness in his voice. "Come on, Craig," she burst out.

His eyes burned into her. "You speak of my father. He wants me to sell up. You know that, of course. In more ways than one."

"Surely…" she began again.

He regarded her, his expression blending invitation and challenge. "First, the property. Who do you think he wants me to sell it to?"

She gave way to the temptation to be flippant. "The devil, perhaps? Or a business management consortium?"

"No. His company. McAllister Bloody Developments. Hell will freeze over first."

"Really, Craig." She lost her patience. "What's so bad about his company owning it? Get real. Surely that's better than losing it entirely."

His eyes narrowed. She hoped he wasn't going to perform his appearance-changing trick again. "Juliet, I've spoken to you before about…"

"…about not getting involved with things that are no concern of mine? Too late. You've involved me. That's the way it is."

He held her in his sights for several seconds. During this time, she found it impossible to gauge his emotions. For one moment, she was convinced he meant to grasp hold of her, crush her to him, and kiss her. But instead, with one swift movement, he was past her. She swung round. Before she could form another word, he strode out of sight.

A little later back in her room, she began reluctantly to pack her bag in preparation for her return to London. And what of Zoe? Would she agree to come with her? Seemed very unlikely. Oh God. This was a mess.

Then her mobile buzzed. Toby. She hadn't been in touch for days. He'd want a progress report, of course. What would she say to him? She was so keen to sell her documentary to him. It would be her big break. But she needed more time. What for, she hardly dared admit to herself.

The mobile kept buzzing, insistent as a trapped wasp. She pressed receive. "Hello."

"Juliet, how's it going?"

"Fine, Toby. Couldn't be better."

"Delighted to hear it. I was beginning to wonder whether your abandoned mobile was ringing out into the charred remains of a torched farmhouse."

"No such drama."

"Will I see you in my office next week? With a mass of great material?"

"Toby, I need to talk to you about that…"

"Not enough interviews? You need more time?"

"Toby, you're a mind-reader. There are still questions I need to ask. I know you wanted to see it next week to decide whether it'll be right for that slot. But … can we make it the following week instead?"

Two or three moments passed. Then Toby said, "You know, something struck me just before I called you. And it wasn't that lump of plaster that fell from the ceiling as I walked into the office."

"Glad to hear it." She breathed more easily. It sounded like he might be lenient about her request.

He broke into her thoughts. "You know what you're up for?"

"Yes."

"Who's your main sticking point?" She took a deep breath. "Your sister?" he asked before she could reply. She felt she'd been handed a perfect opportunity to throw him off the scent. She was about to speak when again he got there first. "In trouble, is she?"

"Kind of. She's in love with Theo. Remember him? Clergyman, ex-broadcaster? I mentioned him to you."

"Ah. Theo Lucas. I was astonished to hear that he had resurfaced. I wish he'd got back in touch with us. I have vivid memories of him."

"You do?" She wasn't sure he'd prove a better topic of conversation than her own emotional involvements here. But it was probably best to play along.

"Yes," said Toby. "He freelanced with us, flew off to Jerusalem, trespassed in the Garden of Gethsemane and nearly got gunned down. That wasn't the original plan."

She became more animated at Toby's mention of this incident. "He told me about that. He scaled the fence, and recorded his thoughts."

"That's right."

"And what were those recordings like?"

"Compelling. Among the best video diaries we've ever received from anybody. He worked with us for a couple of years, and then he just vanished." Toby paused. "So he's back in circulation. And Zoe has fallen for him, has she?"

"Yes," said Juliet. "But I'm hoping he'll be scared off before they reach the point of no return." The idea of her sister as a vicar's wife was the stuff of nightmare.

"Why, what have you got against him?"

"Theo? Nothing. Nothing at all…" Her voice trailed away. In fact, the very thought of Theo and Zoe together twisted her up inside. "That's not the issue. They can do what they like."

"Quite right, Juliet. Leave it to them to decide. Back to your own situation, then."

"My *situation*?"

"Yes," said Toby. "It's plain you've got a special reason for wanting to stay on."

"Just need to sort unfinished business, that's all." She wouldn't allow herself to say more. Fortunately she didn't need to for he changed the subject.

"This material had better be brilliant."

Relief flooded her. "It will be," she laughed.

"What you do next week is up to you, of course, Juliet. But take care. That's my advice."

"Yes, Toby. Understood. Over and out." The call ended.

She took several deep breaths. She'd managed it. She still had a few more phone calls to make, to postpone other appointments. But she'd made her mind up. She was staying another week. Better go and tell Zoe, and Don. And Craig.

Llewellyn looked up as Juliet passed through the sitting room, Nagra slung over her shoulder, microphone in hand, in search of her sister. He was alone, apart from Groucho the parrot, and relaxing in an armchair with a cup of tea, studying a flyer. His eyes glowed at sight of her. He seemed to have forgotten about that incident at his bedroom door.

She turned her mike on and held it up.

"Did you get a voting slip, Juliet?" Llewellyn asked.

"Voting slip?" she said. "What voting slip?" She stared at him, challenging him with her eyes.

"Ah. Sorry, must have missed you out. Before I go on, one question. This is your last day with us. Am I right?"

"In fact no," she said.

He jumped up, nearly knocking the mike to the floor, and gave her a big hug. She fell back, startled, and checked the mike was still OK and set to record.

"Great," declared Llewellyn. "How long will you stay?"

"Probably another week. I'll cancel my appointments."

"Excellent."

"So what's this about a voting slip?" she asked.

"I put one under every door last night," the Welshman said. "Collected them up this morning."

"Oh, Llewellyn, I cannot believe this…"

"You'd better."

She sighed. "Shame you missed me out."

"No problem. I have a spare. I'll go to my room to get it."

"Don't bother," she said. "I can guess the choice. My answer's *Craig*. But what's the point of all this, Llewellyn? What do you hope to achieve?"

For reply, he showed her the flyer. Garishly coloured and presented in a variety of fonts, it announced:

Poetry as Therapy.

Speaker: Llewellyn Hughes.

(Right of admission reserved)

The date on the flyer, she noticed, was the following Saturday. The place, a central venue in Cirencester. As she took all this in, her attention was disrupted by the sound of Groucho shredding a new apple-tree branch in his cage.

"But you can't just take over, Llewellyn."

"Yes I can," he insisted, "if it saves the community."

"Is it up to you to save it?"Juliet asked.

He didn't reply. She noticed he'd unhooked one of Craig's stringed instruments from the wall, and had placed it beside him on the cushion. He now started toying with it.

"What's that?" she asked.

"A balalaika. Craig brought this back with him from Russia." He stroked the strings. "Groucho likes to listen. He'll be out in a minute, once he's finished stripping that branch. Want a go?"

"No thanks," she said, then began again. "Llewellyn, you do respect Craig don't you?"

Groucho began loudly cracking nuts. Llewellyn looked cryptic, and Groucho noisily shook his plumage. The Welshman laid the balalaika down on the sofa beside him. "Come and sit beside me, Juliet."

She did as he asked, mike still in hand, and on record. He studied her for a few moments. Was his mind wandering again, straying into areas best left untouched? Was he about to ask her to turn the mike off? "We were speaking of Craig," she reminded him.

"Yes," said the poet. "Craig's trouble is his father. Not long ago, I suggested Don try and look for what binds him and Craig together, rather than what tears them apart."

"Very wise," she said.

"And the same goes for you and your sister," he remarked.

"Me and Zoe?" She sat up abruptly. "Nothing tears *us* apart – other than Zoe's tendency to fall for the wrong man."

Groucho took off from his branch, and landed on the layer of sharp sand at the bottom of his cage. He began to strut around.

Then Llewellyn said, "Who makes the decision about the right and the wrong man? You, Juliet? Here's my advice: don't. Zoe and Theo are so keen on each other. I know of course that Theo still has much to sort out in his own life."

"As does she," snapped Juliet. "*And* you, Llewellyn, so don't try and distract me."

He threw her a quizzical glance. Then he reached for the balalaika again. "Let me play you some music." He began to pluck at the strings. Groucho made a low soft purring sound.

"Are you serenading me, Llewellyn?" she asked.

He laughed. "Well, I certainly have your full attention."

"And Groucho's."

"Oh yes. He loves music." The Welshman continued to play. "*Follow your instincts,* Juliet. *That's where true wisdom manifests itself.* That's what I'm doing."

"I don't think you are, Llewellyn," she insisted, "I think you're following an impulse that comes from somewhere else. And it's not the right one either."

Llewellyn stopped playing. Groucho hopped out of his cage and onto his perch. The poet got up, and went to stroke the macaw's feathers. Then he turned again. "May I show you a book, Juliet?"

"Of course," she said.

"One of my favourites." He picked the volume up from the armchair he'd been sitting in.

"Is that from Craig's library?" Juliet asked.

"No. My own," said Llewellyn.

"A Welsh poet?"

"You guessed. Listen to this." And he began to read:

The white waves of the breath of peace
On the mountains,
And the light striding
In the distances of the sea.

He kept the book open, and looked at her. She could hear Groucho shuffling on his perch. Was it safe to return Llewellyn's gaze? Or would he believe he'd succeeded in tempting her beyond her professional boundaries again? Not for the first time, she noticed the intelligent, appraising quality in his eyes. Yet the folly of what he was doing seemed to give the lie to that.

"Beautiful," she said. "And of course there's not much peace in this community, but you're unlikely to change that."

"I disagree, Juliet. Just consider the scene at dinner last night. Al knows all about bears that come into houses, in the foothills of western Massachusetts. Last night, a bear came into this house."

"And rampaged round the dining room, in the guise of Rory," she said. "But I still don't see how you're going to improve things."

With a soft laugh, he picked up the balalaika and began to brush his fingers across the strings once more. "Perhaps you'll feel more confident about it all if you join me in the barn later, at nine thirty."

"Why? Is Craig going to announce the results of the vote? And if it's you, what can we expect to happen next?"

"Ah. Something very new. I can't tell you the details now. But please do come, Juliet. You'll have a far clearer picture of what will be going on here from now. I'd love to know what you think."

Exasperation took hold. "You already know what I think, Llewellyn. The question is whether you'll give me any good reason to change my mind."

"Precisely," smiled the poet. "And perhaps you will change your mind when I tell you I first got the idea from Don."

The door burst open. Llewellyn turned. Craig stood framed in the doorway.

"Very dangerous, Llewellyn. I wouldn't advise that at all."

17

Pretender to the Throne

Lunchtime provided Juliet with her first opportunity to start Theo's book. She'd persuaded Patrick to pass it on to her rather than burn it. She was anxious to know what a dodgy book written by a clergyman might be like; especially one that had a conservative evangelical bishop breathing fire, but an archbishop asking for signed copies. Also she wanted to know what Don had said, to give Llewellyn his idea for takeover. Had he set him up for this? Was it all part of a devious plan to separate Craig from this community? She must confront him about it the very next time she saw him.

But meanwhile she concentrated on Theo's book. It was compulsive reading. *Synchronicity*, it was called: *Chance, Coincidence – or the Will of God?* She couldn't understand why the bishop had been so upset. There was a lot about Carl Jung, certainly, and the collective unconscious, and universal archetypes. But this was hardly heresy... Theo just questioned everything, like she did. But perhaps they didn't yet come to the same conclusions.

Despite this, she found his style racy and engaging, with lots of amusing anecdotes. Even with her prior ignorance on the subject, she loved the book. She hadn't expected to feel like that about it. Theo had produced a good read. Did this alter how she saw him? Yes, she supposed it did in some respects; but not enough, perhaps, to change how she felt about him adoring her sister.

Even so, she could hardly tear herself away from the book after lunch. Slipping a bookmark in, however, she set off for a walk with her Nagra. She needed to find someone to tell her about Llewellyn's plans, and how much of a threat they posed to Craig. She left the house, crossed the forecourt and on an impulse unlatched the gate into the vegetable garden.

The sight of all those precise boundaries and regimented vegetable plots, well tended by the group members according to their rota under the supervision of Patrick, would be exactly the thing to marshal her thoughts. Patrick maintained a strict regime here, she'd noticed, in sharp contrast to the emotional anarchy breaking out elsewhere in the community.

One hand on the strap of her Nagra, the other holding the mike, she set off past the runner beans, paying attention to the rhythm of her own footsteps. Somehow, the repetitive movement helped her to process the situation.

Passing the frames, she swung left and took the east-facing pathway. As she reached the south-eastern corner of the vegetable garden, and turned to face north, she saw Rory on his hands and knees weeding under the hedges. She stopped short. Her heart pounded. She and Rory were alone together. Should she turn and flee?

Juliet felt a pang of annoyance at herself. How long was she going to be afraid of him? As long as she remembered his skinny fingers round her neck; and at least until she found out why he behaved as he did.

He'd seen her. She couldn't escape without looking cowardly. She turned her mike on and held it up. "Ah, Rory," she said in a tone which belied how she felt.

She noticed, to her concern, that his face was highly coloured and his eyes held a wildness that reminded her of last Wednesday afternoon in the sitting room. She took a deep breath. It was OK. She had an escape route if necessary. Even so, she drew back, wary and alert. "Sorry, didn't mean to interrupt your work duty. Shall I leave you to it?"

He scrambled to his feet, and snatched her hand. She jerked violently away from him, holding on tight to the mike. "Don't touch me, Rory."

"OK, OK." He managed to look slightly offended. How dare he? She now stood a couple of metres away from him, but still holding the mike out.

"Juliet," Rory said. "You heard Llewellyn's announcement?"

"Last night? Of course I did," she replied.

"And?"

"And what? It didn't make sense at all."

"No? Then I'll explain," said Rory. "A big change is about to take place here."

"Which is?" she asked.

"Craig's no longer top dog. Llewellyn's in charge."

"Llewellyn?" Juliet stared at him. How did Rory know? The result of the votes hadn't been announced yet. She decided to keep her questioning non-controversial.

"What does he offer that's an improvement on Craig?" she queried.

"Poetry Therapy for a start," declared Rory. "He plans to scrap Craig's Dynamic Meditation sessions."

"Oh really? I thought you all enjoyed them."

"Not at all. They disgust *me.* And most of us have voted to overrule Craig."

So that was the result. The group members had made their choice. *Llewellyn over Craig.* How disloyal. For a few moments she was speechless.

"I think this will work much better. Craig's methods were a disaster. And…" here Rory allowed a pregnant pause, "I've begun work. Epic saga. Llewellyn will love it."

"Indeed?" Juliet withheld comment. What was she to make of such a turn of events? A direct challenge to Craig. He'd fight, of course.

"I've told Llewellyn I'll perform tonight in the barn," continued Rory. "You'll come, won't you, Juliet? My debut reading. You can't miss it. Celebratory drinks will follow."

"Well, Rory, I don't know what to say…"

"Don will man the bar," added Rory.

Whilst still digesting this, Juliet took the opportunity to question him further. "You truly feel Llewellyn's methods will work better than Craig's?"

It sounded outrageous. He was a good poet, certainly, but she'd seen no evidence to suggest he could trump Craig on the healing and wholeness stakes.

"Of course," said Rory. "This is quite out of Craig's league." And with that, he plunged to his knees again to continue weeding.

Juliet turned her mike off and quickly walked on. What had inspired Llewellyn to such disloyalty? Don? She couldn't believe he'd encouraged him to stage a coup. And what did this say about Craig's leadership skills? It was bad news. A power struggle between Llewellyn and Craig would split the group.

Then she spotted Theo ahead of her. He was following the path along the eastern boundary, head down, hands clasped behind his back, deep in thought. She raised her voice. "I need your help, Theo."

The cleric stopped and looked round, his expression neutral. Juliet studied him. Had he heard the news? It was time to switch her mike on again and hold it up between them.

His greeting was amiable enough. "Hello there, Juliet. Fine day for a walk."

"Yes. Theo…" She willed herself to draw back. Best to speak calmly about Rory's news. Ah yes. She knew the best subject to start on. "I've just been reading your book."

"That's kind of you."

"Theo, it's great," she said.

He couldn't avoid the light of pleasure showing clearly in his eyes. "Thank you."

"It's a real page-turner."

"I did try to make it accessible," he murmured.

"You succeeded," Juliet said. "But Theo, there's something I'm worried about."

"In my book?"

"No. Here in this community."

"And what's that?" he enquired. "Craig?"

"Well, of course. It's Craig all right. He clams up when I ask him about the past."

"That's not surprising."

"Okay, Theo, so you're not going to be drawn either. But he in turn can't be surprised that I want to know."

"Or rather," said Theo, "that you long to know. For it's not just journalistic curiosity on your part, is it?"

She felt angry. She waited for a moment, taking a deep breath. It was her turn to change the subject, before she exploded in front of the clergyman. "All right Theo. I have another worry. This new turn of events. The vote. Llewellyn's takeover bid."

The cleric's lips curved. "Yes."

"What do you make of it all?" she asked.

"I admire Llewellyn's poetry." Theo inspected the sweet peas for a few moments. "And in ancient Celtic communities, of course, the bard held the highest position in the social structure…"

"Oh, come on, Theo, this isn't an ancient Celtic community," she broke in, exasperated.

"No it isn't, is it."

"But did you encourage him?"

"No," said Theo, "I simply had a short chat with Don. Llewellyn must have overheard. I mentioned it would be good to spend some evenings reciting poems, singing songs and telling stories."

"Sounds lovely. But it isn't what Llewellyn's done. He's staged a coup instead."

"Not a good idea," agreed Theo.

"What do you think will happen next?" she asked.

"Can't say. I stand by consistent leadership. So I've thrown my personal support on Craig's side."

Juliet started. The group was splitting into opposing camps. Seeing her expression, Theo put a gentle hand on her shoulder. "What would you have me do? Remain neutral?"

"But…" she began, then stopped. No, she wasn't going to say it.

"You don't expect me to encourage mutiny, do you?" the clergyman asked.

"No." She threw a quizzical glance at him. "It must be difficult for you to avoid giving advice, Theo."

"True," he said, his manner serene.

She fell in step with him as he turned left and strolled along the west-facing path beside the cucumber frames. The microphone was still live. "Especially now, when Craig needs it more than ever," she observed.

"Yes," Theo said. "But even so, he has to find his own way through this."

Suddenly she said, "You know that colleague of yours who came to the farmhouse before Craig owned it?"

"Yes."

"Are you still in touch with him?" She wasn't quite sure why she asked this.

"I am." A long pause followed.

"You said he had plenty of ideas for how this place could thrive."

"Yes," said Theo. "Additional accommodation and dining room, new uses for the barn and outhouses."

"How did he get these ideas?" Juliet asked.

"He had a vision," Theo replied. "He saw the farmhouse from above. He saw a courtyard with a central sculpture. And the barn was different. Its huge access doorway was a window with a Celtic cross etched in the glass. It was a place of worship."

"But that's extraordinary," said Juliet.

"Yes, isn't it?"

A sudden anxiety took hold of her. "Theo, you wouldn't ever suggest to Craig he should sell this property, would you?"

"No, of course not. I have no such right. And if you're thinking of this colleague of mine with all his bright ideas, well, let me assure you there's no chance of that. He has not the slightest prospect of ever affording it."

She felt she needed space to reflect. She turned the microphone off. When she spoke again, she could only change the subject – and store the mike away for the time being. "Theo, how long will you stay here? Have you agreed to lead that retreat for the Golden Chalice?"

"The answer to your first question is I don't know. And to your second – not yet."

"What does Zoe think?"

"Why not ask her yourself?" said Theo.

Juliet weighed up this reply, trying to work out whether it was evasive or not. Theo it seemed was in no mood either for further chat about his future prospects. He coolly appraised her. "Juliet, you cannot force Zoe's hand."

She flushed.

"Just as you cannot force Craig to tell you about his past," continued Theo.

She said nothing. But she felt mortified.

He allowed a few moments to pass before saying, "Back to you and Zoe. I've watched you both together now on a few occasions. It's not a good idea to confuse your hopes and dreams for yourself, with those for your sister."

"But I'm not doing that," she cried.

Silence fell. A magpie landed on top of a glass frame nearby, and a lively breeze sprang up. She tried to slow her breathing down, by the use of steady inhalations and exhalations. It would never do to have an emotional outburst with Theo, thus giving him yet further scope for his ever-ready counselling skills.

"What do you think would be the best thing to do?" she asked. She braced herself for him to recommend she leave Zoe alone, and go back to London straight away.

"I can't speak for Zoe." Theo laid his hand on hers. "But why don't you just tell her the truth? I mean, your fears and doubts about me. Then wait. And respect whatever choice she makes." And with that, he set off again, walking briskly up the path past the tomatoes, until he was out of sight.

18

Innocence of Morning Flesh

In the great empty space of the barn, Juliet unexpectedly found some peace, despite all that she'd witnessed in it since she'd first arrived at the Centre over a week ago. She needed to collect her thoughts. And for several moments it seemed the quietness of the barn was helping her to do that.

Then she remembered. She'd seen Zoe heading this way and meant to intercept her. They must talk. Leaving the barn again through the great access doorway, Juliet paused inside the buttresses which flanked the arch. Then she saw her sister. Zoe was now making for the house. Breaking into a run, Juliet caught up with her. "Zoe, stop."

Zoe turned and glanced at her. "What's up?"

"Theo. I must have a word with you about him." She couldn't fail to notice Zoe's sigh. Or the wariness that sprang into her eye. It made her sick at heart to recognise Zoe's mistrust. But she pressed relentlessly on. "I had a chat with Theo earlier," she said.

"Oh? You did?" Zoe's tone held a cautious edge.

"And we spoke about you."

"Before you say more, Juliet, listen. There's no way I'll change what I think or feel about Theo to suit you."

"Why do you think I'd want you to do that anyway?" asked Juliet.

"Everything you've said and done in the last few days. Look Juliet, don't think I haven't noticed what's going on between you and Craig."

Folding her arms tightly, Juliet threw a warning glance at her sister. "Craig? What are you…?"

"Still in denial?" said Zoe, tossing her head. "I don't need to suggest what everyone can see. He's crazy about you."

"Crazy about me?" shouted Juliet, before she had a moment to think. "But he won't even…" She stopped, her face burning.

Zoe was watching her intently. "Won't even… what?"

Juliet was silent.

"Now, what advice did you want to give me about Theo?" Zoe asked breezily.

At dinner Juliet avoided Craig's gaze. It was made much easier by the fact that Llewellyn had claimed the seat beside her, and chatted constantly during the entire meal. Tonight she welcomed this. But she also itched to know what kind of power struggle was going on between Craig and the poet. Her curiosity was not yet to be satisfied though, because they both ignored each other. She was tempted on several occasions to look at Craig, but resisted. How on earth had Zoe – in common with Rory – dreamed up the idea that Craig was attracted to her? She was beginning to see how Rory could be so deluded; but not Zoe too.

Looking across the table she caught Don's eye. He smiled at her and immediately she felt an irresistible sense of relief. He was a shining beacon of normality here. Somehow this bluff Yorkshireman who didn't easily share his emotions stood out in the context of this community. Thank God for Don.

She was unprepared for the powerful feelings gathering strength inside her. She longed to be held in dependable arms, safe and protected. What was happening to her? She tried to shake this feeling off, and yet the more she looked at Don, the more it persisted. With an effort of the will she concentrated on the meal instead, and upon the other events unfolding around her in the community.

Mutiny. How would Craig cope with that? But, perhaps, all things considered, it was no less than he deserved. Tonight she'd go to

Llewellyn's session in the barn with an open mind. And she'd reserve judgement until later.

Three of the brightest stars in the sky, framed by the great east window of the barn, emerged into view. *The summer triangle*, thought Juliet, pleased to identify the stellar trio. But nobody else in the barn noticed. Their attention was focused on one star only, of a more earthly nature: Rory. Wearing a rather overdone purple velvet cravat that reminded Juliet of Lord Byron, he paced back and forth across a dais beneath the hayloft, declaiming at the top of his voice.

Juliet had found a spare seat next to Llewellyn and slid into it. She'd attached a clip-mike to Rory's shirt before the recital began. The other mike was in her hand, turned on, and the levels seemed to be behaving nicely so far. She intended to capture all the details of this supposed regime change in the community. Though Craig, she noticed, was absent. Why?

As Rory paused for breath, Llewellyn leaned close, speaking in low, urgent tones as she held the mike towards him. "What do you think, Juliet?"

"Well, Llewellyn..." she began. "You've certainly given Rory a good forum to express himself, and I'm sure that's helped him. But do you honestly believe it is right to take over from Craig like this?"

He looked slightly hurt, moving away from her again. "Take over? Come, Juliet, you don't still see it like that do you?"

"I certainly do."

He fell silent.

A question broke into her mind. Who was he trying to impress? Nevertheless, rather than voice the thought, she judged it best to focus right now on the details of Rory's performance. "Passionate, isn't he?" she murmured. "It's a bit scary here in the front row. I'm afraid he might leap off the podium and throttle me."

The Welshman nodded. "His first epic poem: an amazing achievement in twenty-four hours. And note, too, his subject matter: sex, love, and identity crises."

"Yes. I can feel the raw energy."

Rory launched into the next stanza, tears streaming down his face. Juliet concentrated on his recital until it drew to a close, and he stumbled down from the dais, sweating, to slightly bemused applause.

Llewellyn massaged his chin. "Excellent therapy: far better than Dynamic Meditation. If he finds an outlet for his feelings in verse, he could achieve the freedom he's been seeking in vain for years."

"Freedom from what, or who?" She eyed the Welshman narrowly, microphone poised between them. "Craig?"

He returned her gaze. "Yes. Why not? That's a freedom you probably long for, too, don't you?"

Her mouth turned dry. She hadn't expected such a well-targeted attack from Llewellyn. She flicked the switch on the mike. OK, she could edit this stuff out; but she preferred not to record it in the first place.

"No answer to that," she said.

"Ah. Perfectly diplomatic," he observed. "Credit me with some powers of observation, Juliet. You don't want to fall under Craig's spell yourself, do you?"

"No chance of that. Stick to the point, Llewellyn."

"Willingly. The point is, Craig doesn't like all this. He insists he gives us a creative outlet already, and this is nothing new."

"He's right though isn't he?"

"But, Juliet…" A shadow of disquiet flickered across his face. "Surely you see this is radically different to anything Craig offers. You do, don't you?"

She felt perturbed. Was all this an ill-advised bid for her good opinion? "I left my personal viewpoint outside the entrance gate when I drove in on my first day here." She hadn't used this line before, and now it was out, she strongly doubted whether she'd ever pull it into service again. It sounded hollow.

Llewellyn's next remark confirmed her insight. "Your words put me in mind of something Zoe said earlier."

"Which was?"

"That all this *being objective* of yours is nothing but a front. Underneath you have very strong opinions about everything that's going on here: you're probably more passionate than any of us." He fixed his gaze on her. "Restrained passion is very attractive."

"Is it indeed?" she retorted, choosing to remain non-committal. Despite that, she was aflame with anger. How dare Zoe play the part of *agent provocateur*?

"She also threw out a challenge to me," said Llewellyn, "that I might like to persuade you to open up."

Juliet remained tight-lipped.

"Juliet," he said, "you're among friends here. You need hide nothing. You can trust yourself with me."

And now his expression took on a powerful appeal. She was sorely tempted. If she played Zoe and Llewellyn's game, it might afford some protection against Craig. She was about to respond when she realised everyone else had fallen silent and focused their attention upon her and the Welshman. "Llewellyn," she murmured.

He came to, and jumping up, walked to the front, where he stepped onto the dais, and swung to face the performance poet. She switched her microphone on again. "Thank you, Rory," said Llewellyn. "You're an inspiration to us all." Then he addressed himself to the gathering. "I hope Rory's example has shown you all how poetry, when it comes alive on the air, can be the answer for you, not dynamic meditation – nor any of the futile exercises Craig offers. Creativity, that's the key. Things will be very different from now on. I promise you that. Trust me. Don's waiting at the bar over there. Ask for whatever you want."

Juliet turned to look in the direction he indicated. Don's eyes met hers from his position behind a table at the south west corner of the meeting space, loaded with bottles and glasses. Had this little lot already been in Craig's supply, or did Llewellyn buy them in specially for the occasion, on Craig's account?

As Llewellyn placed his hand on Juliet's arm, Theo materialised before them. "Ah, Llewellyn. A word with you, if I may."

"Of course." Glancing apologetically at Juliet, the poet released his hold on her arm and moved aside with the clergyman.

Juliet hurried across to Rory and removed his clip-mike so she could attach it to her own jacket, enabling her to move around freely, recording a number of conversations.

Al, wearing a magenta shirt unbuttoned almost to the waist, and Laura – in a green smocked dress that looked as if it had come from the children's section of an Oxfam shop – had just left the bar with their drinks and now made their way along to the massive oak table set against the west wall of the barn. The American, raising a glass of whisky, was saying something to her that made her giggle. Beyond those two, Juliet noticed Beth and Oleg, standing apart from everyone else, talking quietly together. She resolved to go and chat to them in a moment. But first she crossed to the bar. "A new role for you, Don?"

"Not so new," he replied. "Pulled the Yorkshire Ruddles in my time, you know."

"Excellent. Have you a Cinzano?"

"Yes." He poured her a measure, dropped ice and lemon in, and handed it to her. She then made her way back along the north end of the barn to join Zoe beside the west staircase.

"What do you think of the poetry workshop idea, Juliet?" asked Zoe.

"Fine as far as it goes. But Llewellyn doesn't run the place," said Juliet. She surveyed Zoe, then flicked the switch once more on her machine. "What's this about you encouraging him to make a big move towards me?"

"Come on Juliet. Lighten up."

"All very well for you to say that. As for Llewellyn, he's a good poet but shouldn't be trying to grab the crown."

"I agree," said Zoe demurely. "But…"

Juliet broke in. "Why did you feed him that rubbish about my supposed *passions*, and then goad him to pounce on me?" She began to feel agitated, and drank her Cinzano too fast. She noticed her sister had the grace to look slightly shame-faced.

"Sorry," said Zoe. "I shouldn't have stirred Llewellyn up. He is trying to impress you, though. Surely you can see that."

"Well, no, I can't."

"A desperate last resort to get your attention," Zoe continued, undaunted. "He saw no other way, what with Craig about to swoop."

"Zoe, stop at once. You make me angry."

"You did turn your recording machine off, didn't you?" her sister asked pointedly.

"Of course. Now listen. I have nil interest in Llewellyn. And the same goes for Craig."

Zoe studied her pityingly. "You seem very on edge about *him.* What's up?"

"Nothing." Juliet snatched a glance back across to the bar, where Don was busy serving drinks to Edgar, Sam, James and Patrick. Sweeping a look round the barn, she saw Craig was still absent. She turned once more to her sister. "Never mind me. *You*'re my main cause of worry."

"Why waste your energy? I'm perfectly happy," said Zoe.

"Don't pretend you don't know what I'm talking about," insisted Juliet. She was about to say more when she stopped. What was it Theo had suggested? *Tell her the truth. Your doubts and fears about me, I mean.* "You and Theo," she continued. "Of course, I like him. And I can see how keen you both are on each other. But is he really your type?"

"Yes he is."

"Zoe, you don't share his faith."

Her sister sighed. "All that matters is that we like each other. Lots."

Juliet stared at her, nonplussed. "That may be good enough for now. But what about later?"

"I'm not thinking about later. I'm living in the present."

Juliet bit back a sharp retort. Her heart pounding, she drained her glass. What also niggled her was the fact that Zoe and Theo did, to the casual observer, make a very compatible pair. She had no intention of saying so to Zoe, though.

Looking again at her sister's face, she decided it would be best to go off and join Laura, Al and James beside the oak table. She made sure she was live again. Upon approach, she saw Al pivot on his heels, bronze medallion bouncing on his chest, and grab the fruit bowl from the table behind him. For a moment she thought he was going to throw it at her.

"Juliet, why don't you go for a peach? One or two strawberries perhaps?" From the sound of his voice, he'd clearly already had more than a few drinks.

Juliet spoke lightly. "I'd be interested in some of those grapes."

"I'll throw a bunch across," Laura giggled. "Here, catch."

Juliet nearly ducked to avoid the missile. But it was unnecessary. James, in a ruffle-front silk shirt, had intercepted Laura's serve, and passed the fruit to her.

"Thanks." Juliet eyed Laura warily. It seemed she, also, had already taken too much advantage of the bar. Perhaps someone had held Don in an arm lock while the rest helped themselves. But then, Juliet guessed, Laura may well have started before she'd even entered the barn. At that moment, she twisted round to look at Don, and the mystery was solved. He'd abandoned his bar duties and gone over to join Theo and Llewellyn. Juliet ate the last grape.

"You downed that yet, Laura?" said Al. As she finished her drink, he took her glass and was about to head back to the bar for a refill. Before he could do so, however, Juliet stepped in front of him. "I think you're being rather irresponsible, Al," she said.

"Not at all. This is a special night," he declared. "The Centre has been reborn as a literary salon."

"Nonsense, Al," protested Juliet. "I don't think this coup of Llewellyn's will last long."

"Sorry, honey. I disagree. In any case, at least it'll blow a little smoke up Craig's butt." And with that, he pushed past her.

Rory and Patrick added themselves to the group surrounding Laura. Rory was, as ever, clutching a glass of water. Considering he was the most violent person here, Juliet found it highly ironical. Certainly alcohol wasn't the cause of his problems. Unless of course he had a secret supply back in his room. Juliet thought he seemed exceptionally smooth and relaxed, now he'd finished his performance. In fact, his manner reminded her of the one he'd adopted at dinner on the evening of her arrival, urbane and charming. She had no doubt at all it was a mask.

Patrick held two tumblers of whisky. Laura stretched out her hand and whipped one away from him; one, Juliet felt, she could well have done without. She sensed a new recklessness in the air, as if an unwritten rule had been breached and now all restraint was thrown aside.

Looking over to the west staircase, she saw Zoe chatting to Sam. Turning to her right she observed Oleg and Beth locked in earnest, alcohol-fuelled conversation with Edgar. She transferred her attention to Laura once more; she was downing the drink Al had brought back. "I feel like the scarlet woman of Babylon," Laura announced.

"To be sure," said Patrick, directing a pointed stare at her, "you're no better than you should be. But that's only to be expected. I put it all down to original sin."

Rory intervened. "Most people put me down to that, too. Don't you worry about it too much, Laura. I expect my sin's more original than yours."

But before Laura could reply to this, she collapsed onto the floor. Al immediately plunged down to her side.

"Can I help?" Juliet started forward.

"No, no, she'll be fine," muttered Al.

It didn't look like it to Juliet. "I reckon she needs to be helped out of here, and off to bed," she said. Then she regretted her words.

"I'm the man for that job," declared Al, raising Laura into a sitting position. She lolled back in his arms, a glazed expression in her eyes. Though Juliet would have much preferred to distance herself from this little scenario, she had little choice but to remain focused on it. And to record the lot. For she couldn't tell which aspect of tonight's behaviour – if any of it – would make good radio or not, unless she kept the machine running.

Patrick chose this moment to continue his previous discussion with Rory. "Think your sin's original, do you, Rory? Tell me: suppose one of those timber beams up above your head was to break off right now and fall on you. If you were to die tonight where would you spend eternity?"

The Irishman was being very provocative, Juliet thought. What made him so confident Rory wouldn't just knock him senseless?

"Haven't the faintest," said Rory, "and I don't suppose you do either."

"Then you suppose wrongly." Patrick declaimed this in ringing tones. He forged on. "Now then, how old are you?"

"That's my secret," said Rory.

"Whatever it is, I'll wager you don't think you're going to die until you're ninety-eight. But what makes you think it won't be in two seconds?"

Juliet held her breath. Surely this was Rory's cue. A well-timed blow and Patrick would be flat on the floor.

"Threatening me, are you, Patrick?" said Rory.

The Irishman threw his arms out, managing to swipe Al in the face just as he'd begun to lift Laura. Juliet watched all this with baited breath. Would the American turn on Patrick? But before he got the chance, Patrick issued a challenge to everyone within earshot. "Having spent so much time here in the Wheel of Love, does anyone actually believe in God?"

Al fell back, and startled by the unexpectedness of the question, let go of Laura and dropped her onto the floor. "What's the deal with you, Patrick?" he demanded. "Believe in God? Course I do. Although …" he hesitated, "…since Llewellyn purloined the driver's seat from Craig, perhaps it's safer to opt for *Don't Know*."

"What does Craig have to do with it?" demanded Patrick.

Al ignored the Irishman as he became busy again, trying to coax Laura to her feet. "Come on, honey," he beguiled her. Then he rushed over to the chairs, grabbed three, and dragged them back to her.

"Since when," continued Patrick, "have matters of faith and doubt, life and death, been dependent upon what Craig tells us? It's what *we* all think that matters."

"Quite right," said Edgar. "And I should know. I've been noting down what every one of us thinks since we've been here."

"And what do we think?" enquired Patrick.

"Ah. Well, let me put it like this," said Edgar. "We don't yet have consensus. But never mind. Look at the mighty cosmos up there: the moon, the stars…" He swept his hand in the direction of the skylights that had been installed in the roof of the barn. Indeed, as Juliet had noticed earlier, the stars were unusually bright and it was easy to identify the constellations.

"I'm glad he's talking of stars," Rory said in her ear.

"Why?"

"Because I hope to be one soon. I feel released to a bright future by my performance tonight."

She wasn't prepared to discourage the newly-inspired poet. Instead, she sought to humour him. "That sounds positive, Rory. How do you see Llewellyn? As the new leader of the Wheel of Love?"

But before Rory could reply, Patrick pulled him aside, clearly intent on developing the theological discussion he'd just opened.

Meanwhile, Juliet's attention was drawn once more by Laura's predicament. She lay flat out across the three chairs which Al had thoughtfully placed there for her, while he kneeled near her head, and cradled it in his arms. Juliet went to join them. "Managing, Al? Need any help yet?"

It seemed not; for as she drew close, she realised they were busy quoting poetry at each other.

"*I was much too far out all my life and not waving but drowning,*" lamented Laura.

"Cool, baby. But try this," said Al. "*I read beneath the innocence of morning flesh concealed, hinting of death she does not heed.*"

"Mmm. Powerful words. Who wrote them?"

"A fellow American. Weldon Kees. They think he jumped off the Golden Gate Bridge in 1955."

"Oh Al, why do we need to be so depressing? Let's go to bed instead," mumbled Laura.

Juliet felt a light pressure on her shoulder. Turning, she saw Theo. He put his free arm around Zoe.

"Good night, Juliet," said Zoe pointedly.

Juliet stepped forward, keen to delay them. "I've been meaning to ask you something, Theo," she said.

"Yes?" he prompted her. What was the matter with him? His eyes, when they rested upon hers, were unsmiling. Had she offended him in some way?

"Enjoy the recital, Theo?" she asked.

He nodded. "Rory did very well."

"Do you still feel Llewellyn was wrong to organise it?"

"Misguided," he said. "If the group continues what he's set in motion here tonight, it will fall apart."

She stared at him, dismayed. "You think so?"

"Certainly. Craig needs to bring it all together again quickly. If not, Don's worst fears will be proved true."

She studied his calm face. "Theo?"

"Yes?"

"What did that visionary friend of yours do next?"

"Went away and discussed his ideas with close friends at his church," said Theo. "But it wasn't possible to take things any further. No money."

She waited.

"I did tell you that before, Juliet," he added softly.

Zoe stood looking from one to the other.

"Come on, Zoe," Theo said. And they left.

Putting her recording equipment onto the bedside table, and throwing herself onto her bed, Juliet thought about what she'd seen and heard this evening. But hard and fast conclusions escaped her. Why wasn't Craig there? He should have been. He needed to wrest back control. But there'd been no sign of him.

And what of Zoe's idea that Craig had fallen for her? If this was true, Juliet needed to make a quick decision. But what *was* she going to decide about Craig? None of it added up. She jumped to her feet and began walking to and fro across her room. Right now, Don seemed a far better option. She thought of Craig as dangerous and unreliable. Don she saw as a haven, a safe place to run into.

But then there was Llewellyn. Surely he hadn't tried to upstage Craig just to get into her good books? That was an appalling thought. At this, there came a knock on her door. She glanced at her watch. It was half past eleven. "Yes?" she called.

"It's me, Juliet." It was Llewellyn's voice.

Ah! Her opportunity to set him straight! She pulled the door open.

"Do you mind?" The poet came through. Amazingly, he still looked fresh and invigorated by the evening's events. He stood regarding her. "Zoe not with you?"

"No, of course not. Why should she be? I would hope she's in bed." And so she probably was; but not on her own, either.

"Come in." She remained standing, and didn't offer him a seat. After the example given him by the other members of the group tonight, she was taking no chances.

"Couldn't go back to my room without a word with you, Juliet," he said. "I imagined you sitting here, perplexed. And I know I'm the one to settle your mind."

"Are you?" She meant to approach this in a reasonable manner. No point in upsetting him by her efforts to make him face the truth. But, having decided this, she burst out, "What are you up to? Craig runs this community, not you."

"He's running it all right. Running it into the ground. Recently, I've had a strong sense that the Wheel of Love may be starting to fall apart."

"So why are you hastening the process?"

"How can you say that, Juliet?" he remonstrated. He searched her face for a few moments. "The community was heading this way well before I got the idea for my little experiment."

"Your *little experiment* as you call it may turn out to be the one thing necessary to puncture the wheel once and for all." Hands on hips, she glared at him.

He wore an injured expression. "You're testing me, Juliet. Surely you admit this evening has opened something up in everybody."

"Yes, but has it been for the good?"

He considered this. "I believe so."

"Perhaps," she went on, "you should have left them for Craig to sort out. Heaven knows, they're in enough of a mess as it is. It's not a task I'd gladly take on, for one."

His eyes held hers. Did he resent her criticism? He gently interlocked her fingers with his. "I apologise for my arrogance."

For a moment, this disarmed her. Then she gathered herself together again, and withdrew her hand. "Apologise to the group, Llewellyn, not me."

"Oh no, I won't do that. They enjoyed it," he said. "And they voted for me."

Juliet fell silent, stung by his unexpected defiance.

"I've been watching you, too, you know." Llewellyn pressed home his point. "Don't think I haven't noticed. I mean, you and Craig."

Not another one! This flash of a knife blade had come entirely without warning. "There's nothing between me and Craig. Why won't anyone believe me?" She felt mortified. She wanted Llewellyn to go. But instead, he remained, the expression in his eyes growing tender.

Before she could translate the meaning of this, he'd stepped quickly forward, and pulled her to him. "Juliet, it's not that… I want you to know… if you say you care nothing for Craig, is there a chance for me?"

Her heart hammered against her ribs. She couldn't believe this. Pure panic shot up inside her. "You, Llewellyn?" she gasped, momentarily paralysed.

"Yes. You know, Juliet, since I came here, I've written poems about everyone. But none more than you."

"I'm glad I've inspired you, Llewellyn. Read me some tomorrow. But go now."

"No, no, Juliet. You can't mean that. What about tonight?"

"No."

"Yes," he said. "*My heart has made its mind up and I'm afraid it's you.*"

Her mind in a whirl, she pushed him away. "No, Llewellyn. Quote poetry all you like. To someone else. But no, it won't be me."

He nearly lost his balance. But when he regained it, he was clearly undeterred, and spoke once more, with fresh resolve. "Juliet, Craig's no good for you. It won't work. You'd ruin your life. And here am I, offering myself to you."

She flared up again. "I told you, you're mistaken about Craig." Even as she spoke these words, she realised how they could be taken the wrong way. "Drop it, Llewellyn. You're wasting your breath. I'm not interested in you." Her arms and hands were trembling, and her face was on fire.

"Please, Juliet. I want you so much." He seized hold of her again.

"No, Llewellyn! Let go. And leave my room."

He behaved as if he hadn't heard. "You care about me, I know you do," he insisted. "You're irresistible." He began to nuzzle her cheek, her ear and her neck with his lips. She struggled, but his hold tightened.

"Let go, Llewellyn," she cried.

"No, Juliet. You're intelligent, beautiful, and have passion inside you," he continued. "Why, don't you realise how perfectly creativity and sensuality go together?"

"I very much expect they do," she said; "with the right person. And that's not me, Llewellyn."

"Oh yes it is." He began to expertly manoeuvre her back towards the bed. She tried to fight him off, but her strength was no match for his. He pushed her onto the bed, and threw himself on top of her. She tried to scream but he silenced her with kisses. "You see," he said after a pause for breath, "you and me, Juliet… we were made for each other."

At that moment there came a loud hammering on the door. Startled, Llewellyn loosened his grip, and Juliet managed to wriggle out from under him and hurl herself across to the door. She wrenched it open and just had time to register the appalled face of

Don, who had clearly glimpsed the dishevelled poet behind her, before she gasped, "We've all had too much to drink this evening. Time for bed."

Don sprang into the room and grabbed Llewellyn. Before she had time to register anything further, Don had propelled him through the doorway into the arms of Craig, who'd been just outside with Don, ready and waiting.

Walking into the kitchen the next morning, Juliet found herself alone with Rory again. Sprawling at the table in a listless fashion, resembling Lord Byron as little as possible, he stirred a teaspoon around in a glass of water. He wore a badly creased T-shirt which looked as if it had been slept in.

She felt emotionally drained. Surely Rory wouldn't try anything so early in the morning? She'd almost lost the will to worry about him any more. And Llewellyn's advances last night had left her in a state akin to shell shock. "Good morning, Rory." She sat carefully at the end of the table nearest to the door, with her Nagra and mike.

His only response was a grunt, whilst he continued stirring. Odd, she thought, especially as he was the one person she supposed to have thoroughly enjoyed yesterday evening's events. Might he already be starting to regret the fact that Craig had been ousted from power?

She set the mike up just beside the muesli packet, and turned it on. "Did you enjoy the poetry workshop last night?" she asked politely.

"I did," he snapped.

"That was a powerful poem of yours," she observed.

"Thanks." He still looked moody.

"But you don't seem too happy this morning."

Rory sipped at his glass of water. "No. It's Craig. He's disappeared."

She felt mystified. "We're not that far into the day. He's probably just gone for a walk."

"After last night," said Rory, looking unconvinced, "you'd think he'd be well in evidence, trying to claw back control."

"Perhaps." Well, she thought, he'd definitely been trying to claw back control in the small hours from Llewellyn, outside her bedroom door.

"Instead, Craig has vanished," went on Rory. "What kind of a leader is that? I used to believe in him."

And yet you voted for Llewellyn, she thought to herself, but didn't say. She still couldn't tell if he might react badly. She considered him, thoughtfully. This was a new Rory, confiding things he'd never admitted to her before.

"So, now," he said, "we look to Llewellyn to lead us."

Before Juliet could query this, the door opened, and Laura weaved her way in. She wore a little floral printed jersey dress with a fleecy cardigan which made her look like something out of the five-to-sixteens fashion section of a major household catalogue. Her hair looked as unmanageable as ever. Juliet watched her as she found her way to the kettle. "Good morning, Laura."

There was no reply.

"Ah, I see things are a little slow in moving this morning," said Rory.

"Surprised?" Laura asked. She and Rory exchanged a fierce look.

"Nothing would surprise me about you now, Laura," said Rory snidely.

"Still sore about last night?" she demanded.

What was all this about? Juliet looked from one to the other in bafflement, but kept the mike live.

Laura, meanwhile, filled the kettle, produced a small plastic bag and removed a sachet from it. Having made her herbal tea, she sat beside Juliet, took a sip from her cup, and said, "I enjoyed last night. Up until the point when Al was about to go and get us some champagne. And was accosted by Rory."

A hand gripped Juliet's heart. Oh no. Not again. What was Laura about to tell her?

Laura lifted the cup to her lips.

Sleek and dangerous, Rory rose from his seat.

"Please sit down, Rory," said Juliet firmly. He obeyed, to her amazement.

"All right, I'll tell the story," he said.

Juliet steeled herself for a completely distorted account. At least she might have got a reasonably accurate report from Laura. Oh well, perhaps she could ask her quietly later. She nodded, and checked the levels on her recorder as Rory spoke.

"At precisely eleven-twenty," he said, "having just escaped a fate worse than death, fending off an attack by both Beth and Oleg as I passed the bathroom…."

Laura frowned. "I didn't know about that." She sounded slightly piqued.

"Maybe you didn't," said Rory, "but it happened. Anyway, I found myself opposite Laura's bedroom door. It stood wide open. Inside Al was trying to convince her he didn't want to take advantage while she was drunk…."

"That's because he's a perfect gentleman," declared Laura, her cheeks glowing at the memory. "So when I told him not to worry because I wasn't *that* drunk…"

"I went in to help," claimed Rory.

Juliet could see Laura's colour rising. She held out a warning hand. But it was to no avail.

"So what business was it of yours?" Laura cried.

"Everything's my business," Rory maintained. "And so, Juliet, back to my story. The next thing I knew, Al rugby-tackled me."

From the sound of it, Juliet didn't blame him.

"Then," continued Rory, "before I knew what was happening, Al had fallen on his face on the floor, and Laura had thrown herself onto me."

"Rubbish," Laura said hotly.

"It was a bit like Potiphar's wife in Genesis, trying to seduce Joseph," said Rory. "I thought, *this is it*, shut my eyes and recited the Lord's Prayer backwards."

"You totally misunderstood the situation, Rory," said Laura.

He shot a poisonous look at her.

Juliet felt she'd heard quite enough by now to build up a pretty clear picture of what actually happened. Rory's interference had been totally inappropriate, and Al's response had been understandable. But she wasn't going to say that to Rory now. Instead, she hastened to defuse the tension between Rory and Laura. She appealed to them both. "Whatever happened, it's all over and done with now, and no one's been seriously hurt."

"I wouldn't say that," said Rory.

Juliet glanced at him. His eyes held a manic glitter. Oh dear, she thought.

"I have been deeply psychologically damaged by last night's events," announced Rory.

Laura and Juliet looked at each other.

Juliet took a deep breath. "Don't you feel, though, Laura," she said quietly, "that last night's antics would never have got so out of hand if you'd all respected Craig's leadership and not encouraged Llewellyn to take over?"

This met with stony silence. A few moments passed. Then Laura got up from her seat. "Llewellyn's in charge now," she said. "End of subject." And she flounced out of the kitchen before Juliet could stop her. As she closed the door behind her, Juliet jumped to her feet, turned the mike off, and picked up her recording equipment. She wasn't going to risk another moment alone in the kitchen with Rory in an irate state.

She was about to follow Laura, when she heard the sound of smashing glass behind her. She spun. Rory had seized his tumbler and lobbed it across to the other side of the kitchen, where it had struck a cupboard door and fragmented.

Juliet froze. "Go easy on the glassware, won't you, Rory."

He stood up, and prowled in her direction. She sprang towards the door and put her hand on the door latch. "I'll stay and listen to you, Rory, if you keep your distance," she said.

He stopped. "All right." He moved back a few inches.

Warily, she stepped forward again.

"Sit down then," he said.

She did so. But every sense was on guard.

"You've been disingenuous about Craig," he said, taking another seat, much closer to her than she liked. "You came to undermine him, and now you leap to his defence."

"I came to do interviews. I only meant to listen, not judge. I shall be sad if the community falls apart."

"I don't believe you." And he reached out and snatched hold of her right wrist. He held onto it so fiercely his knuckles whitened.

"Let go, Rory!"

He didn't respond.

"Rory, I'm warning you…"

"Warning me of what? *You* have no power over *me*."

She managed to twist away from him. "Rory, this is totally unacceptable. Why do you betray my trust in you like this?"

Once more she was on her feet, and hurrying to the door. She was just about to leave when she heard a voice behind her – high-pitched, terrifyingly vulnerable, childlike. It sounded nothing like Rory. It was not the voice of a grown man.

She turned, trembling. All the time she was amazed at her own ability to give him these second and third chances.

He sat, head in hands, back at the table. "I'm sorry," he whispered in the same strange voice. His shoulders were heaving. He was sobbing his heart out.

She felt numb with shock and fear and pity. She swallowed several times before speaking. "Rory, what is it?" she asked gently. "Tell me about it."

Gradually he became more composed. "My problems," he blurted in a voice that sounded like his own again.

"And what are they, Rory?" she asked.

"Come and sit down again first," he pleaded. "Show me you believe I'm not a monster."

Silently she did as he said. Dare she now risk a further question?

"Is it…" she began, then stopped. "Is it… your *thorn in the flesh*?"

He nodded.

"The violent episodes…?" she asked.

"They tend to get out of hand," he whispered, "when I miss my medication."

Her spine tingled. "Your medication?" she asked. "What kind?"

"Antipsychotic," he said. "For schizophrenia."

"I'm so sorry to hear that," she said quietly. "Now I can begin to understand. I mean – about what you've suffered." She rubbed her wrist. It still smarted painfully from his vice-like grip. She hesitated. Dare she plunge in? "Would you tell me more?"

"Willingly," he said, now eager to unburden himself. "I hear voices. They are there to confirm that I'm the passive victim of evil forces. They criticise and torment me, and tell me I'm worthless. They give a running commentary most of the time. They discuss me between themselves."

She listened, aghast. She wondered if the rest of the group knew, or whether only Craig did.

"They threaten me. Sometimes they tell me somebody here wants to hurt me. Then I must defend myself."

As he spoke, she found herself recalling all the occasions since her arrival when she'd noticed odd behaviour in Rory.

There was the evening she first met him, and he said he'd had funny experiences in Gloucestershire which he regarded as an occult county. And he claimed that when Craig spoke to him his own words came out as gibberish. And he described Theo as a *soul mate*, simply because he learned Theo had had a wilderness experience.

Then there was his comment about the need for protection from Satan; and his misrepresentation of his own attack on Oleg as a *near-death experience*. Then there was his assault on Juliet for supposedly *sitting in judgement* on him; and his story about Laura and Al last night. The more she thought about it, the more pieces of the jigsaw puzzle that was Rory fell into place.

His voices were evil, he'd said. "Rory…" she began again.

"Yes?"

"I hope you haven't relied on Craig's methods and exercises and therapy sessions to heal you?"

A few moments passed. He cleared his throat. "Yes, I have," he said; "Largely."

She nodded, and waited for several moments.

"I've got tablets," he admitted, "but try to do without them."

Anger was growing inside her. If Rory was open to mental health services – as clearly he should be – his file would probably be marked *Only to be visited in pairs.* And yet Craig had steered him off his medication, putting everyone – including her – at risk. Rory had nearly killed her. And Craig hadn't warned her beforehand. Why not? She was going to have words with Craig. He had some hard explaining to do. "And… is there anything else?" she asked. "Do you eat properly? I've never seen you eat anything."

"The voices tell me every day that someone's poisoning the food," he replied. "So I wait until the others have eaten to see who drops dead. By the time I realise the food's probably OK because nobody's keeled over, it's too late."

"And Craig knows about this food problem?"

"Yes. He lets me eat in my bedroom. It's the only place I feel safe. I listen to opera on my headphones and drown out the voices."

"This is so sad, Rory," she said.

He relaxed slightly at her empathy, and withdrew a short way, giving her more personal space. "Thank you. Craig understands, too. He's the only one who knows about it."

"But, Rory, I cannot imagine you ever needed to be so secretive. It's not as if it's your fault. If Craig had explained properly… No one would have condemned you."

"I appreciate your saying so. But I had no guarantee of that."

"Did you ask Craig not to tell anyone?"

"Yes."

Silence fell. What was she to make of this? Had Craig been right or wrong? On balance, she believed he had been wrong. Everyone had been in danger. And yet Craig had insisted this was a *safe environment.*

"One more thing," Rory said. "I expect you've tried to puzzle out what I am; when the voices allow me, so have I."

"Indeed?" This sounded curious, and disturbing.

"You'll have noticed how I feel about Craig. I struggle with the wicked things the voices tell me. My feelings have nothing to do with the power of his teachings."

"No?" she said.

"But," he continued, "I never could be sure whether he reciprocated those feelings or not."

She watched and listened with growing pity.

"So now," Rory said, "I've decided to settle the matter once and for all."

The door opened again. She turned. Craig stood there. "And how do you propose to do that, Rory?"

19

Visions Unfulfilled

Juliet was furious with Craig, but she kept it to herself while Rory was in the room, of course.

Craig had managed to dissuade Rory from any drastic solutions. One of his proposals was gender realignment surgery. Craig had convinced him it wouldn't be worth the trouble. Juliet had gently suggested Rory go and take a rest. And start taking his tablets again. Fortunately Rory hadn't exploded again at this. He'd quietly left the room.

And then Juliet turned on Craig. "You knew all along. The poor man. Your methods could never cure him. Can't you see that?"

Craig reached out and took her hand. "Juliet, calm down. I apologise," he said.

"No, Craig, not good enough," she stormed. She snatched her hand away, then flinched – it was the one Rory had gripped. "And don't try and get round me, Craig. You put my life at risk; in fact, you put everyone's life at risk. He needs his medication. What was this? Some crazy experiment? You think you can heal manic depression? Schizophrenia? Psychosis? It's heartbreaking, Craig, but we're talking about severe and enduring mental illness."

As he listened to her, Craig's eyes had darkened, and his face had deepened in colour. "I was wrong, Juliet. I admit it," he said. "But do try and see it from my point of view. The pressure was strong. Rory pleaded with me."

"Maybe he did," she said. "But why did you give in to him? And that's another thing. Rory said he asked you not to tell anyone. But I cannot understand how the group members could have lived for so long with Rory in their midst, without knowing or guessing the truth about him."

"Oh, they're all aware there's something wrong with him," said Craig, "but without specialised knowledge none have been in a position to put a label on him. And I have preferred to keep it that way – to give Rory his best chance."

"But what about the safety of your group members?" she asked.

"Safety from Rory's aggressive outbursts, you mean?" said Craig. "In the past I've managed to contain them – mostly."

"Ah, so I was just unlucky," said Juliet.

He nodded.

"Thank you very much," she said.

"Please don't see it like that, Juliet," Craig begged.

"I'm afraid I do, Craig. And now I'm beginning to understand Don's frustration with you." And with that, she hurried from the room.

After she and Craig had parted company, she went into the library and sank into the chair by the window. Her heart was beating fast. She felt emotionally torn. The same thought kept running through her mind. *Oh, Don, now I know how you feel.*

Craig's attitude almost drove her to despair. She was unable to say how long she sat there. But her thoughts were eventually broken into by voices out in the hall, on the other side of the library door.

The first was that of James. "You'll have to do something about him, Craig."

"I know that well enough," she heard Craig reply sharply. "What do you suggest then?"

"You've heard my ideas," James shot back. Then he lowered his voice. "Look, this isn't a good place to talk about it. How about the gazebo?"

"Fine."

She listened as the front door opened and closed. Then her attention was attracted by movement on the other side of the window. James and Craig were crossing the gravel forecourt together. Craig unlatched the peacock-blue gate, and they both walked through into the garden. They disappeared from sight, undeterred by the light rain that dripped down from the trees.

So they were off to the gazebo for a private conference. She got up and followed. A wander through the shrubbery seemed in order. She had no reservations whatsoever about listening in on conversations not meant for her ears. Devious behaviour seemed to be the only way to get at the truth in this place.

The rain dripped off the lavender bushes as she trod quietly past and approached the gazebo. A hand touched her shoulder. She whirled. "Don," she whispered.

He drew alongside. His eyes held empathy. She felt like throwing herself into his arms and holding him tight. She was going to say, "Don, you're the only sane person in this place; the only person living in the real world." But she didn't. With a strong effort she resisted. That would never do. Neither the words, nor the embrace.

"Same mission?" he murmured.

She nodded. They stole forward a few steps, and peered into the gazebo. James and Craig could be seen through the wet blossoms covering the nearest window. The window was slightly ajar. James's voice floated out. "I agree, of course," James was saying. "Shall I get rid of him for you?"

Juliet held her breath. She and Don exchanged a glance. Who was he talking about? Rory? Then she realised James and Craig could also easily be discussing Llewellyn.

Then Craig said, "I think you'll find that difficult, considering the circumstances."

"What's the alternative?" asked James.

"What I've feared all along," replied Craig. "Do a deal with him."

A deal? Who could they possibly mean? Llewellyn? Rory?

"A deal!" James gave an abrasive bark of laughter. "God forbid! He wants to drag you back to Barnsley. You'll never agree to that!"

Juliet looked at Don. His face had whitened and his jaw clenched upon hearing this. Craig said nothing. Juliet sensed a deep chill cut in between him and James. At that moment, Craig looked up. They both dodged out of sight just in time. Don took her arm, and they moved swiftly away.

"If he's going to do a deal he'd better move fast," said Don grimly, as they headed back across the garden. "The group's days are numbered."

"I think you're right, Don," Juliet said. And she shared with him everything she'd learned about Rory. After she'd finished telling him, he stood deep in thought, shaking his head. "It's even worse than I imagined," he said.

"In view of this, do you think it's possible to do a deal to save the Centre?"asked Juliet.

Don opened the garden gate, and stood aside for her to walk through. "Not in its present form," he said. Hands in pockets, he regarded her.

She waited. Once again, her emotions perplexed her. She felt so ambivalent. Desire and longing battled it out with feelings of anger and hurt and frustration, following on from the whole business with Rory… she knew she was long past any possibility of staying objective. She'd just opened her mouth to ask Don another question, when she heard footsteps behind her. Turning, she saw James approaching. He seemed in a great hurry. He swept through the gateway past Don and Juliet without a word, and across the forecourt and round the side of the house.

What was that all about? Juliet wondered. It was uncharacteristically rude of James. Although she did understand he was probably upset by his recent discussion with Craig. As she thought this, Craig appeared, following behind James. He too looked agitated. However, on sight of Don and Juliet, he stopped.

The restless breeze whipped his dark hair back off his face. He was crushing something in his fist: a ball of paper.

"What's that, Craig?" she asked.

"A plan I'm about to scrap." He swung away. But his father stood in front of him.

"Looks like it's all up, Craig, doesn't it?" said Don.

"All up? What on earth do you mean?" rejoined Craig.

Don shook his head. "You're still in denial, aren't you," he said. "Listen. This business with Rory. Juliet's told me all about it."

"Has she," said Craig, his face stony. "Well, Father, I think you of all people might understand why I had to give Rory his best chance of a decent life, here, rather than out there in the world, where he would become at best *the weird neighbour, the nutter on the bus, the local loony*, or at worst, the permanent resident on the high-security ward in the psychiatric hospital."

Juliet looked from one man to the other, bewildered. Why should Don have a special understanding of what drove Craig's decision? Her bewilderment transformed itself swiftly into intense curiosity. What exactly was Craig saying? As she asked herself this, something snapped inside her.

"We can see you tried to protect Rory, Craig," she burst out, "and yes, I admit that I still want to understand why. Rory's point of view, I understand very well. Rory adores you. He's obsessed with you. He longs for you… but you're not as he is, are you, Craig?"

Craig opened his eyes wide.

"Or are you?" Juliet asked. An inner voice urged her to push the point. She needed to know. She needed to hear from Craig's own lips. "I want to learn the truth about you, Craig," she said. At her side, she felt that Don was tense and watchful. She continued. "I know, Craig, that you don't trust women. Or love. Despite the name of this group you run." Before he could protest, she hurried on. "Let me hear you say it now, Craig. In your own words. The truth."

His eyes narrowed.

Her mouth turned dry. Her fingers and palms perspired. Her neck and shoulders felt tense, and her heart hammered. Several moments passed. Then, unaccountably, she felt the hardness of Craig's will soften.

"Very well, Juliet," he said slowly. "So it's my attitude to women you want to know about. I vowed I'd never marry. Nor will I. If I'm being true to the image of myself I've projected onto the minds of my followers."

She swallowed. An *image*? One he'd *projected*? It didn't add up. "What do you mean exactly?"

"Do I have to spell it out to you?" he said. "The women have come round to the idea that I'm bisexual. The men are all convinced I'm gay."

A hush fell. "And are you?" Juliet asked. *Say it, Craig. One simple word. So I know before I leave.* Though hearing it said would be worse than anything.

"What I mean," said Craig, "is this: their ideas about me are false. I'm not any of the things they believe I am at all. I think you've long suspected that, Juliet."

She said nothing. She felt like strangling him.

Craig went on in a reflective tone of voice. "Although, having played these roles so long for the benefit of my followers, I've almost convinced myself. The roles seem to suit me. And they're certainly better than humouring my father in his delusion that I can be prodded into marriage with a girl of his choice."

Don exploded at this. "Not true, Craig," he began. "I've never…" Then he stopped.

"Surely, Craig," said Juliet, "you oversimplify human beings. You did that in Rory's case, and you do the same with your followers, and with yourself, and your father."

A long silence fell between them. During that silence, many adjustments took place in Juliet's view of Craig. What was he? A skilled inspirational speaker, a charismatic teacher, an adept in the arts of the shaman? Or a young man tripped up by his own ideals?

"I can't speak for my father," said Craig. "Perhaps you're better placed to do that."

"That's enough," broke in Don. He looked straight at Craig. "What's the deal?" he asked. "The deal you have for me?"

With that, Craig seemed to snap. "No deal would work with you.

The truth is you've long tried to control my life."

"I had to do it," shouted Don. "No one else could. Your mother wasn't around. Walked out on us. So it was all up to me. Don't you think I deserve some thanks?"

For some time nobody spoke. Both men were breathing heavily.

Juliet was about to interpose. But she thought better of it.

"No," replied Craig. "She didn't walk, she ran. Before you could break her spirit."

Don's face blanched. Juliet looked from one man to the other, not knowing who to believe. She was almost on the verge of seizing Craig and shaking him till his teeth rattled. She restrained herself in time, stepping back against Don. He wrapped his arms around her, evidently in an effort to calm her.

She missed a breath. She was in his arms. It felt blissful. For a few moments, her mind blanked. She couldn't process any thoughts at all. Shock flashed across Craig's face, as he focused upon the two of them.

And in the next moment, Don released her again. Her face burned and her arms and legs felt weak. She battled the desire to collapse on a fallen trunk. She couldn't handle this. All she saw was Craig's expression. It was icy and taut with fury.

She had no idea how Don was feeling, even when he finally spoke – not to her, but to Craig. "Why that look, Craig?" he asked. His voice trembled. He didn't look at Juliet either.

The question wasn't answered. Moments passed, as all three regained some semblance of poise. Don jerked his head toward the north west. "All right, let's go for a walk. I know the weather's miserable, but it might help us think straight."

Craig coldly considered this. His features were still set – with, she believed, intense controlled anger. Then he led them across the car park, over the stile and along the track that climbed steadily upwards into the cool, moist woodland. As they walked behind Craig, she studied him: his tall, slim figure, his resolute pace, his posture; in fact everything about him. She had no way of telling how Don, behind her, was feeling.

Craig halted. So did she. Don drew level. Then unexpectedly Craig closed in on her, his face holding a curious expression. Was he about to change appearance again? Before he reached her, however, she heard boughs being pushed aside behind them. Turning, she saw a fourth person heading up the track in a rain-spattered denim jacket. Theo. What a relief. Don and Craig couldn't stage World War Three in front of him. Or might she be mistaken in that?

"Hi there Don, Craig, Juliet," called Theo. "Good to see you three. A dreary sky and blustery wind can't put us off, can they? Despite all that's been happening down there." He indicated the house, now well below them.

For several moments no one spoke. Even the trees were subdued. No birds were to be seen, either on the branches, or silhouetted against the opaqueness of the sky.

Don was first to break the silence. "We've got a dilemma. Put it to him, Craig."

Craig didn't speak.

Theo raised his eyebrows. But it seemed none of them needed to explain any further. "You feel hurt, Craig. Because you believe Don has taken Juliet from you."

Juliet's jaw dropped. How could she have been so ignorant of what was really going on? Was it possible that she herself was the most deluded person of all?

Strolling around them and then a short way ahead, Theo turned and faced the three. "I know what it's like to hold all sorts of wrong notions about other people, and what they do and say – and about myself."

Juliet held him in view. But she couldn't trust herself to reply.

"Let's walk on," said Theo. The others silently obeyed as if on automatic pilot. The breeze was much stronger and cooler now. How could she have thought, Juliet wondered, just a few minutes ago, that the atmosphere was still? Now she heard the wind rushing through the tall conifers. "Four and a half years ago," Theo continued, "I started work as a freelance radio broadcaster, alongside my work for the Church. Then, after about two years, without any warning, I quit.

Broke my contract. Cut myself off from friends, family, colleagues."

He tramped on, occasionally stopping to pick something up from the ground – maybe a bird's feather, or a stone, to turn it in his hands and contemplate it as if it aided his thoughts, then to put it back down somewhere else on his journey. "One day, I was more or less OK, the next, a curtain had fallen – a black, thick, impenetrable curtain."

"Depression?" said Don.

Theo glanced at him. "Yes."

"Thought so," murmured Don.

Craig said nothing. Juliet wondered how much of this he already knew.

"I wanted out. So I ran," said Theo.

"Where to?" asked Juliet.

"Rented cottage on the most deserted part of the Norfolk coast. And there I hid for the best part of two years."

"And no one came to help?" asked Juliet.

"No. Once you're in that black state, you don't want help. People tend to steer clear of you anyway. If anyone does offer help you reject it. You're in deep depression. You hate yourself." Theo picked up a small branch from the ground, and twisted and turned it in his hands, feeling the texture of the bark.

"You had no forewarning of this?" asked Juliet.

"Only that for several months, I'd had doubts. Serious doubts."

"About your faith?" asked Juliet.

"Yes. That made me afraid. I was broadcasting as a man of faith. But deep inside, I believed nothing." Theo stared fixedly at the track for a few moments, then lifted his head again. "I'd let everybody down. But I lacked the will to take action. Like you, Craig."

Juliet gazed from Theo to Craig and back again, puzzled. How did this connect with Craig?

Theo soon dropped a clue. Swinging to face the others, he let go of the branch, and spread his arms. "As time passed, I convinced myself that to ask forgiveness from those I'd turned my back on, would earn me nothing but scorn and contempt."

Was this the link? Meanwhile, Craig had picked a cluster of leaves from a nearby shrub, and was flipping them back and forth. Juliet couldn't see his face.

"I had a recurring dream," went on Theo. "I dreamed I'd died, and was still conscious. I realised this must be the afterlife. Dark and silent. An icy waste of nothingness, and no way out."

The atmosphere chilled as Juliet contemplated this scenario. She took the leaf spray from Craig, and began to stroke each leaf.

"Meanwhile, in the daytime, the same half-life continued. I never opened mail," said Theo. "I had the phone line cut off before moving in. No computer, of course. Often, I didn't get up all day."

"And still no faith?" asked Juliet.

"Nil. I believed nothing." He paused. "I didn't even have the energy to be an atheist."

"What?" Don asked. "I never needed any effort for that. Always came naturally to me."

"Atheism is a belief system like any other," said Theo.

Don looked unconvinced.

"The idea of heaven became hollow and meaningless," continued the clergyman. "How can anyone be happy there while the rest of us wallow down here in the mud?"

"I never really looked at it that way," said Don.

"But I did," continued Theo. "And so I concluded that none of it makes sense. It doesn't work. God's got it wrong."

Juliet, Don and Craig all kept quiet.

"But of course," went on Theo, "if He's God, He doesn't *have* to do anything I think He should do." He looked straight at Don and Craig. They both exchanged an uneasy glance.

Craig turned back to Theo and said, "You mean all our expectations might be defeated?"

"I do," said Theo.

Juliet surveyed Craig. He stood slightly apart from them, his expression frozen. She couldn't even guess what he was thinking or feeling.

Don took Juliet's hand and squeezed it. She turned towards him, and responded, putting her hand on top of his. His hands felt warm beneath hers, despite the weather. She looked at him. He was so different. This wasn't the emotionally buttoned-up man she'd known so far. There was feeling in his eyes, real feeling. Something in her heart gave way. What was happening to her? And to Don? Suddenly she saw him as all that was secure, solid, down to earth, trustworthy. Diametrically opposed to much of what she'd found here in this community.

In the next moment she found herself swept into his arms, and crushed close to him. She was stunned. All she could think was, Don, is it you I've wanted, all along?

Several moments later, Don released her. Her breathing came fast now, and she looked around, bewildered. Craig had disappeared. But Theo was still there, damp and windblown. Even the field maples and beeches seemed to have forgotten it was summer. Their leaves hung limp and dejected from the boughs, or so it seemed to her. She looked at Don.

"Juliet, I…" he began. His eyes seemed now to be pleading with her. She guessed he was as confused, overwhelmed as she was. Had he meant to do that? Was he too struggling to come to terms with his feelings and actions, previously totally out of character for him? As, perhaps mistakenly, he'd thought?

Theo strode across to them both. "Juliet, do you have a vision?"

"Yes, Theo," she responded, "you know I do."

"What happened to it then? What are you and Don thinking of? And Craig's gone. What do you suppose he makes of you two?"

"I never meant…" said Don.

Juliet gazed at Theo, appalled by his words. On his face, she read a disturbing mixture of disillusion and bafflement she hadn't believed him capable of. It shook her to the core.

"I don't understand what's happening to me," she whispered.

"You still won't come clean with yourself?" returned Theo. "Or has your goal moved into a region of the unknown you forgot to map?"

Juliet's face burned.

"Well, Don," said Theo, "Your move now."

"How?" asked the Yorkshireman. "When? In what way?"

"In every way that matters," said Theo.

20

Thistle in the Picnic

After Theo and Don had returned to the house Juliet chose instead to walk on for what seemed like miles. One moment she felt ecstatic, the next despairing. Her emotions were chaotic. Don and Juliet … who'd have believed it? She, herself, had certainly never dreamed she was attracted to Don. And yet… more and more she'd felt he was a far better option than his son. Reliable, steady, rooted in the earth…

She did acknowledge she'd grown fond of him. Did she really want him? Yes, and no. What would it mean for the future? Where should she go from here? There was no one to turn to for advice. Zoe would be hopeless. Hardly Don himself. Even less Craig. And she certainly wouldn't ask Theo. She'd heard quite enough from him on the subject already.

And so her imagination freewheeled. By the time she approached the house, she'd exhausted all the scenarios her mind could conjure. Arriving at five-thirty she entered the sitting room. There were two hours until dinner. What would she do? Mental and physical tiredness took over. She sank down onto the sofa, and into a deep sleep.

The next thing she knew she was sitting up, bewildered, staring into the face of Al. The American lounged opposite wearing a flamingo-pink shirt, with a quizzical expression on his good-natured face. He glanced at his watch, a flashy silver affair that had probably been picked up from a cut-price designer watch shop in Hong Kong.

"Ten-thirty," he said. "Say, you've been knocked off centre, haven't you? Missed lunch and dinner. What were you up to earlier?" He gave her a sly wink.

Juliet ignored this gesture. "Is it that late? Why didn't you wake me, Al?"

He paused before replying. "I was a little… preoccupied myself." A self-conscious grin spread across his face, together with a distinct flush.

"What with?" she asked, her attention freshly aroused.

"You know, Juliet…" He jangled loose change in his pocket for a few moments, and recrossed his legs. "When we first met I told you I was here on vacation. Seemed like a good way to cover my trail. But honestly, I came meaning to stay for ever."

"Like most of you," she murmured. "Against Craig's better judgement."

He looked baffled.

"So you feel differently now?" she asked.

"Guess I do. I figured it all out as I chatted to Laura an hour ago." Now his colour deepened yet further.

Juliet began to guess Al's news before he had the chance to share it. "And what did you and Laura say to each other?"

"We discovered we'd both been feeling the same towards each other."

"Feeling the same? So you and Laura…?"

"Yeah, we've both been propping up the bar on a spiritual stopover," said Al, "waiting for our flight to be called. And then I clicked. It was up to me to grab her, and head through that boarding gate."

Juliet caught her breath. Surely this would be just what Craig had hoped for: the willing departure of some of his long-termers, so he could get new people in on proper, fixed-term contracts at the full commercial rate.

"Yep," continued Al. "And Laura… she's a real babe. The plan sounds good to her. She's coming back home with me to the States. She's agreed to marry me, Juliet." And with that, Al's face flooded with pride and happiness.

Juliet jumped up and he too rose to his feet. She flung her arms around him. "I'm so happy for you both, Al."

"Gee, thanks."

She let him go, and he contemplated her with affection. Then he engulfed her in a rib-crushing hug she considered worthy of a grizzly bear.

Juliet was delighted for Laura and Al. And yet she herself was in a state of inner turmoil. What was her next move? She had no idea. "Craig and Don will have to make the best of it," she said, as Al released her.

"Yep. Afraid I draw a blank on that one. Of course, I'll soon be out of the picture. Laura and me, we're pretty much ready to get going." He waited, then added, "The two of them got together in the library after lunch. Had a hunch it was about you."

She tensed at this. "Why?" She gazed at him, hope finely blended with dread.

"One or two phrases I picked up. Afraid I've no idea of the outcome. Don't let it bug you, though." He squeezed her shoulder.

"But it does."

He tried to distract her. "Hungry?"

"Yes."

"I'll go and snitch some leftovers."

"Don't worry, I'll do it," she said.

"Sure? Fine. Be seeing you."

"Bye. And well done, Al."

"Thanks." And he headed off in the direction of the hallway.

Before she could make a move, the door from the dining room opened, and Theo came through. She stiffened.

"Ah," he said brightly. "Just the person I wanted. Where have you been for most of the day? We missed you at lunch and dinner."

"Went for a long walk," she said. "I'm exhausted, Theo. But not because of that. Your comments shattered me."

"Sorry you feel like that. But there are some things you need to hear. Let's not go over that ground again though. I've said enough about Don."

Even as Theo said Don's name Juliet felt a surge of excitement, fear and doubt.

"Ah." He studied her. "As I suspected."

"I don't believe you suspect anything," she said hotly.

"Very well. Enough said, for the moment. Do you plan to return to London?"

"Of course. Friday. You're perfectly free to ask. This is work for me, you know." But she was breathing fast. She must speak to Don. She felt their embrace had changed everything. But did he? She must see him to find out how he felt.

"And your recordings?" persisted Theo, his expression neutral.

"Going great, thanks," she said tightly.

"You're still on track?"

"Of course." Maybe there was one almighty mess with Craig and Don, but even so… She had to carry on. She must complete what she came for – if she could remember what it was. Right now, her brain wouldn't cooperate. Most urgent: speak to Don. Then Craig. But Theo too. She still needed to know Zoe and Theo's plans. "I'll stay for another day or two," she said. She could be sure of that at least. Now for Theo. She needed the facts from him. "Theo, I know you and I…" she began.

"…said more than we meant to, earlier?"

"Yes. But still not enough about the things that matter most."

He lifted one eyebrow in a cryptic manner. "Of course," he said. "I wanted another chat with you too, before going to bed."

Juliet had meant she wanted to talk about Zoe, but wasn't a hundred percent sure that Theo did.

"Craig and I have arranged to meet in the Monk's Room, in ten minutes," Theo said. "May I sound you out about something first?"

She moistened her lips. She itched with anxiety to go and find Don. But OK, Theo was here. Get it over with. She nodded, and he perched on the arm of the chair next to hers. As she looked at him, she saw the midsummer night sky beyond, full of lightness. It surprised her. Everything still seemed slightly unreal, including the time that had passed since the scene up on the woodland track.

"I understand you're worried about Zoe, Juliet," said Theo. "I'll soon put your mind at rest. But as for Don… I stopped you talking about him earlier. But talk about him now if you must. And Craig."

"First, Theo – do you know how Don is feeling right now?"

"I have a pretty good idea. He's on the edge."

"In what sense?" she asked.

"Well, let me put it like this," said Theo. "With Craig rapidly squandering his inheritance – as Don sees it – and bankruptcy looming, Llewellyn trying to take over, and the news that his son has been harbouring a long-term mental-health sufferer with no safeguards in place, Don needed precious little else to destabilise him completely. It took only you to do that."

"Me?"

"Yes. And the same could be said of Craig himself. He was devastated to see you in Don's arms."

"I don't see why he should be," maintained Juliet.

"Of course you probably wouldn't," said Theo. "You didn't see Craig's face. But let's move on from that. I had a few words with Don at lunch. He'd just taken an unexpected phone call. I won't go into the details. But he was called away at once."

"What?" She sat up straight, her heart lurching. "Called away? Where? For how long?"

"Don't know. He spoke briefly to Craig, and disappeared."

"But … why? What for?"

"Sorry. Not allowed to share that with you," said Theo. "Packed his bags, had a bite of lunch, then left."

Stunned, she continued to search his face, hardly able to take his words in. Had Don abandoned her? Did he regret what happened? Was this his answer? Escape? "Back to Barnsley?" said Juliet. "Has Don given up?"

"I promised to say nothing."

For several moments she couldn't trust herself to go on, too angry and hurt to speak. What did this mean? It was a kick in the face. Don was her only real ally here. "But…" She forced words out, in a desperate attempt to make sense of it all. "Then I must see Craig.

And find out what happened. Will he be in the Monk's Room yet?"

"Take it easy, Juliet." He laid a restraining hand on her arm. "You know I'm about to go and join him up there. You come too."

"Let's go." They both got up. She followed him into the dining room, through the doorway by the fireplace and up the narrow flight of stairs to the Monk's Room; that small space within the thickness of the wall which Laura had first mentioned to her, formerly used by fugitives. Theo knocked at the door.

"Who's that?" Craig's voice sounded slurred. Had he been drinking more than usual?

"It's me, Theo. And Juliet too."

Craig opened the door. His hair was in disarray, as if he'd run his hands through it several times. No disadvantage to his appearance though. *He still looks great.* Her eye lingered on him, dressed in dark-blue jeans and a surf-style polo shirt.

"No recording equipment?" he said.

Juliet held her hands out, palms up, and met his gaze.

"OK. Come in," said Craig.

Juliet took a deep breath. She must focus her mind. She needed to find out what had happened to Don. She wanted a hundred percent honesty from Craig for the first time since she'd met him.

It was a very simple room, with whitewashed walls. There was no sign of the Buddha which she understood to normally be the sole occupant. The furnishings consisted only of two chairs and a small table, and the floor was carpeted in purple. She took one chair, Theo another, and Craig the edge of the table.

Craig began first, betraying nervousness by a constant twisting of his wristwatch. "The time's come for us to be straight with each other. I'm sure, Juliet, you're glad to hear that."

"I certainly am," she replied.

Theo's face had now regained some of its characteristic tranquility.

Craig forged on. "The reason why I run a community of emotional misfits is because I am one myself."

"Come, Craig, you're not being quite fair on yourself by saying that," remonstrated Theo gently.

Juliet said nothing. Instead, she studied Craig's face. Was this the real Craig she saw before her, with frank, open expression? Or was he about to exercise his disturbing gift, and shift appearance again? From the sound of his voice, he'd probably had more than a few extra brandies after dinner tonight. But he seemed sufficiently under control to know what he was talking about. Yes, he was being upfront with them both. But even so – the charismatic, charming Craig, describing himself as an emotional misfit seemed completely out of character.

Theo evidently felt he could rescue his friend's reputation. "You do yourself no favour by saying this. I admit, however, that you attract misfits, as evidenced by the members of your group."

"Come on, Theo, let's ditch the pretence," said Craig.

The clergyman was silent.

"Thank you." Craig hurried relentlessly on, perhaps anxious to say all he had to say, now he was in confession mode. "It'll be easier for Juliet to recognise, because she's already quizzed me on my attitude to women."

"Yes," Juliet said. "You say you don't trust them."

"I don't," he agreed. "And yet… I did have a vision for everyone here, men and women, and believed it could work. You see, ultimately, I'm an idealist. I'm a perfectionist, a romantic. I have a Great Gatsby vision of the ideal woman in white chiffon at a riverbank picnic."

Juliet covered her face with her hands to stop herself laughing, then dropped them to her sides and lifted her head once more. "Craig, where does this vision come from? Are you so much influenced by Scott Fitzgerald?"

"I don't believe so," he said, looking slightly ruffled.

"Are you telling me that Laura, and Beth, and Zoe – and me too – in fact, all four of us women, only ever needed to dress in frothy white and carry parasols, in order to transform the community into an ever-turning wheel of happiness and fulfilment?"

"Flippancy doesn't suit you, Juliet," said Craig severely. "And…"

She broke in, persisting with the point she wanted to make. "Let me disillusion you. Picnics, and people, are not like that. At a real-life picnic, you sit on woodlice, flies settle on your sandwiches, and the wind blows your napkins away."

She saw that Theo's face was split by a wide grin. "And you get thistles up your backside and stinging nettles inside your trouser legs," the clergyman said.

"Now listen." Craig was clearly disconcerted by these remarks. "I'm referring to Gatsby's romantic dream, his idealistic vision, the idea of picnics."

"Oh, the idea of picnics is lovely," Juliet persisted. "But – and I'm guessing here, of course, but perhaps Theo might back me up – how often have you, perhaps, in your own life, set out for a picnic, and then perhaps said, *I'm not getting out there. I'm not going to sit on that muddy grass*? How often have you ended up having your picnic in the car, spilling wine over the windscreen, and getting caught up with the gear lever? It doesn't matter how lovely the idea of picnics is, if you actually go on one you'll very often sit on that thistle."

She glanced at Theo. His shoulders were shaking. He was clearly trying to compose himself. She guessed he understood her perfectly.

"Juliet, I didn't realise you held this view of life, and I see I need to do some work on you," said Craig after a long pause.

"No, you don't, Craig," said Juliet. "My grasp on reality is firm. It's yours that's adrift. And by the way, let me remind you of how Scott Fitzgerald chose to end *The Great Gatsby. So we beat on, boats against the current, borne back ceaselessly into the past.* How does that fit in with your ban on *looking back*?"

Craig gave her a hard look.

"Juliet's right," said Theo. "You engage with the past all the time, Craig. And so you will continue to do, until you and your father set things right, and create a new future. Yes, this is a picnic. But the thistle in the picnic here," he insisted, clearly determined to pull the conversation back on track, "as I see it, is the fact that for some time now there's been no agreement between you and Don about how the place was ever meant to work financially."

"We both knew how it was meant to work," said Craig. "People were to come for fixed-term stays, and pay their way."

"And then it went wrong," said Theo. "People took advantage, and you were too kind to throw them out."

"Maybe so," said Craig. "But right now money is the least of my problems."

Juliet stared at him. What an extraordinary statement!

And Theo clearly agreed. "How can you say that, Craig?" he demanded. "When Don spoke to me about it, he even mentioned bankruptcy."

"Out of the question," broke in Craig. "I still believe that through a realistic approach, I can stave off total disaster."

Theo's retort was swift. "What does *realistic* mean, exactly?"

Craig gripped the edge of the table with both hands. "New recruits, Theo, that's what it means."

Juliet made a great effort to put aside her worries about Don, for the time being. "That sounds great," she said. "But will you win them and keep them with techniques like Dynamic Meditation and Dream Yoga?"

"Why not?" Craig fixed her with a steely gaze. "Are you about to make a value judgement, Juliet?"

"Don't go on the defensive," she said. "Just listen to me."

Craig wore a startled expression. Theo folded his hands in his lap, and listened attentively.

"In Dynamic Meditation," began Juliet, "you do your best to hurt people. Oh, I know a few of the group members said they felt *released* afterwards. But you can't ignore those who may be damaged in the long term. What do you say to that? Do you still believe it's the way to earn people's trust?"

Craig smiled enigmatically. "My primary object is not *earning people's trust.*"

"All right then," she continued. "I'll tell you who I do trust, and that's Don."

Craig's expression became impenetrable, as if he was hiding any emotional response. Theo was chewing his lip.

"My father? Why? Even *I* don't trust him," said Craig.

else was close by. Raising her torch, she directed the beam into James's face. He'd followed. She suppressed a shudder. Upright, he looked even more ghastly than he had in a horizontal position. "James, have you come to help?" she demanded. "Or to make things worse?"

How bloodshot his eyes were. Had he rubbed an irritant into them? No, must be contact lenses. For several moments, they both stood transfixed. His stench assaulted her nostrils. Was this the same man who wore bespoke tailoring and Armani aftershave? His tramp's garb had been steeped in some noxious substance. The greasy matted hair dangled around his face.

She willed herself to hold the torch beam steady, picking out his purple features. His theatrical make-up skills were excellent. He still clutched an opened bottle, but it was different from the one she'd seen him with earlier. Turning the torchlight full on it, she saw it bore the label *Dom Perignon*. There was only a small amount left at the bottom.

"James! Have you drunk that all by yourself?" she cried. She astonished herself. After all, at this stage – who cared?

He nodded slowly, a manic grin beginning to form itself on his face. "And very nice it was too," he said. "I only wish you'd joined me earlier, Juliet, and I would have shared some of it with you."

"Oh, shut up, James," she retorted. "Craig's out of his mind and I need your help!"

She spun. Craig was now well into his three-point turn, bringing the Saab round to face the north east corner of the house. With Craig in a distraught frame of mind and not fully in control of his vehicle, Juliet dreaded to contemplate what he'd be capable of once he stepped full on the gas. He'd probably think nothing of mowing her and James down. At that moment, James found voice again.

This time, he hurled a string of expletives – language that, from her brief acquaintance with him, she'd never have believed him capable of. Whether his words were directed at her or Craig she couldn't tell. Perhaps he meant to warn her. His final words convinced her he did. "Get out of his fucking way!" James bawled.

Juliet dived to safety just in time. "James!" she screamed. But he made no reply. Instead, he twirled, and flung the bottle into the woods. It was the swiftest overarm serve she'd ever seen. Then he vanished.

Her thoughts raced. Time was running out. Craig was in reverse, and moving fast. A voice inside Juliet's head said: *He's too close to the barn.* The next thing she heard was a loud bang. Then a sickening crunch of metal being distorted, mangled and giving way. And a fountain of fragmenting glass.

Craig had slammed on the brakes too late.

21

Wheel of Love Retuned

"Drink?" said James. "I think we need one after what's happened."

"You're joking, aren't you?" said Juliet.

She, Theo and James stood together in the entrance hall, gazing at each other. The ambulance had just sped away up the drive, taking Craig to Cheltenham General Hospital. Juliet was still trembling in every limb. After the 999 call James, demonstrating his presence of mind even whilst festering in his rags, had made two further telephone calls, the first to Don to let him know what had happened, and the second to Craig's motor insurance company. The car would be a write-off.

"I should have gone to the hospital with him," said Juliet.

James looked at her severely. "Don't be silly," he said in clipped tones. "I'm in charge now, by the way."

God! What would this mean for the community? A tramp running the place. And Craig with who-knew-what multiple injuries. Suppose he had brain damage? Suppose he became paraplegic? Suppose he… None of it bore thinking about. She swallowed the emotions threatening to seethe to the surface, and felt sick to her stomach.

"You think you're worthy to lead this group, James?" she said. "That would be…"

"Yes, Juliet?" retorted James. "Go on, say it. That would be… what? A farce? An outrage? Or…"

"Words almost fail me," she said, "but in view of your regular appearances as a down-and-out, and your behaviour with the champagne…"

She stopped. He looked at her strangely. And as he did so, a memory nudged her. A conversation between James and Craig in his study. Something about missing bottles…

"James," she said, "while I've been here, I admit I've eavesdropped on a few conversations. And one of those conversations was between you and Craig. It was about some champagne that had gone astray."

Now he stared at her. So did Theo. In the next moment she intended to voice her suspicions. She wondered whether James would call her bluff. After all, it was only her word against his that the conversation had ever taken place.

"You promised to find *the secret indulger*," said Juliet.

"So I did," replied James. His expression gave nothing away.

"Come on. The truth, James."

"The truth? A rare commodity," he sighed. "But on this occasion I will offer it to you, free, Juliet. You want to know who *the secret indulger* was?"

"Yes, I do." She still half-expected him to deceive her.

"It was me," said James.

"But why…? How…?"

"We all have a black hole in our psyches," he said. "Consider Professor Joad, eminent philosopher and debater who fell from grace when he was convicted of travelling on a Waterloo to Exeter train without a valid ticket, and was found to be a frequent fare-dodger…"

Juliet almost gagged in disbelief. "What the hell has Professor Joad got to do with you nicking the champagne, and betraying Craig?"

"Moral bankruptcy," said James sagely, as if it was a badge he wore with pride.

Juliet had had more than enough of his carefully scripted dramatic irony. "James, go and change," she said wearily.

"Of course. Right away," said James, going upstairs.

And not a moment too soon, she thought, as she turned to Theo.

"What do you make of that?" she asked.

"How much champagne was involved?" enquired Theo.

"A case of it, apparently," she said. "A dozen bottles."

The young clergyman shrugged. "Even in the few years of my ministry so far, I've seen and heard things I could never previously have believed. *All have sinned and fall short of the glory of God.* And I admit sometimes I fear the surprises that still lie ahead of me. Still, *sufficient unto the day is the evil thereof.*"

She considered this. "I think you're right. Is there anything more I can do now?"

"No, Juliet, not tonight. I suggest you go to bed," said Theo. "I'll ring the hospital in an hour's time and ask for news."

She had no option but to obey. As she was about to head up the second flight, she heard Theo speak again in the hallway.

"I notice you didn't offer any help, Patrick."

The Irishman's reply was soft. "Thought I'd best keep out of it."

Theo sighed heavily.

"And," continued Patrick in philosophical mode, "What will be will be. Sometimes disaster strikes and there's nothing we can do."

Shut up, Patrick, she said to herself.

"Don should have dealt with all this much earlier," the Irishman added darkly.

"Yes, yes," said Theo somewhat testily.

"Will Craig live?" interrupted Patrick with unmistakeable relish.

A brittle two seconds passed. Then Theo said, "Of course he will."

"Wouldn't bank on it," said the Irishman. "I warned him. *Better make your choice now. Carry on as you are. Or see the light.* And now look at him. It'll be years of purgatory for him all right."

"Be quiet Patrick," said Theo.

"Very well. Only trying to help."

"Well don't."

"Good idea," said Patrick. Juliet heard footsteps crossing the hallway, and the sitting room door open and shut. Meanwhile, another pair of feet ascended the stairs. Theo, presumably. She hurried up to the roof, along the passageway and into her room. She listened to him passing her door. Another door further along the passageway opened and closed. A few moments later, she stole out of her room again.

Fear and shock still gripped her. Would Craig be all right? How badly injured was he? How would Don handle this? Where had he gone, and why? And how exactly should he have *dealt with all this* much earlier, anyway, as Patrick had suggested? Would he now rush straight away to see Craig in the hospital? How could he have retreated from the front line at a time like this? And just after that warm, loving embrace. She felt so confused, so raw and exposed. After all that had happened this evening there'd be no sleep for her, that was for sure.

The sitting room door had closed behind Patrick. He'd still be in there. She probably wouldn't like what he said. But she needed desperately to talk to someone. Returning downstairs, she pushed the sitting room door open and put her head through. Patrick was on one of the sofas. Opposite him in an armchair, one leg crossed over the other, whisky in hand, sat James. How could he have come downstairs again, and dare to be sitting there, looking so urbane, after his recent confession? But, of course, she hadn't told him to go to bed, only to change. And so here he was again, relaxed and composed – and seemingly untroubled by any feelings of guilt.

He was clean and fragrant-smelling. And clad in a velvet needlecord dressing gown. He emanated charm and authority. As she hesitated, he addressed her in an even tone of voice. "Ah, Juliet, what a night." An understatement if ever there was one.

He fixed his eyes on her. She wanted to haul him up from his seat. Bang his head against the wall. But no. She needed his brain intact so he could answer questions. "You rang Don, James," she said. "Where is he? What did he say? Is he going straight to the hospital?"

The academic gazed at her tolerantly. "The answer to your first question is *I don't know.* To your second, *he was incandescent.* And to your third, *I've no idea.* Does that help?"

"No."

"Craig only has himself to blame," remarked Patrick. "No one can say I didn't warn him."

"You warned Craig?" Juliet swung to face the Irishman.

"Yes. He and I had a chat on the forecourt, before dinner on Sunday. We talked about heaven. I must say I was impressed with his grasp. For a non-Catholic, he showed a ready aptitude."

"Did he?" said Juliet.

"Yes. But then he went and lost it. That was when I had a go at him. Sunday night it was, after the poetry recital and party. I told him it was his fault Llewellyn took over."

James muttered something Juliet didn't catch.

"Patrick," said Juliet, "I'm not interested in who you blame, or how many years in purgatory you think he's going to get."

"However," continued Patrick, warming to his subject, "I do think Don should rush to the hospital, if only to make his peace with Craig. Otherwise, if Craig dies with unfinished business, it will increase…"

"Be quiet Patrick," said Juliet, mustering superhuman self-control.

Patrick had apparently not heard. "But silly me, how can I speculate on the number of years? Some of course question how one can count years in purgatory. For time has no meaning after death. And I do accept that."

Juliet steeled herself. "Patrick…"

"Sometimes," the Irishman went on enthusiastically, "I lie awake at night thinking about death. Do you? I've thought about it even more in the last few months – coinciding exactly with the time that I've been here, as it happens."

Juliet had heard quite enough from him for tonight. If he carried on, she'd knock him to the floor, and stamp on him. "Shut up, will you!" He turned hurt eyes upon her. At last, she had his full attention. "Craig is going to live," she shouted.

The Irishman looked pitying. "You've no guarantee of that."

Juliet twisted round to the occasional table behind her and picked up *The Tibetan Book of the Dead.* Then she hurled it at Patrick. He dodged aside just in time. It hit the wall behind and crashed to the floor, where it lay with a broken spine.

"There'll be seven years' bad luck on you for doing that," he said.

At this, James rose. He and Patrick both melted away out of the room.

She stood still, breathing hard. There was nothing for it but to go to bed. She felt bad. Ashamed, enraged, mortified. And afraid for Craig.

Images flashed through her mind as she lay in bed. They included a black-and-white newsreel of James boarding a transatlantic liner ahead of a procession of porters carrying crates of champagne. The fact that James was the one who'd been making heavy use of the *Dom Perignon* for several weeks had escaped Craig. But this hardly mattered now. Damn James, damn the champagne. What of Craig? Would he live? How seriously injured was he?

Some time in the early hours of the morning she must have fallen asleep again. The next thing she knew she was looking at her bedside clock, horrified. The hands now stood at ten a.m.

Leaping out of bed, she dressed, dragged a comb through her hair, and raced downstairs. All was silent. Bursting into the sitting room, she found Llewellyn filling a cup from a cafetiere of freshly brewed coffee. He was alone in the sunlit room apart from Groucho on his perch. As soon as Juliet saw the poet, she froze. The memory of his behaviour on Sunday night flashed vividly before her eyes.

The parrot hopped up and down and ruffled his plumage. Juliet stared at him wildly, then back at Llewellyn. The Welshman regarded her with a grim face. This was their first meeting since that dreadful scene in her bedroom. Would he apologise? She waited. He said nothing. But she really couldn't be bothered to make an issue of it when she had so many other things pressing on her mind. "Llewellyn… how's Craig?"

"Alive. And in not too bad a shape. He'll survive, Juliet. Don got to the hospital two hours ago. Theo told me. Just had a call from Don."

Juliet was stunned by Llewellyn's sardonic tone. "But …"

He interrupted. "Coffee?"

"Oh," she said. "OK. Thanks."

He poured her a cup and handed it to her. She accepted silently.

The poet studied her face, his own a brooding mask. "All right Juliet, let me say sorry about the other night."

She nodded curtly. "Apology accepted, Llewellyn."

"I still cannot believe I treated you like that," he said.

"We all do things we later regret," she replied. Although she admitted to herself that she did think Llewellyn's behaviour towards her also had quite a bit to do with the effect living in this community seemed to have on people. "But never mind," she said aloud. "Let's forget it, Llewellyn, and move on."

He nodded, evidently greatly relieved. A few moments passed.

"Is Don still at the hospital?" Juliet asked.

"I don't know." Llewellyn picked up the set of bronze bellows and began to run his finger back and forth over the embossed design. Then he said something that unsettled her. "Juliet, I feel… now this has happened… it's time I went. You came by car didn't you? Would you give me a lift to London?"

She threw herself onto the sofa beside Groucho's empty perch. It didn't suit her to leave. "No. Sorry. I'm not going today."

"You mean you'll stay? After this?"

"Yes. That's exactly what I do mean," she responded.

"You can't change anything," he said.

"I disagree with you." Though she didn't know why. She looked down at the silk-fringed rug, as if seeking inspiration there.

Llewellyn tried again. "Juliet, please listen to me. Let's both go to London together after lunch."

"No," she said. She gazed at him, mystified. Surely he must see how inappropriate this was? OK, he'd apologised, but the atmosphere was still strained between them. Although she saw nothing on his face to suggest he thought his request out of order.

One further question balanced on her lips. But she couldn't say it. Her own vision of herself and Don together hung in the air, fresh, vivid, real. Then it melted. Don was replaced by Craig. She caught her breath. She fought against it. Felt panic rising, as if any moment now she'd plunge into a chasm.

All the while Llewellyn watched. The two of them seemed set into a freeze-frame. Several moments passed. Suddenly a flash of movement caught her eye. She looked through the window behind him. Sunlight glancing off gloss paintwork. Maroon Bentley. Reversing into a parking space. And drawing to a halt. Don was back.

Without giving Llewellyn time to react, she bounded from the room.

22

Stranger Things

Don unlatched the garden gate, and headed along the path to the shrubbery. Ah, thought Juliet as she followed. The gazebo. That popular place for private chats, here at the Wheel of Love. Don would explain everything: the truth about Craig and the truth about how he, Don, felt for her. And the future would become clear. But as they drew near the gazebo, the signs grew ominous. A heavy, woody smell hung in the cool air. And the low light gave everything a muted appearance.

She now knew that when he'd left the house after lunch the previous day, it had been to attend a meeting of his board of directors in Barnsley. But what had they agreed? Had they made a judgement against Craig? How would the company recover its investment? Of one thing she felt sure: the discovery that Craig had crashed his car wouldn't have helped.

Perhaps she already knew the answers to her questions, even before she and Don settled down on the redwood seats. There was no good news for Craig – or for the Wheel of Love.

And what of her and Don? She longed to know. But she also agonised about the fate of Craig. "Is Craig all right?" she asked.

Don gazed at her, and took her hands in his. "Yes," he said. "No need to worry about Craig. He'll live."

For a moment, Don held her hands tight, then let them go. The look in his eyes told Juliet that he was starting to distance himself. She began to feel the sting of something akin to grief. Her heart filled with foreboding. "Don, what's going on?" she asked. "How do you feel about everything that's happened? Are you trying to protect yourself?"

"Perhaps I am," he said.

"But why? Don, you don't have to."

"Yes. I do."

"I refuse to believe it."

For a long moment, he laid his hand on top of hers. He examined her face, and she his. During their mutual gaze, she felt almost as if he was taking something precious he could keep for ever. Then he withdrew his hand, stood up and walked across the gazebo to the door. She resisted tears as she waited for him to steady himself again and turn.

"Will Craig be out of hospital soon?" she enquired.

He half smiled. "Expect so. Just mild concussion. And whiplash. Supposed to be in overnight. But knowing him he'll discharge himself."

"Don," she said. "Why not let this be your chance to make a fresh start?"

"I can't," he said.

"Why not?"

After several seconds had passed, he said, "I haven't been a hundred percent honest about what happened to his mother. Never even discussed it with Craig."

Juliet became very alert. Craig's mother? She broke the silence. "And what did happen to her?"

A resistance in his face seemed to give way at this question. Some hitherto rigidly upheld line of defence began to crumble. "When she went away," Don said, "it was my fault."

"Oh?" This puzzled Juliet. "Well, wherever she is, I hope she's happy there."

"No. You don't understand," said Don.

"And you don't help me to understand," she countered.

His face had lost colour, she noticed. He cleared his throat. Moments passed as he evidently steeled himself for what was coming next. She could tell this was costing him a lot. But she let the time pass. Some kind of dilemma appeared to revolve in his mind. "Me and Craig," he said. "We've never talked about it."

"Why?"

"I'm afraid of the questions he might ask," admitted Don.

"I'm asking questions now," said Juliet. "Where did Craig's mother go?"

"Gaza," said Don. "Bit like joining the Foreign Legion."

"Gaza?" she repeated, bewildered.

"Community project," he muttered, "To stop violence against women and girls."

"But…" She hesitated, choosing her words carefully. "That sounds admirable. What questions might Craig ask?"

"He might ask, for instance, why his mother chose to champion such a cause."

"Violence against women and girls?" Juliet said.

Don nodded. His eyes met Juliet's. And suddenly, Juliet knew why Craig's mother had left. She looked down at her hands, and began to twist a silver ring round and round on her finger. Physical abuse. It wasn't something she'd ever associate with Don. And yet… What did she know?

"It was years ago," Don said softly. "I've changed."

"I believe you," she replied. A long silence fell between them. Then Juliet said, "But Don, why would Craig's mother walk out and leave her child with you?"

"She didn't," said Don "She took him. But I fought her through the courts. And got him back."

"Why?" she asked, astonished.

For a while he said nothing. They he spoke slowly. "Well, you see," he said, "she was mentally unstable."

"Oh God, no," said Juliet.

"They ruled her *an unfit mother*," Don continued. "And I won custody."

Juliet could hardly believe it. A father who'd been guilty of domestic violence? And yet… Why had Craig never mentioned it?

There again, why should he? Hardly surprising. Even so…

"The alternative would have been to put him in care," said Don. "I didn't want them to do that. So I moved heaven and earth. And I got him."

"You say she was unstable?" repeated Juliet. "Does that explain why Craig…"

"…gave Rory a free rein?" said Don. "Wanting to believe the best of him? Yes. Afraid it does."

She heard someone step through the doorway. They both looked round sharply. Juliet jumped to her feet. She faced Craig, her heart pounding. Out of the corner of her eyes, she saw Don had remained seated.

Craig looked drawn. His face was unusually pale and his jawbone set. There was no sign of any physical injuries. "Juliet. Father," he said, unsmiling.

Don had raised his head, his customary jaundiced expression back in place. Juliet felt a sense of despair – although she now understood why Don put up these barriers. And why he found it so difficult to come clean with Craig. Even now, he remained silent.

She turned her attention to Craig instead, and drank him in. She felt emotionally raw, unsure what to do, or what to say. The sun reasserted itself above a shredded cloudbank in the western sky. Shafts of light slanted through the windows of the hexagon, picking out Craig's dark hair in gold, giving the effect of an aura. For a brief moment, he looked exactly like the spiritual figure he'd long presented himself as.

Was he about to change appearance again? Or had it been a delusion of hers, or a psychological trick? Then the base cloud rose again. The light dimmed once more, and the impression vanished. Craig was Craig again. But who was that? She trusted neither her own judgement, nor her feelings, especially since Don's revelation. But in her imagination she saw Don beating his wife, and she heard her screaming… Then Juliet took a firm grip on her unruly thoughts. Gaza. So that's where Craig's mother went. Perhaps it was Theo's story of nearly being gunned down in the Garden of Gethsemane that had unexpectedly sent an electronic signal to the forefront of her mind.

And then she thought of that emotional letter to Craig. And the piece of charred timber. And the Arabic headdress. Could it be..?

Don, however, was now focusing on another issue. "Craig. Are you fit?"

"Fit as I'll ever be." Craig's eyes travelled to Juliet.

"Fit to talk about something else?" said Don.

Juliet sensed increased tension in the atmosphere.

"This house perhaps?" suggested Craig. He clenched his fists as his arms hung down by his sides.

"You guessed. We've both said enough. We know what the position is." Don halted. Craig and Juliet waited. "We've been through it all," said Don, "over and over. It's out of your control. If you insist on holding on to the house the Official Receiver will have your assets."

Craig's knuckles whitened. A steel-edged silence knifed between them. Don pressed relentlessly on. "There's only one way to dodge bankruptcy. Raise the cash to pay your creditors. In three days. Reckon you could do it?"

Don, Don… said Juliet to herself. She was determined not to interfere. And yet, after what she'd heard, she felt Don was more in Craig's debt emotionally than Craig could ever be in his.

Craig folded his arms tightly across his chest. Juliet thought he should have a plan in mind ready to counter his father's warnings. But no, it seemed he didn't. She slipped across to him and laid one hand on his arm. But he didn't react.

"You'll have to sell the property," said Don.

"No," insisted Craig. "This house will not be sold up and then used by…" He paused, evidently casting around in his mind for a particularly telling example of the kind of unsavoury types who might be lying in wait to snap up a Cotswold farmhouse.

"A disgraced former MP earning his income from celebrity appearances?" suggested Juliet helpfully.

"Internet gambler? Hedge fund manager?" supplied Don.

"Yes, anyone like that," snapped Craig.

Don eyed him keenly. Even now, he didn't yield. "You won't have the luxury of a choice." Craig said nothing. "You can't afford to object to anyone," said Don. "Time's at a premium. You have to sell it to the first buyer. I'd take anyone's offer that was backed by high net worth."

"I'll bet you would," Craig shot back at him. "But aren't you forgetting something? The disgrace of a hasty sale wouldn't be mine alone."

"Don't think I haven't agonised enough about that already, damn you," yelled Don at him, losing patience as he jumped to his feet. Juliet thrust both hands into her pocket, willing herself not to intervene.

Craig appeared momentarily sobered by the power of his father's anger. Moving forward, he threw himself onto a seat. Juliet and Don also sat down again.

"Juliet, what do you think?" asked Craig.

"I'm not going to offer any advice at all," said Juliet. "You decide, Craig." Silence fell.

Don studied the floor for several moments, and then looked up once more. Craig met his glance warily. The two men appeared to be on the brink of something new, something that might move them forward, until Craig abruptly pulled back again. "I'm surprised at your words about the house," he said. "I should have thought *you*'d first seek Juliet's advice…"

Juliet bit her lip. Why on earth should he? And what was Craig about to say now?

"…having after all these years," Craig flung at Don, "fallen for her. The very woman, twenty-five years your junior, the very woman who…"

"Enough," snarled Don, interrupting.

"No," shouted Craig, "the very woman who you had previously chosen for me."

"How dare you?" retorted Don, leaping up once more.

Juliet likewise sprang to her feet. "What gives you two the right to discuss me like this?" she demanded.

The two men remained speechless, breathing heavily, and shooting poisoned glances at each other. Don was first to break into it. "Juliet and me," he said heavily. "We understand each other. There's no future in it. We've agreed to let it be." He turned to her, an expression of gritty acceptance on his face. He spread his hands. "Juliet," he began. "You know what I first hoped for."

She nodded speechlessly.

"But now we both need space." He stopped. Time passed. He looked from Juliet, to Craig, then back again. She seemed to recognise something in their faces.

"I'm off to think," he said. "And to leave you two together. Time. That's what we all need."

He walked to the door. Before leaving, he turned. "And Craig. The house. Think hard. Before dinner." He walked out.

Juliet watched him as he passed the north west window, shoulders hunched and head down, and moved out of sight behind the hydrangeas. She felt a strong wave of sadness. Despite his terse manner, she knew of the warmth, the concern, the sensitivity beneath. But now it seemed he was choosing to keep it hidden.

She swallowed. Tears were not far away. The sense of loss was overwhelming. Only on fleeting occasions had he broken out, when he'd offered himself to her as confidante and ally. Should she hurry and join him? He'd been the one person here with his feet rooted in the real world. Or so she'd thought until she'd begun to glimpse something of his and Craig's story, and how they'd both reacted against each other. No. She stayed where she was, and he walked away.

She turned back to Craig. He hadn't moved from his seat. Was it up to her to say something? She saw the desperation in his eyes vanish. New resolve replaced it. What idea had he caught now?

"I can't stand by, Craig," she burst out, "and watch you and Don mess up your lives like this. If you won't face what's happening between you both, where can we go from here?"

Craig spread his hands wide. She felt despondency settle upon her. But she made one more effort. "Neither of you have any other option. You need to get real with each other."

He reached out and clasped her fingers. She withdrew her hand, already tingling even from such slight contact. Then she took the seat opposite him. But when she looked at him again she saw the hardness and pride in his features begin to evaporate. Immediately she remembered the mystery of his changing face. How did he do it? She still didn't know. Until she did, how could she feel at ease with him?

And yet, with this, she recognised a new defencelessness. It unbalanced her more than any transformation to a carved figure on the gate of an ancient city might have done. But she still struggled to believe this could be so. Go on. Test him.

"Craig, why did you ever put on any shows for me? I don't need that. I only need to know your story."

Moments passed as they both sat there in perfect silence, looking at each other.

"Perhaps I hardly know my own story, Juliet," he said.

She held her hands out, palms upwards, in a gesture of invitation. "Just start by telling it to me. And first – how do you change your face?"

Several moments passed. Then Craig spoke. "Do you know about shamanism?" he asked, "and about shapeshifting?"

She hesitated. "A little," she said cautiously. "Are you saying that this special skill of yours – comes from being a shaman?"

He nodded. "Shapeshifting is part of the Celtic shamanic experience. Shamans are found in all parts of the world. One may be a sage, or a master, or a healer. Another may be a seer of the future, or a prophet, or a spiritual teacher. Yet another may be a shape changer." He paused as she took this in. "Shapeshifting is the ability to alter one's physical appearance; it is the transfer of inner personalities to the outside."

She said nothing. Her mouth felt dry. What was she to make of this?

Craig went on. "When you first noticed my appearance shift, Juliet, you were in a state of heightened perception. And so you saw one of my inner personalities as if transferred to the outside."

Juliet inspected Craig's face, but said nothing.

Then Craig said, "The Welsh bard Taliesin, said to be the father of Celtic shamanism, often alluded to shapeshifting when he claimed: *I have been in many shapes… there is nothing in which I have not been.*"

"If I'd read that before I met you I would have thought it was metaphorical," said Juliet. "But after having seen your face change on more than one occasion… well, let's say for now that I'll reserve judgement until I find out more about it."

Craig smiled but did not comment.

"Good thing Llewellyn didn't quote Taliesin to me," she added.

They both laughed.

"You know," said Juliet, "I can't help wondering what Theo would make of all this. Was Jesus a shaman, do you think? I must ask Theo when I get the chance."

"Do," said Craig. "You'll have an interesting conversation."

"And yet," she went on. "I still don't know you, do I? Who are you? Answer as a human being, Craig, not as a shaman, not as a guru, not as an inspirational teacher. Answer me just as yourself."

"Very well." He rose, crossed to where she sat and drew her to her feet. Taking hold of her hands in both his, he stood gazing at her for what seemed a long time. "Shall I begin by telling you about my mother? Because I believe you've been wondering about her. And instinct tells me my father has already spoken to you about her. So let me tell you now, in my own words. You're only the second person I've spoken to about this."

"OK. Go ahead. Tell me."

"My father and I both know where she is," said Craig. "But we never refer to it. She's in one of the most dangerous places in the world. I've visited her there several times since I found her."

Juliet stared at him. "Gaza," she said.

"He told you."

"Yes."

"My mother is involved in humanitarian work," said Craig. "She risks her life every day."

"I don't understand," Juliet said, "why you and Don never discuss it."

He sighed. "We're afraid, Juliet. Like most people, we fear pain."

She tried again. "You should be proud of her."

Craig's answer came, clear and full of intense feeling. "I *am* proud of her. You wouldn't believe how much."

"And yet…" she felt compelled to play devil's advocate too, "what about her betrayal of you? It's true your father drove her out when you were seven. But why didn't she ever come back to you?"

"She couldn't. And *betrayal* isn't a word I use any more."

"That's because you've forgiven her, haven't you?" she said.

"Yes."

There was a long silence between them.

"What does she do?" asked Juliet.

"She's an activist," Craig replied. "Women's empowerment work. She empowers women and girls for life, not for death."

He looked straight at her. With these words, she saw him totally honest, disarmed, and wide open to love. Hers. She knew she'd willingly give it. Joy rushed in on her unexpectedly. She wanted him to kiss her. But an inner voice spoke. No, first he has to … first he has to do or say what? Have a really open conversation with his father? Agree to turn his back on this shamanism business? Promise to stop running spiritual communities? She didn't know.

He squeezed her hands. Then he let them go. Instead, he moved his fingers to her chin. Then he lifted her face up to his, and their lips met. She surrendered.

Holding him tight, she neither knew nor cared about anything else at all. Not the time that might be passing, nor the decisions that still had to be reached, and not even the questions which remained unanswered. All she knew was the absolute bliss that cocooned her.

Several moments later he withdrew, and said, "Juliet, you quoted the last lines of *The Great Gatsby* to me. Like Gatsby, I've dispensed starlight to casual moths, in pursuit of an empty dream. And you were right. We can never escape our past. We can only come to terms with it." And then he took her hands again.

"Craig..." she began. Everything in his face made an almost irresistible appeal to her. Words were failing her. She no longer knew who was most in debt to the other, Craig or Don.

Though she now felt she was beginning to understand what had made Craig become a guru, an inspirational teacher of personal transformation, and self-appointed healer. Even so, she couldn't escape the fact that no matter how nobly intentioned he might seem to be, skirting the shallow materialism he found so contemptible in others, he'd still allowed his relationship with his father to atrophy to the point where neither felt able to even discuss Craig's mother and what she'd chosen to do.

And as for herself... she would, she realised, have to decide what to tell Toby. After all, she'd gathered more than enough material for one documentary. There was even enough for a novel...

Yet all she had first wanted was to get Zoe out of here.

"And," he went on as if he'd read her thoughts, "your sister...yes, she's seen the light. She's happy with Theo. And he with her."

"But she doesn't share his faith," said Juliet.

"Doesn't she?" asked Craig. "How do you know?"

She swallowed her sense of mortification. It was true. How *did* she know? Had Zoe shared all her feelings with her sister? No. Juliet began to see that in this, at least, Craig was correct. And she would not allow him to provoke or unsettle her, but only to love her.

As she thought this, he seized her and kissed her again. And once more the euphoria arose. She could have stayed like this for hours. This impulse to hide her happiness from Craig and even from herself was a battle she knew she wouldn't win.

Eventually, she broke away. When she'd regained her composure once more she spoke again. "Craig," she said, "you talk of coming to terms with your past. OK. I'm happy about that. But what of your future? The Wheel of Love has stopped turning. What will you do next?" She felt a tremendous sense of relief that she had asked this question.

In response, he looked at her for a very long time. The space between them was not total silence. She could hear his breathing. "I'll be like Zoe," he said, "and see the light."

She was baffled by this remark, even disturbed. Whatever did he mean? Zoe, perhaps, had seen the light by falling for Theo. But what could Craig mean by using this phrase of himself? Surely – her mind whirled – surely he wasn't planning to change course completely and enter a monastery?

Craig pulled her to him again, and began to stroke her hair. She placed her hand on his, and stopped him. He looked down at her.

"See the light? How will you do that, Craig?" she asked. Just then, she heard someone step through the doorway. Together, they turned and faced Theo.

"Ah, Juliet and Craig," said Theo in a benign tone of voice.

Craig held out one hand in welcome. But with his other arm, he still held Juliet. "Hello, Theo."

The clergyman was once more wearing his black clerical shirt with dog collar, as he had done on the evening of his arrival. Zoe wasn't with him. Yet that didn't seem to matter. Theo emanated a strong sense of contentment and peace. Juliet struggled against a wave of different emotions – relief, gratitude, regret, hope…. Which of these were for herself, and which for Zoe and Theo, or Craig… or for Don, she didn't know.

Theo addressed Craig. "I've come to say goodbye."

Craig's arms dropped to his sides. Juliet looked at him. His eyes were full of disappointment. "Are you off so soon?" he asked.

Juliet swung her attention back to Theo.

"Yes," said the clergyman. "It's time for me to go. I'll lead that retreat for the Golden Chalice, and then consider my next move."

"And Zoe?" said Juliet breathlessly.

"She'll return to London with you, Juliet. But Zoe and I will be in touch daily. You can be sure of that." He smiled. "Several times daily, I expect. About the future."

"Your future together?"

"Yes, Juliet." He took Juliet's hands and held them firmly. "And although I don't often give advice, here's a piece of it now, for you. Follow your instincts and obey the promptings of your heart." He inclined his head to Craig as he released her hands. "You've told Juliet, have you?"

"Yes," said Craig.

They all looked at each other. Juliet hardly had time to consider how long Theo had known Craig's life story.

"Stranger things have happened. Much stranger," observed Theo. "Life has its exits and its entrances."

As he said this, Juliet's attention was caught by a flash of movement beyond the shrubbery to the eastern side. She'd glimpsed Oleg and Beth through the blossoms, trudging up the driveway hand-in-hand, rucksacks on backs. Where were they off to? And why now? Was the whole group drifting apart, in ones and pairs? Without saying goodbye? And where was Zoe? She began to panic.

"Time flows on," continued Theo, "carrying with it all sorts of flotsam and jetsam: tragic deaths; amazing success; wonderful flowering; deep disappointments; betrayal." He waited.

"What will you do after the Golden Chalice retreat, Theo?" asked Craig.

"I have a business plan to put to my bank manager," said Theo, "and to a few philanthropic friends who have reason to bear me goodwill."

Craig went on full alert. So did Juliet.

"I have a passion," the clergyman continued, "to open a centre. It will have charitable status. It will be for the dispossessed, and those marginalised by low self-esteem and wounded histories. It'll be a place of empowerment and conflict resolution. Don't know yet when this will be. But it will be an open home where people in need feel free to ask for help. I want to be a person who never turns his back on the lost."

"And Zoe?" asked Juliet.

"I've asked her if she'll be part of it," murmured Theo, "and she's said *Yes*."

"And…" Juliet struggled to contain the tide of emotion threatening to overwhelm her at this news, "where will it be?"

"Again, I don't know. Bristol, possibly. Birmingham."

"Theo, tomorrow the Wheel of Love stops turning," said Craig.

"Mmm," said Theo. "Life is a continual process of loss," he mused, "but by the same token it also brings new things – gifts, visions. I've found it to be so, anyway."

Juliet studied him with quickened interest. A needle of light was beginning to twist its way through the mists in her mind.

"Visions?" she asked.

The clergyman nodded.

"Theo," she said, "Was it you who came to dinner here?"

"Yes."

"And saw the farmhouse as if from above?"

Craig and Theo exchanged glances.

"Yes, Juliet," said Theo. "You realise now it was I who had that dream about this place." He smiled sadly. "But it is not to be."

Craig looked enigmatic. Juliet scanned both their faces, perplexed. What had been going on?

"Theo," said Craig. "It could be."

"How?"

Juliet looked from clergyman to group leader. She hardly dared breathe. Theo bowed his head. Craig took Juliet's hand, and held it firmly in his.

"Because," said Craig, "I want to give this place to you."

Theo's head snapped up again. "You can't, Craig," he said.

"Yes I can."

Juliet swallowed, taking in air at the same time; and was overtaken by a violent fit of coughing. The conversation halted as Craig banged her on the back and Theo drew a tissue from his pocket and wiped the tears from her eyes.

When she was calmer again she said in a husky voice, "Do you realise what you said, Craig?"

"Yes," said Craig.

"Give this property to Theo? Free?" she asked.

"Yes."

"But Craig, it will ruin you. You heard what your father said. You'll be bankrupt."

"There are worse things. I can start afresh. With you, Juliet, I can do anything. And in this way, I'll have peace."

She opened her mouth to speak. But no words came out. Theo had been listening thoughtfully.

Now Craig touched Theo's arm. The clergyman turned to him. "Theo, did you say you'll have charitable status?" asked Craig.

Theo nodded. "You know, there may be ways through this which even your father wouldn't quarrel with."

A look of complete bafflement crossed Craig's face. "How?" he asked.

Theo held his hand up. "All in good time," he said. "You'll need to cover your debts, Craig."

"Yes. I acknowledge that."

Juliet faced him urgently. "But Don will be gnashing his teeth up in Barnsley," she protested. "And so will his board of directors." Craig's eyes met hers. They gleamed. His lips curved. She felt a strong desire to laugh, but just contained herself.

Theo remained quiet for a few more moments. Juliet was amazed that he hadn't said, "Craig, you cannot be serious," or "Are you out of your mind?" or anything like that. He simply bowed his head.

Juliet inspected Craig's face. It shone. This time, she believed, she saw his true self. It was quite extraordinary. His proposal seemed ruinous, for him at any rate. She could only hope – and pray – that Theo would find a way through this financially, and avoid the mistakes Craig had made.

And yet, somehow, she believed he would. Whatever the outcome might be, Craig's face said he understood the implications of his offer; this was his decision, and it was the right thing to do. She kissed him, slowly, seriously – and then turned back to the clergyman.

"With the grace of God, Don will agree to this," said Theo. "And, Craig – with strong financial management, I promise I'll enable you, eventually, to cover your debts."

Juliet found her hand in Theo's. And he now offered his other hand to Craig. They all three stood there, hands clasped. She felt as if a pact was being sealed.

Time passed. No-one spoke. But Juliet thought how curious it was that her sister, whom she'd wanted to take away from this house, would now be staying there for ever.

ACKNOWLEDGEMENTS

I wish to thank the following people who gave guidance, editorial feedback and encouragement at many different stages of this journey; Marie Calvert, William Connelly, John Costello, Hilary Johnson, Jeannie Johnson, Rev James Lawrence, Victoria Lee, Liz Obee, Fay Sampson, and the members of the Kenilworth Writers Group. Also many thanks are due to those who helped me with research: Moira Rawlings on freelance journalists; David Calvert and Simon Chapman on Yorkshiremen and Welshmen respectively; Rev Sharon Jones and Rev Ellie Clack, and ordinand Nat Reuss, for being willing to answer my questions and give me deeper insight into Theo. Thanks are also due to the members of the local community mental health teams in Leamington Spa whose dedicated work with their clients taught me so much, contributing in no small measure to my understanding of certain characters in this story. Inevitably others too deserve my thanks; they are the people who gave me moral support – you have all played your part in keeping me going, by being interested, by asking me about my novel, by promising to buy it when it's published, and by helping me believe in myself as a writer. Thank you to all of you.

DID YOU ENJOY THIS BOOK?

If so why not write a review and recommend it to other readers?

For more from SC Skillman, visit

www.scskillman.com
and
www.scskillman.co.uk

Keep up with the latest writing news at

www.facebook.com/scskillmanauthor

SC Skillman on Twitter

@scskillman

ABOUT THE AUTHOR

SC Skillman was born and brought up in south London. She studied English Literature at Lancaster University. She has previously worked within a BBC production office and later spent four years in Australia. She now lives in Warwickshire with her husband David, their son Jamie and daughter Abigail.

Lightning Source UK Ltd.
Milton Keynes UK
UKOW01f2139161017
311080UK00005B/132/P

9 781999 707309